A Willing Victim

LAURA WILSON

Quercus

First published in Great Britain in 2012 by

Quercus
55 Baker Street
7th Floor,
South Block
London
W1U 8EW

A CIP catalogue record for this book is available
from the British Library

HB ISBN 978 1 84916 311 8
TPB ISBN 978 1 84916 312 5

10 9 8 7 6 5 4 3 2 1

Typeset by Ellipsis Digital Limited, Glasgow

Printed and bound in Great Britain by Clays Ltd, St Ives plc

To my father,
William Wilson
(1924–2010)

'Why, sometimes I've believed as many as six impossible things before breakfast.'

Lewis Carroll, *Alice in Wonderland.*

CHAPTER ONE

31 October 1956

'The Interplanetary Parliament.' Mr Heddon nodded emphatically.

'I beg your pardon?' Behind him, Detective Inspector Stratton heard Feather the duty sergeant trying, unconvincingly, to turn a laugh into a cough.

'The Interplanetary Parliament,' Heddon repeated, apparently oblivious to the barely smothered snorts of mirth coming from behind the desk. Small, dapper and bright-eyed, he was standing in the middle of the West End Central police station entrance hall with an alert and sprightly bearing that made Stratton think of a Jack Russell standing on its hind legs. He tried vainly to suppress an image of the little chap jumping head-first through a hoop with a ruff around his neck as Heddon continued, 'I felt it would be best to alert the proper authorities, to put things on an emergency footing – after all, we can't be caught on the hop, can we?'

'And this is because,' said Stratton carefully, 'you have received information from an alien being about a war between different planets.'

'That's right. The war is imminent. The being came from Venus.

His name is Master Maitreya. I was cleaning my teeth at the time. It gave me quite a turn, I can tell you.'

'I imagine it would,' said Stratton. 'Was there anyone with you?'

Heddon shook his head. 'I live alone.' I'm not bloody surprised, thought Stratton. 'Obviously,' Heddon continued, 'the United Nations will also need to be told.'

'I'm not sure about that, sir.' Stratton fought back an image of a fleet of flying saucers like upside-down soup bowls with little green men peering from their portholes and wondered why on earth he was participating in such a ridiculous conversation. 'I mean, the UN are wonderful in theory, but in practice ... I mean, they don't seem to be doing much good in Hungary, do they?'

'Nevertheless,' said Heddon, to the accompaniment of a choked-off explosion of laughter from Feather, 'they do need to be informed. I trust,' he added, 'that you – all of you – will be treating this matter with the utmost seriousness.'

'We'll do our best, sir,' said Stratton.

'Good. Should I receive any more communications from Venus, I shall let you know immediately.' Turning on his heel, the little man trotted out of the station.

Stratton stared after him. 'I hope it keeps fine for you,' he murmured. Turning to Feather, he added more loudly, 'Fat lot of help you were.'

'Sorry, sir.' Feather, who was big, pink and jolly, sounded anything but apologetic. 'Got a message for you from DCI Lamb. Urgent – wants you to see him as soon as possible. I'll speak to the United Nations in the meantime, shall I? Tell them the Martians have arrived?'

'Ha, bloody ha.'

'Seriously, though.' Feather shook his head, suddenly deflated. 'I dunno why he bothered. Never mind the Martians – any minute now, we'll all be blown to buggery by a bunch of idiot politicians with H-bombs.'

DCI Lamb had softened perceptibly towards Stratton in the last few years. Stratton thought that while this may have been partially due to the fact that his superior was soon to retire and so was, to a certain extent, marking time, the change of attitude dated from three years earlier, when, as the result of an investigation in which he'd taken a hand, an innocent man had hanged. When the real criminal was caught, the case had received a great deal of bad publicity which, as the resulting judicial inquiry was deemed a whitewash, had never, entirely, gone away. Lamb had never said as much, but Stratton knew that it had shaken his superior deeply. That said, he still looked like George Formby, still had the extraordinarily irritating habit of jabbing his forefinger on the desk for emphasis, still wanted everything done five minutes ago, and his recent attempts at chumminess and jocularity were buttock-clenchingly excruciating. This time, though, the interview was brief. 'What kept you?'

'Chap came in to report a visitation from the planet Venus, sir. Apparently, we're to have a war of the worlds. Took a few minutes to get rid of him.'

Lamb shook his head in bewilderment. 'Everyone seems to think the world's coming to an end. But at least that sort are harmless, which is' – he glanced downwards and to the side and Stratton, following his gaze, saw that it was directed at a newspaper sticking out of the wastepaper bin – 'more than you can say for the Soviets. Anyway,' Lamb cleared his throat, 'we've got a suspicious death in Flaxman Court. It's a chap – described as a student, although he seems to have been a bit old for it. Found in his room. Name of Jeremy Lloyd. You and Collins—'

'He's still on leave, sir.' Detective Sergeant Collins had been rushed to hospital with what turned out to be a burst appendix three days before, and Stratton, who'd been to see him, doubted he'd be back any time soon.

'Yes, of course. Poor chap . . .' Lamb stared expectantly at Stratton for a moment, as if hoping he might pull a brand new DS from a pocket in the manner of a conjurer producing a rabbit from a hat, then said, 'Well, take PC Canning with you, then. The death was reported by the landlady, a Mrs . . .' Lamb paused to consult his notes, 'Mrs Jean Linder. She was the one who found him. Says he looks as if he's been stabbed, so we'd better get McNally to him before he's moved. We've been onto Fingerprints, and the photographer's on the way . . . Let's just hope it's not those wretched Teddy boys making their presence felt. Now that really *is* a sign that something's wrong – they've no respect for anything.'

Standing on the steps of West End Central, Stratton stared upwards. Remembering what Feather had said about the H-bomb, he imagined the roiling iron-dark winter sky exploding, spread-eagled, into a mushroom cloud. He thought of the Pathé news-reels he'd seen of the tests at Bikini Atoll, suspended skeins of cloud like the skirts of a gigantic ballerina, the air all around dying in the sunless glare . . . What would be left of England then? Cockroaches and tyres?

CHAPTER TWO

Flaxman Court was less than five minutes away, so Stratton, accompanied by the giant and imperturbable PC Canning, went on foot through Berwick Street market where stalls were being dressed with fresh fruit and veg, treading carefully through the discarded stuff thrown on the road and turned to a slippery, multicoloured mulch by early rain.

'DCI Lamb thinks it's Teddy boys,' said Stratton, as they walked past a Chinese restaurant with its window full of flat, varnished ducks and dried fish that looked like driftwood.

'Been reading the papers again, sir,' said Canning placidly. 'Gives him ideas.'

By and large, Stratton agreed with this. In his experience, Teddy boys didn't do much at all except hang about outside dance halls and cinemas and sneer at people. And preen, of course – they were more conscious of their appearance than girls, although their spotty pallid faces and general air of runtish under-privilege never really seemed to match their dandified clothes. They'd had a few fights on their patch – bicycle chains as weapons, which was a new one on him – a Cypriot café owner beaten up, and a West Indian, and a couple of scuffles down near Charing Cross Road, but that was about it. 'Could be a burglary gone wrong, though.'

'That would just be one of them, though, or two at most. When they're in a group they're ready to tear the place apart, but on their own . . .' Canning shook his head. 'They don't say boo to a goose, never mind murder.'

Stratton was reminded momentarily of his nephew, Reg's son Johnny. Now thirty-six, he'd so far managed – more by luck than judgement – to stay out of gaol. He'd been a car salesmen for a while, in Warren Street, and then there'd been a series of perfunctory trips to the Labour Exchange, yielding nothing, followed by his father's boast that he was fixed up and 'doing well for himself'. Exactly how he was fixed up, Stratton didn't dare ask – in any case, he doubted that Johnny would have told Reg the truth about whatever he was actually doing. Just as well, he thought, that his nephew was far too old to be a member of one of the gangs.

'Anyway, who'd go on the rob in Flaxman Court?' Canning sounded incredulous. 'There's nothing to nick. And it's not the sort of place they'd go just to cause trouble.'

This, Stratton felt, as they turned into the short and dismal-looking alleyway, passing a tramp who was half-heartedly rooting through a pile of refuse and startling a flock of scruffy-looking pigeons, was undoubtedly true. Horribly dilapidated, comfortless and dank even in summer, Flaxman Court consisted solely of a terrace of five tall and grim Victorian lodging houses that looked out onto the high, brick side-wall of a shop on the adjacent street. The house closest to them had a scrubby-looking bit of net curtain in the front window, held in place with what looked like bent forks. A young policeman, who Stratton recognised as the fresh-from-National-Service PC Standish, stood outside the peeling door of number three.

The woman who came to the door had such enormous breasts that Stratton's initial impression was that she had her arm in a sling. 'Mrs Linder?'

He identified himself and, when she stood back to let him enter the narrow hallway, tried to sidle in without making contact with her chest. Close to, she smelt of parma violets and wore so much powder that grains clustered at the roots of her hair in a way that reminded Stratton of grass growing out of sand dunes. Standing between her and the barrel-chested, dense-as-concrete form of PC Canning made him, despite being six feet three and an ex-boxer, feel positively concave.

'I went in this morning and found him in his room,' said Mrs Linder. 'Always keep an eye on the lodgers . . . It wasn't very nice at all, really.' Her tone suggested that she considered finding a dead body to be on a par with discovering head lice or a blocked drain. 'Anyway,' she continued, before he could offer anything by way of condolence, 'It's upstairs. First floor, on the left. I shan't come with you, if you don't mind. Watch your step, won't you?' Having evidently concluded the matter to her satisfaction, she disappeared through the nearest doorway.

'Take a statement,' Stratton told Canning. 'Find out who else lives here. I'll go up.' Left alone, he climbed the dingy stairs. The walls, ceiling and floorboards sloped and bulged alarmingly, and the landing was no better. Lloyd's room was chilly, dusty, and had a smell that Stratton thought of as peculiarly male – the neglect, decay and loneliness of the home of a slovenly over-grown schoolboy. There was no immediate sign of a body, just hundreds and hundreds of books lined on shelves, stacked in tottering piles on, or strewn across, the floor, slewed over all the surfaces, including the narrow, unmade bed; there seemed to be more of them everywhere he looked, giving him the impression that they were, somehow, proliferating by themselves.

A large desk stood in the middle of the room on top of a thread-bare brown rug. Peering over the typewriter and other clutter, Stratton saw Jeremy Lloyd. Dressed in a tweed suit, with the handles of a large pair of scissors protruding from the right-hand side of his neck, he was sprawled on the floor, face waxen, eyes closed. Walking round the desk, Stratton could see that the dead man, who looked to be in his late twenties, was flat on his back with his arms by his sides and his legs bent awkwardly to the right, as if someone had tried to turn him over but only partially succeeded.

Stratton squatted down for a closer look and saw that there were wounds on the chest, too – slits in the tweed and the shirt beneath with small amounts of reddish-brown staining around them. As he leant forward to touch the man's cheek – cold – he saw that what he'd initially taken to be blood on the side of his face was, in fact, a plum-coloured birthmark that disappeared into the dark mass of curly hair. It surprised him that there didn't seem to be much blood at all around the wound, or on the handles of the scissors.

He stood up and looked about the room once more. There was some calligraphic writing, decorated with leaves and vines, in a picture frame beside the grimy window: *The secret of life is to cure the soul by the means of the senses, and the senses by means of the soul.* It didn't actually seem to mean anything to Stratton, although as far as 'the senses' went, anyone searching for physical signs of a perverse sexual appetite would certainly be gratified by the dark circles under Lloyd's eyes and his blue-white pallor – he would lay money on this man's not having been dead long enough for either to be caused by the beginnings of decomposition. This, though, was the room of a scholar. He wasn't going to find a cupboard full of flagellant pornography sent under plain wrapper, or anything like it.

He turned his attention to the bookshelves, reading the spines: *The Secret Path*, *The Projection of the Astral Body*, *Esoteric Orders and their Work*, *In Secret Tibet* and a lot more of the same, interspersed with a few philosophers whose names he recognised, such as Confucius and Plato. Leaning forward to blow dust off the pamphlets strewn across the narrow table under the windowsill, he read: *Within You is the Power*, *The Power to Be Well*, *The Lemon Cure* – blimey – and *Can I Be a Mystic?* by someone called Aelfrida Tillyard. In his case, thought Stratton, the answer was 'not bloody likely' and he didn't need some woman with a daft name to tell him so.

'Mumbo-jumbo.' The voice made him jump and, turning, he saw the elongated and austere form of the pathologist Dr McNally. He nodded towards the 'secret of life' thing in the picture frame. 'Sort of thing that attracts long-haired men and short-haired women. Let's have a look him, shall we? Has the photographer been yet?'

'No. I've only just got here myself,' said Stratton, backing away as far from Lloyd as he could without colliding with any piles of books. 'No sign of anyone from Fingerprints, either, so be careful . . . Lloyd's hair's not too bad, actually,' he added, as an afterthought.

'Still, nothing a short back and sides wouldn't cure.' McNally squatted down beside Lloyd, angling his head for a closer look at the scissor handles sticking out of the side of the dead man's neck. 'And there are plenty of male cranks with short hair, after all.'

'Don't I know it. I had a visit from a chap this morning who said he'd had a communication from Venus about a space war and we've got to be prepared.'

'Well . . .' McNally paused, and looked up at him, a challenge in his eye. 'When you think about it, it's no stranger than the Son of God being born to a virgin, and millions of people believe that, even nowadays.'

'No,' said Stratton, mildly. 'I suppose it isn't, really.'

McNally peered at him, momentarily disappointed, then turned his attention back to Lloyd.

'Do you think someone's tried to move him?' asked Stratton.

'Could be . . . if they did it must have been when the limbs were more pliant, of course. There's some rigor, and he's cooled down a lot . . .'

'Do you think they closed his eyes, too?'

'It's possible.' McNally sounded dubious.

'He couldn't have done this himself, could he?'

'Can't be sure yet – depends if he's left- or right-handed.'

Stratton glanced at the desk. 'Pen and pencil on the right-hand side, but that's not conclusive.'

'Someone'll know. I'd be surprised if he did it himself, though.' McNally stared intently at Lloyd's neck, then said, 'A suicidal stab to the throat is very unusual – I've certainly never seen one. Doesn't mean it's impossible, though, except . . . You didn't touch him, did you?'

'Of course not.'

'Didn't move his head at all?'

Stratton sighed. 'No.' McNally may have been a bloody sight easier to work with than some of the more celebrated pathologists he'd encountered, the types who, treated by the press (and, often, juries) as infallible, were constantly photographed, bowler-hatted and thoughtful, staring down at the gruesome remains of some tragedy or other, but he still asked stupid questions. Stratton was about to add something to the effect that he knew better than to touch anything when a clattering on the stairs heralded the photographer, with Redfern from Fingerprints in close pursuit. The small room now being very crowded, Stratton decided to leave them all to it and went downstairs to find Canning.

'Lloyd's been living here since . . .' Canning, who'd been waiting for him at the foot of the stairs, consulted his notebook, 'April. Hardly ever had visitors, except for the priest from the RC church in Soho Square – Mrs Linder says he came about once a week. No relatives that she knows of, and she laughed when I asked about a girlfriend and said he wasn't the sort . . . Then she said he wasn't the other sort, either. Said she'd often wondered if he wasn't a bit funny in the head, but he'd share his last crust with you and wouldn't hurt a fly. Didn't have a job, but paid his rent in good time . . . Always going on about some book he was writing. Told her he knew Ambrose Tynan.'

'The famous writer?' Stratton had read a couple of Tynan's books – a lot of guff about attempts to take over Britain by sinister foreign powers who could harness dark forces for their dire purposes (but never, of course, succeeding) and some pretty hot stuff about rogering virgins on altar-tops and Satanic orgies and the like. At the time, he'd enjoyed them mainly because they were full of things one couldn't have, such as nice food, wine and cigars. Not that he'd ever particularly enjoyed cigars, but that was probably because he'd never smoked a Hoya de Whatever it was – and nor, come to think of it, was he ever likely to. Tynan's name tended to appear in the society columns of newspapers, along with a lot of oleaginous twaddle about witless baronets and neighing debutantes, and Stratton couldn't imagine what possible connection he might have with somebody like Lloyd.

'That's the one,' said Canning.

'I suppose Lloyd might have written to him asking for advice or something,' said Stratton.

'I had the impression it was a bit more than that. Mrs L. said he'd gone to visit him.'

'And fancied himself part of a secret brotherhood, no doubt.' Stratton sighed, envisioning himself and Canning having to spend the week dealing with a procession of wild-eyed conspiracy theorists and crackpots. 'Did she mention any family?'

'Not so far as she knows.'

'Visitors last night?'

Canning shook his head. 'Mrs L. was at the pictures – A Kid for Two Farthings at the Tivoli. She doesn't recommend it.' Canning's mouth twitched slightly. 'Thinks Diana Dors is vulgar. Anyway, she went with her pal Mrs Heilbron and her husband, and afterwards to the Nellie Dean for a drink . . . It's a regular date, apparently. I've got all the details.'

'And later?'

'Says no one came into the house between quarter past eleven – which is when she came in and went to bed – and half past six, when she got up. Says she's a light sleeper and she's on the ground floor – she heard one of the lodgers come in at a quarter to twelve—'

'How did she know it was a lodger and not someone else?'

'She got up and had a look. Bloke's name is Wintle . . .' Canning turned a page, 'Christian name Harry. Youngish chap, out at work at the moment. Mrs L. says she doesn't know where – he's a painter and decorator and they go all over – but he comes back at lunchtime if he's working near enough. And there's another one she called "Old Mr Beauchamp". He's not been here the last few weeks – on the halls, apparently.'

'Music halls?' Stratton imagined some rouged and wizened horror, tottering night after night through a fifty-year-old routine.

'That's right. Well, what's left of them, anyway. Tours around a bit. Then there's her aunt who lives up at the top.'

'Right-oh. I'll go and see her. Tell Standish to let me know if Wintle arrives. Oh, and ask Mrs Linder if she knows whether Lloyd was left- or right-handed, would you?'

Mrs Linder's aunt turned out to be a hunchbacked crone called Violet Hendry, clad in a musquash coat with a flowery pinny and several cardigans underneath, her extremities covered in fingerless gloves, and socks and slippers respectively, and her legs mottled red from sitting too close to the fire. Once they'd established that she'd heard nothing and seen nothing and that Mrs Linder was very good to her, she volunteered the information that poor Mr Lloyd was a very clever man who *knew about things*.

'What sort of things?' asked Stratton.

'Eh?' Mrs Hendry cupped her hand to her ear.

'You said Mr Lloyd knew about things.'

'He knew about the spirits,' said Mrs Hendry. 'The afterlife. Like my friend.' She fumbled inside her clothes and handed Stratton a dog-eared pasteboard square. *Why Remain in Doubt?* he read. *Madame Beatrice Worth, Famous Trance Medium. Seances and readings. Inspirational Messages by Post. Fees to Suit All. 361 Oxford Street, W1 (over hairdresser's shop).*

'She's marvellous. I've had such comfort since my husband passed on. She talks to the spirits, you see. Really talks to them – doesn't make it up, like some. He understood all that, Mr Lloyd. Writing a book about it, he was. He said that one day . . .' Mrs Hendry lowered her voice dramatically, 'one day, what was in that book would change the world. You know,' here she put a hand as dry and gnarled as a hen's foot on his arm, 'that's probably why they killed him.'

'Who's "they"?' asked Stratton.

'Sorry, dear.' Mrs Hendry cupped her hand to her ear again. When Stratton repeated the question, she peered suspiciously round the room as if there might be spies crouched behind the enamel kitchen unit or under the bed, and then whispered, 'Unbelievers. They were against him.'

'Did he tell you this?'

'Yes. Enemies of truth, he called them. Beset on all sides, he was, like Our Lord. He said it was like the Bible – reviled and persecuted, he was. Reviled.' Mrs Hendry repeated, looking at Stratton intensely, to make sure he was taking it in, 'and persecuted. Aren't you going to write it down?'

Feeling foolish, Stratton scribbled the words hastily in his notebook.

'If you want to find out who killed him,' said Mrs Hendry, 'you look for his papers. Oh, yes.' She nodded sagely. 'You'll find the answer there, all right.'

CHAPTER THREE

Heart sinking, Stratton returned to Lloyd's room and waited while the photographer finished doing his stuff and Redfern made the room even dustier than it was before. Once they'd gone, and McNally had finished his work and was packing his bag, he said – not expecting much in the way of a response – 'Is there anything you can tell me now?'

'Well, it wasn't the wound to the neck that killed him. Look.'

McNally having turned Lloyd's head slightly, Stratton saw that the scissors, blades hardly bloodied, were lying on the rug. 'Did you take them out?' he asked, surprised.

'They weren't in – just wedged between his neck and the floor. We couldn't see because of all that hair. The wound on the neck is hardly more than a scratch. Probably done just before, or just after, death. Accounts for the lack of blood.'

'But there's not much blood anywhere else, either.'

'Puncture wounds – such as those on the chest – don't bleed much, or at least not externally, and unless I'm very much mistaken' – McNally's face suggested that he thought this was most unlikely – 'it was one of those that killed him. That is not, of course, an official diagnosis.'

'Of course,' murmured Stratton. 'And the time of death?'

'Hard to be sure. There's not much meat on him, and the room's not warm . . . Ten or twelve hours ago, maybe a bit more. That's the best I can do.'

Stratton glanced at his watch. 'Midnight?'

'Or it could be earlier. Or later.' McNally picked up his bag. 'I'll get him collected. All being well,' he added, 'I'll be able to let you know my findings in the next couple of days.'

The body having been removed, PC Canning, who'd informed Stratton that Lloyd was, according to Mrs Linder, right-handed, stood in the centre of the room staring gloomily at the sagging bookshelves. 'Blimey. Just look at this lot. Somebody else with too many ideas.'

'You can say that again,' said Stratton. 'He was writing a book, apparently. Told the woman upstairs it was going to change the world. She seems to think that was why he was killed.'

Canning shook his head. 'God help us,' he murmured.

'Well,' said Stratton, grimly, 'it doesn't look like any other bugger's going to be much use. Unless that lodger . . .'

'Wintle, sir.'

'Unless Wintle knows something – but it doesn't sound as if he's going to be here for a bit, so let's get cracking. You can start on the shelves and I'll do the desk.'

Canning stared round the room. 'I like a book myself, but this lot . . .' He shook his head again. 'I'm surprised the floor hasn't caved in. He's got a lot by Ambrose Tynan – I've read quite a few of them, too.' He started pulling them off the shelves as he spoke. '*Who Dines with the Devil* . . . that was a good one . . . *The Fourth Horseman*, *The Curse of Moloch* . . . Tynan's written in this one.' Canning held out a book to Stratton, open at the title page on which was inscribed, in a dashing scrawl, *To my dear friend Jeremy – May the courage and wisdom of the Timeless Ones, who order all things, be your guide, Blessings be upon you – Ambrose.*

'Sounds as if they were quite pally. What was that you said earlier about a secret brotherhood, sir?'

Stratton grimaced. 'Let's just get on with it, shall we?'

Lloyd's desk yielded a heavy book, like a ledger, in which were copied hundreds of aphorisms, none attributed. *In order to be what you are, you have to come out of what you are not*, Stratton read, and *Among thousands of men, one perchance strives for perfection; even among those who strive and are perfect, only one perchance knows* Me *in truth* . . .

Some of them he recognised as biblical, but where the others might have come from, he had no idea. They were obviously meant to be inspirational or, he thought, to be sucked on like sweets, to offer comfort. 'A real spiritual pick-and-mix.'

'Spiritual junk shop, more like.' Canning surveyed the room. 'This is going to take all bloody day.'

After half an hour or so of fruitless pawing through the contents of the room, they heard a noise from downstairs, and a moment later PC Standish appeared in the doorway. 'Someone come to see Mr Lloyd, sir. Padre.'

Relieved to abandon the airless chamber with its dusty clutter of scholarship, Stratton followed him down the stairs. The padre, whom Mrs Linder had ushered into her beaded and brocaded front parlour, turned out to be the visiting Catholic priest she'd mentioned to Canning. His church, popular with the female relatives of local Italian restaurateurs and coffee bar proprietors, was, Stratton recalled, dripping with gilt and crammed with garishly coloured statuettes. Elderly Father Shaw, small, gimlet-eyed, subfusc and drily unsentimental seemed, mercifully, to be the human opposite of the place of worship over which he presided. 'I was concerned about Mr Lloyd, Inspector,' he said, when Stratton asked the nature of his visit. 'I wasn't altogether sure that he was right in the head. I've frequently observed that overmuch lay interest in theological matters can be a prelude to insanity.'

This, thought Stratton, perking up a bit, was admirably frank. 'What form did it take?' he asked.

'Wanting to lecture me on points of doctrine, most of the time.' Father Shaw sighed. 'He was writing a book, you see. Or so he said.'

'So I gather. We haven't found it yet.'

'He talked about it a great deal. Kept it in a briefcase – always carried it with him. I'm sure you'll find the case in his room.' Father Shaw shook his head sadly. 'To be honest, I shouldn't be in the least surprised if it turns out to be nothing more than random jottings.'

'He attended your church regularly, did he?'

'Oh, no. He came two or three times to mass, once for confession.'

'So . . .'

'So why visit him? I suppose, Inspector . . .' Father Shaw stopped and considered, concentrating as if about to negotiate a tricky set of stepping stones in a fast-moving river. 'I felt . . . responsible.'

'Oh? Why was that?'

'Well, for one thing, he was a convert to the Faith. In his youth. It does,' he added wryly, 'have a certain attraction for the artistic temperament.'

'Do you mean,' asked Stratton, straight-faced, 'that he liked the . . . er . . . millinery?'

Father Shaw's mouth twitched. 'I believe that is sometimes a factor, but not, I think, in this case. Lloyd was never vain of his appearance. Certainly, he took pleasure in the ceremonial side, but I think the attraction was more to do with the traditions of the Catholic Church – learning and art and so forth. He'd aspired to the priesthood – unusual for a convert, but not unknown – but unfortunately he was deemed unsuitable.'

'Why was that?'

'I imagine – and he did not tell me this so anything I say must, of necessity, be mere conjecture – that it was because his interest was largely, at least on the surface, to do with dogma and a great deal to do with self-aggrandisement. Not that he wasn't a kind person, and he certainly wasn't selfish or concerned with material wealth, but I cannot imagine there would have been much interest in the *souls* of others, no fineness of purpose or vocation – and certainly not for missionary work. He was too argumentative, Inspector. Unstable. Difficult. The fact is that from an early age he believed himself to be marked out for great things. He said the mark had been put upon him – the port wine stain, you know.' Father Shaw tapped a finger to his left cheek. 'It surprised me that he could regard such an affliction as an indication of divine favour, but there it is. His parents, I understand, believed him to have some talent for music – the piano – and encouraged him, but, despite their paying for him to study at a conservatoire in France, it came to nothing. He was very bitter about this, and expressed the view that his teachers' lack of appreciation for his talents was occasioned by jealousy and spite. It was after this disappointment that he turned his attention to religion.'

'And what happened after he was rejected for the priesthood?'

'Some form of mental breakdown, apparently. He said little about it other than that he'd absconded from the sanatorium where he was being treated.'

'Where did he go?'

'I'm not sure. He told me he'd been taken in by people who'd cared for him, but not their names. He mentioned Ambrose Tynan,' Father Shaw winced as if he'd bitten on a bad tooth, 'the novelist. Said Tynan had helped him a great deal – giving him books, introducing him to like-minded people and so on . . . I'm not sure about the . . . degree . . . of friendship – to be honest, I thought he might have exaggerated it in order to make himself seem important, but I can't say it was the sort of connection I'd have encouraged.'

'Why not?'

Father Shaw pursed his lips. 'Those books of his . . . Sensationalist nonsense.'

'Did Lloyd go in for black magic and that sort of thing?'

'Oh, no. But his interest was rather too . . . wide-ranging, shall we say. Lacking in coherence.'

'I can't imagine that many people would take Tynan's books seriously,' said Stratton, hoping to God that Lloyd hadn't.

'I don't suppose so, but in poor Jeremy's case . . .' Father Shaw sighed heavily.

'Easily influenced, was he?'

'Yes, I'd say so. He wanted to find a meaning in everything, Inspector, and that was the sort of thing that attracted him. I told him that faith is – or ought to be – a simple matter.' Father Shaw looked weary, and Stratton imagined that he must be recalling a series of long and exhausting wrangles over everything from the more obscure points of theological dogma to the meaning of life.

'Did he mention any family?'

'Estranged, I'm afraid. His parents had made little difficulty about his conversion, but they were adamantly opposed to his joining the priesthood. When his rejection was followed by nervous trouble, they – understandably, if inaccurately – blamed the Church. It was they who placed him in the sanatorium. He didn't contact them afterwards. This was, I believe, nine or ten years ago, and I learnt recently that both parents have since died.'

'Who told you this?'

'His aunt. I was most anxious that he should be reunited with his family and begged him for the name of a relative with whom I could correspond – neither of us knew at that point that the parents were dead. He refused to contact his aunt himself, but he gave me her address and I wrote to her.'

'What was his response when you told him of his parents' deaths?'

Father Shaw's face was a drooping mixture of kindness and despondency that made Stratton think of a solitary raindrop making its slow way down a windowpane. 'I never had the chance,' he said. 'I wrote to Mrs Prentice – Lloyd's aunt – last week, and received the answer this morning. That's why I came today. She was most concerned about him. The family solicitor had been trying to contact him to deliver a bequest from his parents, but to no avail, and Mrs Prentice asked me to pass on this information. I have the letter here.' He reached into his jacket pocket and passed a square of lavender-coloured notepaper, folded in four, to Stratton. Opening it, he saw an address in Roehampton written in uncertain, arthritic handwriting in the top right-hand corner.

'Thank you. We'll contact her. However, as she won't have seen her nephew for some years, I wonder if you might be able to provide identification . . .?'

'Of the body? Of course, Inspector. And I would welcome the opportunity to say a prayer, if I may.'

Seeing that the clergyman was about to rise, Stratton said, 'Before you leave, can you tell me if Mr Lloyd had any enemies that you know of?'

'Specifically, no. I'm afraid, when he spoke of enemies, I considered it to be a symptom of his rather, shall we say, *inflated* view of himself. Enemies of Truth, he called them. I should have questioned him more closely about them, but . . .' Father Shaw's eyes flicked momentarily upwards, 'I did not take him entirely seriously. I should have been more vigilant, because one of these enemies caused his death, didn't they, Inspector?'

CHAPTER FOUR

Harry Wintle turned up for his lunch as Stratton and Canning were going through the contents of Lloyd's meagre wardrobe. Leaving Canning examining a threadbare jacket that smelt strongly of camphor, Stratton interviewed Wintle in his room. Around thirty, stout and ham-faced, dressed in paint-splashed overalls and steel-capped boots, with a grubby bandage wound inexpertly round the end of one finger, he'd received the news of his fellow lodger's demise with violent raisings of his eyebrows and huffing noises made through pursed lips, accompanied by bulging cheeks. After a moment, clearly feeling that he'd reacted enough, he turned his back on Stratton and set about heating up a tin of tomato soup on his solitary gas ring.

'Can't say I knew him well. We didn't have a lot in common, did we?'

Looking round Wintle's spartan accommodation, which was entirely devoid of books and decorated exclusively with film stars torn from magazines with 'come hither' eyes and breasts jutting provocatively from swimsuits or low-cut gowns, Stratton had to agree. 'Did he tell you that he was writing a book?'

'Told everyone. Kept it in a briefcase, didn't he? Pages and pages in there . . . you never saw him without it. Never showed me, though, or anyone else so far as I know. Wouldn't surprise me if the whole lot was blank.'

'Why do you say that?' asked Stratton, remembering what Father Shaw had said.

'He was a bit of a crank, wasn't he? Harmless enough, though, and he'd have given you his last penny if you'd asked. Can't see why anyone would have wanted to do away with him. For one thing, he never went out, and he never saw anyone, either, unless you count that padre.' Judging from his expression, Wintle clearly didn't. Then he frowned, and peered into his saucepan as if seeking inspiration – or perhaps confirmation – before adding, 'I did think something might have scared him, though.'

'Why?'

Wintle glared at the soup again, so intently and for so long that Stratton half expected a miniature hand with a sword to rise out of the viscous orange puddle, then said, 'He give me a photograph, didn't he? It's on there.' He jerked his head towards the mantelpiece, where, among a litter of string, tools, a half-bald shaving brush and a cracked saucer, was a large brown envelope. There was no writing on it, and it looked new.

Inside was a photograph of a very attractive woman who looked to be about twenty-five, standing on a lawn, with part of a tree – Stratton could see the white candelabra of a horse chestnut – and the corner of what looked like a large building behind her. Turning it over, Stratton saw the initials *L.R.* written on the back. 'Did he tell you who she was?'

'No. And I'd remember if I'd seen her. Smasher, ain't she?'

She certainly was, and looked as if she knew it. Dark-haired, with sculpted features and enormous eyes, black and liquid, there was an assured sexiness about her that, despite the demure frock, rivalled the flashier beauties on Wintle's walls.

'Did he say anything about her at all?'

Wintle shook his head. 'Just that I was to keep it. Then he said

I might not see him again. When I asked if he was leaving he just said he'd try to contact me. "In another way" was what he said. Then he went off back to his room.'

'He said he'd try to contact you in another way?'

'Those exact words. I didn't know what he was on about, unless he meant a letter, because there's no telephone in this house. To be honest, I didn't think nothing more of it. He was always a bit mysterious – acting like he'd got some secret the rest of us didn't know ... Like I said, a crank. Come to think of it, that was the last time I saw him.'

'When was that?'

'Couple of days ago. Hold up ... Saturday, it was. I remember that because it's the day I did this.' He held up the bandaged finger. 'Got a splinter, didn't I? Big bugger. I was trying to get it out when he come in, so I didn't pay too much attention ... Still in there, some of it, and now it hurts like hell.'

'Were you here last night?'

Wintle nodded. 'Wasn't back till, oooh ... half past eleven, twelve, something like that. Took my girl out, didn't I? She thinks I ought to see the doctor about this.' He cradled his injured finger in the other hand. 'I was working in a place where they've had horses and she's worried about tetanus.'

Stratton took the photograph downstairs, where he found Father Shaw still there, sitting with a baleful-looking Mrs Linder. He was obviously attempting to comfort her, although Stratton thought that by the looks of him it should have been the other way round. Neither of them recognised the woman, and nor, when he went up to Mrs Hendry's garret, did she. PC Canning, having given the photograph a careful once-over and a low whistle, told him that he hadn't come across any photographs in Lloyd's room at all, nor any reference to a name with the initials L.R.

'What about a briefcase?' said Stratton. 'Or anything that looks like a manuscript?'

'Nothing like that, sir. I've looked everywhere – the only place left is under the bed.'

'Fair enough.' Stratton got down on his knees and lifted up the edge of the candlewick bedspread, where he found a pair of dirty sheets, rolled up, and a large wooden box with a padlock.

'Could be the answer to the mystery, sir,' said Canning, as he hauled it out onto the rug.

'If the manuscript actually exists,' said Stratton. 'Father Shaw and Wintle both knew about it, but they seemed to think it was make-believe.'

'Well,' said Canning, 'if it's anywhere, it's here. And look what I found . . .' He leant over and lifted up one corner of the pillow to show a key. 'Nothing else here with a lock on, so . . .'

Stratton watched, expectant now in spite of himself, as Canning turned the key, removed the padlock, and threw back the lid with a flourish.

The box was empty.

CHAPTER FIVE

Stratton gazed up at the iron-girdered roof of Harringay Arena, and then at the floodlit platform decorated with baskets and urns of flowers, where an enormous choir of women in white blouses and men in dark suits stood waiting under the square black eyes of a battery of film cameras. The place was filling up quickly – audiences of up to twelve thousand, Stratton had heard. Watching the fervent expressions of the people near him, most of whom were twenty or less, he had, despite the preponderance of damp mackintoshes and the crescendo of phlegmy coughing, a sudden, disturbing memory of the newsreels he'd seen of Nazi rallies, the youthful, eager supporters with their upturned faces, waiting to receive the Führer's message.

He had to admit that the choir's singing, when it got under way, was magnificent. 'Guide Me, O Thou Great Jehovah', conducted in a flamboyant style that made Stratton think of a Cup Final. Then Billy Graham himself appeared, slim and handsome, with golden hair that waved back from his brow, made almost a halo by the bright lights. Stratton's first impression was that he was very small, but then, he told himself, in contrast with the stylised portrait of the face – radiating clean-cut health and strong-jawed sincerity, and a hundred times bigger than life

– that had eyeballed him from every street corner for the last month, he would be small, wouldn't he? Actually, when measured against the other men on the platform, he seemed pretty tall, with an air of smart athleticism – a sportsman in his Olympic suit. When he began to speak, Stratton noticed that he had a microphone attached to his tie, its flex trailing from his jacket, and he suddenly wondered how Jesus had managed to address the five thousand without amplification. Odd that whoever wrote the Bible hadn't thought to mention that that in itself was a miracle – feeding the buggers, Stratton thought, was nothing in comparison. After all, you could get loaves and fishes from anywhere . . . For God's sake, he told himself, pay attention. You're here, so you might as well listen.

He and his brother-in-law Donald had been dragged along to the meeting by their other brother-in-law, Reg. His daughter Monica was there, too, but that was only because she'd made a date to see him that evening and expressed mild curiosity about tagging along when Reg had insisted on his attendance. Reg's urging had surprised both him and Don; his attendance at church was limited to weddings, christenings and funerals, plus the odd duty visit at Christmas and, although he was capable of talking balls by the yard on just about every subject under the sun, religion had never, as far as either of them could remember, been one of them. It was odd, too, that it wasn't his wife or his sisters-in-law to whom Reg had appealed, only himself and Don.

Stratton wondered what, if anything, *he* was expecting. In so far as he'd ever given serious thought to God, he supposed he believed in a general, informal sort of way . . . or at least he had until his wife Jenny had been killed twelve years earlier. After that, his feelings were more like hatred – although in a confused way, because he felt guilty, too, about not having got there fast enough to prevent her death. The only time he'd discussed this was with Don, who'd opined that people believed in order to explain, or at least dismiss in safety, those bits of the universe that they didn't understand. Then, as Don had pointed out, science explained some of the bits and people believed less, or, alternatively, science failed them and they went back to religion. That, Stratton thought, was probably about the size of it, although God seemed to him to be somehow more factual than this allowed for; not uplifting, and certainly not consoling, but just sort of 'there'. Not that he'd ever attempt to explain any of that to Don, of course, but he couldn't imagine, aged fifty, that life – or indeed anything that he might hear this evening – was going to show him any different.

Stratton glanced at Reg, who'd been uncharacteristically silent since they'd met up in the queue outside the arena, and wondered what he was thinking. He saw that his brother-in-law's coarse-grained face had a closed, intense look and his usually high, varnished colour seemed dull. He turned his attention back to Billy Graham, who was in the middle of some personal anecdote about being in an aeroplane – there'd obviously been something about losing radio contact, because now he was talking about making contact with God. 'You say,' he intoned briskly, "Billy, how can I make contact with God?" Jesus said, "I am the Way, the Truth and the Light." There is only one way back to God – through Jesus Christ!'

It seemed to Stratton that the man, though undoubtedly likeable, lacked the gift of oratory – hence, he thought, his own lapse of concentration. He wasn't the only one, either – from somewhere behind him he could hear fidgeting and whispering and once, a muffled laugh. The delivery was rapid, almost staccato, and, because of the microphone, tinnily mechanical. Although he strode about a fair bit, there were no expansive gestures. Now there was some stuff about God's eye being always upon us, but with a good deal less turgid doom-mongering than he remembered from the Sunday services of his youth, probably because it was garlanded with a lot of stuff about hope and forgiveness and opening your heart. He certainly seemed to know his Bible, too – he held it all the time as he quoted, slapping it for emphasis but never once looking at the pages, and interspersing the stories with a lot of rhetorical questions of the 'Who is God? What is God? Does God matter?' variety. As far as Stratton could tell, it seemed to be mostly New Testament stuff – parables and the like. He guessed that the reason for this was that the Old Testament – at least, in his recollection – was either incomprehensible or full of foul-tempered characters doing disagreeable things, with God the worst of the lot.

Stratton glanced at his daughter and brothers-in-law. Don was frowning and Monica seemed to be staring at her feet. Reg was leaning forward with the sort of strained expression which could have denoted anything from total concentration to stifling a fart. After about forty minutes, Graham, who'd been talking about what he called 'getting right' with God, opened his arms wide and, after a dramatic pause, intoned, 'Come and give yourself to God! Declare yourself for Christ! If you want Christ, you need Christ. You want Him to change your life. Come to the front . . .'

After some initial reluctance, a trickle of people began to move towards the platform. Graham repeated his exhortation, and, slowly, more people followed. Stratton did a quick headcount: one hundred, two hundred, three . . . They seemed to display no emotion, although, as they passed, he noticed that one or two were in tears. As the choir began to sing an anthem, he saw, out of the corner of his eye, that Reg had stood up. Monica, looking surprised, moved out of his way, as, after leaning down to whisper briefly in Don's ear, he began making his way towards the front.

Stratton raised his eyebrows interrogatively at Don, who, giving a disbelieving shake of the head, muttered, 'He says not to wait for him after.'

'Fair enough.' Stratton watched as Reg and the other stragglers were marshalled to the side of the platform, where a group of dark-suited men with what looked like badges on their lapels waited to lead them out of sight. Stratton supposed that these must be the counsellors he'd read about in the paper, who encouraged people in their faith. He tried to imagine what sort of conversation Reg might have with such a person, failed, and then, detaching himself from the proceedings, sat back with his arms crossed, waiting for the thing to end so that they could go home.

'What did you think?' he said to Monica. They were standing under the overhang of the vast building, sheltering from the drizzle as they waited for Don, who'd got stuck behind a knot of people, to make his way through the crowd.

His daughter, who'd been adjusting a headscarf over her long black hair, paused for a moment, biting her lip. 'Don't know, really. It's a bit ... well, *much*. For me, anyway.'

'I know what you mean.'

'I'm surprised about Uncle Reg. Being so keen on it, I mean.'

'Me too.'

'Is he all right? I thought he looked a bit under the weather.'

'He's probably coming down with a cold or something. How about a cup of coffee? There must be somewhere open round here.'

Monica knotted the scarf under her chin. 'Better get back. If I miss the ten o'clock train, the next one's not for ages.' She leant forward and gave him a peck on the cheek. 'I'll give you a ring.'

'All right, then.' Stratton patted her on the back. 'Keep safe, won't you?'

'Course. You too, Dad. Night, then.'

Stratton watched her weave through the crowd until her slender figure was lost to sight, wishing, not for the first time, that she'd find a nice chap and settle down. His niece Madeline had been married for a few years now – Don and Doris were grandparents – but Monica, at twenty-six, showed no signs of doing the same. She seemed happy enough, working as a make-up girl for a film studio in Essex and renting a tiny cottage nearby with a girl who worked for a fashionable London milliner, but there'd been a lot of trouble over a young film star called Raymond Benson, who'd proved to be a complete shit, and married, to boot. He worried that the experience – not to mention her subsequent miscarriage – had put her off men for good. It couldn't be for lack of offers, because she was lovely looking, just like his wife Jenny had been at her age except for the hair colour, which was like his – or like most of it, anyway. In the last year, he'd suddenly noticed that he was greying at the temples. Still, at least he *had* all his hair, which was more than could be said for Don. His brother-in-law's head, as he bobbed towards him through the throng, looked, in the harsh light cast by the lamps outside the stadium, like a large, freckled egg.

They walked away in silence, and it was only when they reached the tube station that Don broke it by asking, 'Well, what did you make of it?'

'I'm not sure, really,' said Stratton. 'Pretty impressive, I suppose. You?'

'I'm not sure, either. I don't know that he's making that many converts, though. I got the impression that most of the people who declared themselves, or whatever you call it, were pretty fervent already.'

'Not Reg, though.'

'No.' Stratton, who was puzzled and irritated by Reg's behaviour, and all the more irritated for knowing the irritation was unreasonable – after all, it was none of his business what the man did – hoped that Don would enlarge on this, but he didn't. Instead, as they stepped into the train, he said, 'I suppose, with everything that's happening, the appeal isn't so surprising.' He grimaced in the direction of a man reading a newspaper and Stratton saw the headline ALL SET TO GO IN, and, underneath, *Egypt rejects, Israel accepts ultimatum. British and French Forces Ready to Take Over Suez Canal Bases.*

'That and the Soviet troops in Hungary,' said Stratton.

'That's another bloody mess, if you ask me. I can't help remembering how ... well, *romantic*, I suppose ... we were about Communism before the war.'

'Were we?'

'I think I was,' said Donald, ruefully. 'Naive, anyway. Thinking it would be fairer and so on.'

'Yes, I suppose we were,' said Stratton, although he didn't think he had been, particularly. 'You were never a party member, though, were you?'

'No, but I remember thinking, when they all went to Spain, that if I hadn't got a family and so on ...'

'Maybe,' said Stratton, 'but I reckon a lot of them'll be tearing up their party cards now. Even the real diehards are going to have a hell of a job pretending that the Soviets are invading to protect Hungarian workers. Talk about The Light That Failed.'

'I know ... But the thing is,' Donald returned to the previous subject with an air of having escaped to safer ground, 'that people are bound to want certainties at a time like this, and Billy Graham's got them, hasn't he? All that stuff about the Bible solving your problems.'

'Do you think that's how Reg sees it?'

'God knows.' Don laughed. 'There, you see? It's like any situation in life – illness, death ... annihilation ... somebody must know. They don't, of course, so we're stuck with God because if He doesn't, we're buggered.'

'I think,' said Stratton, nodding in the direction of the newspaper, 'that we're buggered anyway, so far as that goes.'

'Yeah . . . the Empire on which the sun never sets. Famous last words.'

'Pete's going. Got a letter yesterday.'

'You didn't say.' Don looked as if he were groping for words, then said, quietly, 'Bit rough, that.'

'He doesn't think so.' Stratton's son, who'd decided to stay on in the army after National Service, had seemed, judging by his letter, to be relishing the prospect. 'Says he can't wait to get stuck in.'

'Does Monica know?'

'Yes, he telephoned her.' Stratton wondered if, trains aside, not wanting to talk about it was why Monica hadn't elected to stay. They'd discussed it briefly, before the meeting, and he knew she was worried about Pete, though she'd hidden it well.

'Well,' said Don grimly, 'let's hope he comes back in one piece.'

'I just hope to God . . .' Stratton stopped, unable to put his feelings into words. He and Pete may not have too much to say to each other, but the idea of losing his son as well as his wife was . . . well, unthinkable. Fortunately, the train pulled into Turnpike Lane station, so he was saved from having to try to explain. 'Our stop,' he said. 'Come on.'

To Stratton's relief, Don didn't mention Pete again. Instead, as they were walking to the bus stop, he said, 'You do realise that being born again in Christ is pretty well guaranteed to make Reg even more irritating than he already is, don't you?'

Stratton nodded, gloomily. 'I always thought that one thing you could say about Reg was that at least he was predictably awful.'

'Insulting you and then saying "Can't you take a joke?" you mean?'

'Exactly.'

'That way of speaking he has, as if he's got inside knowledge of the workings of the world that he can't share with you because you're too stupid to understand?'

'That as well.'

'Holding the telephone right away from his ear and shouting into the mouthpiece as if he's encouraging a horse?'

'Yup. And the way he always calls rice pudding "Chinese wedding cake" and every other bloody thing he says and does. But we *expect* him to be like that, and now . . .'

'Now he's wrong-footed us . . .'

'And,' concluded Stratton glumly, 'he'll probably start looking at us sorrowfully – "Father, forgive them, for they know not what they do" sort of thing. Secure in the knowledge that he's been saved.'

'*Shriven*,' said Don. 'Do you think that's possible? Forgiveness of sins, no matter how bad they are?'

Stratton thought about it for just a moment. 'No,' he said, shortly. 'I don't. Some things aren't forgivable.'

CHAPTER SIX

I did not see anyone come in or go out of the house during that time, read Stratton, *except for when Mrs Linder came back at just after eleven which I know she did because we had a word when I went to put the cat out and it was* ... Stratton turned the page ... *persistently importuning men for an immoral purpose in Leicester Square, paying four visits to public lavatories in the area in the course of ninety minutes* ...

'Quite a cat.' Swearing quietly to himself, Stratton sifted through the jumble of statements on his desk, trying to find the right page. He and PC Canning and PC Standish had spent the morning doing the rounds of the neighbours in Flaxman Court and the adjoining streets but no one appeared to have seen anything out of the ordinary. No unusual visitors to Flaxman Court, no strangers hanging about the place, nobody fleeing into the night. Many of them knew Lloyd, or at least recognised the description, but nobody seemed to have seen him out and about with anyone except Mrs Linder or Father Shaw. He didn't frequent the Nellie Dean or any of the other local pubs and generally seemed – Stratton sighed deeply – to have kept himself to himself. All of them thought him an oddball, if a kind one. There were a lot of mentions of carrying shopping and running errands and so on, but nothing above the level of mere acquaintance.

They'd got soaked for their trouble, too – hats and coats steaming on the stand beside the paraffin heater which, despite much fiddling with the wick, smelt strongly. Stratton shivered – his feet were damp and the draught from the slightly open window (a necessary measure against asphyxiation) was blowing directly down his neck.

'The man must have had *some* friends,' he muttered, pawing the papers into a rough heap and putting anything that didn't apply to the investigation on one side. He read through the statements again, double-checking that nothing interesting had slipped past him unnoticed – it hadn't – then flipped disconsolately through his notebook. Two people – Mrs Linder and Father Shaw – had mentioned the writer Ambrose Tynan. Mrs Linder had told Canning that Lloyd had visited him, and the priest had said he'd 'helped him a great deal and given him books', one of which they'd seen in Lloyd's room, and also that Tynan had 'introduced him to like-minded people'. Stratton wondered who they were. Not anyone that Father Shaw would approve of, by the sound of it. A telephone call to Tynan's publisher had elicited the information that their star author lived in a village called Lincott, in Suffolk. Stratton decided he'd better go and see the man. Given what Father Shaw had said, he suspected that the connection was more important to Lloyd than it was to Tynan, but – aside from the aunt, Mrs Prentice, who DI Grove had gone to Roehampton to interview – it was the only lead he had.

'Lincott in Suffolk?' said Grove, round his pipe. With his pouched eyes and increasingly pendulous chops, the older copper's appearance was becoming, in Stratton's opinion, more and more like that of a friendly bloodhound. Now, he wore the expression of a dog that had got a scent. 'Let's have a butcher's at that map.'

When he'd shambled round to Stratton's side of the desk, he said, 'I thought it sounded familiar. That's where Ballard went when he left us. Round there, anyway.' He jabbed a finger at the string of little dots on the green background. 'Cambridgeshire borders, I remember him saying.'

'Is it?' Stratton had regretted his former sergeant's departure, two years ago, from West End Central, but he'd understood it all right. The ostensible reason was Ballard's little girl ... Kitty? Katy? ... who had weak lungs and needed clean air. Must be five or six now, he thought. Time flies ... And there was Ballard's promotion, of course, to DI, but Stratton knew there'd been more to it than that. The hanging of Davies, for a crime he almost certainly had not committed, had taken its toll in self-reproach and a loss of confidence, both in his ability as a copper and in the institution as a whole. Stratton had experienced it too, but it had been worse for the younger man, and he could see why he'd welcomed the chance of a fresh start in a different place. He felt that he should have remembered where Ballard had gone. Grove, kindly and avuncular, always remembered things like that. 'Yup,' he said now. 'You could give him a call.'

'I certainly shall. What was Mrs Prentice like?'

'Very respectable, and smart with it. Had the *Radio Times* in an embossed leather cover. Nothing peculiar about *her*.' Grove nodded in agreement with himself. 'She confirmed what your priest said: the parents were pretty cut up when Lloyd went AWOL from the sanatorium they'd put him in – well, you can imagine – and of course the poor souls died without knowing where he was or what had happened to him. He was their only child – born in ...' here, Grove flicked through his notebook, '1928. There was a sister – born two years later – but she died when she was a baby. Mrs P. said he'd had a difficult personality since he was a boy. "Awkward" was the word she used.'

'Sounds about right, from what I can gather.'

'The parents spent all their savings paying for him to learn the piano.' Grove glanced down at the page again. 'They felt that his religious obsession had taken him away from it, so there was a fair degree of bitterness towards the church, which they saw as having encouraged him to give up on the music.'

'But presumably,' said Stratton, remembering Father Shaw's words, 'Lloyd must have been a bit potty to get so wrapped up in the church in the first place. I mean, they couldn't have turned him into a religious nutcase without something to work on, could they?'

'Shouldn't think so. Anyway, Mrs Prentice thought it was more a case of his not having enough musical talent – which was what that priest said, wasn't it?'

'Pretty much. Was she aware of the contents of the parents' wills?'

'Yes. She told me they'd left £200 to her, and the rest of the money and the house to him in the first instance, and in the event of his death to the RSPCA. Solicitor confirmed it – the total estate, minus the aunt's money, came to . . .' Grove consulted his notebook, '£7,217. So, nothing there unless you believe the RSPCA makes a practice of bumping people off.'

'He didn't have paid employment,' said Stratton. 'At least, not as far as I know, so I wonder how he got by? There was no evidence that he had a bank account, and the only money I found in his room was a bit of loose change, but the landlady told Canning he was always paid up with the rent.'

'No idea . . . Oh, before I forget, she gave me a couple of photographs. That one' – Grove proffered a photo of a serious-looking kid in flannels and a school blazer – 'probably won't be much use, because he's only sixteen or thereabouts, but this,' he laid another photograph, clearly recognisable as Lloyd the man, on the desk, 'might come in handy.'

'Thanks,' said Stratton, gazing at them abstractedly. 'I suppose,' he added, 'that too much self-belief is as bad as none at all. Mind you, you could say that about belief in anything. There must be some sort of decent middle ground.'

'Still,' said Grove, 'it's normal to want to make sense of the world, isn't it? I mean, old son, you could say that's what we do.' Seeing Stratton's confusion, he added, 'Our job, I mean. Finding answers to questions.'

Both men considered this for a moment before making a silent, mutual decision that there was nothing more that could sensibly be said on the subject, and beating a hasty retreat to the altogether less taxing topic of Mr Heddon. 'Barmy,' said Grove. 'Mad as a hatter. Still, it could be a lot worse. Remember that chap we had in March who was so frightened of living under the Russians that he clobbered his wife with a claw hammer and stuck his head in the gas oven?'

'Vividly, thanks,' said Stratton, picturing the dead woman's caved-in face and punctured eyes. 'But as fears go, that was a bit more realistic, wasn't it? I mean, the Soviets actually exist. Unlike the little green men.'

'Ambrose Tynan probably thinks they do.'

'That's what I'm afraid of,' said Stratton gloomily, thinking of the regularity with which articles about evil cults and threats from outer space by the author appeared in the newspapers. 'More bollocks.'

'I'm not at all happy about having you chasing round all over the country, but seeing as you don't have anything else, you'd better get up to this Lincott place tomorrow and find out who these people are,' said Lamb, when Stratton had explained the situation.

'Suffolk's not far, sir, and Lincott's on the Cambridge border.'

Lamb grunted. 'I suppose I ought to be grateful that you're not proposing to go traipsing up to Norfolk.' He made it sound as though Stratton had chosen the destination by blindfolding himself and sticking a pin in a map.

'I understand from DI Grove that Lincott may be on DI Ballard's patch, sir.'

'Good officer, Ballard.' Lamb looked fractionally more approving. 'I was sorry to lose him,' he added, in obituary tones.

'So was I, sir.'

'If that's the case, you might have a chat with him while you're there – he'll know the lie of the land. I'll give his superior a call – fill him in about it.'

'Yes, sir. Thank you.'

'Off you go, then. Stay overnight if it's necessary. And try to make some sort of progress, won't you?'

CHAPTER SEVEN

Seated in the corner of a small Italian restaurant on the edge of Soho, Stratton sipped gingerly at a glass of vinegary red wine and contemplated the Alpine scene, rendered in smeary oil paint, which stretched the length of the adjacent wall. What he really wanted was a decent pint of beer, but that wasn't available. The choice of edible food – edible, that was, without risking a lot of spilling and mopping and making a fool of oneself – was limited too, which was a shame because it wasn't half bad once you actually managed to get it into your mouth. However, Diana seemed to like the place, so it was where they came. He thought wistfully of the Lyons Corner House where he'd taken Jenny when they were courting – meat, two veg and a nice fruit pie afterwards – but, try as he might, he couldn't imagine doing the same with Diana. He and Jenny had been comfortable with each other, right from the start. Their differences – the fact that she was a Londoner and he'd grown up on a farm – had been a source of amusement. Her mimicry of his (then much stronger) Devon accent and his pretending to think she believed milk came from tins had been fun. Safe. He'd always known where he was with Jenny, what to expect, how to *be*. But he supposed, when she'd died, that the self he was with her had died as well . . .

And Jenny's family had welcomed him, hadn't they? He'd never met any of Diana's family, but he knew bloody well that, had they been alive and her ancestral home not sold off for next to nothing, it would have been strictly tradesmen's entrance only for the likes of him. And, but for the war, he'd never have met Diana in the first place. Besides, he and Diana weren't *courting*, were they? Quite what they were doing, he wasn't sure, but since they'd begun doing it – a little over two years ago – he'd schooled himself not to examine it too closely.

Gradually, in the years after Jenny had died, 'we' and 'us' had been replaced in his mind by 'I' and 'me', but he couldn't think of himself and Diana as 'we' and 'us'. The chasm between them was too great. He couldn't have existed in her world, nor she in his – the idea of her standing in the scullery of his home in Tottenham, washing up at the sink, was preposterous. They both pretended, when together, not to be aware of such things, but often – although he was, frankly, still dazedly proud to be with someone who looked and spoke as she did – he had a sense that they were inside a bubble which might burst at any moment.

He lit a cigarette, remembering the vertiginous feeling he'd had the first time they'd kissed. Astounded by his daring, he couldn't believe that she was allowing him – encouraging him, even – to put his lips on hers, and as for the rest ... The first time he'd seen her naked had been wonderful, of course, but at the same time rather frightening, because of the almost impossibility of it. Taking another sip of the nasty wine, Stratton remembered his dry mouth and sweaty hands, as though she were his first. He pushed his chair back, resting his head against the wall and staring up at the ceiling, where the muralist had continued the view as a blue sky clotted with improbably solid-looking clouds, and wishing he'd brought a paper with him. Waiting for Diana to arrive – he always took care to be at least a quarter of an hour early, so that she would never be forced to sit alone –

made him feel ungallant, a heel, but she refused to let him meet her in public and escort her there. They'd argued about it, and she'd told him, sharply, that she wasn't going to hang around for him on a street corner or in a tube station as though she were a prostitute. He'd protested, in vain, that he'd never keep her waiting, but she wouldn't have it. In any case there was, he knew, a more important reason: theirs was, by unspoken mutual agreement, a clandestine arrangement. He hated this, too, but he'd never spoken of Diana to his family, just as she, he was sure, had never told her friends about him.

'Edward, I'm so sorry!' Looking up, he saw Diana in front of him and jumped up, making the candle wobble precariously on the small table. As always, her beauty made him catch his breath. Tall and elegant, with shining blonde hair and huge, luminous eyes, she was graciously receiving the attentions of two waiters who were falling over themselves to help her off with her coat, pull out her chair and provide her with a drink. Penned in by furniture and knowing he was surplus to requirements, Stratton sat down again, feeling sheepish. He'd often noticed that people always rushed to Diana's assistance, made allowances, and generally put themselves out. He did it himself, didn't he? Watching her now, he found himself wondering whether she realised such solicitousness on the part of others was the exception rather than the rule – but then, he reasoned, to her it was entirely normal.

'I'm afraid I got held up at work. It's this film I told you about, with the alligator. It's supposed to be a girl, but this afternoon we realised that the one we've got is rather *obviously* male at times. Apparently it's impossible to tell unless they get, you know, *excited*, and I suppose it didn't occur to anyone to ask the owner. The problem is, there are lots of close-ups with the leading man holding it and so on . . . They're trying to find a female one from a zoo or something, but it meant rescheduling everything and a lot of fuss about different costumes, and that's why I'm late.'

Stratton raised an eyebrow. Since Diana had started working in the design department at Ashwood Studios, she'd come back with a few tales, but ... 'Well, as excuses go, it's certainly original.'

'You're not angry, are you?' Diana looked distressed. 'I did my best, but—'

'I'm joking! It's almost the weirdest thing I've heard all day. Couldn't you give it some bromide?'

'I don't suppose it works on alligators. So what's the weirdest thing you've heard all day?'

Once they'd ordered and been served, Stratton told her about Mr Heddon and the message from outer space, and then a bit about Jeremy Lloyd. 'We've found his aunt, the only next of kin, and he seems to have been friendly with Ambrose Tynan. Didn't they make a film of one of his books at Ashwood a few years ago?'

Diana nodded. '*Such Men Are Dangerous*. But that was an early spy one, not one of those witchcraft things. I met him.'

'Did you?'

'Yes, he came to the studio. Terribly *grand*. Went about handing out copies of his books. The one I got was some nonsense about flying saucers.'

'When you say *grand* like that,' said Stratton, 'do you mean "common pretending to be upper class"? Not quite "one of us"?' This came out with rather more of an edge than he'd intended, and Diana flushed.

'It sounds horrible when you put it like that – snobbish. I suppose it's true, though. I met someone who knows him in the country recently, and they said – oh, dear ...' Diana's colour intensified and she looked down at her plate. 'They said he's been acting the part for so long that he'd probably be genuinely horrified to find his name wasn't in *Debrett's*. His wife's was, though – or her father, anyway, because she was the Honourable Dorothy Lambton before she married. Came to the studio with him – I got the impression she didn't take him very seriously. I did wonder if the money mightn't have played quite a part in it, because they got married quite late on, after he was successful, and her family was stony broke, but I rather liked her. She died a couple of years ago. Cancer, I think. But *anyway*,' Diana rolled her eyes, still slightly embarrassed but trying to make a joke out of it, 'what I was trying to say was that he seemed to me – and I could be wrong because I only spoke to him for about five minutes,' she added hastily, 'to be, well, sort of invented. By himself, I mean.'

'Doesn't everyone invent themselves as they go along?'

'I don't quite mean that. It was more . . . well, as if . . .' Diana thought for a moment, toying with the stem of her glass, then said, 'As if he'd decided at about sixteen what kind of person he was going to be. As if he'd written it all down or something, like a, a template, then set about forming himself into that. Oh, look, I'm probably talking rubbish. Take no notice. What is interesting, though, is that he knew Colonel Forbes-James. Worked for the Secret Service during the war.'

'Surely he shouldn't have told you that?'

'He didn't.' Diana's cheeks, which had returned to their usual colour, went pink again. 'Claude Ventriss told me.'

'Oh, yes?' Stratton tried to quell the surge of aggression that welled, unbidden, inside him. Ventriss had been Diana's lover during the war, when she'd been married to her first husband. Stratton had hated him on sight, a feeling which had intensified after the way he'd treated her later on, when she was all but destitute after her second husband had deserted her. 'What did he say?'

'Only that Tynan wrote papers about defence and things like

that. I remember Claude saying that he'd never seen one, but if they were anything like his conversation they must be quite mad. Claude said he was always talking to F-J about mind control and astral projection and things like that.'

Stratton wanted to ask Diana if she thought that Colonel Forbes-James, the section head to whom he'd been seconded during the war to work on a sensitive murder case, believed in such things, but he didn't fancy hearing 'Claude said this' and 'Claude said that' again and again. In any case, Forbes-James wasn't an easy topic of conversation. Stratton was fairly certain that he'd committed suicide, and pretty sure that Diana knew far more about the circumstances than he did, but as she'd never alluded to it he'd judged it best not to ask. One way or another, he reflected, there were a hell of a lot of things between them that were off-limits. Not just the stuff about Forbes-James and that bastard Ventriss, but the fact that, three years before, he'd seen Diana at her lowest ebb, distressed, dishevelled and homeless, and he was careful never to say anything that would remind her of it. It wasn't only that he hated to think she went on seeing him because she felt indebted, but he also knew that someone seeing you like that made you vulnerable, which could lead to your resenting them, and—

'What is it, Edward?' Diana had put down her knife and fork and was looking at him in consternation.

'What is what?'

'You've been glaring at me for the last two minutes.'

'I'm sorry. It's not you, it's just this case ... I've got a horrible feeling it isn't going to be at all straightforward.'

'I suppose you'll have to interview Tynan, will you?'

''Fraid so. Still, it means a change of scenery – he lives in Suffolk.'

'In quite a ...' Diana laughed, 'grand house, I believe. I remember his telling me about it. He collects all sorts of art. Quite a wine cellar, too, judging by what he said.'

'Got to be better than this stuff.' Stratton grimaced at his glass. 'Still, I shan't be offered any. Or asked my opinion of his collection.'

Diana, looking anxious, said, 'Oh, I didn't tell you. I saw Monica today. She's working on the stage next to the alligator film.'

It was an obvious change of subject, but Stratton, who adored his daughter, was quite happy to be drawn. 'A comedy, she said.'

Diana nodded. '*The Cabbage Patch*. It's set on a farm. They're doing the interiors at the moment – barns and what not. At least,' she added, 'our alligator hasn't scoffed any of the props.'

Stratton laughed. 'Monica'd like that – the animals, I mean. She and Pete were evacuated to a place with a farm, and they loved helping out. That was in Suffolk, come to think of it.'

'I don't suppose she has that much to do with the animals – I mean, they don't need make-up – but she certainly looked happy.'

'Oh, she is. At work, anyway.'

As if guessing what was in his mind, Diana said, 'You needn't worry, you know. She's doing fine.'

They finished their dinner and sat talking about nothing in particular over cups of coffee – only marginally nicer than the wine – until it was time for him to find Diana a taxi and catch the bus home. Dozing off in the warm fug, he found himself in a half-memory, half-dream of himself and Jenny walking arm in arm down the pier at Brighton with the sea pounding beneath their feet so that they could feel it through the soles of their shoes. When they reached the end of the pier, the sea had calmed, and they stood watching the sunset, the scudding pink clouds . . .

The revving of the engine woke him, and he sat up quickly, self-conscious and feeling dizzy and disconcerted, as if he'd suddenly found himself in the middle of a tightrope walk, a long, long way from the ground.

*

This sensation, or at least its uneasy aftermath, returned the following morning, when, on the way to the station to catch the train to Suffolk, he encountered a solemn-looking elderly bloke with a soup-strainer moustache who was wearing a sandwich board reading, 'The End is Nigh'. On the back it said, 'God Wants You', which made Stratton think of Kitchener. The old boy was being followed by a tramp with a beard so densely matted that it looked like felt, and whose lack of teeth and missing shoelaces made him, with the tongues lolling out of his boots, appear to have come undone at both ends. 'How can I find Him, then?' he was shouting. 'Has He got a telephone number? You got His number, have you? Eh? Eh?' The God bloke, clearly embarrassed by the noisy attention, was hampered in his efforts to escape by the board, which hung down to his knees. After watching for a moment, Stratton intervened, identified himself, and sent the tramp on his way, much to the relief of the God chap, who shook his hand repeatedly and started talking about Billy Graham.

'I've been,' said Stratton, attempting to free his fingers.

'Ah,' said the man, 'then you *know*.'

'You've got the wrong bloke, mate,' Stratton muttered, as he walked away.

As the train pulled out of the station and picked up speed, Stratton stared out at the dirty backs of houses, gapped with bomb sites where the past had been knocked down and the future hadn't yet arrived. That's assuming that there's going to be a future, he thought. Who knows?

As the tunnels of blackened bricks and the backs of houses gave way to flat-roofed asbestos prefabs and finally to country-side, spooling past him through the carriage window, Stratton reflected that the more you thought about religion, the less sense it made. That stuff about having 'sure and certain hope of the Resurrection', for example. It simply wasn't possible – hope, by its very nature, was neither sure nor certain . . . Still, if you puzzled over that sort of thing too much, you'd probably end up as barmy as Lloyd had evidently been. It was all far too bloody complicated. Shame about the weather, he thought, looking out at muddy fields and waterlogged thatch, but it's nice to get out into the country – and he wasn't half pleased at the prospect of a drink and a chat with Ballard. He'd telephoned his former sergeant before he'd left, and, behind the ribbing about Stratton's encroaching on his patch, he'd sensed that Ballard was looking forward to their reunion as much as he was.

Soothed by the rhythm of the train, he leant back in his seat and closed his eyes.

CHAPTER EIGHT

Standing in his back garden, Detective Inspector Ballard could see, over the wall, a large stone angel on a pedestal, her head bowed low in prayer, and, on the far side, brown fields, some still dotted with pillboxes, vanishing over the horizon. His wife Pauline hadn't liked the idea of living so near a graveyard, but as Ballard had pointed out, at least their neighbours were quiet, and Katy, their daughter, enjoyed playing in there.

There was no doubt that moving to Suffolk had done her good. Now a sturdy six-year-old, there were roses in her cheeks and – thank God – her breathing had improved no end. Pauline, although she'd missed her family badly at first, seemed to like it here too, and so, on balance, did he. Of course, there were things he missed about West End Central – and, come to that, about Putney, where they'd lived – the people, the busyness of the place, the feeling of being at the epicentre . . . But, set against the biggest thing of all, they seemed trifling.

In the aftermath of the Davies and Backhouse cases, the suffocating weight of 'if onlys' had made him doubt his thoughts and instincts to the point where he seemed to be suffering from a sort of creeping mental paralysis which all too often gave rise to a jeering inner chorus of self-disgust. Geographical distance was, he knew, no substitute for mental distance, but it had certainly helped not to be seeing the same people – DI Stratton, DCI Lamb and the rest – every day. The constant I-know-you-know of guilty knowledge and the horror of 10 Paradise Street that lurked, unacknowledged and never discussed, at the corner of the station's collective eye, had proved in the end too much. When he was offered the chance of transferring to the country, he'd accepted immediately, without waiting to consult Pauline. This, he realised afterwards, was wrong, but he'd done it unthinkingly, as a drowning man would grab at a lifebelt. Presenting it to her as a fait accompli, he'd argued that promotion meant more pay, which had gone down well, and the point about Katy's welfare had gone down even better. When Pauline had advanced an argument of her own, that the healthier air of the countryside might help her conceive the second child she so desperately wanted, Ballard felt he was home and dry. The matter of a sister or brother for Katy didn't bother him one way or the other, but as long as it remained at two children (still affordable) and didn't become three or – God forbid – four, he didn't really mind. He'd been sorry when Pauline's second pregnancy, back in 1953, had ended in a miscarriage, but if he were honest his feelings had been more to do with concern for his wife's grief than anything else. Since then, each month had brought more disappointment, and, as Pauline had made it clear that his attempts at reassurance were pathetically inadequate, he had for the sake of sanity closed his mind to the problem, reasoning that either they would have another baby, or they wouldn't, and there was nothing – apart from the obvious – that he could do about it. And that was quite bad enough, thanks to the pamphlet Pauline had sent off for, with its helpful diagrams and instructions which had to be followed to the letter and made him feel more as if he were carrying out a medical procedure than participating in sexual activity.

The other good thing about being in the country was that, as now, he could occasionally nip home at lunchtime; such a luxury which would have been out of the question in London. Ballard lit a cigarette and stared past the angel to the church with its squat Norman tower and a fussy little porch – a Victorian addition, he thought – that was festooned with long rosters of the names of flower-arrangers, brass-polishers, linen-launderers and the like. To the left, he could see an ancient cottage, topped with dark, soggy thatch that sagged in the middle like an old and ill-bred horse, and beyond that, more fields. This morning, a piece of the past in the form of DI Stratton had telephoned, saying that he was coming to interview Ambrose Tynan. Good luck with that one, mate, thought Ballard. Tynan, he knew from experience, was the sort who insisted he didn't want any special treatment and then raised merry hell if he didn't get it. Ballard had arranged a car to collect Stratton from the station, and agreed to meet him for a drink in the George and Dragon in Lincott – conveniently, just a quarter of a mile from his house – in the evening.

He was looking forward to seeing Stratton again: not only had he learnt a hell of a lot from him in their years together at West End Central, but he also admired and liked the man. He'd always be grateful for his erstwhile superior's discretion when he and Pauline, who'd been a policewoman, were courting, as well as for the constant unspoken support and the camaraderie. There was also the fact that – unlike some other senior officers he could think of – Stratton had never claimed credit at Ballard's expense, never belittled and never patronised. A part of him couldn't help wishing, though, that Stratton belonged to any other bit of his life but work. There was always a danger that the subject of Davies and Backhouse might come up, and, even after three years, it wasn't something Ballard wanted to discuss. He'd done his best, since they'd moved here two years ago, to pretend that none of it had happened. When he'd arrived, there'd been a fair few sly digs from fellow coppers who'd resented him as an incomer, but time and proximity having both accustomed and resigned them to his presence, such comments had all but ceased.

He hadn't told Pauline about Stratton's visit – why, he wasn't entirely sure – only that he'd be working late. There was also the fact – nothing to do with Davies and Backhouse, this, but possibly part of the tangle of obscure reasons why he hadn't mentioned it – that, having passed his fortieth birthday and feeling, for the first time in his life, that his personal fulcrum had tipped over into middle age, the promise of a nostalgia session with Stratton definitely added to the sensation that he was somehow passing into his own past. He'd had his strongest impression of it yet the previous evening when he was washing up the dinner plates for Pauline and suddenly recalled his father standing at the sink in their Holloway home, holding up a plate or colander or something and saying, 'I wonder how many times I've washed this up?' Then, looking down at his hands and arms with the shirtsleeves turned back twice and folded precisely, in exactly the same way as Dad had done, he'd suddenly thought: is this all there is?

Thinking about this, another memory surfaced: of his father, six months before his death last year at the age of sixty-six, making his wheezy way along the pavement, stopping to hang onto lamp-posts while he recovered his breath. He hadn't lived long after his retirement. His mother was like most of the older women in the street – be-cardiganned, with National Health teeth and spectacles (for all he knew, some of them had wigs, as well), living on, sharing the house with her also-widowed sister. As far as he could see, the pair of them spent their time matching privations and ailments while poor Dad, in the cemetery, crumbled slowly away to dust.

Ballard had read somewhere that the death of a man's father

broadened his horizons and emboldened him, but in his case, it had been simply unnerving. All he could think was: you're next in line, chum.

This miserable and isolating train of thought was abruptly derailed when he caught sight of a shapely thigh with a hint of stocking-top coming over the stile at the end of the graveyard. The rest of the woman lived up to his first glimpse. Even from a distance he could see that she had a strikingly pretty – no, beautiful – face and a cloud of dark brown curls, and that the outdoor clothes she wore could not disguise her slender curves. Seeing him, she made no move to cover her leg or clamber down, but straddled the stile in a deliberate pose that reminded him of an exceptionally saucy wartime propaganda photograph of a landgirl, and gave him a cheerful wave.

'Fancy giving me a hand?' she shouted. 'I seem to be stuck!'

Instantly galvanised into action, Ballard vaulted over the wall, forgetting – bloody hell! – that there was a patch of stinging nettles on the other side, and, leaping over the listing grave of Sir Thos. Harsnett, Bart, and His Relict, Anne, ran to help her. Close to, he saw that she was a few years older than he'd originally thought; twenty-nine or thirty, perhaps, but quite as much of a knockout. When he gave her his hand, she climbed down with graceful ease and it was only after a moment (at least, he hoped it was only a moment) when he was aware of nothing else but her shining dark eyes and the warm sexiness that seemed to envelop him, that he realised she hadn't been stuck at all. His gallant dash struck him as absurd and he stood rooted to the spot, aware that he must look just as foolish as he felt, but still caught, tongue-tied, in the strongest force field of sexual magnetism he had ever experienced.

'You must be Mr Ballard.' The voice had a touch of huskiness to it – proper enough, but with a hint of mischief. 'Sorry, I mean *Inspector* Ballard, don't I?'

As she spoke, Ballard felt the discreet snap of something closing in on him; as if, he thought, she had him in her sights. 'At your service.' Oh, Christ, why had he said that? And how the hell did she know his name? 'How . . . I mean, I am, but—'

'Pauline's told me all about you.'

'Has she?'

'Oh, yes.' She flashed him a wide, happy smile. Her teeth were white and even. 'I'm Ananda.'

'Amanda?'

'A-*nan*-da.'

'That's unusual.'

'It means . . .' She hesitated deliberately, as if waiting for a drum roll to finish, then said, triumphantly, 'Bliss!'

Pauline can't have told me about her, thought Ballard. I'd have remembered *that*. He felt pleased if his wife had made a friend, though. Although she'd never complained, he knew she found it lonely at times. Not only were the locals wary of incomers, but they seemed to feel – understandably, Ballard supposed – that the wife of a policeman, even if he wasn't actually the village bobby, needed to be kept at arm's length. 'How did you meet Pauline?' he asked.

'The same way I met you – out walking.'

'Do you live nearby?'

'Just the other side of Lincott. The Old Rectory.'

'The Foundation?'

'That's right.' She giggled. 'Don't look so surprised! We do come out sometimes, you know.'

'Yes . . . I . . .' Feeling more foolish than ever, Ballard finished, 'Of course you do.'

'Bless you.' Ananda regarded him for a moment, head on one side, then leant forward and kissed him on the cheek. He caught a whiff of perfumed soap as her curls brushed against his face, and then she was gone, nipping between the graves. At the gate she turned and gave him a wave before disappearing down the road.

Ballard stared after her. After a moment, the tentative beginnings of an erection gave way to a jolted, fearful feeling, as though he'd narrowly escaped being run down by a bus. It took some minutes of standing quite still, followed by the soothing powers of another cigarette, for it to dispel so that he could think clearly once more.

In the two years he'd lived there Ballard had never, so far as he knew, actually met anyone from the Foundation for Spiritual Understanding, unless you counted Tynan, who had some connection with it, although he wasn't quite clear what form it took. All Ballard knew about the Foundation was that it was home to a bunch of people who practised some sort of religion. The vicar, Reverend Sewell, had described it to him – with a disapproving sniff – as 'esoteric' and, when he'd looked the word up, he'd found that meant a philosophical doctrine that was 'only for the initiated' and 'not generally intelligible'. In other words, secret and inward-looking. Certainly, the Foundation's inhabitants could occasionally be glimpsed performing strange exercises in the grounds of the Old Rectory, but they never seemed to mix with the villagers. They were popular with the local shopkeepers because they placed large orders, and because they'd never been involved in any trouble Ballard had never had reason to step inside the gates.

The Old Rectory itself, however, had long had a reputation. A series of newspaper accounts of ghostly sightings in the 1930s, illustrated by suspiciously blurry photographs, had earned it the title of 'the most haunted house in England'. Even now, in the summer, more than a few trippers would ask for directions to the place. Ballard had no idea whether or not they were admitted. He had the impression that most of them didn't wish to be, but were content to gawp and take photographs from the road. Gothic, looming, and reputed to be built on the site of an ancient nunnery, the house certainly looked the part but, unlike haunted houses in films, derelict with broken windows, banging shutters and cobwebs as thick as blankets, the Old Rectory – nowadays at least – was well maintained, with gleaming paint and a lovingly tended garden. Of course, there was no shortage of locals who, for the price of a pint, were willing to tell tales of tragic nuns, grey ladies and, for all he knew, headless horsemen as well.

Ballard opted for the longer way back to his house, where – without mentioning either Stratton or the strangely named Ananda – he said goodbye to Pauline before making his way back to the police station. He spent the afternoon investigating a series of thefts of farming implements, but all the time *she* lingered at the back of his mind, saucily perched on the stile, smiling and flashing those gorgeous legs.

CHAPTER NINE

The asphalt on the platform at Lincott station was cracked like the top of a cake. Alighting, Stratton was about to tap on the smeary window of the stationmaster's office and ask for a taxi when, to his surprise, a driver sent by Ballard appeared and put himself at Stratton's disposal for the rest of the day. The man's slightly resentful air made Stratton wonder how easy it had been for Ballard – a true Londoner, unlike himself, not to mention being CID – to fit in with the local force. Reverting to the accent of his childhood, he said, 'I appreciate that – I'm afraid I don't know these parts at all.'

The man narrowed his eyes for a moment, suspecting mockery, and then, after looking up and down the empty platform, said, 'You *not* from London, then?'

'Not originally,' said Stratton. 'I grew up in Devon.'

The man nodded, apparently satisfied. 'Sergeant Adlard, sir. If you'll follow me . . .' Picking up Stratton's suitcase, he led the way to the car.

Adlard kept up a running commentary as they drove through the centre of Lincott village – self-contained and quiet, with cottages ranged around a green and along the road, and more, just visible, dotted about behind, a couple of shops, a church, a school fenced with hooped iron railings, and a pub – and into open country. 'Hardly ever see that, now,' he said, gesturing at a field where a man was ploughing with two horses. 'Most of the farmers round here got tractors. Beautiful, aren't they?'

'Yes,' said Stratton. He'd loved his father's patient, majestic Shire horses, Blackie and Dora; how they smelt at the end of the day, when they were hot, and how he'd stood on an upturned bucket to brush the dried sweat from their necks as they'd mumbled hay from the rack in the stable . . . 'I grew up on a farm.' Remembering, too, the generations of labourers literally worked into the ground, their tiny, damp cottages teeming with lousy children and the old people with goitres from years of drinking pond water, he added, 'A bit of modernisation's no bad thing, though.'

'I suppose so. New council houses over there, look.' Adlard gestured at a group of raw, box-like brick buildings, exposed in the middle of a flattened, barren field at the top of a hill, their gardens marked with concrete posts and chain-link fencing, one with an H-shaped television aerial protruding from its chimney. 'Just gone up, they have. London must have been quite a change for you, sir – don't mind my saying.'

'Well, I've been there a while, now, but it did take a bit of getting used to at first.'

'Not surprised. Only been there a couple of times myself. You can taste it in your mouth, can't you? All sooty and gritty. And city folk think you must be stupid if you sound like you're from a village.'

'Oh, they're all right when you get to know them.'

Adlard nodded, as if assenting to an unspoken request, then said, 'You know what I'd miss if I lived in London? The stars. Just stand outside my back door and stare up at 'em, sometimes. You can't imagine where they end, can you?'

'I missed them, too. Mind you, it wasn't till the blackout – you could see them sometimes, on a quiet night – that I realised it.'

After this, both men, discomfited by this sudden and inexplicably lyrical outburst, retreated into silence for the next few minutes, until a high brick wall came into view, and Adlard said, 'Mr Tynan's place.' They drove past what felt like, but couldn't actually have been, miles of wall, coming to a halt in front of impressively large wrought-iron gates flanked by posts on top of which animals of some unspecified heraldic species sat upright, as if begging for scraps.

Ambrose Tynan's house, situated at the end of a longish drive, was a big, square affair which Stratton thought was probably Georgian. It had obviously been built for some long-ago country squire with the dual aim of getting one over on the neighbours and putting the peasantry in their place. If his own reaction was anything to go by, Stratton reflected, then as far as the second bit was concerned, the bloke had definitely succeeded. Standing beneath the giant portico, he felt common as muck and about six inches high.

The door was answered by a manservant with a bearing so stiff that he might have had a tray stuffed down the back of his jacket. Although Stratton was expected – and had readjusted his accent – the chap's tone as he repeated the word 'Inspector' suggested that he was holding some particularly unpleasant article between his finger and thumb, just before dropping it in the dustbin. He ushered Stratton into a vast hall, decorated with wine-red flock wallpaper and heavy mahogany mouldings, and left him to contemplate the grand, curved staircase, hung, as far up as the eye could see, with gilt-framed oils of Tynan's – or somebody's – ancestors. Unless they were his wife's family, Stratton supposed he must have bought them as a job lot and then adopted them, as it were, backwards.

After about five minutes, the man returned and led him past a series of half-open doors through which he could see glimpses of bronzes and marble busts and what he thought were Russian icons, cheek-by-jowl with paintings and framed maps as well as the usual furniture. Stratton remembered that, besides all the cigars and brandy and what-have-you, Tynan's books were full of descriptions of fine things of just this type. He also remembered what Diana had said about the man's art collection, and the particular way she'd described both him and his house as 'grand'. Stratton could see what she'd meant. It did all seem a bit, well, *staged*, somehow.

Tynan was waiting in his library, a large, high-ceilinged room at the back of the house with tall windows that looked out onto a terrace. Below it was a geometrical arrangement of low hedges that Stratton thought was called a parterre. As they entered, he rose from behind an enormous desk, a large man with a fleshy face and thick white hair swept dramatically off his brow, tweed-suited and wearing a tie that Stratton would have bet his last penny had some educational or military significance. The desk, like the rest of the furniture, was heavy, dark, and looked to be Victorian. Despite the fact that Tynan couldn't have been more than ten years older than he was, the room, with its rows of leather-covered books stamped in gold and a plum-coloured smoking jacket hanging behind the door, had the air of belonging to someone from another age.

'How do you do?' said Tynan. At least, Stratton guessed that was what he'd said, and replied accordingly. Not only did his heavily jowled face have the sort of peering, disgruntled expression that indicated a member of a privileged social group having to deal with a troublesome underling, but he spoke in a sort of fluctuating whinny with half the words swallowed back in just as they were coming out.

'I've asked my man to bring us some tea,' said Tynan, indicating that Stratton should take a seat. Settling himself on the opposite side of the desk (in a considerably higher and more comfortable chair), Tynan leant forward and, steepling his fingers, closed his eyes for a moment and inhaled deeply. As he did so, his hands twitched slightly, as if an electric current was passing between the tips of his fingers. This performance over, he opened his eyes wide in an expression of almost malevolent intensity and said, 'I understand you wish to ask questions about poor Jeremy Lloyd. We met on a number of occasions. Not socially, of course.'

Heaven forbid, thought Stratton. 'How did you meet him?'

'At the Foundation.'

'The Foundation?'

'The Foundation for Spiritual Understanding. A group of individuals who are, shall we say, Seekers After Truth.' He pronounced the last three words in audible capitals.

Must be the 'like-minded people' mentioned by Father Shaw, thought Stratton. 'When you say "truth" . . .?'

Tynan laughed indulgently. 'What is truth, said jesting Pilot, and would not stay for an answer. As most of us don't these days, I'm afraid. They are based near here. In fact, I was instrumental in acquiring a house for them. I admire their work enormously.'

'And their work is . . .?'

'Their *aims*,' said Tynan, with the air of one imparting a revelation, 'are to discover and put into practice a precise system of knowledge about man's place in the universe and his spiritual evolution. There is no reason why an ordinary man should not develop spiritually. One does not need to be a yogi or a monk in order to do so . . .' Bloody good job for you, mate, thought Stratton, eyeing the fine-grained luxury around him. 'However,' continued Tynan, raising his voice in a clear rebuke to Stratton's waning attention, 'some form of guidance is needed. The vast inheritance of spiritual wealth from the East has – until comparatively recently – been ignored by the West.' His speech, with its authoritarian rhythms and occasional startling emphases, reminded Stratton of DCI Lamb at his most dictatorial and bullying. Clearly, being a successful and

revered novelist, Tynan was well used to being listened to unchal-
lenged. It was only, Stratton thought, the stroke of good fortune
that made his stuff popular that separated him from the fate of
being – as Lloyd, he felt, undoubtedly had been – not only a crank
but a bore as well. 'The ancient sages of the East,' Tynan continued,
'have much to teach us, if only we will listen.'

'Such as?' enquired Stratton in his blandest tone.

'Philosophy. That is the love of wisdom. One can find wisdom
through self-knowledge, but first one must free oneself from illusory constraints such as character, likes and dislikes, joy, sadness,
pain. One can live unaffected by the world, yet play one's part
in it. The secret is,' Tynan leant forward conspiratorially, 'to see
that it is *all* a play. When you see that your own life is a play
and the whole work of society is a play, you gain independence
from it because you can step away from it. It cannot touch you.'

Stratton felt that was a bit much coming from someone who
was so keen on this 'play' that he had, as Diana had said, very
obviously designed an impressive part for himself in it. 'And Lloyd
was a student of this philosophy, was he?'

'Very much so. He was one of the first.'

'So he would have come to the Foundation when?'

'Nineteen forty-seven, I should think. Around that time.'

'Presumably there's a religious component to this . . . way of
thinking.'

'Religion?' Tynan threw his hands in the air in a 'what can
you do?' gesture. 'Religion is based on duality. Me down here,'
he gestured at the parquet floor, 'God hovering around somewhere,' he jabbed a finger at the elaborate cornicing, 'up there.'
No wonder Lloyd didn't elaborate on any of this to Father Shaw,
thought Stratton.

'The philosophy,' continued Tynan, 'is the way of unity. We
are separated from our true selves not only by our ideas of God,
but by the distractions of the world.'

Bit rich coming from a man with a mansion full of worldly distractions, thought Stratton, wondering when the tea was going to arrive. 'So this takes the form of lectures, does it?'

'Yes, and study. There are exercises, too, and coming under discipline through a measured programme of physical and spiritual activities, early rising, segregation of the sexes, obedience, and so forth ... but those are only for initiates.'

'Initiates?' This, Stratton thought, sounded suspiciously like one of Tynan's own books, with robed people walking round in circles intoning things before waving their hands over sacred flames. 'So they have ceremonies, do they?'

Tynan smiled indulgently. 'It's really very simple,' he said. 'The exercises and activities help people to gain understanding – to connect them to their true selves.'

'And this is a community, is it? I mean, the initiates live at the Foundation?'

'About twenty of them. Others visit on a regular basis.'

'And the finances? Upkeep and so forth?'

'The students pay modest fees, of course, and gifts are given by those, such as myself, who are able to afford it. I can assure you that no one is asked to contribute beyond their means.'

'Did Lloyd pay fees?' asked Stratton, wondering how he could have afforded to have done so.

Tynan shook his head. 'In some cases, we are able to make provision.'

'And what about when he left? Did the Foundation pay for his lodgings in London?'

'I don't believe so.'

'A benefactor, perhaps?'

Tynan gave a dismissive shrug. 'I have no idea, Inspector.'

'I see.' Stratton produced the photograph Wintle had given him and slid it across the desk. 'What about this lady? Is she a student, too?'

The novelist looked down at the photograph and Stratton saw the beginnings of what looked like a dreamy smile – a memory of carnality, perhaps? – quickly replaced by a more serious expression. 'Yes, she's a student.'

'What's her name?'

'Ananda.'

'An—? Could you spell it, please?'

'A, N, A, N, D, A,' said Tynan, as Stratton wrote. 'It's a Sanskrit word – means "bliss". Sanskrit is the most ancient of languages. It's not only the root of Hindi, but of all—'

'She doesn't look Indian,' said Stratton.

'She's as English as you or me,' snapped Tynan, clearly irritated at being cut off in full flow. Hardly surprising, thought Stratton, as he obviously wasn't used to it. 'It was the leader, Theodore Roth, who called her Ananda. He said it reflected her true nature.'

'Do you know her original name?'

'Mary.'

'Surname?'

'Milburn. Mrs Milburn.'

'Do you know if she went by any other name? There are some initials on the back of the photograph.'

Frowning, Tynan turned it over, and then his face cleared. 'I should imagine that L.R. stands for Lincott Rectory. That's where the picture was taken – where the Foundation is based. It's not far from here.'

Remembering a newspaper headline, Stratton said, 'Wasn't that—'

'The most haunted house in England? That's the one. All that was before the war, of course. I've written a bit about it myself, as it happens – articles for newspapers, and so on. We got it for a song at the beginning of 1947 because it was in such a mess, and of course it was far too big for a modern vicar and cost a fortune to heat.'

'If twenty people can live there,' said Stratton, 'it must be enormous.'

'The larger bedrooms have been made into dormitories,' said Tynan. 'And we've managed to use some of the loft space, but you're right,' he chuckled merrily, 'it can get a bit crowded, especially with all the visitors. Everybody mucks in, you know. Bit like the army.'

Oh really, thought Stratton. Everything he'd ever heard about the army suggested that it was the Poor Bloody Infantry who did all the mucking in while those in charge ponced about with swagger sticks and gave orders. More to the point, he felt, might be something Pete had once said to him about army logic being completely different to the ordinary sort, to the extent that it was either mind-numbingly contradictory, or missing altogether.

'The church put the place up for sale,' Tynan continued, 'but nobody wanted to take it on – too big, and it hadn't been inhabited since before the war. The current incumbent had moved into a much smaller place, so it was just left to rot. The students have really worked hard on it, though, and done wonders. No ghosts now, of course.'

If there ever were, thought Stratton. God Almighty, there was quite enough airy-fairy stuff to wade through without adding apparitions and poltergeists and Christ only knew what else. Indicating the photograph, he said, 'Do you know her well?'

'I wouldn't say "well".' Tynan sounded defensive.

'Has she not been at the Foundation long, then?' asked Stratton.

Tynan peered at him suspiciously. 'She came to live at Lincott Rectory about a year after we bought it, to help Mr Roth. I suppose you might say she's his Right-hand Woman.'

'So you've known her since 1948,' said Stratton. 'Eight years. That's quite a while.' Affecting not to notice that Tynan's look of suspicion was now tinged with outrage, he asked blandly, 'Do you know anything about her background?'

Tynan frowned for a moment, and then, with a relief at having attained safe ground that he could not quite manage to disguise, he said, 'That is the past. What matters is the present.'

'I've found,' said Stratton, in as neutral a voice as he could manage, 'that in a murder investigation the past often has a hell of a lot of impact on the present, so it would be helpful if you could tell me anything you know.'

'That is the point,' said Tynan, as if explaining something to an exceptionally backward child. 'I know very little about Ananda because I have never considered it important to enquire. That is not what our work is about. One thing,' here, he smiled at Stratton as if conferring a favour, 'that I do know, however, is that she'd lived at Lincott Rectory before. She was the vicar's wife.'

'That would be . . .' Stratton glanced down at his notebook, 'the Reverend Milburn, would it?'

'That's correct, yes.'

'Quite a coincidence, her coming back.'

'If you choose to believe in such things,' said Tynan, 'then yes, it is. When one looks beyond the surface, one sees that everything happens for a reason. Ananda came to the Foundation with her son – he was a baby then – and she stayed.'

'And the reason for her coming back?'

'Those things,' said Tynan, loftily, 'that float into the mind of the individual who is attentive and still, and whose mind is open to them, are the gifts of the wise.' In other words, thought Stratton, you've got no idea. 'It has been said,' Tynan continued, 'that they set an idea in the atmosphere which is appropriate to the time and wait for some open heart to pick it up. It has been said that the man who picks it up has the ability to feed others in the spiritual sense.'

Stratton would have dearly liked to retort that it has been said that the moon is made of green cheese but that had turned out to be bollocks as well. Instead, he said, 'What about the vicar – the one who was her husband. What happened to him?'

'I have never asked. And,' Tynan held up a hand as if stopping a flow of traffic, 'before you say anything, I know nothing at all about Lloyd's background.'

'I see. And what is . . .' Stratton glanced at his notebook, 'Ananda's relationship with Mr Roth?'

'Purely platonic. I give you my word on that. Anything else would be unthinkable . . .' He tailed off purposely, leaving words to the effect of 'you grubby little man' hanging soundless in the air.

'And her relationship with Jeremy Lloyd?'

'There was no relationship. At least, not in the way you're implying. That sort of thing is not allowed,' he added, with what Stratton felt was unnecessary vehemence. 'It acts as an impediment to progress.'

Doesn't stop you fancying her, though, does it? thought Stratton. Somehow, he doubted that someone as obviously keen on worldly things as Tynan was would stint himself when it came to women, whatever this Mr Roth and his teachings might have to say about it. Remembering that Diana had said Tynan's wife had died not long before, he thought, You tried your hand, didn't you? And Miss Ananda didn't want to know . . .

Before he could ask anything more, the butler, or whoever he was, arrived with a tray and made an elaborate and unnecessarily servile performance of pouring tea and offering milk and sugar. While this was going on, Tynan proffered an ornate box of expensive-looking cigarettes ('The best in the world – I have them imported') before inserting one into an amber holder for himself. As he was clearly not prepared to continue with the interview until the man had left them, Stratton took the opportunity to think up a list of questions phrased in ways he hoped wouldn't lend themselves to more portentously vague answers.

The tea, though doubtless also the best in the world, was weak, nastily perfumed stuff, which Stratton suspected was drunk by those in the know, like Tynan, without either milk or sugar. He swallowed, managing not to grimace, and taking a pull on the fag (which actually wasn't half bad), said, 'Was Mr Lloyd living at the Foundation?'

'Yes, for quite some time.'

'Since 1947?'

'I believe that was when he arrived.'

'Do you know when he left?'

'Earlier this year, I believe.'

'And when was the last time you saw him?'

'Sometime in the spring, I think.' Tynan closed his eyes for a moment and did the steepling, twitchy thing with his hands again. 'Yes, that would be right. We went for a walk together in the grounds. He was proposing to write a book about the Foundation's work.'

'Had he been asked to write it?'

'I had the impression that it was his idea, but I imagine he would have sought approval for the project.'

'Who would give the approval?'

'The leader. Mr Roth. A man of remarkable qualities.'

'How did he seem to you? Lloyd, I mean.'

'He seemed . . . himself.'

Stratton was tempted to ask if Tynan meant his true self or his other one, but Tynan continued, 'By that I mean he was as he always was: a devoted servant of the cause. He wasn't doing it for his own fulfilment, but to educate, to enlighten, for the greater good. To make a difference . . . to bring about change, understanding . . . You see,' he added, after a pause, 'the servant is the master. The performance of service is an important part of the teaching. It is given . . . it flows from the higher to the lower.' Then, seeing Stratton's puzzled expression, he said, 'I could, perhaps, have expressed that more elegantly,' and gave him a piercing look which indicated that, even so, it was a bloody sight more elegant than anything Stratton could have managed.

'Did he tell you that he was planning to leave?'

'No. I don't think he *was* planning to, not then.'

'So something, or someone, must have made him change his mind later on?'

'He would have received instruction.'

'From the leader?'

'Yes. Mr Roth understands the true nature of all the individuals who have placed themselves under his discipline.' Here, Tynan opened both arms wide to demonstrate an infinity of care. The grand gesture was somewhat marred by the fact that, as he did so, a finger of untapped ash dropped off, scattering itself across the desk. Pretending he hadn't noticed, Stratton said, 'What can you tell me about him?'

'Mr Roth came to England as a refugee, just after the war. He'd been in a concentration camp, and was very lucky to be alive. He'd spent his youth studying under the great masters in Tibet, and was determined to bring the knowledge to Europe. He used to hold evening classes in London, which is where I met him. It was shortly after my mother died. She was over ninety years old and I suppose I must have thought, in my arrogance,' he let out a quick bark of laughter, 'that she would go on living for as long as I wanted. She was always a very healthy, very robust woman, but one day . . .' Tynan shook his head. 'I experienced the most terrible grief. I hardly knew what to do with myself. I couldn't bear the thought that I would feel like this for the rest of my life.

'I would spend hours walking on Hampstead Heath, on my own. At one point I found myself by one of the ponds, watching the children with their toy boats. And then, suddenly, it came to me that, although one is entirely alone, one is also connected to everything in the universe. I felt as though I was a part of the children, the ducks, the trees and everything around me – all one and the same. Not just the same matter, but the same spirit in all of us.' As Tynan broke off to puff on his cigarette, Stratton wondered how many times he'd told this particular story. A fair few, he thought. Oddly, it seemed less a memory than something to be recited by heart, even though it was coming out with exactly the right degree of spontaneity.

'My misery was replaced by a sensation of peace, of oneness, that I remembered long after it had left me. I was desperate to reconnect with it, because it seemed to me that it contained the very essence of life – that everything else was just a sham. When I came upon one of Mr Roth's advertisements in the paper I wondered if he might be able to provide the answer, so I went along to the meeting, and listened, and asked questions. Mr Roth was able to explain to me that I was attached not to my mother, but to the *notion* of loving her – and unless I accepted that this was only an idea in the mind, I would never be able to free myself from it, to progress. As he was speaking, I knew that here was a man who understood me in a way that nobody ever had before.' Tynan stopped, shaking his head in wonder.

Stratton had no idea what sort of response was expected – hysterical shouts of 'Alleluia!' perhaps, or a standing ovation – but settled for 'I see.'

'Do you think,' he asked, 'that Lloyd had experienced something similar on meeting Mr Roth?'

'Undoubtedly,' said Tynan. 'Mr Roth has changed the lives of many people. Those who are *receptive* will find a true meeting of minds, and that is how the work of self-realisation begins.' His face as he said this suggested that Stratton was unlikely to realise himself, or, come to that, anything else.

'Well.' Stratton pushed back his chair. 'Your Mr Roth sounds quite something. I think I'd better have a word with him.'

CHAPTER TEN

As Adlard drove him the short distance to Lincott Rectory, Stratton reflected that what Mr Roth sounded most like was a thumping great confidence trickster, getting Tynan to buy him a house and set him up like that. There had to be a bit more to it than mere trickery, though: Tynan, whatever else he may be, clearly wasn't stupid, and, judging from the tosh he wrote in the papers, he considered himself to be pretty hot at spotting wicked, mind-controlling cults and things. Equally clearly, he wasn't that keen on talking to anyone he couldn't patronise, and Roth had obviously made a huge impression on him. An individual, or a way of thinking, seeming to provide all the answers – he could see the attraction of it, all right. And so could thousands of others; one look at Billy Graham confirmed that.

If Lloyd had moved into this Foundation place in 1947 or '48 and only left in the spring, then he'd lived there for seven or eight years, which was quite a chunk of anyone's life, and he'd known Mary/Ananda for almost the same length of time. Add to that the possibility of a manuscript – which, if it existed, was definitely missing – about the work of the Foundation ... This Stratton felt, definitely constituted some progress, even if it did mean listening to people talking in riddles.

The driveway to Lincott Rectory was shorter than Tynan's and flanked by bare-branched trees that Stratton thought were mostly horse chestnuts like the one in the photograph. Adlard slowed the car to a crawl and began staring unashamedly around him. Although it was chilly, there were plenty of people in the grounds. A solitary man was looking at the trees in open-mouthed wonderment, as if it had only just occurred to him that there were different sorts, and several groups of both sexes were standing about in a way that made Stratton think of unsuccessful players in a game of musical chairs. As the car drew nearer, he noticed that their eyes were closed. Further off, across the grass, another group was engaged in chopping wood and ferrying it away in wheelbarrows. Seen from a distance, under a sky which, during the time Stratton had spent with Tynan, had turned an ominous metallic shade, the house, with its rambling outline, irregular roofs and tower had a haunted, sinister look, but as the car pulled up outside the front porch, he could see that it was spick and span and nothing like the Victorian wreck he remembered from newspaper photographs. A loud bellow of 'Stop!' from somewhere behind them made both men jump. Assuming it must be directed at them, Stratton looked round and, to his astonishment, saw that the wood-choppers were frozen in mid-action, two with axes raised high above their heads, others stooped in the act of gathering logs from the piles on the ground. As the seconds became a full minute, and then two minutes, and they continued to hold their positions, it dawned on Stratton that this must be one of the exercises mentioned by Tynan, although what it was supposed to achieve – besides aching arms and a sore back – he couldn't imagine. Then there was another shout, and they all carried on as if nothing had happened.

Before Stratton had a chance to press the bell, the door was opened by a diminutive middle-aged lady, clad in immaculate tweeds, with the small plain face and flattened hair of a peg-top doll. Beaming, she said, 'How may I help you?' in a well-modulated sing-song which reminded him of the woman who did the *Muffin the Mule* television programme. When Stratton introduced himself and said that he'd like to speak to Mr Roth, she introduced herself as Miss Kirkland, explained that Mr Roth was speaking to some students, but that she would let him know when the session ended in ten minutes' time and asked if he would like a cup of tea while he waited.

Stratton, hoping that it would be the normal sort and not the strange stuff he'd been given at Tynan's, assented, and, having led him into an anteroom, she trotted off, leaving him alone. The room was sparsely furnished – chairs pushed against the walls as in a waiting room, a rug and a small table – but spotlessly clean, with a burnished parquet floor. Despite what Tynan had said about Eastern philosophies and what not, there wasn't anything unusual in evidence. In fact, the only ornaments were two framed texts on the walls, very like the one he'd seen in Jeremy Lloyd's room. One read, *When a machine knows itself, it is then no longer a machine*, and the other, *For a man to become conscious, a big stick is necessary*, and both were ascribed to someone called G.I. Gurdjieff. Stratton decided that G.I. Gurdjieff, whoever he might be, was a bully and, by the looks of it, probably a sadist as well. And, seeing that being thumped with a big stick was more likely to result in *unconsciousness* than the reverse, he clearly wasn't too clued up about cause and effect either. Then again, it probably wasn't meant to be literal; the 'machine' quotation obviously wasn't. But surely some things in life – digging the allotment, having a shit and so forth – had to be done mechanically, didn't they? Not that those things weren't enjoyable, of course, but if you stopped to question or examine every action, it would take you a bloody long time to get anything done at all.

Miss Kirkland reappeared with a tray of tea and, as she poured it for him, Stratton noted the delicately embroidered cloth, fine bone china and the almost reverent precision of her movements. He expected her to leave when she'd given him the cup, but instead she took a seat beside him and perched in silence, bolt upright and utterly unmoving, as if in church. It made Stratton feel self-conscious enough to return his cup, half-drunk, to the tray – a pity, because this tea was pretty good – and, more for something to say than anything else, bring up the subject of the big stick. 'Bit dangerous, that, I should have thought.' This comment was rewarded with a smile of impenetrable sweetness which he took to mean that she was possessed of higher knowledge about the matter but wasn't prepared to argue. After a few more minutes' silence, during which Stratton tried to imagine what it would take to shake her out of her complacent repose and concluded that nothing, up to and including bawling obscenities and getting his cock out, would do the trick, Miss Kirkland glanced at her wristwatch and said, 'Please follow me.'

The rest of the house, though less grandiose in terms of size and proportion than Tynan's place, was pretty impressive, and looked to be just as scrubbed and polished as the anteroom. Stratton stared in wonder at the wooden panels in the hall and on the staircase, which seemed, even in the thin winter sunlight, to glow like fire. 'It is beautiful, isn't it?' said Miss Kirkland. 'When we came here, it was covered in layers and layers of ancient varnish. We had to scrub it off with wire wool ... But,' she continued, looking so joyful that Stratton thought she might burst into song, 'that is why we are here. To strip away the layers and reveal the truth.'

Never mind bell, book and candle, thought Stratton, no ghost would stand a chance against this lot. The house did have an odd atmosphere, though. The two sets of doors they'd passed through to arrive at the hall were, he thought, a bit like the decompression chambers of a submarine, with any sounds from outside banished or muffled. There were obviously plenty of people about – he could see several well-dressed women crossing the wide landing, some with trays and others with things like buckets and scrubbing brushes, their steps careful, apparently making a supreme effort not to interrupt or distract someone or something. He couldn't hear a single human voice and, despite the wooden floors, barely the sound of a footfall. A monastery must be like this, he thought, hushed and reverential, but that would seem right in a religious context – here, it was eerie, as disconcerting as if he'd put a seashell to his ear and heard nothing at all.

Miss Kirkland paused in front of one of the doors on the landing and turned to face him. Her hands fluttered as though she were barely managing to restrain herself from brushing lint from his suit, so that Stratton found himself glancing down at his lapels and shoulders to check that they were presentable. Beaming, with an isn't-this-fun? expression on her face, as though Stratton was a child about to be given a surprise birthday treat, she breathed, 'Ready?' When Stratton nodded, she took a deep breath, squared her shoulders and closed her eyes momentarily, in the manner of one summoning mental and emotional strength, and knocked on the door.

CHAPTER ELEVEN

Theodore Roth was, Stratton guessed, in his mid sixties or there-abouts. Sallow of skin, with eyes as sunken as if his face had sucked them in like quicksand, staring fiercely from beneath bushy eyebrows, he had a slightly hooked nose and prominent chin that reminded Stratton of Mr Punch, and a noticeable paunch. His suit was clearly an expensive one but, in contrast to the neatness of Miss Kirkland, it had a crumpled look, the lapels sprinkled with ash. Being in his presence, Stratton thought, was like a meeting with a great actor must be: the sonorous voice, the air of natural authority, and the way he drew the eye and filled the room, so that one was barely aware of anything else. Glancing round him, he saw that there was not, in fact, very much else to be aware of, because the room was almost as sparsely furnished as the one downstairs, containing only an armchair, two hard chairs and a small sofa arranged before the fire, and a side table with leaves and berries arranged in a vase. The sole ornament was a framed print of the Virgin Mary by one of the Old Masters, blue draped head inclined slightly to one side, eyes downcast to the chubby figure of the infant Jesus that lay on her lap.

Roth's manner, and the way he said, 'Be seated'. as if they were in church, gave Stratton the feeling of being granted an audience.

This was intensified when Miss Kirkland, seating herself on one of the hard chairs, assumed a tilt of the head exactly like that of the Virgin on the wall, which position, though minus drapery and halo, combined devotion and attention in much the same proportions. Roth himself took the armchair closest to the fire, and said nothing further. Clearly, small talk and spiritual enhancement didn't mix. Determined not to be put on the back foot, Stratton said, 'I've come to ask you some questions about Jeremy Lloyd. He was found dead yesterday.'

Roth gazed at him intently for a moment. Then, producing a silver cigarette case from his waistcoat pocket, went through the process of selecting one, tapping it, lighting it, inhaling smoke, holding it and then, very slowly, exhaling. There was something theatrical about the whole performance that suggested that while it was going on, Roth was building himself up for some incredibly weighty pronouncement. 'So I understand,' he said, finally.

Stratton, who found that he'd been holding his own breath, exhaled in his turn, with the sensation of having expended great effort to lift up an enormous dumb-bell and found it made of balsa wood. 'How do you know?' he asked.

'Mr Tynan telephoned me. He was good enough to tell me I might expect you.' Roth gave a lofty smile, as if the whole thing was some sort of mildly amusing cosmic joke.

'Did he also tell you,' asked Stratton, tight-lipped, 'that Lloyd was murdered?'

'He did.' Roth's accent was foreign. Stratton couldn't place it, but the thickness of speech reminded him of the Polish servicemen who'd been in London during the war.

'He was one of your students, I understand.'

'He was here for a time, yes.'

'When did he leave?'

'In April.'

'Why?'

'He had ambition. An idea in his head, shall we say. That was really his defining feature, a striving after greatness. He believed himself to be marked out for it – literally.' Roth tapped his cheek, reminding Stratton of Lloyd's birthmark. 'It took the form of wishing to write a book about esoteric practices, such as the discipline we follow here. To enlighten the world.' Roth smiled his all-knowing smile and shook his head indulgently.

'That's not such a bad thing, surely?' said Stratton. 'I mean,' he glanced about him, 'you had the ambition – the idea in your head – for *this*, and the aim is the same, isn't it?'

A flicker of irritation in the other man's eyes, and Miss Kirkland's momentarily pursed lips told him that the two things simply did not bear comparison, but neither was prepared to say so. 'Lloyd seems to have told several people that he was writing a book,' said Stratton, 'but we were unable to find a manuscript. Have you ever seen it?'

'No. I did not ask to see it. He had allowed this . . . compulsion . . . to dominate his personality, and I took the view that it was something he needed to get out of his system.'

'So you didn't approve?'

'I neither approved nor disapproved.' Roth's tone was lofty.

'Did you think him capable of writing a good book on this particular subject?'

'He was certainly capable of insight, but as to the necessary discipline and clarity of thought . . . No.'

In other words, nothing half as good as anything you could produce yourself, thought Stratton, wondering if Lloyd's presumption had been a factor in his departure from the Foundation. 'Are you paying for his lodgings in London? His upkeep?'

Roth looked as though he found the question distasteful. 'I am not.'

'Do you know who is?'

'I have never enquired. That is – was – a matter for him.'

'And have you any idea as to *why* someone might have murdered him?'

Roth did some more theatrical smoking, during which Stratton became conscious that he was holding his breath again, and irritated with himself for doing so.

'I'm afraid not,' he said, sounding anything but. 'But then . . . I am not a detective.'

Ignoring the clear implication that he wasn't much of one, either – which, Stratton thought sourly, was right at that moment, absolutely fucking spot on – he asked, 'Did he quarrel with anyone here?'

This won indulgent smiles from both of them – clearly, it was the type of question only to be expected from one so unenlightened – before Roth said, 'We try to create harmony, not division. Our students work to free themselves from their likes and dislikes. Such a thing would not have been tolerated.'

'If you had known about it,' said Stratton, after a pause.

'I should have known, even if it had been unspoken. Conflict brings about a change in the atmosphere. One can sense it.'

'Not always.'

'*Always*,' said Roth, with finality.

Giving up on this as a bad job, Stratton said, 'We found a photograph of a woman who has been identified as Mary Milburn – you call her Ananda. What was his relationship with her?'

During the next loaded silence between Roth's inhaling and exhaling of smoke, he looked at Miss Kirkland, and saw a tenseness to her face which definitely hadn't been there before. Freeing oneself from likes and dislikes was obviously easier said than done. Roth, on the other hand, was positively beaming. 'Everyone loves Ananda,' he said.

Stratton glanced back at Miss Kirkland, who flushed slightly under his gaze but did not look up. Oh, really? he thought. There's one who doesn't love Ananda, and she's right here under your nose, mate.

As if reading his thoughts, Roth said, 'People need to overcome resistance in themselves, of course. Our work is not for the faint-hearted.' Miss Kirkland's colour deepened at this indirect rebuke.

Keeping his tone deliberately neutral, Stratton said, 'But love can take many forms.'

'It can. And some of them' – here, Roth's even-toned detachment was suddenly and disconcertingly replaced by a jolt of anger that caused Miss Kirkland to start involuntarily – 'are debased and gross.' He leant forward and gestured with his cigarette, sending a shower of ash across his trousers. 'Slavish following of the sex impulse is not tolerated – students must come under discipline in order to learn to self-regulation.'

'I shall need to speak to Mrs Milburn,' said Stratton.

'I'm afraid that won't be possible. At least, not at the moment. She's left.' A twitch of Miss Kirkland's eyebrows told Stratton that this was news to her.

'When did she leave?'

'This morning.'

'But she was here before that?'

'Yes, she was.' Miss Kirkland nodded her head in confirmation.

'No unexpected absences?'

'Not unexpected, no.'

'But she went out?'

'Yes, a few evenings ago. The thirtieth of October.'

The night Lloyd was killed, thought Stratton. 'Where did she go?'

'The pictures, with Mr Tynan.'

'He didn't mention it.'

'Did you ask him?'

'No,' admitted Stratton, cursing himself. In all the business about the Foundation and the various dates of people's arrivals, it hadn't occurred to him.

'Do your students often go to the pictures? Isn't it contrary to your ... discipline?'

'I don't encourage it, and most of them do not wish to go, but ...' Waving his cigarette hand, Roth treated him to a tolerant smile, 'some of us need a little diversion, every now and then.' Miss Kirkland's tight expression said very clearly that she was not one who needed diversion. It also conveyed, Stratton thought, the fact that Ananda, whom everyone loved, was treated with rather more indulgence than the rest of the community. 'This isn't a prison, Inspector.'

'Do you know where they went?'

'Ipswich. It was a documentary film – *Seven Years in Tibet*.'

'I see. And she came back the same evening?'

'Of course. But you can't imagine that Ananda had anything to do with ...' another waft of the hand, this time sending a gentle rain of ash down the front of his jacket, 'the matter in London.' It was very much a statement, and not a question.

'When are you expecting Ananda back?' asked Stratton.

This got him a repeat of the tolerant smile. 'I have no expectation. When she feels the need to return, she will.'

'Where has she gone?'

'That I can't tell you.'

'Why not?'

'Because I do not know. People come and go as they wish.' The smile returned with full force. 'As I said, Inspector, this is not a prison. We aim to make people free, not to confine them.'

'Has her son gone with her?'

'She prefers to leave him in our care. This is, after all, his home.'

As Miss Kirkland trod nimbly down the stairs beside him, Stratton reflected that denying the existence of something, however vigorously, didn't mean that it stopped existing – especially if that thing was the sex instinct. A group of students were gathered around the wide fireplace in the hall, sipping tea and making hushed, earnest conversation, a drift of complacency hanging over them like cigar smoke at a smart boxing event. That's all surface, he thought, eyeing them as he went past. They were high-minded all right, as well as genteel, and – now he thought about it – curiously sexless. But underneath . . .

Instinct told Stratton that, although the students might be none the wiser, whatever *had* happened in London – plus Tynan's warning of his own arrival at the Foundation – had resulted in the very rapid disappearance of Lloyd's pin-up girl.

CHAPTER TWELVE

'Rum bunch, aren't they?' said Adlard, when Miss Kirkland had escorted Stratton back to the car.

'You can say that again.'

'There's been a bloke out here scrubbing that lot.' Adlard jerked a thumb at the red tiles on the floor of the porch. 'All dressed up in a suit, he was. Didn't even take his jacket off. Never used soap, either, just water. And I've been watching that lot over there,' he jerked his head in the direction of the wood-choppers. 'Not a clue! None of 'em look like they've ever held an axe in their lives.'

'Probably up from London,' said Stratton, settling himself in the passenger seat. Most of the students, he imagined, would be the sort of town-dwellers for whom everything to do with nature and the countryside had profound spiritual significance, who thought – God help us – that manual labour was noble and uplifting.

'Helpful, were they?' said Adlard, starting the motor.

'Not the word I'd have chosen.' Stratton grimaced, and then, spotting something out of the corner of his eye, said, 'Hold up,' and got out of the car. Running across the grass towards the house was a boy of eleven or perhaps twelve years old. Stratton did a rapid calculation – Tynan had said the place was bought just after the war, and Ananda and her baby son had arrived a year later, so that would make him about the right age . . .

As the boy came closer, Stratton could see that he was handsome – exceptionally so, in fact – with an eager, shining face and blond hair that, even in the weak winter sunshine, seemed to glow about his head.

The boy stopped, looking puzzled, when he saw the car and Stratton standing beside it. There was a neatness about him – well-pressed suit, spotless shirt and conker-shiny shoes – and an awkward solemnity which, together with the long trousers, made him seem older than he actually was. Before either of them could speak, Miss Kirkland bustled past and took his arm. 'You're late for your Greek lesson, Michael. Mr Hardy's waiting.'

As she spoke, a man appeared round the corner of the house, looking breathless, a schoolmaster's gown flapping crow-like at his shoulders. 'There you are, Maitreya. Let's get cracking, shall we?' Acknowledging Stratton with a bob of his head, he put an arm round Michael's shoulders and led him inside. When they reached the door, however, Michael suddenly stopped and, detaching himself from his teacher, ran back to where Stratton and Miss Kirkland were standing. Putting a hand on Stratton's sleeve, he stared into his face with blazing blue eyes and said, 'You are carrying a burden. Your burden is guilt. If you shed your burden, then you will be happy.' Before Stratton could collect himself enough to reply, the boy grinned at him, revealing a gap in his teeth – a sudden flash of unadulterated childhood – and ran back into the house.

There was nothing playful about what he'd said, however. Evidently intelligent – as well as photogenic – he'd obviously meant it. 'Is that Ananda's son?' he asked Miss Kirkland.

'That's right. Michael. We're educating him here.' As she gazed at him in her rapt, intense way, it occurred to Stratton that she had more of the child about her than the boy had. He, Stratton thought, was not so much young, as *new*. 'How wonderful,' gushed Miss Kirkland, 'that you were able to meet him.'

Stratton raised his eyebrows. 'But the man – the teacher – didn't call him Michael.'

'Yes . . . Maitreya. It's a mark of respect.'

'Some sort of title, you mean?'

'Well . . .' Miss Kirkland frowned, caught on the horns of an inner dilemma that Stratton imagined must have something to do with an injunction from Roth about not discussing things too much with the uninitiated. 'Maitreya means a spiritually advanced being – a master of ancient wisdom. When he grows up, Michael will be a great teacher . . .' She hesitated, and then, apparently unable to stop herself, said, 'A teacher such as Buddha, or Jesus.'

'Without the immaculate conception, I presume?' asked Stratton, flippantly.

He expected a rebuke or at least an indulgent, all-knowing smile from Miss Kirkland, but got instead a deeper frown that crenellated her entire forehead. He had the distinct impression that she was genuinely at a loss to know how to answer him. Eventually, she gave a little cough, said sharply that it was not a suitable subject for discussion, and beat a hasty retreat into the house.

Stratton stared after her. She can't *really* believe he's the product of virgin birth, he thought. Then again – as he very well knew – there was no limit to what people would believe. The boy was just an ordinary kid – except that he obviously didn't live like one, and what he'd said to Stratton about the burden of guilt hadn't exactly been ordinary, had it? Then again, if everyone expected him to come out with things like that all the time, perhaps he'd just got into the habit of it. But he'd been right, hadn't he? Stratton did feel guilty. He'd felt guilty – in varying degrees, admittedly, but it was always there – ever since Jenny had died. Was it so easy to spot? Or did the boy use some sort of technique like that of a medium giving a 'cold' reading, feeling his way from vague assertions to something more concrete by studying his subject for silent clues? If that were the case, then he had it down to a fine art.

All the same, it was bloody odd. Presumably it was Roth who'd marked Michael out as 'great teacher' material, Stratton thought, scribbling notes, and, going by what had just happened, the kid must think so himself – or perhaps he just had a strong inclination to self-dramatisation. That sort of thing would be enough to give anyone a superiority complex.

As Adlard drove to the pub in Lincott where he'd arranged to meet Ballard and stay for the night, Stratton wondered what age Michael had been when Roth had come to this conclusion. It was, he supposed, fairly recent. Vague memories of lessons at Sunday school reminded him that Jesus had been twelve when he stayed behind in the temple in Jerusalem to talk to the people there and amaze them.

Stratton stared out at the trees and fields, greying and softening in the dusk, and wondered what Jeremy Lloyd, who believed himself marked out for greatness, had thought about Michael.

CHAPTER THIRTEEN

Stratton took a pull on his pint and sighed appreciatively. The George and Dragon looked the part, all right. Thatched, with wooden beams, worn flagstones and a roaring fire, it was empty but for himself, an old man in one corner, his skin cross-wrinkled by years of outdoor work to resemble the neck of a tortoise, and the landlord who stood behind the long bar, hands resting wide apart on the polished wood in the attitude of a priest. This aside, he looked the part as much as his pub did: corpulent and ruddy, with a flamboyant moustache and a scarlet handkerchief spilling from his jacket pocket. The sort, Stratton thought, who was accustomed to pouring out tall stories as easily as pints, with an equal amount of froth. 'Denton,' the man boomed, by way of introduction. 'Call me George. And this,' he gestured towards his wife, small, grey and clad in beige, who had just entered with Stratton's sandwiches, 'is the Dragon.' Mrs Denton, who'd obviously heard this many times before, smiled wanly. 'Otherwise known as Maisie. She'll look after you.'

'Stratton,' said Stratton, adding 'thank you,' to Maisie Denton, who bobbed her head in acknowledgement before scooting back to the kitchen.

Denton held up a large hand as though conferring a blessing, before holding it out to be shaken. 'A warm welcome to you.' He gave Stratton a cheerfully calculating look – Albert Pierrepoint guessing his weight – before saying, 'Business or pleasure?'

'Business, I'm afraid.'

'Thought so. I saw the car. You with the police, are you?'

'That's right.'

'Just come from the rectory, have you?'

'Yes.'

'Joe there' – Denton gestured at the man in the corner, in the manner of someone hailing a taxi – 'spotted you on his way over.'

'Quite a bush telegraph, then.'

'Oh, yes. Anything happens, we'll hear about it sooner or later.'

'In that case,' Stratton produced the photograph from his pocket, 'can you tell me about her?'

Denton looked at the picture, raised his eyebrows, and mimed a whistle. 'Oh, yes. I can tell you about *her* all right. She was married to the old vicar, Reverend Milburn. Doesn't look like a vicar's wife, does she? Didn't behave like one, either, by all accounts. Makes me think of Tommy Trinder.' Here, he drew his hand down his chin as if to elongate it, and gave a passable imitation of the comedian's leering smile. '"Beautiful girl, they call her Nescafé . . . She's so easy to make!" Man mad, she was. Never tried it on with me, mind . . .' Here his glance flicked in the direction of the kitchen. 'More's the pity. She was quite something, I can tell you. What you might call a piece of work, though.' Glancing round, Stratton saw that old Joe, in his corner, was all ears and nodding in vigorous agreement. 'In trouble, is she?'

'Nothing like that. But we do need to speak to her.'

'She not at the rectory? We heard she'd come back to live there. Not that I've seen her – you won't catch any of that lot in here.'

'Oh?'

Denton shrugged. 'I suppose it's against their religion – whatever that's supposed to be. Mind you, if a bit of the other' – he gave Stratton a conspiratorial leer – 'isn't on the cards either, I don't suppose she'd be likely to stay around too long.'

'But she lived at Lincott Rectory when it had the reputation of being haunted?'

'That's right. And there's a lot round here who'll tell you that was her doing, as well.'

'How do you mean?'

'There's ways of faking these things.' Denton nodded sagely. 'She'd come up with these tales of things flying across the room and mysterious figures floating round the garden. Old Joe there, his sister-in-law Ivy used to work in the kitchen. Told me it used to frighten her to death, saucepans tumbling off the shelves, bells ringing, dirty words appearing on the walls, pins put on her chair . . . Lot of nasty tricks.'

'Sounds like something a child might do.'

'Exactly – easy enough to set up – and the place had a name for it before, didn't it?'

'Did it?'

'Oh, yes. There was a nunnery there originally. Medieval times, I think – all gone now, of course. There's all sorts of tales about that: a girl who'd been locked up because she wouldn't marry the man her father wanted, so she took her own life, and a nun who'd fallen in love with some farmer's son and was planning to run away with him, only she got killed when he lost control of his horse . . . Mrs Milburn claimed she'd seen them both, and the chap on horseback. All nonsense, although you'd probably find one or two in the village who still believe it. Mind you, all that old stuff was more or less forgotten until the Milburns came, but after it all started again we had men from the newspapers, trippers, the lot. She wrote to the papers, you see, and there was this chap who made a business of investigating ghosts and mediums – Maurice Hill, his name was – and one of the papers gave him a lot of money to come and write about it.'

'When was that?' asked Stratton.

'Couple of years before the war.' The photograph must have been older than he'd originally assumed, thought Stratton.

'Hold up,' said Denton, reaching beneath the bar to retrieve a shoebox. When he lifted the lid, Stratton saw a pile of newspaper cuttings. The topmost had a headline that read *SÉANCE HELD IN HAUNTED HOUSE. MYSTERIOUS RAPPINGS IN THE RECTORY OF LINCOTT.* It was dated 15 June 1938. 'They came here about a year before that,' he said. 'She didn't lose any time and of course, she got her picture in the papers as well . . . Some said she and Hill were carrying on and they were in it together. Wouldn't surprise me if they had been. I mean, look at it from his point of view.' He spread his hands in a gesture of open-mindedness. 'He'd spent all his life showing how ghosts don't exist and how mediums are tricking people, but if he could show that a ghost *did* exist, well, that's a much better story, isn't it?' Denton paused to swipe at his nose with his scarlet handkerchief, 'I didn't do so badly out of it, either. Hordes of sightseers – me and the missus were run off our feet. Almost as good as the war, it was. Do you know, half the time those GIs just left their change on the bar, couldn't be bothered with it, so—'

Realising that this could go on for some time, Stratton said, 'What about the Reverend Milburn?'

'That was a funny old thing . . .' George shook his head. 'We all read these accounts in the papers, and it was always her saying she'd seen these things flying about, not him. He said things about having pins placed on his chair and belongings not being where he'd put them – she could have been doing that easy, same as the pans falling off the shelves in the kitchen and scaring poor old Ivy. No one really knew how Reverend Milburn felt about it. I remember some story about him dousing the place in holy water, but that could have been because the dean told him to – the dean and the bishop didn't like it at all, you see. Sensational, they said. Gave the church a bad name. But Reverend Milburn, well . . . He was a lot older than she was. Sixty if he was a day. They'd married when she was very young – not much more than a schoolgirl – and frankly, he wasn't too well when he came here. I'm not a churchgoer myself, but the wife goes along–' He broke off and, leaning through the doorway to the kitchen, bellowed, 'Maisie!'

Mrs Denton appeared, looking resigned and wiping her hands on her apron. 'Come here a minute, love.' Denton put an arm round her thin shoulder. 'Mr Stratton's asking about Reverend Milburn, what he was like in church.'

'I don't know what stories George has been telling you . . .' Maisie Denton frowned at her husband.

'It's all right, love,' said Denton, instantly placatory. 'Mr Stratton is a policeman.' Seeing her look of alarm, he patted her with a huge paw and said, 'There's nothing wrong. He just wants to know about the Milburns, that's all.'

'Well, I suppose it's all right,' said Maisie, sounding doubtful. 'One thing I will say: his sermons were always very moral. A lot of talk about sin. Everything he saw was sin, and he was always very hot on that.' To Stratton's astonishment, a sweetly mischievous smile lit up her face. 'A bit surprising when you consider the way Mrs Milburn used to carry on. I felt a bit sorry for him, really, the way people used to talk about the pair of them behind their backs . . . And you could see he wasn't well. He used to get muddled, forget what he was talking about halfway through the sermon. A bit bumbling, really, and it got worse over the years so you never knew what you were going to hear next. And then when he collapsed in the pulpit . . . I'll never forget it. A couple of the choir carried him through to the vestry and there he was, laid out, with his head propped up on a hassock while they fetched the doctor. He'd had a stroke – we all thought it would kill him, but it didn't. He retired after that, though, and the pair of them moved away. I did hear that he'd died, but I don't know where or when it happened.'

'What was he like when he wasn't in church?'

Maisie Denton screwed up her face in thought, then said, 'Do you know, I couldn't really say. He kept himself to himself – we never really saw him out much, which is a bit unusual in a place like this. I think he was too ill to do much visiting in the parish. You know, I always thought he liked doing the burials best. Much better than marriages. I suppose that must have been because of Mrs Milburn.'

'What did you think of her?'

'Well . . .'

Seeing his wife hesitate, Denton said, 'Not much, is the answer. None of the women here liked her. Didn't trust her near their husbands.'

'There was a bit of that,' admitted Maisie. 'Jealousy, really. Because she was nice-looking – *fancy*-looking, if you know what I mean. A bit flashy. Well, maybe not for London, but for here . . . always seemed to have new clothes . . . And you did hear a lot of stories – but I don't know how true they were.'

'And these lovers she was supposed to have had – was that just gossip?'

'Well . . .' Maisie flushed. 'There was certainly plenty of talk about that journalist or psychic investigator, or whatever he was supposed to be.'

'What about Ambrose Tynan?' asked Stratton.

Maisie shook her head. 'He wasn't here then.'

'Came just after the war ended,' boomed Denton. 'Down from London, although I did hear he had a place over at Otley, as well.'

'Where's that?'

'Village near Woodbridge. About forty miles, by road.'

'Mrs Milburn had other visitors, too,' Maisie put in, 'men from London—'

'Shouldn't be surprised if some of them had been in on the haunting business as well,' Denton interrupted.

'But the vicar would have been present, wouldn't he?' asked Stratton. 'If these visitors were staying in the rectory.'

'Well, yes,' said Denton, 'but he was getting very doddery by then, and she'd got him right under her thumb, so . . . Perhaps he was afraid she'd up and leave him in his old age if he made a fuss about the other chaps. The fact is,' he added judiciously, 'we don't really know what was going on. Stand behind a bar long enough and you'll hear stranger things than that, though . . .'

'I always wondered,' said Maisie, 'if that was why he talked about sin so much. As a warning to others.'

'Did they have any children?'

'Not when they were here,' said Denton, 'and I don't suppose they did later on, either, not with him being so ill. There's a boy stays up at the rectory now, though. Doesn't go to the school, but I've seen him a few times in the village. Nice-looking lad. I've heard he's her son, but if she got married again, we certainly never heard of it, so heaven knows who the father is.'

CHAPTER FOURTEEN

'. . . And I suppose it's possible,' concluded Stratton. 'Mind you, it's one thing to get people believing that your house is haunted, and quite another to convince them that your son is the product of immaculate conception. And even if the Reverend Milburn was too old and feeble to consummate his marriage, there seem to have been several others who were happy to fill the breach – as it were – so it's not as if she's a virgin.'

'That's just gossip,' said Ballard, hotly. 'Old women in the village. Jealousy, pure and simple.'

Struck by the alacrity with which his former sergeant leapt to Mary Milburn's defence, Stratton said, 'So she's worked her magic on you as well, has she?'

Stratton had worried that his meeting with Ballard – the first since he'd left West End Central – might be awkward, but after a couple of minutes' wariness, they'd slipped back into their old relationship, but with Ballard expressing himself more boldly than hitherto (and without the 'Sir'). Pretty much, anyway: Stratton was aware that, in the ten minutes or so they'd spent reminiscing about old times, neither man had – by mutual but unspoken agreement – brought up the subject of Davies. Certainly, he'd felt no hesitation in telling Ballard all the facts of the Lloyd case, including what the boy had said to him about feeling guilty, which he'd relayed in what he hoped was a suitably light-hearted manner. They were sitting in a corner of the snug, away from the trickle of early evening drinkers who, clustered around the bar, talked in low tones and glanced over their shoulders from time to time to check that Stratton and Ballard weren't eavesdropping.

Embarrassed by his outburst, Ballard stared into his pint. 'Anyway,' he said finally, 'I don't see what it's got to do with your inquiry.'

'Probably nothing,' Stratton conceded. 'Well, that part of it, anyway. But I'll lay good money that Mary/Ananda herself – whose photograph Lloyd treasured so much that he gave it to Wintle for safe keeping, remember – has a lot to do with it. What's more, she's disappeared.'

At this, Ballard jerked his head up. 'No she hasn't. I saw her this morning. Well, at lunchtime.'

'You seem to be the last one who did, then. Roth didn't seem to know where she'd gone or when she'd be back. But she's clearly,' he raised an enquiring eyebrow, 'fresh in your mind.'

'She did make quite an impression,' said Ballard ruefully. 'You haven't met her yet. She has the most extraordinary sex appeal – you almost can't breathe, let alone think of what to say. It was like being bloody seventeen again.'

'That bad?' Stratton grinned. 'She sounds quite something.'

'You wait till you meet her. You'll see I'm not pulling your leg. But she can't have gone far. Perhaps she's just gone to stay with friends or something.'

'Well, if she has, she didn't tell them at the Foundation. Or *they* didn't tell *me* – which seems a lot more likely. She seems to have an alibi for the night Lloyd died, though. Went to the pictures with Mr Tynan, apparently. I had the impression he was rather keen on her.'

'That's hardly surprising,' said Ballard. 'But there's no reason – other than Lloyd having her photograph – why she should be a suspect, is there?'

'None at all,' Stratton agreed, remembering Roth's certainty about the matter. 'At least, not at the moment.'

'I'd no idea she'd been married to the vicar,' said Ballard, thoughtfully. 'She's obviously quite a bit older than she looks.' He narrowed his eyes in calculation. 'If they were newly married when they came here in . . . 1937, you said, didn't you, and she was, say, twenty . . .'

'And the landlord here told me that Reverend Milburn was at least sixty,' said Stratton.

'Blimey. So if she was twenty in 1937 she'd be – what? – thirty-nine, now. She doesn't look anything like it.'

'Some women don't,' said Stratton, thinking of Diana.

'Ten years younger, at least,' said Ballard.

'I don't suppose you've noticed any anaemic-looking virgins knocking about the place, have you?'

'Very droll. You'd think someone would've mentioned about her being the vicar's wife, wouldn't you? Mind you, I never asked.' Ballard shrugged.

'Bit mean about sharing information, are they, the local coppers?'

'They can be. Part of it's like anywhere – thinking that CID will take over anything where they think there's a chance of clearing it up, then take all the credit, so you can understand that. But part of it's the place. It takes a bloody long time to be accepted. Parsons – he's the village bobby – he told me that when he came here it was six months before anyone spoke to him voluntarily, other than to say good morning, and he's only from Ipswich – but now that he is accepted, he's gone like the rest of them, not interested in anything that happens outside the parish boundaries. Anything *inside* them is a different matter, of course.'

Here, Stratton had a sudden memory of how, when he was nine, one of their neighbour's cows had given birth to a two-headed calf, which had been discussed with a level of excitement and urgency never accorded to the impending war.

He rolled his eyes in sympathy. 'Don't I know it! I grew up in a village, remember.'

'Well, it came as a bit of a shock to me. You always hear that people in the country are like that, but I thought it was just something that town people said about them. I mean, it's not as if people here have *never* been anywhere – most of the men went away to fight in one of the wars – but you wouldn't know it to listen to them.'

'Do you get much crime?'

'It's not like London, that's for sure. Every village of any size has its bad family.' Ballard put quotation marks round the last two words by raisings of his eyebrows. 'Well, not so much bad as stupid, really, although of course they don't see it like that. Always up before the beak for nicking lead, poaching, falling behind with the never-never, driving uninsured ... Small stuff and pretty dull, but a hell of a lot of it. My guv'nor's all right, though. Told me DCI Lamb'd had a word with him about all this,' Ballard jerked his head in the direction of the Old Rectory, 'and says I'm to "render assistance as necessary". Talks like a book, but he's a good sort. Anyway, getting back to that odd business of the boy being ... you know, like Jesus or Buddha ... people believe those things because they want to, don't they?'

'I imagine that Mr Roth can be pretty persuasive,' said Stratton, thoughtfully. 'He's got quite a presence. And if people are willing to be persuaded, that would be half the battle.'

'They must do,' said Ballard. 'It's like women who go to seances because they're desperate to contact their dead husbands or sons.' He chuckled. 'That reminds me. You'll never guess who I saw a few weeks ago.'

'At a seance?' Stratton grinned. 'What were you doing – raiding it?'

Ballard looked sheepish. 'Pauline wanted to go.'

Stratton must have looked disbelieving, because Ballard, clearly feeling the need to explain said, awkwardly, 'It's because she wants another baby. The doctor can't explain why it hasn't happened, and she thought the medium might be able to tell her – sort of like a fortune-teller, I suppose. I told her I thought it was daft, but she kept on about it and I didn't want a row, so—'

Stratton held up a hand to stop him. 'I'm sorry. I didn't mean to pry.'

'No, *I'm* sorry. I shouldn't . . .' Ballard shook his head, more at himself than Stratton. 'Anyway,' he continued, with a determined effort to regain his former levity, 'you'll never guess who the medium was.'

'Go on.'

'None other than Big Red.'

'You've got to be joking.' Until she'd left a few years back, Big Red, otherwise known as Peggy Nolan, had been a fixture in Soho for as long as Stratton could remember. Nicknamed for the improbable magenta colour of her hair and known for scrapping with other girls over punters, she'd been a constant and often violently unwilling visitor to the station, and by the time she retired had racked up over two hundred convictions for soliciting.

'I'm not. Her hair's grey now and she's thoroughly respectable. She didn't let on she knew me, but she asked us to stay afterwards. Said she had something particular to tell us. Her card said she had "many unsolicited testimonials". I bloody nearly gave the game away when I saw that, I can tell you.'

'Didn't Pauline recognise her?'

Ballard shook his head. 'She worked at Marlborough Street, remember? Big Red was on our patch.'

'And you didn't tell her who she was?'

'I couldn't, could I? She'd been so keen to go, and then she was disappointed because Big Red didn't have any message for her – you know, from the spirit world or whatever it's called – and I thought if I told her who she was she wouldn't believe me and . . .' He tailed off, shaking his head.

'I understand,' said Stratton. 'Difficult subject.'

'It was funny, though. Funny peculiar, I mean, not funny ha-ha. We'd eyeballed each other as soon as I came in – she's Madame Sabra now, by the way – and I knew she knew and she knew I knew. I thought she might take advantage of it, knowing what I did for a living, but she didn't. When she asked us to wait, I thought she just wanted a natter for old times' sake and I thought I was going to be for the high jump with Pauline for not telling her, but it wasn't like that at all. She pretended she didn't know me from Adam and she told Pauline she knew how much she was longing for a child – said she could sense it – and then she told her she'd have one in time and she had to be patient and not worry about it. And that was it. Afterwards I kept trying to think if there was anything we'd done to give the game away, but I couldn't see how . . .'

'Like that business with the kid I was telling you about,' said Stratton. 'Shakes you up a bit, doesn't it?'

'Certainly does.'

'The thing is,' Stratton continued, 'with the usual run of villains, whether it's murder or pinching sheep or nobbling prize bulls, you know what you're up against, don't you? I mean, you've got some idea of why they do it, whether it's need or greed or lust or envy. But with this lot, I don't know where to start. All this about renouncing your feelings . . . What sort of a world would we have if everyone did that?'

Ballard stared thoughtfully into what was left of his pint, then said, 'Well, there'd be no wars, would there? And we'd be out of a job because there'd be no crimes committed.'

'No . . . but there wouldn't be anything else, either. No emotion, no love, no sense of attachment to anyone or anything. D'you remember Shitty Sid?'

'That tramp from round the back of the news cinema? What's he got to do with it?'

'He used to preach in the early thirties – bit before your time. I heard him once, at Speakers' Corner. He'd talk about his visions of the Apocalypse, how it was coming soon and the world would be swept away and only the righteous would be saved. He had quite a few followers. Pretty respectable types, some of them.'

'Bet they followed at a safe distance.' Ballard grinned.

'He wasn't so bad in those days. Lived on the streets even then, but they used to bring him new clothes and food and what-have-you from time to time. Turned out that he could have done with a bit of soap and water, though – his leg started rotting last summer, great festering wound from his knee to his ankle. By the time we got him into hospital the smell was enough to knock you off your feet. Too late even if they'd amputated, but Sid never complained and he never stopped smiling. Just accepted it – dying, everything. It didn't bother him. What Tynan and Roth were saying reminded me of him.'

Ballard shrugged. 'Sid was *feeble*-minded, not . . . *high*-minded. But in any case, if everyone was like him – accepting things – then, whether it was because they were simple or holy or what-ever else, there'd be no progress, would there? No inventions, no cures for diseases. We'd still be living in bloody caves. The world we've got now may not be perfect, but it's got to be better than *that*.'

'I'll say. Just as well, really, as it's the one we're stuck with and it's not likely to change, is it?'

'Not unless the Soviets drop the bomb on it.' Ballard rose, draining his glass. 'Fancy another?'

CHAPTER FIFTEEN

Stratton had a not-more-than-averagely revolting meal of corned beef rissoles and greens boiled to sludge followed by tinned Empire fruit with synthetic cream, reflecting as he ate that Tynan was, at that moment, undoubtedly dining off lobster bisque with sherry and partridge with foie gras, all washed down with vintage wine. He spent the night at the George and Dragon in a room tucked under the thatch with sloping whitewashed walls and a latched wooden door so low that he had to bend almost double to enter.

The following day, he and Ballard – who, he suspected, was relishing the chance to get his teeth into something more exciting than the usual round of rural crime – arrived at the Old Rectory to question the Foundation's twenty-odd residents about Lloyd and Ananda. This time, the door was answered and the tea fetched by a man who, despite being no more than about twenty-five, had the air of one who'd accumulated enough wisdom to deal with anything life had to throw at him. Just you wait, chum, thought Stratton. You may be sure of yourself now, but life will have you, just like everyone else.

The young chap, who smoked, showily, in imitation of Roth, had evidently been charged with keeping tabs on them while they interviewed the rest of the students, because he seated himself outside the door and returned at intervals, accompanied by a gentle, moon-faced woman who got in the way, apologised constantly, stated the obvious, and at one point spilt scalding hot tea agonisingly over Stratton's crotch. All the time she was doing this she smiled down at the pair of them like an angel of mercy on a particularly bloody battlefield, so obviously selfless that it was impossible to show even the smallest sign of irritation.

'You look as if you're in quite a bit of pain,' Ballard murmured when the woman, still apologising, was dispatched to fetch a cloth to mop up the mess on the table.

'I'll live,' said Stratton, through gritted teeth. 'Let's have the next one, shall we?'

This proved to be a spruce middle-aged man who exuded a version of Miss Kirkland's joyousness and enthusiasm so great that he seemed to be permanently leaning forwards. So keen was he to tell them about the Foundation's 'power for good' that they had a hard job getting him to say anything about Lloyd at all. His story of his first meeting with Roth was, Stratton thought, not dissimilar to Tynan's, and told in much the same language, except that the death of a beloved mother was replaced by a general disillusion with the state of the world and a feeling of powerlessness to change either it, or himself. He talked of a new experience of 'oneness' with his surroundings, a heightening of his senses and a consciousness of a deeper level of existence.

There was a lot more of this as the morning progressed – a procession of straight-backed, smartly dressed individuals who, although giving every appearance of being helpful, were actually much more interested in telling Stratton and Ballard how the Foundation had changed their lives for the better than in shedding even the smallest light on why Lloyd might have been killed. They had all arrived at the Foundation after him, and after Ananda and Michael. None of them had seen Lloyd since he'd left in April, none of them had given him money, and none of them seemed to know anything about his writing a book, either. They expressed disgust at the idea that he might have had any sort of intimate relationship with Ananda, and, although she'd told several of them about the film she'd seen on the 30th, none of them seemed to have any clue at all as to her present whereabouts. Whether Roth had instructed them to tell him nothing, or whether they genuinely didn't know, Stratton wasn't sure, but the whole thing had a curiously stage-managed feeling. He imagined Roth sitting upstairs, the all-seeing, all-knowing presence, and the students reporting back to him after they'd been interviewed. He was reminded, oddly, of the annual village concerts of his boyhood – the muttered tension behind the scenes as each child was pushed through the curtain to sing or recite in front of a throng of proud but anxious parents. And – now he came to think of it – those occasions were always full of the same stuff, too: sentimental for the girls, rousing Victorian patriotism for the boys.

A male student spoke, with an ease born of practice, of having had a drink problem, another of being dogged by illness; a woman spoke about grief at the death of her fiancé, another of a feeling of hopelessness, another of a feeling that she could sense things that other people did not, and several of both sexes, including Miss Kirkland, of a feeling that there must be 'something more to life'. They seemed, too, to have a collective dislike for the personal pronoun, replacing 'I' with 'one' at every opportunity. Over and over again Stratton heard the same words and phrases – truth, wisdom, unity – until, two hours in, he felt that, barring changeable particulars, he could have recited their scripts for them without too much difficulty. Besides the revelation of meeting Roth, a marked theme was the futility, stupidity and general crappiness of the outside world, from its politics to its popular music. It was clear that at the Foundation they felt themselves safe, in their straight-laced, well-ordered world, with all forms of vulgar modernity kept at bay. That, thought Stratton, was presumably the reason Michael was taught here – to ensure that he remained as unsullied as possible.

Left alone for a few minutes between the departure of one student and the arrival of the next, Ballard, who looked as punch-drunk as Stratton felt, murmured, 'They don't blink much, do they?'

'Perhaps it's something they've learnt.'

'Downright creepy, if you ask me. And have you noticed how tired they look?'

Stratton, who'd noticed a lot of pinkish eyes, nodded. 'Perhaps that's part of it, too.' He waved a hand at the quotation on the wall about the big stick. 'From what they're saying, it sounds like a pretty full programme – manual labour as well as lectures and meditation and what not. Must be the discipline that Roth was telling me about when he suddenly blew up about sex.'

'They're all sincere, though, don't you think?'

'Yes, I do. True believers – I think they can't understand why everyone isn't doing it. They're well-intentioned, too. And I can't really see how you could say they're brainwashed when they obviously *want* to believe that this is a higher way of life or whatever you want to call it. I mean, it works for them, doesn't it?'

'Yes.' Stratton rubbed the back of his neck. 'But it's not getting us very far, is it?'

Ballard shook his head despondently. 'Give me a decent villain, any day.'

'I suppose,' said Stratton, remembering what Tynan had said about how the place was financed, 'that most of them must have private means. If they had to work for a living, I don't see how—'

'If they had to work for a living,' said Ballard dismissively, 'they wouldn't have time to muck about with all this. After all, if you've got money, it's easy to say that material possessions don't matter. Rise above the daily grind, and all that.'

'Not the only thing they're meant to rise above,' said Stratton. 'Roth said the sex instinct was . . .' He leafed through his note-book. '"Debased and gross." He said something about not being a slave to one's impulses, as well. Still, if Mary/Ananda is as sexy as you say she is' – Stratton pretended to ignore the slight flush that had crept into Ballard's cheeks – 'then she must have caused a bit of a stir, at least. Perhaps Lloyd was having an affair with her and one of the other chaps was jealous.'

'It's not impossible, I suppose, but they don't seem the type, do they? I mean, if one of the blokes we've seen this morning was jealous, I should have thought he'd be more likely to have the spiritual equivalent of a cold shower than get on a train to London and do his rival in. I've never met this Roth bloke, but I can sense his presence all right.'

By the end of the morning, Stratton felt himself having to make a supreme effort not to slump in his chair as the last student arrived. Like the others, Miss Banting was polite, well spoken and middle class, but she seemed a different type, several years younger than nearly all of them and dressed not in tidy tweeds but un-seasonably, in the sort of clothes Stratton thought of as 'arty': a dirndl skirt and a blouse in the peasant style with a parti-coloured woollen shawl flung dramatically over her shoulders. Her eyebrows, above thick spectacles, were painted in arches of surprise – or possibly menace – and she wore a necklace which looked as though it had been made out of chunks of wood, and a bracelet which seemed to have been constructed for the purpose of noise-making. She was, Stratton realised, the first student he'd seen who looked distinctive: she'd retained the trappings of her former life and personality, whereas the others, to a man and woman, were unadorned and bland.

Despite this, her composure and responses were as uniform as the others' had been, with much made of her need to find a meaning to life and wish to connect to a higher awareness – until Stratton asked her whether she'd seen Jeremy Lloyd since he'd left the Foundation.

Her eyes widened in outraged surprise. 'Of course not!'

'Why "of course"?' asked Stratton.

'One does not communicate with those who leave.' Her tone was vehement. 'We are told—'

Here, the man who had seated himself outside the door gave a discreet but audible cough. It was an innocuous sound, but it stopped Miss Banting in her tracks as absolutely as the shout of 'Stop!' Stratton had heard on his previous visit to the Foundation had arrested the woodcutters in mid-chop. For a moment she froze, mouth partially open and then, as swiftly as if a light had been extinguished, the passion left her face. She glanced apprehensively upwards, much, Stratton thought, as a medieval peasant might, who feared he had angered heaven and would bring down the wrath of God upon himself – or, in Miss Banting's case, the wrath of Roth.

'I simply meant,' she said, after a moment, 'that I had not seen him. I'm afraid that one has rather a habit of complicating things. We were told that he had gone to live in London, so of course, being here, there was no opportunity to see him.'

'I see,' said Stratton. And he did see, very clearly, that leaving the Foundation meant excommunication, in the manner of the Catholic Church. Either you were in or you were out, and there were no halfway measures – except, of course, for Tynan, but then he'd paid for the place and, equally clearly, had a foot in both camps. But for all Roth's insistence that he'd 'neither approved nor disapproved' of the fact that Lloyd was writing a book, the leader had cast him out as surely as Adam and Eve had been expelled from Paradise.

CHAPTER SIXTEEN

Returning to London with a sense of futility, Stratton thought that this, after Lloyd's knock-back from the priesthood, must have come as a double blow. Nodding off at home over the *Daily Express* – *EISENHOWER: SUEZ ATTACK AN ERROR*, alongside adverts for Nestlé's Condensed Milk and Craven A – he was trying to summon up the energy to go upstairs to bed when a thunderous banging on the front door announced Pete. 'Penny for the guy, guv? Remember the fifth of November, and all that.'

'Last time I looked, it was only the third.' Stratton stood back to let his son enter. 'I wasn't expecting you, was I?'

'No. Sorry, it's so late.' Dumping his kitbag on the hall floor, Pete headed for the scullery, saying, over his shoulder, 'I came by earlier but you weren't in and I've lost my key, so I went to the pub. We're shipping out tomorrow. I'd have written, but they've been mucking us about so I wasn't sure . . . Don't mind if I stay, do you?'

'Course not.' Stratton followed him, stifling a yawn. 'If you're looking for beer, there's some under the sink.'

'Oh, good show . . . Join me?'

Reflecting that this was pretty well par for the course – for the last few years the only conversations he had with his son seemed to take place when Pete, on leave and glassy-eyed from the pub, crashed in late at night – Stratton said, 'Why not?'

Stratton looked at Pete, settled in the armchair opposite, and wondered why it was that the sheer size of him – a good inch taller than his own six feet three and, thanks to all the army's training, he seemed almost to pulsate with muscularity and health – continued to be a source of wonder. It was, he supposed, because he saw the boy – although, at twenty-four, he was hardly that any more – so infrequently. He seemed, Stratton thought, to have sprung full-grown a few years ago from National Service, fathered anew by the army, and the beer he'd consumed made him sprawl, so that he took up even more space than usual.

'. . . do you think he's all right?' Pete was saying.

'Sorry, old chap, I'm not with you. Do I think who is all right?'

Pete gave him a sharp look – obviously not as tipsy as all that, thought Stratton – and said, 'You haven't heard a word I've said, have you?'

'Bit tired,' said Stratton apologetically. 'Been a long day. Who are we talking about?'

'Uncle Reg.'

'Why shouldn't he be all right?' asked Stratton, remembering, belatedly, that Monica had said something about Reg looking 'under the weather'.

'I don't know, really . . .' Pete frowned. 'It's just that he was in the pub, so we had a chat about going to Egypt and all that, and . . . Well, you know how he's always got an opinion about everything?'

Stratton grimaced. 'Don't I just.'

'I thought he was bound to start pontificating about it, giving me a lecture – you know, the World According to Reginald Booth – but he didn't. Just wished me luck, and . . . Well, that was all, really. And he's not so fat as he used to be, either.'

'Isn't he?'

'Haven't you noticed?'

'Can't say I have. But that's good, surely? Mind you, if he's been on some sort of . . . slimming cure, you'd think we'd have been treated to a lot of stuff about the joys of rabbit food and . . . I don't know . . . charcoal biscuits.'

Stratton thought Pete might laugh at this, or at least smile, but he didn't. Instead, he said, 'He's not looking well, Dad.'

As Pete's attitude to his uncle had always been – much like that of the rest of the family – either resigned or irritated, Stratton was pricked by his obvious concern. 'If he's put himself on some faddy diet, it's hardly surprising. He's probably just feeling a bit out of sorts.'

'It was a bit weird, though . . .' Pete didn't look convinced. 'Usually, you can't shut him up.'

'Thank God for the rabbit food, then,' said Stratton. 'Mind you, he did drag your Uncle Don and me off to see Billy Graham a couple of days ago.'

'The God bloke?' Pete raised his eyebrows.

Stratton nodded. 'Come to think of it, I thought he was a funny colour then.'

'There you are, then. You might ask him if he's all right, Dad. Next time you see him, I mean.'

It was unlike Pete to be so solicitous, but Stratton, recalling something he'd heard about the forces asking men to make their wills before going into theatres of war, decided it must be to do with that. He tried to push away the image that accompanied this train of thought – his son's broken body lying in the desert – but it lingered on, stubborn, in the corner of his mind's eye. The Pete sitting opposite him looked too solid, too *vital*, even to *be* mortal – but then millions of fathers must, over the years, have felt the same thing about their sons and been proved horribly, heartbreakingly, wrong.

Stratton drank some beer and was trying to think of a subject of conversation that was far enough away from their respective jobs not to have anything to do with impending or actual death when Pete said, 'What's all this I hear about you having a girl-friend, then?'

Whatever else he expected his son to say, it wasn't that and, caught in mid-swallow, Stratton choked.

'Blimey, Dad!' Pete jumped up, narrowly missing the occasional table and, before Stratton could raise a hand to stop him, began bashing him between the shoulder blades. It was like being hit with a shovel.

'Steady on,' he spluttered, eyes bulging. 'I'll be fine.'

'You've gone puce. Here, have a cigarette.' Pete lit it, took one for himself and stood surveying him for a moment before resuming his seat. 'Serious, is it?' He eyed his father specula-tively.

'Not a girlfriend,' said Stratton, between gasps. 'Who told you, anyway?'

'Monica. She said she's called Diana Carleton and she works at the studio and you've been there to collect her.'

Stratton, who thought they'd been very discreet on the few occasions he'd done this, meeting Diana down the road in a place where they couldn't be seen from the gates, was impressed by his daughter's powers of observation but wondered why she hadn't mentioned it to him herself. He wondered if Monica, taking it as a sign of disloyalty to her mother, was upset by it. Both she and Pete had found Doris and Lilian's attempts – pretty much given up now, thank God – to push local widows in his direction more risible than anything, so he didn't think it could be that . . . Monica knew Diana, of course, but his memories of their few conversations on the subject suggested that she rather liked her. It was Pete, he thought, who'd be more of a problem, given his feelings – made all too obvious in the past, although, it had to be said, not recently – about the manner of Jenny's death and Stratton's failure to prevent it.

Pete, however, was smiling. 'Well, well, well . . . You are a dark horse, aren't you?'

'I told you,' said Stratton, 'she's not a girlfriend. More a . . . a . . .'

'A *what*, exactly?'

'We go out together sometimes, that's all. For meals and things. We met on a case during the war, and—'

'Oh, yes?' Pete's eyes narrowed.

'Oh, *no*,' said Stratton firmly. 'Nothing like that, so don't get ideas. We were colleagues, and then, a couple of years ago, we met again, and now . . . Now we're friends. We just meet up sometimes, and . . . And that's all.'

'So you always had an eye for her,' said Pete. 'Monica says she's beautiful. And,' he added in clipped, upper-class tones, 'terribly posh.'

'Yes, she is,' said Stratton. 'Both those things. But I never . . . I loved your mother.' Stratton ducked his head. Why was he being so defensive? Yes, he had fancied Diana – fancied her like mad – any red-blooded male would have felt the same. But there really hadn't been anything *like that*, not when Jenny was alive and not for a number of years afterwards, either. The idea was ridiculous.

He was just about to say something to this effect when he saw that Pete was grinning. 'I know that, Dad. I'm teasing. Still . . .' he leant over to grind his cigarette out, 'it's nice to know you're human like the rest of us.'

The trouble was, thought Stratton, that he never knew if Pete *was* teasing or not, and Monica, he suspected, felt much the same way. Still, if Monica had mentioned Diana to him, the two of them were obviously getting on all right, which was a good thing.

'You want to be careful,' said Pete. 'She sounds strictly officer class to me.'

Stratton sighed. 'I've told you, there's nothing—'

'It's all right, Dad.' Pete stood up and stretched. 'I'd better turn in. Early start, I'm afraid. I'll be gone before you're up.'

Stratton got up too, and drained his glass, and they stood awkwardly on the rug in front of the fireplace, facing each other, close enough to embrace. Pete took a step back. 'Don't worry, I'll leave everything tidy.'

'Thanks . . .' There was another pause, before Stratton, feeling the need to touch his son, extended his arm, aware that he must look stiff and absurd, and gave him a clumsy pat on the elbow. 'Keep safe, won't you?' he said.

'I'll do my best,' said Pete, looking down at Stratton's hand, which was still on his sleeve. 'Don't worry, Dad. I'll probably end up guarding some rotten munitions dump.'

'Yes, well . . . Be careful,' said Stratton, gruffly. 'You watch out for those camels. Nasty things, camels. They spit.'

'I'll keep out of their way, then.'

'Good.' Stratton gave Pete's elbow another pat before disengaging himself. 'Because I'm really quite fond of you, you know.'

Pete's mouth crinkled into a smile. 'You're not so bad yourself. Night, Dad.'

'Night.'

CHAPTER SEVENTEEN

'Your lucky day, sir,' said Feather when Stratton arrived at West End Central the following morning, 'There's a pretty girl waiting to see you. Says she's got something for you and she won't give it to anyone else.'

Stratton introduced himself and escorted his visitor to an interview room. She was indeed pretty, with a mop of dark hair and enormous limpid brown eyes, but too young for her face paint and dressed in what looked like a party frock, so that he took her, until she began to speak, for one of the passive, sullen types you saw about with the Teddy boy gangs.

'It's about Mr Lloyd,' she said briskly, as they sat down. 'I've just seen it in the paper and I thought I should come straight here. I knew him, you see, and—'

'Let's start at the beginning,' said Stratton. 'What's your name?'

'Albertine Russell. I know,' the girl rolled her eyes. 'I ask you! People usually call me Bertie.'

'Well,' said Stratton, 'if you don't mind, I shall call you Albertine. I think it's a nice name.'

'It's not, it's *dreadful*. My dad's name was Albert. I don't really remember him,' she added matter-of-factly, 'because he was killed in the war, but Mum told me he chose it. I suppose he thought it was funny or something, but honestly . . .' She gave a gusty sigh.

She was so bright, so expressive, and – compared to just about everyone else he'd interviewed on this case so far – so resoundingly *normal* that Stratton found he was thoroughly enjoying himself. 'How did you meet Mr Lloyd?' he asked.

'Well, I'm a waitress in the Irani. That's the new café in Old Compton Street,' she added proudly.

'I know it.' Stratton frowned, thinking of the hard, bright café opposite the bomb site. It was full of plastic and Formica, with rubber plants, an enormous, steaming Italian coffee-making machine and a huge American jukebox that played music with a crude, stupefying beat to which the absurdly young customers bounced and gyrated. How Albertine managed to negotiate her way around them without spilling the dishwater coffee they served, he couldn't imagine. He much preferred the Italian cafés with their rough, whitewashed walls, wooden furniture and gingham tablecloths, but he supposed that to people of Albertine's age they must seem dull and old-fashioned. He couldn't think, offhand, of a place that more accurately symbolised the modern world from which the Foundation's members were hiding than the Irani Café. 'I wouldn't have thought it was Lloyd's sort of place at all,' he said.

The girl laughed. 'Oh, it wasn't. He was *far* too old.' Suddenly fearing she'd given offence, her eyes widened and she put her hand up to her mouth. 'Oh, I'm sorry. I didn't mean—'

'That's all right.' Stratton grinned at her. 'Carry on, young Albertine.'

'Ohhh . . .' She wrinkled her nose at him. 'He came in one day a few months back. Said he'd seen me through the window and he knew me. I said I didn't know him, because I'd never seen him before in my life, and he said – you're going to think I'm off my rocker, but he really did say it – not in this life, but the

one before. Said I'd been his sister but I'd died when I was little.'
She laughed. 'I didn't know what to say to that.'

'I'm not surprised,' said Stratton.

'He was very strange,' said Albertine. 'We started talking, and
he was smiling at me, and I thought it was just, you know, being
friendly, so I smiled back, but then he just carried on smiling
like that . . . I had to go and serve some customers, and when I
turned back to him again he was still smiling right at me in just
the same way. He always did that – every time I saw him. I know
that sounds silly,' she added quickly, 'and I'm not saying he was
mad or anything – well, perhaps a little bit – but . . .' She shook
her head, bewildered by the memory.

Stratton, remembering Miss Kirkland, said, 'It doesn't sound
silly at all. You became friends, did you?'

Albertine screwed up her face. 'Sort of, I suppose . . .'

'Did you, for instance, ever visit him at home?'

'Hardly.' She stared at him as if he'd just grown a second head.
'He just used to drop by and say hello from time to time – he
never stayed long or talked much – or sometimes he just stood
outside and waved at me. Sometimes he gave me things – choco-
late or a banana or something. He didn't, you know . . .' Albertine
looked uncomfortable, 'want anything in return. The manager
didn't like it because he never bought anything, but it didn't
bother me. I mean, you could see he didn't mean any harm. And
I felt sorry for him, because he obviously didn't have many friends.'
The kind sincerity with which this was uttered reminded Stratton
of Monica. 'So he was just, you know, *there*. But last week he came
in and gave me this.' She held up a string bag.

Seeing an orange and a packet of sandwiches, Stratton said,
'His lunch?'

'*No* . . .' Albertine gave a half-groan, half-giggle that reminded
him of Monica again. Reaching in and pulling out a large brown
envelope with staples across the top, she said, '*This*. He said it

was important and I was to keep it safe in case anything happened to him. He told me not to look at it or show it to anyone, but when I saw the newspaper, I thought I ought to tell the police.'

'You were quite right.' Stratton took the envelope. 'Did you look at it?'

'No. Honest. He'd done it up like that, you see,' she indicated the staples, 'and I thought if he came and asked for it back, he'd know if I had looked, so . . .' She wriggled. 'I was curious, though. I tried holding it up to the light, but I couldn't see anything, so I just put it in a drawer in my bedroom.'

'And when he said "in case anything happened to him", did he say what he thought might happen?'

Albertine shook her head. 'I should have asked, shouldn't I? Only we were very busy, and . . . But it did happen, didn't it? The paper said he was killed. I wish I had asked him,' she said, sadly. 'I mean, I might have been able to do something, or . . . I don't know. But I didn't. I just said I'd look after the envelope if he wanted. I didn't take it seriously.' She looked overwhelmed and tearful. 'That was wrong.'

'Listen,' said Stratton, passing her his handkerchief. 'No one could blame you for it. Mr Lloyd was a strange man, wasn't he? He said strange things. And I suppose he must have given this to you because he thought you were a reincarnation of his dead sister. I'd say that's fairly odd, wouldn't you?'

Albertine, who'd been blowing her nose vigorously, nodded. 'He said he knew I wouldn't let him down because I was family.'

'There you are, then. And – strictly between ourselves – he seems to have said strange things to quite a lot of people.' Stratton gave her an encouraging smile. '*Old* people. And they didn't take him seriously either – or if they did, they didn't know what to do about it.'

'Really?' Albertine looked, if not comforted, then less distraught.

After a moment, curiosity getting the better of her, she said, 'Aren't you going to open it?'

'I think we'd better, don't you?' Holding the envelope close to his chest, he ripped open the top and carefully – making sure it was facing him – slid out a small photograph. Taken outdoors, with part of what might have been a horse chestnut tree in the background, it showed a boy from the knees up, hands on hips, grinning triumphantly as if he'd just won a game of something. The grin, and the two crescent shapes of his smiling eyes, were partly obscured by a frenzy of scratches, but Stratton recognised Michael Milburn all right.

'What is it?' Albertine was leaning forward eagerly.

Stratton put the photograph on the table. 'Do you know him?'

'No. I've never seen him before. At least, I don't think I have, because you can't see his face properly. It looks as if someone did that on purpose.'

'Yes, it does.'

Albertine frowned. 'If Mr Lloyd hated him that much, you'd think he'd just rip up the picture and throw it away. Do you know who it is?' A sudden thought made her stare at him, round-eyed. 'It wasn't this boy who killed him, was it?'

'I very much doubt it.' It wasn't impossible, of course – but he couldn't imagine that the kid would ever be let loose in London (or anywhere else, come to that) by himself. 'We don't know *who* killed him, yet.'

' But it is a clue, isn't it?' Albertine turned the photograph over. 'His name's Michael. It says so here. And something else . . . *Art . . . Ant . . .* I can't read it.'

Stratton picked it up. The word Michael was written in neat block capitals, with 14.9.55 beside it. Underneath, in large, hysterical scrawl and with a full-stop stabbed into the paper after it, was a word that Stratton had to peer at for several seconds before he made it out.

'What does it say?'

'I think,' said Stratton slowly, 'that it says Anti-Christ.'

'That's terrible,' said Albertine, goggling at him. 'Do you think Mr Lloyd wrote it?'

'I don't know,' said Stratton, thinking that if he had, it certainly answered the question of what he'd thought of Michael. 'We'll have to compare it to a sample of his handwriting.'

'He must have been completely mad,' said Albertine, 'not just a bit. I thought,' she added, more slowly, 'that he was ... you know ... a bit touched, but all right really. But he wasn't, was he?'

'Not really,' said Stratton. 'But I'm sure he wouldn't have done you any harm. And,' he added, patting her hand, 'you've done the right thing, coming here.'

Stratton stared down at the scratched black-and-white face with its ruined eyes. If Lloyd had defaced the photograph himself, then it was presumably Michael, and not Mary/Ananda or anyone else at the Foundation, who was the principal target of his anger. But if he had hated Michael so much, why had he not only kept the photograph but given it to Albertine for safe keeping? Judging from what everyone had said about him, Stratton thought that he probably was potty enough to believe she really was his dead sister, but all the same ... It would, however, make more sense – at least to someone possessed of what might be termed ordinary logic – if someone else had done it and Lloyd had kept it as a form of insurance because he, too, had cause to fear them. After all, he had said to Albertine that he was giving her the envelope in case anything happened to him ...

Was it possible, Stratton wondered, that Lloyd was Michael's father? That was unlikely, but it wasn't impossible. Stratton leafed through his notebook. Lloyd's aunt had said that he was born in 1928, so if Michael was now eleven or twelve, he'd have been born in 1944 or 1945 when Lloyd was sixteen or seventeen. A boy could father a child at that age, and Mary/Ananda, who'd married a man fully forty years older than herself and was said to be 'man-mad' into the bargain, might not give two hoots about how old her partner was ... But that meant that the two of them would have had to have met during the war, before the Foundation was set up, which didn't seem particularly likely. All the same, he made a note to check if Grove knew, or would find out, what Lloyd had been doing in 1944 and '45 and where he'd been doing it.

If it were true, of course, then Lloyd might have grown to hate Mary/Ananda for colluding with Roth in erasing him from Michael's family tree. Perhaps he'd grown to hate his own son, too, for supplanting him when he felt himself to be the 'chosen' one? But in that case, why not deface both the photographs? And why stay at the Foundation for so many years, accepting – or at least keeping quiet about – the fiction about Michael's conception?

None of it made sense. And surely, even for such a strange bunch as he was dealing with, none of that was very likely. One thing, however, was likely: if anyone other than Lloyd had defaced that photograph, then Michael – and possibly Mary/Ananda, who must have had some reason to flee the Foundation – might well be in danger.

CHAPTER EIGHTEEN

'We don't want to take any chances with this,' said Lamb. 'I'll get in touch with the District Superintendent in Suffolk about providing a police guard for the boy. We need to track down the mother, too – get that photograph in the newspapers. And we'd better have some copies made of both those pictures of Lloyd, as well.'

Wonders will never cease, thought Stratton, surprised and relieved by his superior's acceptance of his argument, entirely without the bollocking-plus-finger-jabbing routine.

'I'll suggest you continue to liaise with DI Ballard,' said Lamb. 'I also think it might be a good idea for you to contact the Psychical Research Society about this Foundation place. I'm told that they keep tabs on that sort of thing.'

Stratton felt his heart sink: more cranks. Something of this must have shown on his face, because Lamb said, 'I realise that they may seem a somewhat, er ... *eccentric* crew ... but apparently they're the best source of information about this type of outfit, as well as,' Lamb's smile was open and genuine, 'about the fairies at the bottom of the garden.'

Back in his own office, Stratton had just discovered that the

Psychical Research Society had its headquarters off Kensington High Street and was wondering if one of Lamb's Masonic chums might have told him about it, when McNally telephoned. 'Cause of death was loss of blood resulting from puncture wounds,' said the pathologist. 'The haemorrhage was internal, which is why you didn't see much blood, and—'

'Whoa,' said Stratton, fumbling in his jacket. 'Let me get my notebook.' Digging about in his pocket, his fingers came upon the envelope Albertine had given him. Feeling something crackle and move inside, he realised that it contained a hitherto unnoticed second item, taped flat to the inside. Detaching it, he saw that it was a death certificate for the Reverend Edward Granville Milburn, with the date given as 17 May 1945. The informant was a Suffolk physician, Dr James Slater. Stratton, glancing at the information given under cause of death, shook his head in disbelief.

'Right,' he said, putting the telephone receiver back to his ear. 'Sorry about that. You're a bit keen, aren't you, working on a Saturday?'

'I said I'd give a talk to one of the university science clubs,' said McNally, 'where I am due in half an hour, so we'll need to hurry this up. I assumed you'd like to know sooner rather than later.'

'Yes, absolutely. Fire away. Internal haemorrhage and ...?' Stratton started writing.

'Yes, internal. The assailant wouldn't have had much blood on him at all, unless he – or she, I suppose – was injured. All the blood samples we took are O Positive – the most common group ...' McNally began reading from his notes at high speed, so that Stratton struggled to keep up. 'Wounds on the hands commensurate with an attempt to defend himself. Traces of blood under the nails – O Positive, as I said – and twelve wounds to the chest which didn't penetrate the cavity, plus two that did. One of them punctured his left lung. A quantity of blood had escaped into the cavity of the pleura, which would have begun to impede respiration fairly quickly, but what actually did for him was a puncture wound to the left side of the chest, five and a half inches deep. Penetrated the right ventricle of the heart and death was caused by blood loss. Mind you,' he added, 'the wound to the lung would have finished him if the other hadn't – it would just have taken a bit longer to do the job. Judging from the blood flow, both of the wounds were inflicted when Lloyd was horizontal. The others could certainly have been done when he was standing up ... with the scissors, if only one blade was used. There's not much blood on them, but with a rapid blow or plunge the vessels are compressed so bleeding takes place when the pressure is removed with the withdrawal of the weapon, and of course sometimes the weapon is effectively wiped clean on the edge of the wound or against clothing as it's withdrawn—'

'And the traces on the scissors are O Positive too, are they?' asked Stratton, more to slow things down because his hand was beginning to cramp than because he hadn't understood.

'Yes, as I've said.' McNally's voice rose a peevish semitone. 'Judging by the position of the scissors, the minor wound to the neck was inflicted last ... It seems to have been a pretty frenzied attack, so perhaps the assailant didn't realise that Lloyd was done for. You'll get a report in due course, but now, if you don't mind—'

'Just one more thing,' said Stratton, who was still scribbling frantically.

'If it's quick.'

'It will be. Nothing to do with Lloyd but, if you saw a death certificate where the cause was given as ...' Stratton clawed the piece of paper towards him, '"bed sores, exhaustion and rheumatoid arthritis," what would you think?'

'I'd think someone was playing a prank. Or that he didn't know what he was doing. Why?'

'I've got one here. It's for a sixty-eight-year-old man who died in 1945. The informant is his doctor.'

'Man must have been an idiot, then. Bed sores can cause septi-caemia, which could certainly be a cause of death, but then it should say so on the certificate. Rheumatoid arthritis may be unpleasant, but it doesn't kill you, and exhaustion would need to be qualified.'

'So you'd say it was insufficient.'

'I most certainly would. As I said, the doctor's a fool. And, if the need had arisen, he'd never have got it past a coroner – or not unless *he* was a fool, too. Now, if there's nothing else, I have to be on my way.'

Stratton replaced the telephone receiver and was trying to collect his thoughts when a phlegmy rumbling noise heralded Grove, who ambled in with his pipe clenched firmly between his teeth and a sheaf of paper under his arm. 'We widened the area of inquiry – done all the streets between Shaftesbury Avenue and Oxford Street – but there's bugger all to show for it. Everyone was either out, asleep or away, and no one saw a bloody thing. We've had another chat with everyone in the house at Flaxman Court, too, but . . .' Grove shook his head gloomily. 'I took a copy of that photograph, but no one recognised the woman.'

'At least we know who she is.' Stratton proceeded to fill Grove in on his visit to Lincott. 'We also know, I'm afraid, that she was at the pictures in Ipswich the evening of the night Lloyd was killed, with a friend. The manager remembered her. He said that the programme ended at half past ten, and he saw them leaving. Wait a minute, though – now I think about it, I don't think anybody actually said they'd seen her when she got back to the Foundation . . .' Stratton leafed through his notebook. 'No, they didn't. So I suppose she could have come to London afterwards, if she'd taken a late train or got a lift or something.'

The older man listened carefully, sucking his nicotine-stained teeth at intervals and shaking his big grey head. 'Not impossible. We'll keep showing the photograph, and I'll get them to ask if anyone's seen a strange car. You'd think someone would remember – not so many people around, late on. I'm afraid,' he added, 'that the news from Fingerprints isn't very good, either. The ones on the scissors are Lloyd's and so are most of the prints in the room. Those that aren't belong to Mrs Linder. There's only one set – well, a palm – unaccounted for, and it doesn't match anyone in the house or anything on the files.'

'Where did they find it?'

'On the desk. Redfern says that from the look of it, someone was either leaning against the edge of the desk or was pushed back against it. Of course, it doesn't mean they had anything to do with Lloyd's death. Could have been months old – from the sound of it, he didn't go in for housework.'

'That's true,' said Stratton, remembering the state of the room. 'By the way, do you know what he was up to in 1944 and '45?'

Grove made a frog face, turning down the corners of his mouth and raising his eyebrows. 'Haven't the foggiest. His aunt would know though – want me to give her a ring?'

'Please.' Stratton stood up, stretching. 'I've got to pay a visit to the Psychical Research Society – yet more fun.'

'You might ask them what the wife's Auntie Annie did with her teaset,' said Grove. 'Only electroplated nickel, but it had great sentimental value and she'd always said the wife could have it when she'd—'

'I'll electroplate you in a minute,' said Stratton, reaching for his coat. 'And you get your lot to find something useful for me down Wardour Street, or I'll tell the Psychic blokes to send *you* something that goes bump in the night.'

*

The headquarters of the Psychical Research Society proved to be next door to a drab vegetarian restaurant. Stratton, who was feeling peckish, glanced at the flyblown menu card in the window. Headed with the words 'Fleshless Food', the items on offer included sorrel salad, something called Nuttolene which he didn't even want to think about, and 'health-giving' Granose biscuits. Despite it being lunchtime, there seemed to be very few customers and Stratton found he had no desire to join them.

The building occupied by the Society, spruce and gleaming with fresh paint, seemed positively welcoming in comparison. There was a book shop on the ground floor, with a neatly arranged window display of the society's journals and books with titles such as *The Way of Attainment*, *Photographing the Invisible*, and *Science Hammers on the Church Door*. The middle-aged lady behind the till was rather wispy and dressed in trailing, sludge-coloured clothes, but at least she didn't go in for penetrating stares or everlasting smiles. On hearing why Stratton had come, she conducted him briskly through to a cramped, filing-cabinet-filled back office to meet her boss, who had the reassuringly corporeal look of a scruffy, aged Billy Bunter and whom she introduced as Dr Thorley.

'Mr Lloyd hasn't come to our attention,' he said, when Stratton had explained the situation, 'and I'm afraid we know very little about Theodore Roth's background. There's the connection with Ambrose Tynan, of course,' here Thorley gave an indulgent smile, 'but we don't, for example, know where he was born, or very much at all about his life before he came to England.'

'That was after the war, was it?' Stratton pulled out his notebook.

'That's right. I assume, from his name – if, of course, it is his real one – that Mr Roth is Jewish. So, if he came from Europe, then he must have been lucky enough to escape the persecution.'

'I understand he'd been in a concentration camp,' said Stratton, remembering what Tynan had told him.

'It's quite possible. We think he came originally from Eastern Europe. He claims to be Russian, which is certainly possible. It's often difficult, with these sorts of people, to disentangle fact from fiction. He also claims, for example, to have studied in Tibet.'

Stratton flicked back through his notebook to the notes from his conversation with Tynan. '"In his youth, under the great masters",' he read. 'And they would be?'

'Your guess is as good as mine. In fact, we don't know whether they exist at all. But it's not an unusual claim, by any means. Madame Blavatsky, who founded the Theosophical Society in the last century, told people she'd travelled to Tibet on her own and lived there for over seven years. It's never been substantiated but an awful lot of people swallowed the story on remarkably little evidence.' Thorley shrugged. 'They believed because they wanted to. It was the same with G. I. Gurdjieff. He founded an organisation very similar to Roth's, and made the same claim about studying in Tibet – but again, there's no proof he went anywhere near the place, just as there isn't with Roth. Blavatsky, incidentally, was Russian, and Gurdjieff was born in Armenia. There are an awful lot of stories about both their lives which I doubt would stand up to examination.'

Stratton nodded, remembering the quotation about the big stick he'd seen at the Foundation. 'Presumably, between the wars, it would have been quite hard for a foreigner to get into Tibet.'

'Heinrich Harrer managed it, of course, during the war.'

'Harrer?'

'Austrian mountaineer, visited the country and became the Dalai Lama's tutor. Wrote a book called *Seven Years in Tibet*. Very popular.'

'Oh, yes.' Stratton recalled seeing the title in the windows of the bookshops on Charing Cross Road. It must, he thought, have been the basis for the documentary film that Roth had said Tynan and Mary/Ananda had gone to see on the night Lloyd was killed.

'Harrer was the exception. It was very much a closed country – still is, of course, now the Communists have got it. Very few Western travellers, and the natives have little contact with the outside world, so they can't tell us. And of course much is made of the secrecy surrounding these great masters.' Thorley's fat hands pawed quotation marks in the air around the last two words. 'Or the "Great White Brotherhood", as Madame Blavatsky called them. Which is,' he added sardonically, 'especially convenient if – as we suspect – they don't actually exist.'

'Forgive my saying this,' said Stratton, 'but I thought you'd be more . . . well, receptive to this sort of thing.'

Thorley wagged a portly finger at him. 'The society holds no collective opinions, Inspector. Some of our members are sympathetic to spiritualism, claimed mystical connections and the like, others are more sceptical, not to say hostile . . . and others, of whom I hope I am one, are dispassionate and committed only to scientific investigation.'

'Did you investigate the hauntings at Lincott Rectory?'

'Twice, as a matter of fact. I,' he added, with a modest dip of the head, 'was one of those chosen to direct the second investigation, which took place in 1946.'

'As late as that?'

'It was just before Roth's Foundation for Spiritual Understanding purchased the rectory. When I heard about it I thought that perhaps they might try to capitalise on the hauntings. Even when they were no longer what you might call hot news, there was still quite a lot of interest. I have to say,' he added, 'that there's no evidence that this happened.'

'Did you meet Mary Milburn?'

Regretfully, Thorley shook his head. 'We were unable to find

her. The Reverend Milburn was dead, of course – as, unfortunately, was Maurice Hill, the original investigator—'

'Who must,' Stratton interrupted, 'have made a fair packet out
of all those newspaper reports.'

'Oh, undoubtedly. And there was the book, too, in 1940 – *The
Most Haunted House in England*. Came out before paper rationing
started and sold thousands ... Money could have been the sole
reason, and Hill was a journalist so of course he wanted sensational copy, but motives in these cases can be surprisingly mixed,
you know. It wouldn't surprise me if he'd been keen on Mary
Milburn.'

'Did you speak to people who'd known Mary before she'd left
Lincott?'

'Oh, yes. But no one knew where she'd gone. I only received a
couple of pieces of new information about her.' Levering himself
out of his chair with difficulty, because he was a tight fit, Thorley
turned his back on Stratton, almost sweeping the contents off his
desk with his backside as he did so, and began rummaging in one
of the filing cabinets. After some minutes he surfaced, waving a
folder and then, seating himself once more, began to leaf through
the pages. 'Here we are. It was a Mrs Dixon. She told me that Mary
Milburn's involvement with her brother – a Dr Slater – left him
a physical and emotional wreck. Complete mental breakdown, by
all accounts. Unfortunately, I wasn't able to speak to him directly,
but Mrs Dixon said Mrs Milburn had made him believe that she
was a medium and could give him messages from his dead wife.
She also,' here, Thorley's eyebrows raised so far above his round
glasses that they almost disappeared into his hair, 'appears to
believe that Mrs Milburn murdered Reverend Milburn, her husband.
There's a letter here, with the details ...'

'May I?' Stratton took the letter, and, skimming it, saw the
name 'Dr James Slater' halfway down the page. The death certificate, he thought. Had Mrs Dixon's brother, Dr Slater, been Mary's

unwitting accomplice? 'Did you show this to the police at the time?'

Thorley shook his head. 'Perhaps I ought to have done, but her claims are unsubstantiated and the tone of the thing is – as I'm sure you can see – rather wild . . .'

'Fair enough. I'd like to keep this for the time being.'

'Of course, Inspector. Mrs Dixon also told me – this was on the telephone – that she'd heard that Mrs Milburn had become a GI bride just after the war ended, and was living in America.'

Remembering that the Reverend Milburn's death certificate had been dated some time in mid-May, Stratton said, 'Well, if that's the case, she can't have wasted much time . . . What conclusion did you reach about the Lincott hauntings?'

'Quite bogus. We decided that the phenomena were either faked by one of the occupants of the house – possibly with the connivance of Hill, who, as you pointed out, stood to make quite a bit of money – or were due to natural causes: rats, acoustic effects and the like.'

'And your conclusion about Mrs Milburn?'

'That she was behind a lot of it, certainly. We were by no means the only people who thought so. It's hard to say, never having met the woman, but, judging by what people who *did* know her had to say, she wasn't reliable and had difficulty in separating truth from fantasy. Whether this was sheer mischief or evidence of a hysterical need for attention, I couldn't say. Mrs Dixon certainly believed it to be something more sinister, but she was influenced by Mrs Milburn's bad treatment of her brother.' Nodding at Stratton's coat pocket, where he'd stowed the letter, Thorley added, 'She does become rather . . . *emotional* on the subject.'

'Were you aware that Mary Milburn had returned to Lincott Rectory?'

Thorley sat up as sharply as if he'd been jabbed with a compass, and his eyes grew even rounder than before, so that he looked more Billy Bunterish than ever. Stratton half expected him to yelp 'Yarooh!'

'She lives there with her son,' said Stratton. 'Or at least she did until a couple of days ago. We're very keen to speak to her, but at the moment we don't know where she is.'

'Well, if I hear anything I shall let you know immediately, of course. Her son, you said. The child of the GI, presumably?'

'At the moment, we're not sure. The general consensus seems to be that he's unlikely to be Reverend Milburn's son.'

'Yes . . .' Thorley coughed and a spot of hard colour appeared on each cheek. 'I'm afraid she was described to me several times as a nymphomaniac. Constantly trying to seduce men, and very often succeeding.' He said this with a mystified air which made Stratton think that, in his world, there was little place for sex. 'Dear, oh dear . . .'

'In fact,' said Stratton, 'I was told at the Foundation that there's an idea going round that the boy's conception was, er . . . divinely aided. The students – some of them, at least – appear to be believe that he is one of these great masters, or whatever they're called.'

'Really?' Thorley chuckled. 'Dear oh dear. It never ceases to amaze me what people will believe. It's like Blavatsky's lot, grooming boys as future saviours and making claims as to who the students had been in their previous lives . . . It was all written up in the *Theosophist* magazine, a series of articles called "Rents in the Veil of Time", and then it was issued as a book. Really set the cat amongst the pigeons, because of course some people had been written up as more important – nearer to the leader – in their former incarnations than others.' Thorley chuckled. 'A sort of spiritual *Debrett's*, if you like. It's quite extraordinary – people will strain at a gnat, but they'll swallow a camel without a second thought . . .'

Afterwards, waiting for a tube train to take him back to the West End, Stratton reflected that he couldn't have put it better himself.

CHAPTER NINETEEN

Ballard was frankly delighted when Stratton's call came, because it gave him an excuse to avoid – or at least put off – dealing with a case involving a family in a village some miles from Lincott, of the type which always made his heart sink. They were a bony, unkempt bunch, with a look of ingrained malnourishment that Ballard imagined would take generations of roast beef to eradicate. The mother had died and the eldest daughter had taken her place in all senses of the word, an arrangement the rest of the family seemed to consider perfectly normal and which would have gone on indefinitely but for the intervention of a neighbour, concerned that the girl would become pregnant. Ballard had dealt with several cases like it and wasn't relishing the task of explaining why the arrangement was illegal, immoral and couldn't go on to a man who was only fractionally less animal than the beasts he tended. Stratton's Dr Slater, driven by Mary/Ananda to a nervous breakdown according to his sister, Mrs Dixon, was a far more interesting – as well as a far less revolting – prospect.

Ballard's first impression on seeing him was of an elderly bulldog dismayed by the sudden removal of its bone. Rheumy-eyed, jowly and grey-faced, he sat, surrounded by other leftover Victorians, in the sanatorium's enormous conservatory. Swathed in rugs, Slater's face was turned upwards to the weak winter sunlight that was struggling to penetrate the murky skylight and windows. He was positioned between a woman whose face, impossibly wizened and puckered by age, was grouted with thick powder, and another, equally ancient, whose long grey hair was incongruously plaited into two childish pigtails. Ballard would have preferred privacy, but the matron had assured him that while neither lady had sufficient mental capacity left to understand anything of his conversation with the doctor, their presence was necessary for his peace of mind. They remained silent throughout, but took turns in glaring at Ballard and patting Slater's knees and stroking his hands when he became emotional, which, in the course of the interview, was often enough to make Ballard feel a complete bastard for asking the questions in the first place.

Using the information given him by Stratton, he'd run the old boy to earth in a genteel but rundown establishment on the coast, just outside Aldeburgh, about sixty miles – all of them on narrow, twisting country roads – from Lincott. Mrs Dixon, who'd reluctantly given the address, had seemed to think he was long past talking to anybody about anything, but the matron, when applied to, had been more optimistic and, thus far, she'd been proved right.

Although adamant that he'd never met, or even heard of, Jeremy Lloyd, the mention of Mary Milburn's name had, to Ballard's consternation, caused Dr Slater to burst into noisy tears. When his sobs finally subsided, he said, 'I've never told my sister everything that happened. I couldn't bring myself to . . . It was because of Daphne.'

'Daphne?'

'My wife. When she died, I was . . . I missed her so much. All the time we'd been married, I couldn't believe my luck. She was lovely and we were so happy that when it came to an end – Daphne had cancer, you see – it was as if the world, my world, had ended. I could see no logic in the fact that I was still alive, when she . . .' Dr Slater shook his head in slow bewilderment. 'I thought, if I could contact her somehow . . . I wanted a sign that she was still with me, because I was so lonely without her. I wanted her to stay with me . . .' Slater buried his head in his hands.

'I am sorry to distress you.' Ballard was aware, as he said this, that it was a hopelessly inadequate response, but he couldn't think of anything better. 'When was this?'

'January 1944, she died.'

'And were you acquainted with Mrs Milburn at that time?'

'Not until about a year later, when I began attending her husband – as his doctor, of course. He was bedridden by that time, crippled with arthritis. One can try to alleviate the pain, but in Reverend Milburn's case the condition was pretty well advanced, so that he had difficulty in feeding himself and so forth, and the treatment is fairly limited.'

As he spoke, Ballard caught a glimpse of the professional man he'd once been. 'And this was at Lincott Rectory, was it?'

'No. The Reverend Milburn had retired by then – he would have been quite unable to continue his duties – and they'd moved to Woodbridge. I knew of their connection to Lincott Rectory, of course, and that was why . . .' The watery eyes were full of anguish. 'All I wanted was to feel that Daphne was near me. I didn't want anything else.'

'What did you do?'

'Well, I knew that Mary Milburn was a medium, you see, because I'd read the book about the hauntings at Lincott, so I asked if she could help me to contact Daphne. She wasn't keen at first, but I didn't want to let it go, if there was a chance . . . And I suppose I was quite . . . Well, she was rather attractive. The most beautiful eyes ... Not that I ... I mean, she gave me the impression of being devoted to her husband and there wasn't any idea in my mind of anything ... *untoward* ... I do hope you understand that.'

'Of course.' Ballard, who, despite his appreciation of Mary/Ananda's undeniable charm and good looks, now felt nothing but sympathy for the man, nodded solemnly. 'I do understand. When did the seance take place?'

'I don't remember exactly, but sometime in the spring. Before the Reverend Milburn died, certainly. Mary came to my house – I was also living in Woodbridge at the time – and during the seance she said she had a message – messages – from Daphne. Then she embraced me. She said it was Daphne, that Daphne's spirit was coming through her and wanted to kiss me ... I let her, and it really did seem ... I mean, I thought I felt Daphne, that she was there with me ...' Mouth agape, Slater stared at him through woebegone, red-rimmed eyes.

'Through the medium of Mary, you mean?'

'Yes. This happened on several occasions, and each time, there was more ...'

'You had intercourse with her?' Ballard glanced uneasily at the two women, but neither seemed to register what he was asking.

'Yes ... But it was with Daphne. I mean ... that's what she told me, and ... I believed her. I felt that she – that *they* – had rescued me. I'd felt as if I was drowning, and they'd rescued me together. I suppose you could say I was in love with Mary, but it was only because of Daphne. Daphne came back to me through her, or so I thought ... She made me believe it and I wanted to believe it, Inspector. I wanted my wife ...' Slater broke down in deep, racking sobs, and his two attendants pawed at him with soothing whimpers, as a dog might place its comforting head on the knee of a crying child.

'How often did you ... did this happen?'

'Several times. Five or six, I think. I lived for those meetings, Inspector. It was all I had, that connection ... It meant everything to me.'

'I understand. What happened next?'

'She – Mary – hadn't contacted me for two or three weeks. I tried to speak to her. They didn't have a telephone, and when I went to the house, no one came ... Several times, I thought she must be there – I heard noises, but she didn't answer the door, and I was desperate ... Then she came to see me. She said that her husband was dead, he'd died in the night. She told me that his condition had deteriorated, and that she'd been busy nursing him. When I asked her why she hadn't contacted me – about Reverend Milburn, I mean – she said I'd told her there was nothing I could do for him and she hadn't wanted to trouble me.'

'Did she seem upset?'

'That was the worst thing. She was so cold. Ruthless. She said she wanted a death certificate. I said I must see the body before I could do it – I hadn't seen Milburn for at least a month, and it was against the law – and then she said that it wasn't necessary. She said I ought to trust her because we were lovers. I tried to explain – we weren't lovers, it was because of Daphne – and then she said ... she said ...' Unable to speak, Slater sat clutching the women's hands, tears coursing unchecked down his face. There being no nurses in sight, Ballard leant forward, proffering his handkerchief, which was twitched from his hand by the crone in pigtails. Slater sat passively and allowed her to dab his face, which she did with the infinite tenderness of a mother ministering to a sick baby.

'She said I'd taken advantage of my position to seduce her. I realised then that she'd tricked me, that she'd only pretended to contact Daphne and go into a trance and that it was all a put-up job. She'd lied to me and I'd ... I'd ... *betrayed* ... my wife ... insulted her memory ... I couldn't bear it. I know I should have insisted on seeing the body but at the time my whole concern was to get away from her. She was demonic . . . her eyes as she said those things . . . You can't imagine . . . I made up a death certificate – I can't even remember what I wrote. It was the first thing that came into my head. I just wanted her to leave me alone. I remember I asked her to return some letters I'd written her, and there were some things of my wife's – jewellery – that I'd given to her, but I never had them back . . . I broke down after that. I gave up my work . . . I was terrified that Mary would black-mail me . . . It haunted me, and the terrible thing I'd done to Daphne . . . to my beloved wife . . . I couldn't bear it . . .'

Ballard stared at Slater, appalled. Mary had targeted the man at a time when, almost deranged by grief, he was supremely vulnerable. Had she married the much older Reverend Milburn in order to manipulate him, too? And, more importantly, had she got Slater to cover up the fact that she'd murdered her ailing husband – a man for whom she had, presumably, no further use?

'Just one more question, Dr Slater. Did Mary have a child?'

'Yes, a son. Little more than a baby.'

'Do you remember his name?'

Slater drew his brows together in the effort of recollection.

'Was it Michael?'

'I don't think . . . No,' he said, more decisively. 'Not Michael. Something else. But I'm afraid . . .' He shook his head, defeated.

'Thank you.' Ballard rose. 'You've been very helpful. I'll leave you in peace.'

Bloody stupid thing to say, thought Ballard as he left. He'd rarely seen a human being so bereft of peace as Slater. Picturing the poor man, stripped of all dignity and without hope in either this world or, if it existed, the next, broken and shaking between his two senile and uncomprehending attendants, he fervently hoped that no one would suggest charging Slater with aiding and abetting. He was lucid enough, yes – he'd even remembered Mary's Woodbridge address – but whether he was physically or mentally fit to stand trial was a different matter, and would, Ballard thought, be simply cruel. Also, given Slater's condition, and the utterly fantastic nature of the story he'd told, he very much doubted they'd have enough to justify disinterring the Reverend Milburn – assuming that he'd been buried and not cremated – for forensic examination.

Sitting alone in the car, Ballard took his copy of Mary Milburn's photograph out of his pocket and stared at it, remembering the feelings he'd had on meeting her. They'd unsettled him then, exacerbated the other feelings he'd been having, that his life was being lived but somehow unspent. Not that he'd imagined some glorious epic, taking place against a background of heroically soaring strings, like a film or something; it was more a feeling of being due something . . . well, just something *more*. Of course he couldn't imagine actually being with anyone else but Pauline, in the sense of living with and married to – it wasn't that, or even being on the lookout for someone to have an affair with, as some men did. In any case, he told himself, you're more than a bag of glands, for God's sake.

It was just that Mary/Ananda had, in a way that he couldn't quite put his finger on – and wasn't, in fact, going to allow himself to pinpoint, because that way lay danger – represented an opportunity. Something happy, something simple, something different; something that wasn't tied up with all the business of failing to get pregnant and the concomitant disappointment, grief and the obscure, but increasing, feeling of being blamed that seemed, nowadays, to colour his life with Pauline . . .

Recalling the vitriolic terms in which Mrs Dixon had referred to Mary in the letter, Ballard had no hesitation in agreeing that the woman was an 'absolute bitch'. And Slater had said that his

sister didn't know the half of it . . . If what he'd said was true –
and, extraordinary though all of it was, Ballard had no reason
to disbelieve the poor sod – then Mrs Dixon's description of
Mary/Ananda as 'ruthless and amoral' didn't begin to cover it.
But – he looked again at the photograph – she was so beautiful,
so sexy. Ballard felt himself enveloped in disappointment. Mary
had, in some indefinable way (after all, she owed him nothing
– what was he to her or she to him?) *let him down* and this sensation, no matter how ridiculous and illogical, refused to go away.

Wishing the feeling would go away, but knowing that any
resolve not to think about it or feel like it was impracticable and
bound to be ineffective, he pulled out the choke with an unnecessarily brutal yank and started the car.

CHAPTER TWENTY

'I doubt we'd get an exhumation order,' said Stratton, when Ballard telephoned to report on his meeting with Dr Slater. 'Was he buried locally?'

'Hasketon. That's just outside Woodbridge, where they lived. Reverend Milburn was pals with the vicar there.'

'Did you talk to him?'

'Yes. I called him from the station at Lincott. He didn't think there was anything untoward ... I got the impression he didn't think much of Mary/Ananda, though. Flighty was the word he used. Quite polite compared to some of the stuff we've been hearing, but then he is a man of the cloth.'

'No help there, then,' said Stratton. 'The death certificate is certainly unusual – and McNally's right, it wouldn't have got past a coroner if he'd had to examine it – but it's all so ...'

'Bizarre,' supplied Ballard.

'It's that, all right. And unless someone else comes forward to tell us about it, or the bloody woman confesses when we find her, there's not going to be enough evidence to do anything about it.'

'On a slightly different subject,' said Ballard, 'Slater was sure that the boy's name wasn't Michael, and I was just wondering if Roth might have given him a different name, along with his mother.'

'Yes, but "Ananda" is meaningful. To them, anyway.'

'So's Michael,' said Ballard. 'I nipped home and looked it up in Pauline's book of baby names. It means "like the Lord".'

'Only *like* the Lord? I'm surprised they stopped there. But they do call him something else, don't they? Wait a minute . . .' He put the receiver down to flick through his notebook. '"Maitreya". Mind you, Michael was an archangel, wasn't he?'

'Yes. Oh, by the way, Lamb spoke to my guv'nor and we've sent a policewoman up to the Foundation to keep an eye on him. Still no sign of Mary/Ananda . . . We'll just have to hope the picture in the papers does the trick.'

Stratton was massaging his temples and wondering what the hell to do next, when Grove lumbered in and stood in front of his desk, grinning.

'What have you got to be so bloody cheerful about?' asked Stratton.

'Turn up for the books, old son. Your pin-up girl made the late edition and someone's just called about her. A Mrs Dora Wheeler, lives in Suffolk. Dunwich, so you're in for a trip to the seaside tomorrow, because she says she's got some *very* interesting information about your Mrs Milburn. Wouldn't tell me any more, other than that she's been trying to find her for years—' Grove stared at Stratton. 'Give us a smile, for God's sake – it's good news.'

'Sorry,' said Stratton. 'I know it's good news, but I've got a horrible feeling it's going to lead to more complications. The woman's a menace. Leaves a trail of destruction wherever she goes.' He told Grove about Dr Slater and the suspicious circumstances of the Reverend Milburn's death.

'Bloody hell! Obviously chooses her prey carefully, though – vulnerable old men . . .'

'Lloyd wasn't old. And Roth – that's the chap in charge at the Foundation – certainly isn't vulnerable, although I did get the impression he was pretty taken with her, in his way.'

'Perhaps it's all men, then. Oh, I managed to get hold of Lloyd's aunt this afternoon. She says he was still at school in 1944, evacuated to Wales. You said your woman was in Suffolk then, so a meeting seems pretty unlikely.'

'Never mind. It was just a thought. Thanks, anyway.' Stratton stood up. 'Right, I'd better clear this little jaunt with Lamb, then.'

Reading the paper at home after a piece of his sister-in-law Doris's steak-and-kidney pie – *EDEN FACES GRAVEST HOUR* – Stratton suddenly remembered that he'd made a date with Diana for the following evening. Lamb had been remarkably sanguine about Stratton's visit to Dunwich, suggesting that he drive to Lincott afterwards to see Ballard 'in case of developments' and adding that he should stay the night and return to London the following morning.

When he telephoned Diana in Chelsea and explained the situation she announced, to his utter amazement, that if he had to spend any length of time in Suffolk, she'd be happy to join him. 'A friend of mine has a cottage down there. She hardly ever uses it, and she's always telling me I can go whenever I like. I've never taken her up on it before, but now ... well, it might be fun.'

Diana, thought Stratton, *would* know people with country cottages going spare. 'Ordinarily,' he said cautiously, 'I'd like nothing better, but I'd be working, so there wouldn't really be any time—'

'Not during the day, but you'll be free in the evenings, won't you? I can take a few days off – the alligator crisis has passed, thank goodness – and I'd enjoy playing at keeping house for you.'

'It's a lovely idea,' said Stratton, 'but – even if I had to spend some time up there, which I don't know, because I've no idea how the thing's going to pan out – the local police would need to know where I was, and I could hardly tell them I was . . . you know . . .' Stratton tailed off, aware that he sounded ungrateful and churlish.

'I know you couldn't, darling, but they're not likely to want to contact you in the middle of the night, and you can always go back to wherever you're supposed to be staying in the morning, can't you? Of course, if you don't want me to come . . .'

After a bit more of this, Stratton had agreed to a provisional arrangement, at the same time hoping that the circumstances in which it might happen wouldn't arise. It wasn't that he didn't want to see Diana – he did, very much – and the idea of actually spending the night with her was tremendous, especially as it was something they'd only managed a couple of times before. It just seemed a bit of a hole-and-corner way to go about things, and mixing up work and Diana was bound to cause problems. She could be so impulsive, and this tendency – at least where it concerned men – had, in the past, led to disaster. Not that *he* was anything like *those* men, of course, but this time it might have disastrous consequences for him. What if he and Diana were together in Suffolk and Ballard were to find out? He supposed it wouldn't be the end of the world – after all, Pete had seemed more amused than upset – but all the same, it wouldn't look very professional. God knows what Ballard would think about it, and if – God forbid – he mentioned it to anyone else, Stratton really would be for the high jump. Besides which, he had a lot on his plate and he needed to concentrate on it.

He turned back to the *Daily Mirror*, trying to shrug off the feeling of uneasiness. In any case, he told himself, it would probably never happen so there was no sense in getting steamed up about it. *The House of Commons will hold an emergency session to hear whether or not the Prime Minister will obey the ceasefire order of the United Nations Assembly* . . . Stratton's eyes strayed past advertisements for Magic

Margarine and Bear Brand nylons to the bottom of the page. *Eden tries to justify his war by calling it a police action . . . The truth is this: There is NO treaty, NO international authorisation, NO moral sanction for Eden's War.* He wondered what Pete was doing. On a troop ship somewhere, presumably, sailing towards Christ knew what. We're all so powerless, he thought. We don't control anything – we're just shunted through life like pieces on a chessboard. Sighing, he turned off the gas fire and trudged upstairs to bed.

CHAPTER TWENTY-ONE

Stratton, who'd learnt to drive after the war, had brought his own car, a black Ford Popular, purchased when they came out a couple of years earlier. Driving to Dunwich, he wondered if Lamb's insistence that he stay the night at Lincott might not have been something to do with his superior's concern about his ability to get back in the dark in one piece. It would be a bloody long drive anyway – Dunwich was at least a hundred miles from London, and Lincott, being right on the other side of the county, was a good sixty miles again.

Heading towards the coast, he squinted into the bright winter sun and thought, as he always did when in the car, how much Jenny would have enjoyed the ride. Arriving, he parked by the shingle beach and walked back, past the pub and the post office and down a row of cottages until he found Mrs Wheeler's house, which was next door to the village school.

Apparently oblivious to the yells coming from the narrow, muddy garden, where a large number of children were playing some sort of complicated game involving a ball, a cricket bat and a lot of chasing and dodging and tagging, Mrs Wheeler sat Stratton down in the back parlour which, spotlessly clean – if, despite the fire in the grate, a little chilly – was clearly the room kept nice 'just in case', and went to make a pot of tea. Bright-eyed and cheerful, with a comfortably middle-aged figure, Mrs Wheeler settled herself on the sofa opposite him and accepted a cigarette. 'I couldn't believe it when my husband showed me the picture in the paper. We thought she must be dead because she never came back or wrote or anything.'

'Why did you want her to contact you?' asked Stratton.

'My husband said . . .' She broke off, looking anxious. 'He said I shouldn't telephone because you might take him away, and I have to say I was in two minds myself, which is why I didn't want to say too much when I called, but I felt we had to tell you, really.'

'Take who away?' asked Stratton. 'I think,' he added, with an encouraging smile, 'you'd better tell me everything from the beginning.'

'Yes, of course.' Mrs Wheeler's hands twisted nervously in her lap.

'It's all right,' said Stratton. 'Take your time.'

'Yes, well . . . Mrs Milburn was a neighbour, you see. When we lived in Woodbridge. I don't know if you know Suffolk at all, but that's about twenty miles from here – we lived there after we were married, up to the middle of 1946. I never knew Mrs Milburn that well, but we'd pass the time of day, you know . . . Anyway, a couple of weeks after VE Day, she came to my house with the baby and asked if I'd look after him for a couple of days because she had some business to attend to. She didn't say what it was, but her husband had died the week before so I thought it must be to do with that.'

'Did you know the Reverend Milburn?'

Mrs Wheeler shook her head. 'I'd only seen him once or twice. He was an invalid, hardly ever left the house. The doctor was always calling. There were some people who said he was going to see her, not her husband, that they were carrying on, but it was just gossip and I don't think there was any truth in it.'

Clearly, thought Stratton, Mrs Wheeler was a woman with a kind and unsuspicious nature. 'Anyway, she came along with Tom—'

'That would be the baby, would it?'

'That's right. He was about eighteen months old at the time. I agreed to look after him for her, so she brought his clothes and that – my twins were just over a year at that time, so their things would have been too small – then off she went and that was the last we saw of her. We never had so much as a postcard.'

Stratton produced his photograph of Mary Milburn. 'And it was definitely this woman who left the child, was it?'

'Oh, yes. No question about that. Very nice-looking she was, and always well turned out. When she didn't come back, my husband went round to her house but it was empty and the people next door hadn't seen her for days. We went to the police, but they couldn't find her. Then we paid a solicitor to search for her, but he didn't do any better, so in the end we decided to treat him as a gift from God and bring him up as one of ours. We had to ask at the surgery to find out when his birthday was – Dr Slater was gone by then, of course. So I've got five of my own, and Tom. I'm thinking,' she added shrewdly, 'that you haven't found Mrs Milburn, or you wouldn't be here, but when you do, will we have to give him back? She never registered his birth, you see, and he's got no idea – he thinks he belongs to us. The police said we had to go to court about it, but the magistrate said we could keep him – it's all in the records. He was only a baby then, of course, but he's nearly twelve now, and if he had to lose his whole family . . . As far as the others know, he's their big brother. I know that would be pretty unlikely, given their ages, but they're not old enough to understand things like that yet . . .' Eyes round with distress, Mrs Wheeler put a hand to her mouth. 'I can't bear to think of him being taken away.' She took a handkerchief from the sleeve of her cardigan and began dabbing her eyes.

Stratton stared out of the window while she composed herself. Children – Mrs Wheeler was obviously minding others as well as her own – seemed to explode in all directions in a blur of muddy knees, flying wellingtons, flapping scarves and apple-red cheeks. Their excitement and glee were infectious, and Stratton found himself grinning. In the middle of the mêlée, one boy, who looked to be about ten, had upended a smaller girl and was tickling her mercilessly, so that she yelped and shrieked with laughter, and two identical tow-headed boys were helping a taller, dark-haired boy to his feet. Impressed by the evident solicitousness of the pair, Stratton, looking more closely, saw that the dark-haired boy wore a calliper on one leg.

Following the direction of his gaze, Mrs Wheeler said, 'That's Tom. He caught polio when he was eight. The epidemic . . . He was lucky, really, that it's only down one side. We were terrified he'd end up in an iron lung.'

'I'm not surprised,' said Stratton, thinking of the monstrous metal carapaces he'd once seen on a polio ward, whoosh-whooshing rhythmically as they 'breathed' for the poor sods incarcerated inside, only their heads visible as they'd stared, endlessly, up at the ceiling. 'Wouldn't wish that on your worst enemy.'

'They've always looked out for him,' said Mrs Wheeler. 'Ever since he got ill – Johnny, my youngest, was only three at the time, but even he knew he had to be gentle. I was always worried about him getting knocked over, because they don't half tear about, but they're very careful. And,' she nodded in Tom's direction, 'if he does fall down, they help him back on his feet.'

'I'd like to meet him,' said Stratton. Mrs Wheeler looked at him fearfully. 'It's all right,' he reassured her. 'I'm not going to take him away.'

Mollified, Mrs Wheeler opened the window and shouted for Tom to wipe his feet and come inside.

Pale-faced and freckled, with dark brown hair flopping over his brow, Tom was as neat featured as the woman who'd given birth to him, but without either Michael's breathtaking good looks, or his air of solemnity. His damaged right leg gave him a curious rolling gait and up close, Stratton could see that his right shoulder was lower and narrower than his left, and his right arm, un-muscled, hung limply. Not wishing to embarrass him, Stratton held out his left hand. Tom looked at it for a moment as if puzzled, and then, at a nudge from Mrs Wheeler, wiped his grubby left hand on his shorts and held it out to be shaken, with a diffidence that reminded Stratton of Pete at the same age.

'I'm Detective Inspector Stratton,' he said. 'How do you do?'

'I . . .' Panic leapt in Tom's brown eyes. 'I . . .' He turned to his mother with a speed that made him lurch, off balance. 'I've done nothing wrong,' he said. 'Honestly, I haven't.'

'I know that,' said Stratton. 'I was paying a call on your mother, and I wanted to meet you, that's all. That's not so terrible, is it?'

Tom ducked his head and blushed a delicate shade of pink that made Stratton think of strawberry ice. He was clearly of a similar age to Michael – could Mary have had twins? – but he had none of the sophistication and polish. He was a nice, ordi-nary kid. Stratton found himself thinking that, despite the handi-cap, Tom might well have been dealt a better hand in life than the boy who was, presumably, his brother.

When he'd returned to the garden, Mrs Wheeler turned to Stratton. 'Why are you trying to find Mrs Milburn? Has she done something wrong?'

'We're not sure yet, but we are concerned about her safety.'

'Do you need to tell Tom about her? That he's not ours, I mean. Even if she doesn't want him—'

'Even if she did,' said Stratton, 'I very much doubt that any court would give a child back to a woman who'd abandoned him as she did, especially when he already has a good home.'

Especially, he added silently, one who'd very likely murdered the kid's father and then blackmailed the family doctor into falsifying the death certificate. 'And I don't think you need tell him.' At least, he thought, not for the moment. 'I can see,' he added, 'that he's very happy here.'

'Yes, yes.' Mrs Wheeler nodded vigorously. 'He is. And what he doesn't know can't hurt him, can it? My husband – he's out at work – he'll be ever so pleased. He's a blacksmith, though it's more fancy ironwork than horseshoes nowadays. We're not rich – can't be rich with six children, can you? – but we get by.'

Stratton smiled at her. 'Looks to me as if you do rather better than that. Tell me, when Mrs Milburn came to your house with Tom, did she have another baby with her?'

Mrs Wheeler shook her head. 'Just him.'

'Did you ever see her with two babies?'

'No. She only had the one child, I'm sure of it. I never heard anything about a brother or sister. She didn't leave another child with someone else, did she?'

'Not as far as we know,' said Stratton, thinking that if she had he wouldn't be surprised. 'When's Tom's birthday?'

'Twentieth of December. He was born in 1943.'

'And you're sure he didn't have a twin?'

'Sure as I can be,' said Mrs Wheeler. 'I mean, he might have had a twin who died – it happens sometimes – but I never heard of it. They didn't mention it when we asked at the doctor's surgery about Tom. I suppose there's no reason why they should have told me, but all the same . . .'

Stratton returned to his car and sat staring out at the slate-grey sea, washing down the fish-paste sandwiches he'd brought for lunch with cold tea from his thermos flask. Then he took out his notebook and flipped through it until he found the notes he'd taken when Ballard reported his interview with Dr Slater.

The doctor's account tallied with Mrs Wheeler's, and there was no reason to believe that either one of them was lying. Dr Slater had said that Mary's child was 'little more than a baby' when the Reverend Milburn died in May 1945. A child of eighteen months, which Mrs Wheeler had said was Tom's age when Mary'd left him with her, was almost a toddler. That could mean 'little more than a baby' couldn't it? And Ballard had said Slater had been pretty clear that the kid's name wasn't Michael. Perhaps his impression that Michael was about twelve had been wrong. Perhaps he was younger – tall for his age – and Mary had had him the following year. Or Michael was Tom's twin – they weren't always identical – and Mary had, for some reason, kept him hidden. But why? It wasn't something a normal mother would do, but Mary, as was becoming increasingly evident, was anything *but* normal, not only as a mother, but as a human being.

He must find out Michael's age – but first, he'd stop off in Woodbridge and question Mary's former neighbours. There were bound to be one or two who remembered her. Whether it had any reference to Lloyd, he wasn't sure, but he had a feeling that Mary was, whether directly or indirectly, a key part of the whole thing, and, in any case, it was the only lead he had. Remembering Ballard's 'give me a decent villain any day', he set off wishing, not for the first time, that he didn't feel quite so adrift in a sea of Christ only knew what.

CHAPTER TWENTY-TWO

In Woodbridge, those neighbours who remembered Mary Milburn took a dim view of her goings-on. There were several disparaging mentions of her and Dr Slater – the general consensus seemed to be that she'd 'led the poor man on' – and several more about her treatment of the Reverend Milburn, who, they felt, had been neglected. At least two of the people Stratton spoke to thought that Milburn was Mary's father, not her husband, and that the baby (always one infant, never two) was the offspring of a spouse who was away fighting (or in one case, missing presumed dead). What they all agreed on, however, was that Mary often went to dances at the nearby American airbase, 'carried on' with one or more of the men stationed there, and danced the hokey-cokey in platform shoes night after night when she should have been at home with her family.

By contrast, their memories of Mrs Wheeler were positive. The consensus confirmed Stratton's impression – that she was a good neighbour and a kind woman who'd taken in Mary's child and 'done her best' despite having little money and a large family of her own. He'd also shown around the photographs of Lloyd, just to be on the safe side, but was met with an entirely and, he thought, genuinely, blank response.

He drove to Lincott with the phrase 'no better than she should be' ringing in his ears. It was, he thought, a pretty stupid expression – how good should anyone be? Were some people supposed to be better than others? But if it meant that the neighbours hadn't expected Mary to behave well in the first place and she'd lived up to their expectations, then he had to agree with it. And why had she told some people, or led them to believe, that Milburn was her father? What with the haunted house business, the picture he was getting was of a compulsive liar who told stories for the hell of it, manipulated everyone she met, and had little feeling for others, including, apparently, her own child.

He'd agreed to meet Ballard in the George and Dragon, where he'd booked a room for the night. By a quarter to nine, he'd had a bath and a meal of watery soup which tasted primarily of salt, and a stew consisting of a lot of potatoes garnished with scraps of grey meat, and the pair of them were comfortably ensconced, pints to hand. It being Guy Fawkes' night, most of the village was attending the bonfire on the green, so the place was – for the time being, at least – practically empty but for a few thickset, ruddy-faced farm workers who clustered about the bar, ignoring them.

'But why would anyone dump a child like that?' said Ballard, when Stratton had told him about his visit to Mrs Wheeler. 'I mean, it wasn't as if the boy was illegitimate.'

'As far as we know,' said Stratton.

'No, but what I mean is, she'd had a husband, hadn't she? She was a perfectly respectable widow. All right,' he added, 'maybe not respectable according to the neighbours in Woodbridge, but the kid had a name, didn't he? And as far as the world knew ...' Ballard shook his head. 'I don't understand it.'

'Me neither,' said Stratton. 'And as for what it might have to do with Lloyd ... I mean, I know he'd kept the photographs, but ...'

'It's got to be to do with that Foundation place, hasn't it? I can't believe that somebody there doesn't know *something*.'

'Fair enough, but—' Stratton got no further because at that moment a policeman – who he assumed from the sudden hush that had fallen on the few other people in the place must be the village constable – appeared. As he made his way across to them, the drinkers edged away as if in danger of contamination.

'I need to speak to you outside, sir,' he said to Ballard. 'Got a message.'

'DI Stratton is a colleague, Parsons. You can tell me here.'

'Rather go outside, sir.' Parsons stood by the table, his stolid form shifting uncomfortably, aware of the small knot of rustics at the bar, alert, with sausage-like fingers clamped round now-forgotten pints of beer. 'Very well.' Ballard inclined his head, indicating that Stratton should follow.

'For heaven's sake,' said Ballard, when Stratton had shut the door behind them and they were standing in the cold night air. 'What is it?'

'Couple of fishermen, sir. Found a body in the woods on the edge of Mr Tynan's place. It's a woman, and she's been shot in the head.'

CHAPTER TWENTY-THREE

'We don't know how long she's been there, sir,' said Parsons, when they were in the car. 'The fishermen who found her – they're staying at the pub, as a matter of fact – said they'd left it a bit late packing up and got lost on the way back from the lake. They'd been blundering around in the wood for a good half hour before they stumbled across her, and then of course it took some time for them to get back to the village and find me and explain where she was . . . The desk sergeant was trying to contact the police surgeon when I left, but he's coming from Ipswich, so that'll take some time.'

'So no one's identified her?' said Ballard, from the back seat.

'No, sir.'

Stratton twisted his head to look at him. 'Mary Milburn?' he asked. Then, 'You've still got someone looking after Michael, have you? Overnight?'

'Yes.'

'Because if it is her, then—'

'Yes,' said Ballard tersely. 'I know.'

Shut up, Stratton told himself. It's his first suspicious death and he doesn't need me stating the bleeding obvious. After a couple of minutes' tense silence, Ballard said, 'Who's there with her?'

'PC Harwood, sir,' said Parsons, adding, apologetically, 'apart from the desk sergeant, he was the only one at the station.'

Stratton was surprised when Ballard tapped him on the shoulder and murmured, 'Our version of Arliss.'

'Ah,' said Stratton. That explained Parsons' tone. PC Arliss had been, until his retirement a couple of years earlier, notorious as West End Central's most incompetent policeman. Dim-witted, ignorant and unplagued by apprehension, responsibility, doubt, or anything else except his bowels – with which he was presumably still locked in mortal combat – Arliss's working life had been one gigantic skive. 'Everyone's got one, I suppose.'

Parsons turned off the road and onto a rough track, where they bumped along over ruts and furrows for several minutes before the way became too narrow for them to continue. 'I'm afraid we'll have to walk from here, sir.'

They squelched across waterlogged ground in the dank and chilly darkness. Although there was a full moon and a clear sky, the density of trees, even at this time of year, made torches very necessary. As they entered the crude, narrow path through the wood, Stratton, dodging thorny bushes that dragged at his clothing and swiped his face, wondered how the hell they were going to get the body out, never mind the car, which had seemed, as he'd got out, to be sinking into the sticky mixture of black mud and leaf-mould that was all around them. They tramped on for several minutes before Parsons said, 'Over here,' and motioned them towards a small clearing on the edge of which a stout constable – obviously Harwood – stood leaning against a tree, wearing an expression of vacant moroseness with which Stratton was only too familiar. Thinking he was unobserved, the constable was amusing himself by shining his torch on different parts of his anatomy. On the other side of the clearing, a pair of orange eyes appeared in the darkness – a fox – and then vanished, soundless in the undergrowth.

'Where's the body?' asked Ballard, causing Harwood to jump and drop his torch, which shattered on a protruding root. 'See what I mean?' he muttered to Stratton, while Harwood grovelled about on the ground.

'At least he's managed to stay awake,' said Stratton.

'Only because it's too bloody wet to sit down. For God's sake,' he added to Harwood, 'Parsons'll help you find it in a minute.'

'Yes, sir.' The constable straightened up with a grunt. 'Just behind there.' He indicated a tree to his right.

The woman was lying face down. Her hair was covered by a headscarf, and she was wearing a camel-hair coat, stockings and wellington boots. On the bare nape of her neck, in the gap between coat and brightly patterned scarf, Stratton saw, by the light of his torch, a neat round hole that looked as though it had been made by a small calibre bullet.

'Entry wound, presumably,' said Ballard, 'seeing as she's fallen on her face. Doesn't look as if anyone's tried to move her – no drag marks.'

'Doesn't look like an accident, either,' said Stratton, staring at the dark staining and peppering of propellant particles around the edge of the wound. 'I'd say that was done at close range. Not touching, but pretty damn near ... There should be a shell case somewhere, unless whoever did this picked it up,' he added, shining his torch on the leaf-mould around the woman's head.

'Or unless Harwood's gone and trodden it in.' Ballard squatted down and peered intently at the ground. 'Oh no, here we are.' He pointed to a small object a couple of inches away from the woman's feet.

Stratton shone his torch on the tree directly in front of the body. 'This is the logical place if she was shot from behind ... Yes, here's the bullet, embedded in the bark. Must have come out through her face.'

There was a moment's silence as both men contemplated what this might look like, before Ballard said, 'Those'll help us, anyway. No sign of a gun, though. We'll keep Harwood here overnight – he'll love that – and make a thorough search in the morning. You know . . .' He stared down at a curl of hair which had escaped from the scarf. 'It definitely could be Mary Milburn, although I don't think her hair was quite so dark.'

'But it was brown, wasn't it?' asked Stratton, remembering the photograph.

'Yes, but this is almost black. Mind you, she seems to be the right shape and size, although it's hard to tell in that thick coat.' Ballard shone his torch on the surrounding tree roots. 'No handbag that I can see. Odd to come out without one, I'd have thought.'

'Perhaps whoever shot her took it away with him. Did Mary Milburn have a handbag when you saw her?'

Ballard thought for a moment, then shook his head. 'Can't remember. She did have a coat on, but she was wearing shoes, not boots.'

'So you noticed her legs, then?'

'Hard not to.' Ballard, looking sheepish, avoided Stratton's eye. 'She was climbing over a stile.'

'Very observant,' said Stratton, wryly. 'It sounds,' he added, lowering his voice in deference to the dead woman, 'as though you got quite an eyeful.'

'Yes.' Ballard drew away from the body as he said this. 'It was rather hard not to. If this is her, then . . . Well, she may have been an absolute bitch, but she was lovely, you know . . . Captivating.'

'She'd have to have been standing up,' said the police surgeon, Trickett, who'd arrived twenty minutes later, accompanied by an assistant who was struggling with a portable lamp and a stretcher. Trickett, a stocky, elderly man with the face of an unlucky boxer, was immediately proprietorial, refusing to engage with either Ballard or Stratton until he'd completed his examination, sketched, photographed and recovered the bullet and shell case. 'Trained by Spilsbury himself,' Ballard had murmured, when they'd withdrawn to the clearing, leaving him to it. 'And never misses the opportunity to remind you of it.'

They stood in silence, smoking, until Trickett beckoned them forward to look at the body, which he'd turned over. Despite the bluish-white colour of her face and the leaf-mould that clung to the edges of her hair, Stratton could see that she'd been attractive, with neat features and long, dark eyelashes. As they'd guessed, there was a hole to the side of the woman's right nostril, larger than the one at the back of her neck, but almost as neat. As Stratton looked down at her, an earwig detached itself from the muck by her ear and began crawling across her cheek. Averting his eyes, he looked a question at Ballard, who responded with a tight shake of his head followed by a slight raise of the eyebrows and a barely discernible shrug. They hadn't found Mary Milburn, but an unknown woman.

CHAPTER TWENTY-FOUR

'Entry wound at the back,' said Trickett briskly, as if delivering a lecture. 'Came out there,' he pointed a stubby finger, 'point three two, Eley shell case. I'll pass them on to the lab. You've not found the weapon yet, have you?' Without pausing for a response, he continued, 'The ballistics people'll tell you if it was a pistol or a rifle, but I doubt it was a hunting accident because she's been shot at close range. No apparent marks of the muzzle touching the skin, but whoever shot her couldn't have been more than a few feet away. She was standing up at the time – the track of the missile is horizontal – and she fell forwards. I understand she was found at around seven o'clock.' Here, Trickett shot a look at Ballard, who nodded confirmation. 'She could have been killed at any time up to three hours before that.' Putting his hand up in a traffic stopping gesture, he added, 'Can't tell you anything more at this stage.'

'So that's any time after four, is it?' asked Ballard.

'I'd say so.'

'Still be light at four,' said Stratton. 'Starts getting dark about half-past, though.'

Harwood, who had limited his contribution to the occasional grunt and sniff, said, 'Mr Tynan takes potshots at rooks out of the windows.'

'Wrong direction.' Ballard jerked his thumb over his shoulder. 'Tynan's house is that way.'

'Well,' said Harwood sulkily, 'There's poachers come in these woods all the time.'

'As I said,' snapped Trickett, 'an accident is extremely unlikely.'

'But if she'd come up on them unawares . . .' said Stratton. 'I suppose they might have thought it was an animal, but people make a hell of a lot more noise than foxes—'

'I'm off now,' said Trickett, peeved that he was no longer the centre of attention. 'Can your man help with the stretcher?'

'Just a moment.' Ballard squatted down and, wrapping his hand-kerchief over his hand, began examining the pockets of the woman's coat. 'Nothing here . . . I wonder if whoever killed her went through her pockets as well . . . Wait a minute, there's a tear in the lining – something behind it . . . Here we go. Shine your torch down a bit, Stratton, can you? It's a library card for a Mrs Rosemary Aylett. Local . . . well, Suffolk, anyway. That should narrow things down a bit.'

'Assuming it's hers, of course,' said Trickett. '*Can* we get moving, please?'

'Back to square one,' said Stratton, when they were back at the George and Dragon. Ballard had telephoned his boss from the station and, as it was after hours, they were drinking in Stratton's room, having spoken to the two fishermen, who were rather the worse for wear after downing several restorative whiskies each. The men had explained that they were after an enormous pike which, having managed to evade the attentions of anglers for years, had become an object of fascination to the fishing commu-nity, and George Denton had confirmed the truth of this. They'd heard several shots during the time they were fishing, but assumed them to be sportsmen or poachers.

'Which they probably were,' said Ballard. 'All but one, anyway.'

Stratton, who'd kept quiet during the interview because it wasn't his investigation, said, remembering the guns his father and elder brothers had had on the farm, 'You'd use a twelve bore for partridge or pheasant, but that would usually be a shotgun. A rifle's more for deer, but I should think there'd be some of those round here.'

'I'll talk to Tynan about it tomorrow,' said Ballard. 'And I need to find out what the hell Mrs Aylett – if that's who she is – was doing in the wood.'

'Back to London for me,' said Stratton. 'And I'll just have to hope there's been some response to the house-to-house enquiries, because there's bugger all else to go on.'

CHAPTER TWENTY-FIVE

After a queasy breakfast, avoiding Pauline's eye – they'd put away far too much of the bottle of Scotch Denton had sold Stratton after hours – Ballard rang the station to tell Parsons to contact the library service about Mrs Aylett's address, and headed off to see Ambrose Tynan. Neither he nor his staff knew who she was, and none of them had seen or heard anything strange on the previous afternoon or evening. Tynan had condescendingly confirmed that yes, he did own – amongst other things – several shotguns, which were all licensed and, as he put it, 'present and correct', and that he did 'pot the odd rook' from an upstairs window, adding that the boy Michael frequently came over for lessons in shooting outdoors, although he had not done so yesterday. He'd said this with a teeth-baring smile of statesman-like *noblesse oblige*, so that Ballard was left in no doubt as to the superiority of his marksmanship. Tynan had even taken him up the grand staircase to show him the best place to shoot from, which proved to be on the opposite side of the house to the wood where they'd found Mrs Aylett's body.

He was about to leave when Tynan's manservant, who was quite as stiff as Stratton had said he was, with a good long nose for sneering down as well, told him there was a call from the station and directed him to the telephone in the kitchen corridor.

'Found an address for Mrs Aylett, sir – Wickham Market,' said PC Parsons. 'The librarian was most helpful. Confirmed the description – says she's a big reader, keen on romances. A widow, she said, lives by herself, always stops to chat.'

'Wickham Market's what? Forty miles away?'

'I'd say so, sir.'

'What was she doing coming all the way up here for a walk, then?'

'No idea, sir. If she was keen on romances, perhaps she liked nature, too. Or she was visiting someone.'

'Did this librarian happen to know if Mrs Aylett had any relatives?'

'A sister, sir, a Mrs Curtin. Muriel. She's a member of the library, too.'

Before Parsons could list the sister's literary preferences, Ballard said, 'Address?' and took it down in his notebook. 'Does she have a telephone?'

'No, sir. I checked with the exchange.'

'Right, I'm on my way.'

By the time Ballard arrived at Wickham Market, driving with the car windows open to get a good blast of fresh, cold air, his hangover was beginning to wear off and with it, the concomitant feelings of lethargy, self-disgust and the rest. Anxiety, it was true, remained, but that was the case – wanting to prove to himself that he could investigate a suspicious death without fouling it up – which was probably the main reason he'd drunk too much Scotch in the first place. The main reason, he thought, but not the only one – his father's death, Pauline and the baby she couldn't conceive and fancying Mary/Ananda so much were all factors too, no matter how hard he tried to put them out of his mind. The other, and for the time being, more pressing, reason was that

he was about to tell this poor bloody woman that in all proba-
bility her sister was dead, and ask her to identify the body. He'd
never actually uttered the words himself, but he'd been present
enough times when they'd been said, and he could remember
all of them, clear as day. That soundless split-second – often
before the officer had opened his mouth – when they *knew*. The
bad news. The end of hope. The moment that kept coming back
to you whether you wanted it to or not. When he'd heard that
his dad had died, Ballard had felt an actual physical jolt, as if
he'd just stepped off a merry-go-round while it was still in motion,
a horrible sensation he'd never forgotten. At least he'd known
that his father was ill – for poor Muriel Curtin, he thought grimly,
it was going to be a great deal worse.

Her address turned out to be one of a row of gentrified farm
workers' cottages on the outskirts of the small town. To Ballard's
surprise, the door was answered by a youngish local policeman
who, when he identified himself, had given his name as PC Carter.
Carter explained with admirable succinctness that he was there
because Mrs Curtin had reported her sister as missing an hour
ago, but he'd only just arrived and hadn't yet got the full details.
'I'm here,' said Ballard, sotto voce, 'because we're pretty sure
we've found her, and I'm afraid it's not good news. There was a
body in the woods over at Lincott that matches her description,
with a library card in the pocket. Death caused by a shotgun
wound, but that's as much as we know at present.'

The young policeman nodded, solemn as an undertaker, only
a slight tightening of his face betraying any excitement. 'Dreadful
thing to happen, sir. Mrs Curtin's close to her sister. Mrs Aylett
only lived two doors down.' He gestured to his left and Ballard
saw, beyond the neat gardens of Mrs Curtin and her next-door
neighbour, a rank and overgrown patch with a messy hedge and
a clutter of unoccupied chicken coops. Following his gaze, Carter
said, 'Let the place go a bit since her husband died.'

'Is Mr Curtin here?' asked Ballard.

Carter shook his head. 'Widowed, sir. Two daughters – one here, one in London – neither of them on the telephone. I did suggest getting in touch with the local one, but she keeps saying she doesn't want to be a bother.'

'Might be a good idea to get hold of her, once I've . . .' Ballard paused, clearing his throat. 'We can get the address later.'

Muriel Curtin, neat, unremarkable and, Ballard thought, about forty-five, was sitting in an equally neat and unremarkable kitchen, an untouched cup of tea on the table before her, eyes narrow and muddy with worry. Even before Ballard had finished introducing himself, she'd summed up his serious face, his suit, his whole demeanour, and, recognising him as a carrier of despair, had pushed back her chair, hands out as if trying to ward off the unspoken words. 'You've found her, haven't you? You've come to tell me . . .'

'I'm sorry, Mrs Curtin. We have found a body, and we have reason to believe that it may be that of your sister, Mrs Rosemary Aylett.

'Oh, no, no . . .' Ballard recognised that this was not a refusal to cooperate, but an automatic negation, as if mere iteration could un-happen the fact of her sister's death.

'I am sorry,' he repeated helplessly.

Muriel Curtin shook her head rapidly, and he could imagine the frantic scenes whirling through her mind – Rosemary, who loved romances, broken in a ditch, hit by a car, violated by a madman. 'Where is she? How . . .?'

'She was found at Lincott, and she's been taken to—'

'I told her not go without me.' Mrs Curtin buried her face in her hands, then looked up, eyes raw and face bagged with grief. 'We had a row about it. We never argue, but we did. It was the last thing she said to me: "If you won't help me, I'll do it myself."

I should have been there, gone with her, but I didn't. If I'd just
...' Mrs Curtin shook her head again, violently. 'This is all my
fault.'

PC Carter, who'd been standing behind Ballard, moved round
the table and helped the sobbing woman back into her chair
with calm, soothing movements. 'Shall I fetch Mrs Curtin's
daughter, sir?' he asked, over the woman's bowed head.

'Yes, please,' said Ballard gratefully. 'If you could just tell us
where she lives, Mrs Curtin?'

PC Carter having departed, Muriel Curtin looked at Ballard as if
seeing him for the first time, and with flustered, automatic good
manners said, 'Of course. I'm so sorry ... Would you like a cup
of tea? There's some just made, and ...' She half-rose, staring
round the kitchen as though looking for something she couldn't
remember, then sat back down. 'I'm sorry, I don't seem ...'

'That's all right, Mrs Curtin.' Partly of necessity, and partly for
something to do in order to put off the moment of telling the
woman that her sister had been shot, Ballard said, 'Why don't I
make some fresh tea, for when your daughter gets here? I'm sure
she'd like a cup.'

'Yes ... It's all ...' She gestured towards the kettle on the hob,
then shook her head again. 'I'm sorry. It's all ...'

'Please,' said Ballard. 'Let me. You've had a terrible shock.' He
refilled the kettle, lit the gas, found some cups and saucers in
the cupboard, set them on the table. Mrs Curtin stared at them
for a moment, then said, 'That one doesn't match. One of the
saucers got broken, you see, when I was cleaning.' She stopped
in confusion. 'I'm sorry, I don't know why I'm telling you this.'

'That's all right,' said Ballard. 'Look, I've found a matching one.
You've still got five of them. They're very nice,' he added, point-
lessly, as if this could make up for the loss of a sister.

'Yes, aren't they?' Mrs Curtin put out her hand to one of the cups and turned it gently round, staring at it. 'They were a wedding present – that's why I was so sorry. They don't make this line any more, so it can't be replaced ...' She looked up at Ballard, who was waiting for the kettle to boil. 'How did she die, Inspector?'

'I'm afraid ...' Ballard swallowed. 'It was a gunshot wound. We think it might have been an accident, but obviously we need to—'

'Someone shot her?' Mrs Curtin's mouth gaped.

'Yes. But it would have been very quick. She wouldn't have suffered.'

'But what was she doing?' Mrs Curtin looked bewildered. 'I mean, where ...?'

'She was found in the woods.'

'But what was she *doing* there? That wasn't ... Oh, I *knew* I should have stopped her.' Her voice rose in a wail.

'Why did Rosemary go to Lincott, Mrs Curtin?'

'She wanted to find her boy.'

'Her boy? Do you mean her son?'

'Yes – Billy, his name was.'

'And he was lost? Had he run away?'

'No, no ... Oh, it's all so complicated. I told her not to, I told her ...'

'I'm afraid I don't quite understand, Mrs Curtin. Why did you tell her not to?'

'Because she didn't even know if it was him. It was some stupid letter.'

'A letter from her son?' asked Ballard, thoroughly confused.

'No, we don't know who it was from, that was the trouble. You see, she gave Billy away. When he was a baby.'

CHAPTER TWENTY-SIX

The kettle began to hiss and clatter, and as Ballard got up to make the tea, PC Carter returned with Mrs Curtin's daughter Mrs Allardyce, a small, shrill woman in her early twenties, who exploded through the door, arms outstretched, and rushed to her mother's side. 'The policeman told me what happened, Mum. I'm so sorry. You should have come round to me if you thought Aunt Rosemary was missing. We could have . . .' She stopped, evidently not knowing what they could have, but glaring at Ballard as if it would have been a lot better than anything he or Carter could have. 'What was she doing in Lincott, anyway?' she demanded. 'It's miles away!'

Ballard wondered fleetingly if Muriel Curtin hadn't wanted Carter to fetch her daughter when she thought her sister had disappeared not because it would be a bother, but because she was clearly someone who was only ever an instant away from pop-eyed indignation. 'Detective Inspector Ballard,' he said, repressively. 'Please sit down.'

Jennifer Allardyce allowed herself to be steered to a chair by Carter, who looked cowed, presumably because he'd had a strip torn off him already, and sat down, staring at Ballard with an outraged expression, as though the whole thing were his fault.

'Now,' said Ballard, 'I think we should all have a cup of tea – if you wouldn't mind, Carter?'

In the brief interval while the young policeman poured and handed round the sugar, before retreating to stand in the doorway, he noticed that Muriel Curtin had put a placating hand on her daughter's arm. 'Your mother,' he told her, 'was just explaining why Mrs Aylett went to Lincott.'

'Yes . . .' Mrs Curtin glanced nervously at her daughter. 'You know about some of this, dear, but not everything. It's about Rosemary's son Billy.'

Jennifer Allardyce frowned, and Ballard could see the aggression, which had subsided, shooting back. 'I don't see why you need to go into all that, Mum. If it was an accident—'

'They don't know that it was an accident yet, dear,' said Mrs Curtin, wearily. 'Besides, Billy was the reason why Rosemary went to Lincott. She was trying to find him.'

'But why on earth would he be in Lincott? I thought—'

'Mrs Allardyce.' Ballard held up a hand for silence. 'Please, Mrs Curtin . . . Just take your time.'

'Well,' said Muriel Curtin, 'we've always been close, Rosemary and I. Her husband died about six months ago, and since then she's been more . . . well, reliant, I suppose, on me. She's not a weak person,' she added quickly, 'but it was quite a wrench after so many years – not that it was ever easy, what with the . . .' She stopped, wet-eyed and blinking rapidly, to dab at her eyes with a scrap of lacy hankie pulled from the sleeve of her cardigan.

Seeing, or possibly just sensing, that her daughter, who'd leant forward, was about to launch into a tirade against Ballard, Mrs Curtin hesitated for a second and then, drawing breath and bunching her shoulders like a swimmer about to take a dive, plunged into speech. 'It all happened a long time ago – during the war, in fact. Bert – that's Rosemary's husband – was away in the forces, and she . . . well, you know how things happened then,

things that wouldn't have happened if the men were here ...'
She paused, shaking her head at what was evidently a well-
remembered tangle of loneliness, uncertainty, confusion and
moral imperatives. Her daughter, who by Ballard's calculation
would have been about ten at the time, sat back in her chair
with lips pursed and arms crossed in condemnation.

'There was an American base near here then,' said Mrs Curtin,
'and Rosemary became friendly with one of the airmen. Not a
pilot,' she added, in a bid, Ballard thought, to demonstrate that
her sister wasn't a silly girl who'd simply fallen for some glam-
orously heroic fighter-boy and his promises of nylons and candy.
'He was older. One of the ground crew – looking after the planes
and what not.'

Ballard nodded slowly, to show he understood her need for
elaboration. 'What happened?'

'The usual thing, I'm afraid. She became pregnant and had a
son. She found out she was pregnant in 1944 – Billy was born in
December, a few days before Christmas. We didn't tell Bert.
Rosemary couldn't face it – he'd have known immediately that
the child couldn't possibly be his. I tried to persuade her to tell
him, but in the end it was her decision, not mine, and I'd never
have gone behind her back. My husband was away too, in the
navy. I think if he'd have been here he'd have pretty well *made*
her write to Bert. He took Bert's part afterwards – not that I
blame him for that. Anyway, when Bert was demobbed, well ...
I should think all the neighbours must have heard the shouting.
They knew, of course – they could add up as well as anybody –
but they had their own troubles, and ... Well, you know how it
was, everybody trying to readjust and get on with their lives.
Except that Bert couldn't accept the child as his. They'd no children of their own – never did have, more's the pity – and he said
that he wouldn't have this ... cuckoo ... in the nest, that he'd
leave Rosemary if she didn't get rid of it. Of course, he didn't

mean anything *bad* by that, just that she must find a home for this baby. There was a fair old to-do over that, of course, but in the end she agreed, as long as Billy didn't end up in a children's home. I wanted to take him myself, but my husband wouldn't hear of it. He and Bert were quite firm that the baby couldn't stay nearby – out of sight, out of mind, I suppose – and besides, we had two of our own by then, and that was a struggle because money was tight . . .' Mrs Curtin shook her head, blinking away tears.

'Come on, Mum.' Jennifer Allardyce murmured, reaching out to give her mother's arm a little shake. 'It's all right.'

'But it wasn't all right!' Mrs Curtin rounded on her, yanking her arm away. 'It wasn't all right at all!' Jennifer recoiled, as affronted as if she'd been hit, as her mother turned back to Ballard. 'My daughter's too young to understand, Inspector. She doesn't remember what it was like. In the end, Rosemary and I agreed to find someone who'd adopt Billy. We were going to ask the district nurse how to go about it, but then this woman just turned up on the doorstep, out of the blue. Very smart, well-dressed – beautiful-looking. She said she knew about Billy – well, that wasn't surprising, because people do talk, whether you like it or not – and she desperately wanted a baby and couldn't have one of her own. Her name was Mrs Carroll, and she told us she was married to an American soldier and was going back to the States with him. Well, we thought this would be a solution – Billy was bound to have a good life in America, especially as she'd told us her husband's family were wealthy people – and it was certainly far enough away . . . Rosemary didn't like that so much, but she wanted to stay with Bert, and how could she bring up Billy by herself with no work?'

'And Mrs Carroll took the baby, did she?'

'Yes. She took him . . .' Mrs Curtin's lip trembled. 'Took him away.'

'When was this?'

'I can't remember the exact date, but it was the summer of 1945.'

About six months old, thought Ballard, so he'd be almost twelve now. 'And Mrs Carroll adopted him, did she?'

Mrs Curtin shook her head. 'It wasn't done formally. We saw her several times, of course, and she was very good with Billy. You could see that. We both liked her. It should have been done properly – of course it should – but Bert kept on at Rosemary, he wanted the baby out, gone, and if she didn't hurry up and do it, he'd leave . . . It was a terrible time, Mr Ballard. Rosemary was desperate, and this woman seemed like the answer to our prayers. We never met the husband – she said he was already back in the States, and their army would make the arrangements for her and Billy to join him.'

'But how could she, Mum?' This was clearly a bit of the story that Mrs Allardyce didn't know, and curiosity had obviously triumphed over moral high ground. 'If she had no papers for Billy?'

'Well, there was a birth certificate. She had that. She said we weren't to worry because she could do the rest.'

'How?'

Mrs Curtin looked at her daughter blankly. 'How?'

'Well, the birth certificate would have had Rosemary's name on it, wouldn't it? Not hers. And if she couldn't show that Billy was her child, I don't see how she could have taken him out of the country.'

'She said that the baby's name could be put on her passport.'

'But surely that would still involve proving that he was her baby?' Mrs Allardyce looked at Ballard for confirmation of this.

'But if your sister thought that Billy was in Lincott,' said Ballard, 'perhaps he never went to America at all.'

'I just don't know,' said Mrs Curtin. 'It did cross my mind at the time, the business over the passport, but I've never had one, you see, so I don't know anything about it. I remember Mrs Carroll saying there were ways round these things . . . I suppose we should have gone into it a bit more, but she was very persuasive, and Bert insisted. Rosemary didn't feel she had any choice, and Mrs Carroll said she'd keep in touch, let her know how Billy was doing . . .' Mrs Curtin's voice cracked. 'When you think back, what you'd have done different . . . Last night, when Rosemary didn't come back, I couldn't sleep for thinking of it, how I should have done something so that Ernie – my husband – would agree to us keeping Billy, but I don't see how I could have . . . It was a terrible time. The war did dreadful things to families, Mr Ballard. All those poor children . . .' Engulfed by the memory, it took a moment before she emerged, reminding Ballard again of a diver in a pool, shaking her head and wiping her eyes with the hankie, which was now wadded into a tight, soggy ball. Wordlessly, Jennifer Allardyce fumbled in her handbag and handed over a clean linen square.

'Thank you, dear.' Mrs Curtin blew her nose.

'Did you hear from Mrs Carroll again?' asked Ballard.

'Never. Not a word. And when Rosemary did start trying to find Billy again . . .' She turned to her daughter. 'That was after your Uncle Bert died, dear.'

'You never said anything.'

'No, dear.'

'Why didn't you tell me?' Jennifer Allardyce looked affronted once more, and Ballard, who could imagine exactly why Mrs Curtin hadn't told her, said quickly, 'And she traced him to Lincott, did she?'

'She thought she had. She'd never forgotten him, you see, and I was the only one she could talk to. I tried to talk her out of it – I mean, Billy was too young to remember her, and if Mrs Carroll hadn't told him anything . . . But she was adamant. She said, "I'm going to find him if it's the last thing I do." And it was, wasn't it? The last thing . . . and we don't even know if she saw Billy, or if it was Billy at all . . .'

Jennifer Allardyce patted Mrs Curtin on the back and stared balefully at Ballard while her mother wiped her eyes. Ballard's mind was racing – beautiful, well-dressed, persuasive, and the boy was at Lincott – it seemed crazy, but with Mary/Ananda's record, anything was possible . . . But then, why would she want another child when she had just – to all intents and purposes – given her own away? 'Can you tell me,' he asked, 'exactly how you went about tracing Billy?'

'Well,' said Muriel Curtin, 'I didn't see how she'd be able to find him if he was in America. We had a copy of his birth certificate, but where do you start? Rosemary contacted the American Embassy, and they put us onto the forces people, but they told us there was no record from that time of anyone called Carroll who'd married an Englishwoman, so we were stuck. I told her it wasn't meant to be, but she wouldn't let up. She wouldn't talk about anything else – nothing mattered but finding Billy. Then, about a week ago, she showed me a letter she'd had – I remember there wasn't a date, but she said she'd got it the day before – and it said that her son was living in Lincott. There was a photograph, too, a boy, very handsome – Rosemary was certain it was Billy. We had a row about that as well, because I said I didn't see how she could be sure, because he didn't look like her – not that she wasn't attractive, of course, but he was fair. Fair hair, and Rosemary was dark.'

'What about the father?' asked Ballard.

'Patrick – that was his name, Patrick Brennan – he had fair hair. Sandy, I suppose you'd call it. Rosemary did have a couple of photographs of the two of them, but she got rid of them before Bert came back, and I haven't got any, so . . . I only met him a couple of times, and . . . He wasn't a bad-looking man, but I can't

really remember exactly what he looked like. Tall, well-built . . .
Yes, quite a smasher in his way. I do remember thinking he was
a lot better-looking than Bert.'

Mrs Allardyce stared at her mother, apparently astonished by
this nod towards carnality, and Ballard, careful not to let his
excitement show, asked, 'Who was the letter from?'

'There was no name, just "A Well Wisher" written at the bottom.
And it didn't say Billy's name, either, just "your son who was
born in the war". It wasn't nasty or anything, but because it
wasn't signed I said it might just be somebody making trouble
– although I don't see who'd want to, not after all this time.'

'Where was it posted?'

'London, she said. I never saw the envelope.'

'And she took the letter with her, did she?'

'Yes, and the photograph. She had them with her when she
left, in her bag.' Mrs Curtin frowned. 'You must have seen them.
I mean, isn't that why you . . . why you're here?'

'We didn't find a bag, only a library card in her pocket with
her name on it.'

'They must have taken it, then. Whoever shot her must have
stolen it . . . D'you think that's why she was killed? To rob her?
She didn't have . . . I mean, she wasn't rich. She was just . . . just
Rosemary.' Mrs Curtin stared at Ballard with hurt, baffled eyes.

'We don't know yet,' said Ballard, gently. 'But we'll find out.
What you've told me is very helpful.'

'Why did she have to go like that, on her own?' wailed Mrs
Curtin. 'I'd told her I'd go with her – and I would have done –
only I thought we ought to make some enquiries first. I know
Lincott's only a small place, and the letter mentioned a school
there. Odd name – the Foundation.'

'The Foundation?' echoed Ballard, not quite believing his ears.

'That's right. I suppose it must be one of those progressive
places you hear about. I told her she couldn't just walk in and

say "that's my child", but she was too excited to listen. I said to her, what about Mr and Mrs Carroll? They weren't mentioned in the letter, it was just "If you want to find your son, I know where he is." She accused me of not wanting to help her. Said I was like Bert and Ernie and I just wanted to forget all about it."Blow you, I'll go by myself," she said. Then she left.'

CHAPTER TWENTY-SEVEN

Ballard and Carter left Jennifer Allardyce bossing her mother into a coat and hunting out a photograph of her aunt to pin up in the Lincott village post office, and went down the road to Rosemary Aylett's house. As he let them in through the kitchen door with keys given by Mrs Curtin, Ballard wasn't sure what, if anything, he was expecting to find, but, telling Carter to search upstairs, he went into the sitting room to have a look round. Despite the dilapidated state of the garden – obviously Bert's department, thought Ballard – the house was clean and neat, the fresh dust only just beginning to settle. Specks, he thought, of Rosemary Aylett's skin – all that remained of her, in the corners of the rooms, beneath the bed, on the tops of curtain rails and doors . . . all that was left. A book bound in green cloth, the page – 73 – neatly marked with a hand-embroidered strip, lay on the occasional table beside an armchair. Ballard glanced at the spine: *Cotillion*, by Georgette Heyer. A slight, almost imperceptible indentation on the antimacassar where her head had been as she'd sat dreaming of a reunion with Billy . . .

Ballard made a cursory search of the room and, returning to the kitchen, looked in cupboards and opened drawers, but found nothing unusual. One plate was slotted into the drying rack above the sink and, on the wooden drainer, placed in a line, were one cup, one saucer, one knife and one fork.

Carter appeared at his elbow. 'Come and look up here, sir. There's nothing in the lady's bedroom, but – well, you'll see.'

Ballard followed him up the stairs and across the cramped landing seeing, as he passed, a bedroom – Rosemary's, judging by the pink eiderdown and the scent bottle and powder puff glimpsed on the fussy dressing table – and a gleaming bathroom. Carter stopped in front of the first of two doors adjacent to it. 'In here, sir.'

Ballard caught his breath as Carter swung the door open. Inside, pristine and crammed with things so brand-new that they almost glittered, was the perfect bedroom for a twelve-year-old boy. Boxed Airfix kits, Escalado, bagatelle, a football, a pile of I-Spy books and adventure stories, Dinky toys in their boxes, with a Supermarine Swift jet fighter and a Gloster Javelin as well as a number of cars and lorries, and a Hornby Dublo locomotive, also in its box. A Davy Crockett cap hung from a hook on the back of the door, over a boy's tartan dressing gown. Ballard stared round the room in amazement. 'She's thought of everything,' he said. He pulled open the topmost drawer in the chest of drawers and saw new flannelette pyjamas, neatly folded, alongside socks and underwear. There were more clothes in the wardrobe – trousers, blazer, raincoat . . . even cricket whites.

Carter picked up a copy of an *Eagle* annual, its cover showing a picture of Dan Dare, Chief Pilot of the Interplanet Space Fleet, with his manly jaw and curiously shaped black eyebrows. 'Trains, spacemen, cowboys . . . it's everything a boy could want,' he said, looking round. He tapped the annual. 'This year's, too. Everything bought pretty recently, I'd say.'

'I agree,' said Ballard. 'She must have been sure, mustn't she?'

Carter looked up from a brightly drawn strip of Dan Dare bravely facing down the evil Mekon with its heavy lidded eyes and enormous green cranium. 'She wanted him so badly,' he said. 'That's why she believed he was in Lincott.'

'Did you look in the room next door?'

'Not yet, sir.' Carter relinquished the annual with, Ballard thought, some reluctance.

The next room, which was tiny, contained nothing except a gleaming and obviously new Raleigh bike. 'Blimey,' said Carter, standing at Ballard's shoulder. 'I'd have killed for one of those.'

'Me, too,' said Ballard. 'She was set on making it up to him, wasn't she?'

'I'd say so, sir.'

'I'm betting,' said Ballard, 'that Mrs Curtin didn't know anything about this.'

He was right. Muriel Curtin and her daughter stared at the Aladdin's cave in astonishment. 'I had no idea,' said Mrs Curtin. 'None at all.'

'How could she afford it, Mum? All this stuff must have cost a fortune.'

Mrs Curtin took a step into the room, her fingers quivering over the lid of a giant Meccano set. 'Bert left her a little,' she said, quietly. 'And I know she used to keep back a bit from the housekeeping. Never said what it was for, though.' Turning to Ballard, she added, 'My sister was always a good manager. She'd have made sure Bert never went short.' She reached over and picked up a cricket bat, turning it over in her hands, stroking the wood. 'Poor Rosemary. All her plans, all this . . .' Her damp-eyed gaze travelled round the room, seeing, Ballard thought, her sister's imaginings – the handsome boy, clattering up the stairs after a day's school or play, happy, sturdy, vigorous, hungry for his tea – 'All this *belief*. All this *hope*.'

CHAPTER TWENTY-EIGHT

'Yes.' Mrs Curtin looked down at the waxy, blue-white face, then turned her head away. 'That's Rosemary.'

'Thank you.' Ballard led Mrs Curtin out of the mortuary's viewing room and back to her now very subdued daughter. Earlier, while they were waiting for Trickett's assistants to lay out the body, the pathologist had taken him aside. 'Not much more to report, really,' he had said, clearly unhappy not to be able to make some pronouncement of infallible wisdom in the manner of his celebrated mentor Spilsbury. 'She's in her forties, and she's given birth to a child, and I stand by what I said about the timing. As I said, there was no muzzle impression on the neck, but I've examined the marks round the entry wound – the effect of the gases – and the weapon was definitely fired from no more than two inches away. I've had a report from the ballistics chap – the bullet is a .32, marks matching the cartridge case, and there were six right-hand grooves of the Browning type. Weapon turned up yet?'

Ballard shook his head. 'Neither has Mrs Aylett's handbag, assuming she had one ... So ... going back to what you were saying, she must have been aware of her assailant?'

'I'd say so. I suppose he could have hidden behind a tree to shoot her as she came past if he'd known she was going to be there, but she'd have been so close she must have known he was there. Unless she was deaf, I suppose, but even then . . .'

Ballard took Mrs Curtin to the Ipswich police station to make a formal statement. They went through everything again over a cup of tea, a kindly policewoman taking notes, while Mrs Allardyce waited outside. Muriel Curtin's brave, jerky smile and solemn eagerness to cooperate made him want to put his arm round her. Rosemary, she told him, could hear perfectly well and always carried her handbag with her. 'It's the same as mine,' she said, holding up solid-looking brown crocodile bag with slightly sloping sides and a gold clasp. We bought them at the same time, a year or so ago. In Ipswich. We went to the pictures afterwards . . .' She blinked, obviously remembering a happy occasion. 'We saw *The Runaway Bus*. Rosemary always liked Frankie Howerd.'

'How would she have got to Lincott? Did she have a car?'

Mrs Curtin shook her head. 'She'd have taken the bus. Unless she'd accepted a lift from somebody, and they . . .' She tailed off, a smiling motorist turning into a gun-toting maniac in her head. 'But,' she added, firmly, 'Rosemary *wouldn't* have accepted a lift. Not unless she knew the person. And what I don't understand is why she was in the woods in the first place.'

'Did she like walking?'

'Not particularly. I mean, I've never known her just take herself off for a walk. Was it near the school?'

'School?'

'That Foundation place.'

'The Foundation's not really a school. At least, not for children. I suppose you'd call it a religious centre, really.'

'You mean some sort of church thing?'

'Not exactly. More . . . spiritual. Esoteric.'

Mrs Curtin looked at him blankly. 'Well, I don't know anything about that sort of thing. Why would Billy be in a place like that?'

'I'm not sure,' said Ballard, 'but I'd like you to have a look at a photograph and tell me if you recognise the person.' He slid the picture of Mary/Ananda onto the table.

'That's the woman who took Billy!'

'Are you sure of that?'

'Yes, it's unmistakable. But . . .' Mrs Curtin looked from Ballard to the policewoman and back again, confused. 'How did you know?'

'I'm afraid,' said Ballard, 'that I can't tell you that at present because it's something to do with another case. We're looking for this lady at the moment. You said she came for Billy sometime during the summer of 1945 . . . that's right, isn't it? Can you be more precise?'

'Well . . .' Mrs Curtin's face screwed up with the effort of recollection. 'I do know it was sometime around the date of the Japanese surrender, because there was a holiday announced and Ernie hadn't gone to work and there'd been a big bonfire and what not . . . I think it must have been couple of days after that.'

'So, the seventeenth or eighteenth of August.'

'Thereabouts, yes. Not before, because I remember Rosemary saying it was a pity Billy was too young to enjoy the fireworks. It was very hot, and when I went over to Rosemary's, she and Billy were in the garden and she was lifting him up to see the hens and making clucking noises. Funny, the things that stick in your mind, isn't it?'

'You said Billy was born a few days before Christmas?'

'That's right. Twenty-first of December, it was. Rosemary'd always come round to me and talk about him, every year, and end up crying . . . I was the only one she could talk to. I did feel sorry for her, because it broke her heart, having to give him away . . . I don't like to speak ill of the dead, but her Bert was a difficult sort of man. Always falling out with people, so if you were his friend it was hard to go on being friends with them because he'd think that was disloyal ... And of course when he found out about Billy, that was Rosemary being disloyal and he didn't want me and Ernie even to speak to her. I said, "I'm not having that, she's my sister no matter what she's done", but he wanted us to take sides. He was very difficult all round really, but Rosemary stuck to him. I never thought he deserved it, but then again, she didn't have anywhere else to go ...'

'What was Billy's full name, Mrs Curtin?'

'William Thomas Aylett.'

'You mentioned a copy of the birth certificate – was that in your keeping, or your sister's?'

'Rosemary's. She had it in her handbag when she left ... I know because she showed me. We gave the original certificate to Mrs Carroll.'

'And you're positive that this' – Ballard tapped the photograph – 'is Mrs Carroll, are you?'

Muriel Curtin nodded. 'I'd know her anywhere. You don't see many people as good-looking as that. There is something else, though – perhaps I should have said before, but I didn't see why it mattered ... Well, it probably doesn't matter, and you'll probably think I'm silly, but ...' She looked at him doubtfully, seeking permission to continue.

'I don't think you're silly at all,' said Ballard firmly. 'Tell me.'

'Well, it was just something I thought at the time. I didn't say anything to Rosemary, and she didn't mention it, so then I thought, well, I'm imagining it. But each time we saw Mrs Carroll – that was three times, as far as I remember, three different occasions – I thought she looked as if she was in the early stages of pregnancy. Very early, because you couldn't tell it from her shape, but she had a sort of glow about her, that women sometimes get. But then I thought, why would she tell us she couldn't have children and go to all the bother of adopting one if she was having one of her own? That made no sense at all, so I decided I must have imagined it, but I remember it was quite a strong impression at the time, and I wouldn't say I was a fanciful person, not at all. Do you think it could be Billy, Inspector, at that funny place?'

'I don't know,' said Ballard, grimly, 'but I'm going to do my best to find out.'

'Because if it is,' Muriel Curtin's face was creased with anxiety, 'well, I'm – I mean, we are – his next of kin, aren't we? And I can't just *leave* him, not after . . . You don't think he had anything to do with Rosemary's death, do you? I don't mean killing her, but . . . It's probably talking out of turn, but you said that you were looking for Mrs Carroll, so if she's a . . . a criminal of some sort . . . then . . . well, presumably they're looking after him at this place, but . . .'

Ballard reached across the table and patted her hand. 'I do understand, Mrs Curtin. I shall be looking into it, and we will keep you informed, I promise you.'

'We thought we'd done the right thing when he was a baby, but . . .' She shook her head, tight-lipped. 'I couldn't imagine – well, I didn't want to imagine – what Rosemary must have been feeling all those years, but when I saw that room . . . I just want to do the right thing by him, that's all. Him *and* Rosemary.'

CHAPTER TWENTY-NINE

After making a note to ask Parsons first thing tomorrow about getting hold of a copy of Billy's birth certificate and finding out whether the US army had any record of a serviceman called Carroll who'd married an Englishwoman in 1945, Ballard drove slowly and thoughtfully out of Ipswich and home through the dark, narrow lanes.

Mary Milburn was a loose cannon, all right, but somehow he didn't think that she'd acted on a mere whim in taking Billy from Mrs Aylett. If what had happened with Dr Slater was anything to go by, the woman tended to have a purpose to her actions, no matter how illogical or bizarre it might seem to others. But what that purpose might have been, he couldn't imagine. What if Lloyd were the writer of Rosemary Aylett's anonymous letter? If he was, then he'd somehow managed to discover the boy Michael's true origins.

It was possible, Ballard supposed, that Mary might have told Lloyd that she'd taken Billy and brought him to the Foundation under the name of Michael, but given her apparent disinclination for telling the truth that too seemed unlikely. Besides, the last thing she'd want was for Michael to be revealed as just an ordinary kid. Presumably Roth had spotted Michael's 'specialness' early on, and that, in turn, had conferred status on her.

Could she, perhaps, have started off by colluding in the Michael mythology, and ended up actually believing it? Ballard supposed that stranger things must have happened, although he couldn't, at that moment – driving past farmyard walls in dripping, dung-scented darkness – think of any.

They hadn't asked the students at the Foundation about Michael – no reason to – but Ballard suspected that if they had, their questions would have been met, despite all the bright intensity, with guarded responses. In a place where the very air was thick with significance, Michael's divinity would, Ballard was sure, be the most significant thing of all: proof to the students that they were following the true path and had access to something extra special that was denied to others by their inferiority or ignorance. That they considered themselves superior, he had no doubt – with Michael, of course, the most superior of all. People have killed to preserve their status before now, thought Ballard, and Mary/Ananda's status depended on Michael's . . .

If Lloyd's manuscript *had* existed, then it might have contained information blowing the whistle on the pair of them. Mary/Ananda might have been able to get to London to kill him, and removed and destroyed the manuscript in order to keep it quiet, and she might have killed Rosemary Aylett, too, if she'd encountered her. Or Lloyd could have told Mary/Ananda that he'd sent the letter and they could expect a visit, couldn't he? Roth would have had good reason to want the manuscript suppressed, too – and he'd hardly have welcomed Rosemary . . . Did he have so much power over his students that they would kill in order to protect him and the Foundation? It was hard to imagine any one of that almost absurdly genteel bunch murdering somebody, but that didn't make it impossible. If only we could find the bloody woman, he thought, crunching the gears as he turned off the village's main road and into the lane that led to his house.

*

'You didn't tell me Inspector Stratton was here.' Pauline, up to her elbows in washing-up, was clattering the dishes with unnecessary violence. She'd been spiky all through supper, monosyllabic and challenging by turns. Now, Katy was in bed and Ballard, cloth in hand, was waiting to dry the supper things, feeling – as he had all evening – waves of something a lot like hostility and doing his best to ignore them. Silence, he'd decided, was the best policy. All his attempts at conversation, however banal, had so far placed him immediately and absolutely in the wrong. Now, Pauline's tone was positively accusing, as if he'd deliberately concealed something from her – which, of course, he had, although he wasn't really sure why he'd done it.

'I didn't think you'd be all that interested.'

'Well, I am. He's been asking questions at the Foundation, hasn't he? About that man who was killed in London.'

'Heavens.' Ballard kept his tone light. 'News does travel fast.'

'I read about the man in the paper, and I do occasionally talk to people – the ones who'll speak to me, anyway. And then there was that woman killed in the wood . . .'

'Yes, but that's nothing to do with Stratton's inquiry,' said Ballard, 'at least, not at the moment.'

'Well, it's all over the village, anyway. And about the one who's disappeared and had her picture in all the papers. Not that anyone's thought to ask me about it, of course.'

Ballard remembered what Mary/Ananda had said about meeting Pauline out walking, but an obscure fear that he'd somehow give himself away made him say, 'Why, did you know her?'

'Yes.' Pauline banged a plate onto the wooden drying rack. 'As a matter of fact, I did.'

'Oh?'

'I met her at the Foundation.'

'Did you? But . . .' Ballard stopped himself. This definitely wasn't the time to contradict her. Instead, he asked, 'What were you doing there?'

'I went to a few talks. They do these introductory courses. Anyone who's interested can go along.'

Vaguely recalling that he'd seen a notice to this effect in the village shop, Ballard said, 'I didn't know you'd done that.'

Another plate crashed into the rack. 'Well, you didn't ask.'

Deciding to let this go, Ballard said, 'What did you think of it?'

'It was interesting. They're nice people. Kind. They're not all posh types who sit about being self-indulgent, you know. They're up at dawn, and they work really hard – cooking and cleaning and gardening. They're even going to build a new wing themselves. And you can talk to them.'

Passing over the implication that she couldn't talk to *him*, Ballard said, 'What did you talk about?'

'That's not important.'

'You're making it sound as if it is.'

'What I mean is, they don't have any stupid ideas about me being the wife of a policeman and therefore the enemy.'

'Unlike some of the people in the village, you mean.'

'Yes. And it's peaceful there. It's . . . *good*.'

'Inspector Stratton found it a bit creepy.'

'He *would*.'

Ballard was taken aback by this. Pauline, so far as he knew, had always liked Stratton. 'It was just his impression,' he said. 'And I have to say I thought they were a pretty rum lot myself.'

'But you only talked to them about one thing, so you're not really in a position to judge, are you?' She narrowly missed his hand with the upended teapot, spraying him with water. 'You're just accusing them of things when you don't know anything about them.'

'No one's accused them of *anything*, Pauline. Did you meet the leader, Mr Roth?'

'Not yet, but they're always talking about him. I suppose you think he's done something awful, too.' A glass crashed against the edge of the sink, hard enough to break. Taking a step back, he said, 'What's all this about, anyway?'

'We never talk properly any more. We can't seem to have a conversation without it turning into a row.'

'I wasn't the one who started it.'

'I didn't say you did. Now you're just being childish.'

'Oh, for God's sake.' Ballard threw down his drying-up cloth. 'I've had enough of this. Are you going to tell me what it's about, or aren't you?'

'I'm trying to! The teacher at the Foundation said that we're all – all of us – tangled up in our own little worlds, and we don't communicate properly or honestly or anything, so we go round and round in circles and we don't say anything that matters because we're full of preconceived ideas, and that's how wars start, people getting the wrong ideas about each other, and it's true, isn't it?'

'Are you saying I've got the wrong ideas about you?'

Pauline took her hands out of the soapy water and rested her arms on the edge of the sink. 'It's not just about you and your ideas, you know.'

'Clearly a lot of it is, or you wouldn't be angry with me.'

'Oh ...' Pauline sighed, flicking her fingers at the soapsuds, the momentum of her anger gone. 'I don't know. It all seemed so clear when she said it, and when she was talking about the ideas we have about ourselves – what kind of people we are – but trying to explain it now ...' Pauline shook her head. 'I've been thinking about it for the last few days—'

'Since the lecture?'

'Yes. And I thought that if I could just get rid of the wrong ideas and not worry or have negative thoughts, everything would be all right – because that makes sense, doesn't it? It ought to work, and I really felt as if it would – I was sure. But then this morning – after you left–' She stopped, tugging at the pushed-up sleeve of her cardigan for her handkerchief and dabbing her eyes frantically.

'What happened this morning?'

'I got the curse. I was so positive, this time. I even *felt* pregnant. The teacher at the Foundation was telling us how the mind affects everything – the subtle world, she called it – she said it governs the physical world and if we think the right thoughts we'll be in tune with nature and know our true selves. I've never heard anyone say anything like that before, and it made so much sense, but ...' The next few words were lost as Pauline blew her nose violently and turned to look at him with damp, red-rimmed eyes.

Ballard, who had managed to follow some, if not all, of this, said, as gently as he could, 'I don't think mind over matter is quite as simple as that.'

'You think I'm being stupid, don't you?' Pauline glared at him. 'About wanting another baby. You don't understand it.'

'No,' said Ballard. 'I don't. I mean, it would be nice ... lovely ... if we had another child, but it won't be the end of the world if it doesn't happen. And if you want a positive thought, what about Katy? We're lucky to have her – some couples can't have children at all.'

'Yes,' snapped Pauline, 'I know that. And of course I love Katy. I just ... I can't help it, Ben. I think about it all the time.'

'You know,' said Ballard, thinking about what Pauline had just said about the lectures she'd attended, 'that business about people having the wrong ideas about themselves ... Well, perhaps your idea of yourself having to be the mother of more than one child is wrong?'

'So I've failed myself as well as everyone else, you mean?'

'No, I don't mean that at all.' Ballard who a second before had been feeling rather pleased with himself, gave up trying to extricate himself and settled for a vehement shake of the head.

'I have, though. You' – here, Pauline held up a hand to forestall any argument – 'and Katy as well. She was asking me the other day why she didn't have brothers and sisters like the other children in her class.'

Ballard held up his hands in a gesture of surrender. 'I *am* sorry, Pauline. It's hard for me to know what to say . . .'

Why was it *so* hard, he asked himself later. The rest of the evening had been spent circling each other at a wary distance, only volunteering the most anodyne of comments. He sat on in his armchair after Pauline had gone to bed, not wanting the proximity just yet. Part of it, he knew, was being ashamed – ashamed of not being more supportive to Pauline, ashamed of not being bothered about another baby; ashamed, too, of wishing the whole problem would just *go away*.

He knew he'd been distant and uncommunicative; knew, too, that Pauline felt isolated, which made it all the more unforgivable. No wonder she'd turned to the people at the Foundation. Although he'd worried about Pauline being lonely, it hadn't occurred to him that she'd want to make new friendships – not deep ones, anyway. After you were married, he'd reasoned, you didn't need them. You had each other, didn't you? Or you were supposed to . . . Perhaps that wasn't how it worked, after all.

He found himself wondering why Mary/Ananda had told him she'd met Pauline while out walking, and not at the Foundation. Perhaps it was just an example of the mysteriousness they all seemed to go in for, or perhaps Pauline had asked her not to tell him – or perhaps Mary/Ananda, a compulsive liar, was simply acting true to form.

Driving away, by an almighty effort of will, a vivid and astonishingly arousing image of Mary/Ananda, skirt hiked up and straddling the stile, Ballard levered himself out of his armchair and, guilty and sheepish, went upstairs to join his wife.

CHAPTER THIRTY

Unable to sleep, and tired of staring into the dark and listening to Pauline's breathing, Ballard went downstairs, made himself a pot of tea, and, thinking he might as well do something useful, sat at the kitchen table and began writing down the sequence of Mary/Ananda's doings that he'd managed to piece together so far. At the end of half an hour, he had:

20th December 1943 – Mary/Ananda gives birth to Tom (assuming T is her child!)

21st December 1944 – Rosemary Aylett gives birth to Billy

17th May 1945 – Death of Revd Milburn

Around 22nd May 1945 – Mary/Ananda leaves Tom with Mrs Wheeler

Around 17th August 1945 – Mary/Ananda 'adopts' Billy, saying she's married to an American serviceman called Carroll

Some time in early 1948 – Mary/Ananda and Billy arrive at the Foundation (B. would have been 3 years old)

5th November 1956 – Rosemary Aylett comes to find Billy and is killed

If Mary/Ananda had become desperate for a baby three months

after she'd abandoned her own, why not simply go back and get him? Why go to the bother of finding another one? Unless, he thought, looking at Tom and Billy's respective birth dates, it was to do with the *age* of the child ... If Mary/Ananda was worried that somebody might find out she'd done away with Milburn (or caused his death by neglecting him), then she might well target an American serviceman in the hope of becoming a GI bride – America was nicely far away from gossip and suspicion (not to mention Dr Slater) after all ... And what better way to ensure a hasty marriage than claiming to be pregnant? Presumably she was having an affair with this Carroll while Milburn was still alive – Stratton had said the neighbours in Woodbridge had told him how she was always going to the American dances ...

If Carroll had gone away to fight in Europe, he wouldn't have realised that she'd never been pregnant, and it was hard to tell the age of a baby just by looking at it. He might have accepted a one-year-old baby – Billy – as being younger, but by almost two, which was Tom's age in November '45, they were beginning to stagger about and say things, weren't they? Mrs Curtin had said she thought Mary/Ananda was pregnant, although she hadn't looked it. She must have been mistaken, thought Ballard, because, as she'd said herself, it made no sense at all.

Perhaps Mary/Ananda had married Carroll and gone to America with him but the marriage had failed and she'd returned home with the child. What had Stratton told him after he'd been to see the chap at the Psychical Research place? Thumbing through his notebook, he found: *Thorley unable to find Mary M. when re-investigating Lincott Rectory haunting in '46. Slater's sister said MM was GI bride.* Mary/Ananda arriving at the Foundation in early '48 would make sense if she'd been to the States and then returned.

Ballard went into the hall and took the photograph of Rosemary Aylett that Jennifer Allardyce had given to him out of his coat pocket. It showed an attractive woman posed in front of a rail on a promenade somewhere, the sea behind her and the wind ruffling dark hair about a smiling face. Rosemary, who'd been married to grumpy old Bert, and who'd liked romances and Frankie Howerd. Who'd salted away bits of the housekeeping for years to buy a boy's treasure trove for her long-lost son. He thought of Katy, snuggled asleep upstairs with her golliwogs Sammy and Topsy beside her, and remembered when she was born, Pauline's fierce, protective love for her. He'd felt the same, but not, he knew, with the same intensity. Ballard studied the photograph again. *It broke her heart, having to give him away* . . . Such love, he thought. All this belief, Mrs Curtin had said. All this hope. Everything she must have felt as she'd set out, armed with an anonymous letter, a photograph and a birth certificate, to try to reclaim her Billy. She and Lloyd were linked by the Foundation, and – if Lloyd were the writer of the letter, by Mary/Ananda and Billy/Michael, too. It was possible, Ballard reasoned, that Rosemary Aylett's death was an accident, but, if so, why had whoever killed her taken her handbag and gone through her pockets? Robbery could be a motive, he supposed, but it seemed equally, if not more, likely that whoever killed her had wanted to conceal her identity. Was that to make sure that there was no possible link to the Foundation? And if Lloyd had written the letter, might the two of them not have been killed by the same person – someone who was desperate for Michael's true origins not to be revealed? The obvious candidate was Mary/Ananda who – according to Dr Slater, anyway – had killed once before . . . And, judging from all he'd heard about her, she was ruthless enough . . . The one good thing about it, he supposed, was that if she were the murderer, she wasn't likely to attack Michael, because that would be killing the goose that laid the golden eggs.

He'd talk to Stratton first thing tomorrow: there was a definite case, he thought, for making the two murders into a single inquiry. If only they could find the bloody woman . . . Thumbing through his notebook once more, he wrote:

1947 – Lloyd arrives at the Foundation
April 1956 – Lloyd leaves the Foundation
30th/31st October 1956 – Lloyd killed

He stared at this for a while, then put the tea things in the sink and went back to bed. The rigidity of Pauline's body as he climbed in beside her told him that she was not only awake, but still upset. Excusing himself on the grounds that talking to her would only lead to another argument, he affected not to notice and, turning away from her, closed his eyes and tried to sleep.

CHAPTER THIRTY-ONE

'We don't yet have a statement from anyone who saw Mary/Ananda returning to the Foundation after seeing that film on the night of the thirtieth. I haven't talked to Tynan about it, either.' Stratton, who'd relayed the information about Rosemary Aylett that Ballard had given him straight away, fully expected that owning up to these omissions would earn him a top-class bollocking, and thought he was about to get one when his superior gave a snort of disgust. 'The woman must be deranged,' he said.

'She certainly seems to be pretty strange,' said Stratton, feeling relieved.

Lamb raised his eyebrows, which had the effect of making him look even more like a man reflected in a tap, then said, 'Sounds as if "strange" is the least of it. But I agree that it makes sense to treat the two deaths as a single inquiry, so I'll be speaking to DI Ballard's superior officer. Meanwhile, it looks as if you're going to do more good up there than down here, so you'd better get straight back home to pack. Grove can manage things at this end. Just make sure you report back.'

Stratton folded a couple of shirts on top of the things in his suitcase, closed it, and took it downstairs to put in his car. Then he made himself a cup of tea, and, taking it into the sitting room, sat listening to *Mrs Dale's Diary* while he drank it, knowing as he did so that he was simply putting off the moment. If he didn't phone Diana to say he was going to be in Suffolk for a few days, she might find out from Monica at the studio, and be hurt that he hadn't told her. He'd had to tell Doris that he'd be away for a few days, to stop her and his other sister-in-law, Lilian, bringing his dinner round. He could hardly ask Doris not to tell Monica he was going, and as for telling Monica not to mention it to Diana – what on earth would she think if he were to say that? No, it was impossible. Stratton stood up, cut off Ellis Powell in the middle of being rather worried about Jim, and, striding purposefully into the hall, picked up the phone and dialled, all the while hoping that Diana would say she was too busy to join him.

She wasn't. They'd arranged to meet at the cottage she'd borrowed in a place called Halstead Wyse, which, when Stratton consulted his map, proved to be not too far from Lincott but far enough, or so he hoped, for his daytime and night-time activities to remain entirely separate. When he'd raised questions about the logistics of the thing, in a weak bid to put her off the idea, Diana had told him she'd arrange to borrow a car from one of her colleagues, and would arrive the following day with groceries and the like. All he needed to do was to turn up.

He wanted to see her, of course he did. He just wasn't happy about it being like this. The problem, he thought, as he drove through drizzle down a stretch of dual carriageway, was the idea that one's life should be divided, as far as possible, into water-tight compartments, so that one thing (in this case, Diana) did not encroach on another (such as work or family). Sensing a possible breakdown of the system gave him an unpleasant feeling of lack of control. While he knew that, ordinarily, the success of the watertight business depended on the leakiness, or otherwise, of the person concerned, he didn't like matters being taken out of his hands in this way ... Just then, the new lights overhead, which were being tested, flickered then switched themselves on, bathing the dull grey day in an eerie yellow glow. Stratton wondered briefly if radiation might not be that colour – hard to tell if you'd only ever seen the mushroom cloud in black and white. Of course, his worries would be meaningless if they all got blown to buggery ...

Thinking of the newsreels he'd seen – the mysterious explosions that unfolded themselves above Pacific atolls while he sat watching in the dark, Stratton thought that the carnage they'd all seen during the war had been only a preview before the main feature. At least, he supposed, fumbling in his coat pocket for a cigarette, that sort of thing put everything else well and truly into perspective.

CHAPTER THIRTY-TWO

'There's a message for you,' said Maisie Denton, when Stratton arrived at the George and Dragon. 'DI Ballard said I was to ask you to telephone as soon as you got here.' She dug a hand into the pocket of her cretonne overall. 'He said he was just on his way home – I've written down the number for you here.'

Stratton followed her down the passage that led from the bar. The phone was fixed halfway down, and a vast sneeze like a distant trombone told him that George Denton was situated in the room – a kitchen, judging from what he could see through the half-open door – at the end.

'She's turned up!'

'What?' The line crackled and Stratton held the receiver hard against his ear, trying to block out the parping crescendo issuing from the kitchen.

'Mary or Ananda, or whatever her bloody name is! She's here!'

'Where?'

'Tynan's. He rang the station. I told him you were on your way – got a message from On High – and we'd come over when you arrived. I did wonder if it mightn't be a good idea to get them both down to the station, but I thought we might get a better idea of things if we saw them on home ground – his home ground, anyway ... Look, do you want to come up here first? I'm sure you'd like a cup of tea or something.'

'What if she scarpers?'

'Tynan was adamant she wouldn't. I told him I'd hold him responsible if she did. Also ...' Ballard sounded sheepish, 'I promised I'd read the nipper a story before bed.'

'Fair enough.' Stratton fished his notebook and pencil out of his coat pocket. 'Won't take me a minute to get organised here. What's the address?'

Stratton followed Ballard's instructions and ended up crawling down a narrow lane, his headlamps illuminating the thin rain falling on the shabby, spiky leftovers of hedges and bushes that were no more than straggles of dead sticks. Apart from a church next door, Ballard's cottage seemed isolated. Stratton found himself wondering what historical anomaly or human stubbornness had resulted in the place of worship being a good quarter of a mile from the heart of the village it served.

There wasn't enough light to get much impression of the place, but Stratton noted the beds laid out on either side of the path in the front garden, the overhang of a thatched roof and crisscross leading on the windows. Pauline Ballard answered the door, minus the uniform but otherwise very much how he remembered her – pink and white and strapping, looking, even in her thirties, every inch the sort of girl who'd be jolly useful on a sports field or tennis court. Now, she threw the door wide. 'Ben's upstairs reading to Katy, but he won't be long. I've got the kettle on.'

'Thanks.'

Pauline helped him off with his coat. 'You won't mind sitting in the kitchen, will you?'

'Not at all. Nice place you've got here.'

'Not too quaint, I hope.'

'Nothing wrong with a few roses round the door. Mind if I pull up a chair?'

'Please . . .'

It was disconcertingly intimate, Stratton thought, to see inside the home of someone you worked with. He'd been invited to Ballard's wedding and Katy's christening, but, other than that, he had only ever seen him – and Pauline, too, in the days when she was Policewoman Gaines – in the context of work. Catching a glimpse of an upright piano through the door of what was, presumably, the sitting room, he decided it must be she who played, as his former sergeant had never given any indication of being musical. Bit late to ask now, he thought, imagining Pauline, buxom on the piano stool, entertaining Ballard of an evening.

'How's country life suiting you?' he asked, as she busied herself with the tea things. 'Must be a bit different from Putney.'

'It's been wonderful for Katy. She's ever so much better now, with the fresh air, and she's getting on well at school.'

Remembering what Ballard had said about it taking a long time to be accepted in the community and Pauline desperately wanting a second child, Stratton didn't press the issue of whether or not *she* liked country life, but said, 'I must say, I'm glad of a bit of fresh air, too. Don't seem to get out of London much these days.'

'Ben said you grew up on a farm.' Pauline placed a cup and saucer on the table in front of him. 'Sugar?'

'No, thanks. My brother runs the place now. Farming's changed a good bit, mind you, since I was a boy . . .'

Ballard appeared several minutes later, a brightly coloured storybook tucked under his arm. 'Sorry about that. Katy's just about asleep,' he added to Pauline.

'I'd better go and kiss her goodnight, then. Leave you in peace.'

'Thanks, love.'

Ballard looked somehow softer than usual, Stratton thought, recalling the rare occasions on which he'd been at home at the right time to read to his own children, his words dropping into the special silence that surrounded them as they drifted off, sealing themselves into sleep, before returning downstairs afterwards to a cup of tea with Jenny.

Extricating himself from this thought – and all the thoughts that, if unchecked, would be bound to follow it, he said, 'What did Tynan say?'

'He's a cool customer. You'd have thought he was inviting me to a garden party or something. Said she was staying with him for a few days.'

'Did he say where she'd been for the last four days?'

'Went to London, apparently.' Ballard rolled his eyes. 'Wanted to get her hair done.'

'You're joking!'

'I'm not.'

'For Christ's sake . . .'

'Odd, isn't it, that the rest of them at the Foundation are busy at all hours with this great programme of theirs, and she just comes and goes as she pleases.'

'Bloody odd,' said Stratton. 'I don't know about you, but for all Roth's speechifying about how the place isn't a prison, he struck me as someone who's pretty intent on controlling people's lives . . . and she seems to do pretty much as she likes.'

'I suppose that's because of Michael. Gives her special status.' Ballard gave him a meaningful look.

'Quite. Mother of the Deity, and all that. So she didn't go back to the Foundation, but went straight from London to Tynan's place?'

'That's what he said. I had a word with PC Briggs. He's been doing the bodyguarding at the Foundation, along with another chap called Jackson. The guv'nor brought them in from Sudbury.

Briggs is on the day shift, so I asked him if there'd been a sighting of Mary/Ananda – he's seen the photograph – and he said there hadn't. I got him to check up, but apparently no one's seen her since she went off. We made a search of her room this morning, too – didn't find anything significant. Precious little there at all, in fact. Briggs and Jackson are pretty fed up, by the way – said the place was creepy and they'd be bloody glad when the job was over. They're both from round here, so I suppose they must have grown up with all the ghost stories.'

'The power of suggestion,' said Stratton. 'Much like everything else about the place . . .'

'I take it,' said Ballard, with an expression of the utmost seriousness, 'that you don't believe in ghosts.'

'No. Not the sort that go bump in the night, at any rate.' Stratton finished his tea and stood up. 'We all set, then?'

'Yes. And I think it may be better,' Ballard said this casually and apparently spontaneously, but Stratton had a feeling he'd thought about it, 'if – on this occasion – you do the talking. Parsons has made enquiries at US Airbase HQ about a serviceman called Carroll, and they're going to ring back when – or if, I suppose – they turn up anything. And I'm having copies made of the photograph of Mrs Aylett for a house-to-house around Lincott – Mrs Curtin seems to think she came here by bus, so somebody might have seen her getting off it – but we haven't started yet, and I haven't released the name, so I'd say Mary/Ananda might be in for a bit of a shock.'

CHAPTER THIRTY-THREE

'You're not going to be ...' Mary/Ananda gave Stratton an up-from-under look, accompanied by a slight suggestion of trembling lower lip, 'unkind to me, are you?'

From the moment he'd seen her making her way towards him down Tynan's grand staircase, high-heeled, made-up, the curves and planes of her body swaying gently in a tight sweater and skirt, making him think of a darker version of Rita Hayworth in that film where she sang in a nightclub, Stratton had felt the woman's presence as sharply as air on a naked nerve. He could see now what Ballard had meant when he'd said it was like being seventeen again. Mary/Ananda, even at forty-odd, and with her obvious awareness of the drama she was creating, all the lip-biting and the eyelash-batting, was, quite simply, sexual dynamite, and any man who did not react to her must be made of stone.

He and Ballard were sitting opposite her on over-stuffed armchairs in one of Tynan's grandly furnished rooms, complete with a display of flintlock pistols and elaborate Moorish-looking swords, several cabinets with displays of silver-framed photographs on top and, benevolently presiding over it all from his corner, a large and smiling bronze Buddha. Tynan had wanted to remain while they conducted the interview. Fussing proprietorially over Mary/Ananda, he'd only consented to leave once she had assured him, for perhaps the tenth time, that she'd be fine. Stratton had been unable to work out, from their exchanges, whether he was worried that she might be bullied, or concerned that she might talk out of turn.

'No,' said Stratton, heavily. 'We're not going to be unkind, but we do need to ask you some questions.'

Mary/Ananda's enormous, limpid eyes widened. 'Mr Tynan said . . . you were looking for me. He said you put my picture in the papers.' She sounded gratified by this.

'Yes, we did.'

'I didn't see it.'

Despite all the glamour stuff, there was something childlike – although definitely not childish – about her, thought Stratton, but whether it was real or put on, he couldn't tell. 'You must have been hiding yourself away, if you were in London,' he said, 'because nobody seems to have seen you.'

'I didn't go out much,' she said. 'I was staying with a friend.'

'But I understand you went out to get your hair done.'

'Oh, no . . .' She gave a tinkling laugh. 'The friend I was staying with – she used to own hair salons. She did it for me at home. Do you like it?'

Ignoring this, Stratton said, 'And what's the name of this friend?'

'Mrs Astley. She lives in Wimbledon.'

'Where, exactly?'

Mary/Ananda produced an address book from her handbag and handed it over. 'You'll find it under "B" for Bettina.'

Copying it down, Stratton said, 'Wimbledon's not exactly out of the way. Surely you must have known we were looking for you?'

'No.' The eyes widened again, the expression one of total candour. 'But Mr Tynan explained about poor Jeremy.'

'You knew him well, didn't you?'

'I don't think anyone knew him well. He was terribly clever, you see. Intellectual. But . . .' she sighed. 'I don't think he was ever very happy.'

'What makes you say that?'

'Well, Mr Roth always said he thought too much. His ego . . . Think-think-think-think . . .' She made little circular motions with her hands. 'Interfering.'

'Mr Roth thought Mr Lloyd was interfering with his work?'

'Oh, no!' Again, the tinkling laugh, this time coupled with the wide-eyed candid thing. Stratton had a strong impression that that she was checking herself, as in an invisible mirror, to gauge the effect she was having. 'That wouldn't be possible. The truth cannot be affected by anything. It is . . .' she paused, frowning slightly as if trying to remember something, then said, 'immutable.'

'Mr Roth's words, I take it?'

Mary/Ananda nodded. 'He puts things so well. Much better than I could.'

'And what did you think about Mr Lloyd?'

'Oh, I agreed with Mr Roth.'

Stratton and Ballard exchanged glances. Here we go again, he thought, remembering the other students and the sheer impossibility of getting them to deviate from the Foundation's 'party line', until she suddenly giggled and said, 'I thought he was a bit . . . you know. Homosexy.'

Taking this to mean that she'd been unable to twist the man round her little finger, Stratton said, 'When did you first meet Mr Lloyd?'

Mary/Ananda looked surprised. 'At the Foundation.'

'You didn't know him before?'

She screwed up her face in puzzlement. 'No, of course not.'

The 'funny look' was, Stratton felt, genuine. The woman was

too aware of herself for it to be otherwise. 'Where were you when Mr Lloyd was killed?'

'Mr Tynan said it happened the evening we went to the cinema in Ipswich.'

'And what did you do after that?'

'We came back here.'

'So you spent the night here, did you?'

'Yes, in Michael's room. Really, Inspector . . .' another little laugh, clearly meant to indicate that his inference was absurd, 'I don't know what you must be thinking of us.'

'Michael has a room here, does he?'

'He stays here sometimes, yes.'

That would appeal to Tynan's vanity, Stratton thought. Exclusive access to the Boy Wonder. Perhaps he was thinking of writing a book along the lines of *Seven Years in Tibet* about his time as guide and companion to the young Maitreya. But Roth had said Mary/Ananda had returned to the Foundation after seeing the film, hadn't he? Which meant that he either hadn't known, or hadn't wanted to admit that he knew, that something different had happened. It certainly explained why none of the students had seen her that night, but why – assuming that Roth did know she'd come here – hadn't he said so? Aloud, he said, 'And Mr Tynan's staff will be able to confirm this, will they?'

'Of course.' Yet another laugh. 'I wasn't creeping up and down the back stairs like a thief in the night, Inspector.'

'It's important that you take this seriously, Mrs Milburn.'

'I am, Inspector. Really, I am.'

'Are you aware,' asked Stratton, 'that the body of a woman was found on the fifth of November in the woods about half a mile from here?'

'Yes, Mr Tynan told me.'

'Did he tell you that she'd been shot?'

'Yes, poor thing. But . . .' Mary/Ananda nibbled her lower lip, looking bewildered, 'I don't know anything about it. I was in London.'

'We believe,' said Stratton, 'that you knew the dead woman. Her name was Rosemary Aylett.'

CHAPTER THIRTY-FOUR

Mary/Ananda blinked at Stratton several times, into a deep silence that seemed to seal itself around the three of them like an airlock, shutting out the murmurs of the house. She looked from Stratton to Ballard and back again, several times. Trying to tell which of us will be more sympathetic, thought Stratton, gazing stonily back at her. He made sure he kept his eyes only on her face, although he was almost preternaturally aware of the rest of her body as it made small, agitated movements, offering itself – breasts, hips, legs – for his attention.

'I don't.' Mary/Ananda looked as if she were about to cry. 'I wish I could remember her, but I really can't. It doesn't seem much to ask, does it, when someone's dead, but I'm afraid ... I'm so bad with names, and ... Well, everything, really. Was it someone who came to the Foundation?'

For a moment, as she was saying this, Stratton found himself thinking that it was entirely possible she didn't remember, but then, catching a flicker of what looked a lot like calculated vagueness, he changed his mind. 'Mrs Aylett,' he said, slowly and clearly, 'is the mother of Billy, the boy you took from her in the summer of 1945. You were calling yourself Mrs Carroll at the time. We have reason to believe that she returned to Lincott this week with the intention of reclaiming her child. We also have reason to believe that that child is now called Michael, and that he is the boy you refer to as your son.'

Mary/Ananda had turned white under the carefully applied make-up. Her mouth opened and closed soundlessly several times, as though being worked by some hidden and external mechanism, and her eyes darted from Stratton to Ballard and back again.

'You're going to say it's all my fault,' she said breathlessly. 'I know you are. But it wasn't . . . I didn't . . .'

'How could it be your fault,' said Stratton, blandly, 'if you were in Wimbledon with your friend Mrs Astley?'

'I didn't mean that.' Her voice had risen a semitone. 'I meant if this Mrs . . . What was her name?'

'Mrs Aylett. Rosemary. Who gave you her son when he was eight months old.'

'Yes . . . Well, if she came back and somebody shot her by accident.'

'We don't think it was an accident, Mrs Milburn.'

'But it must have been!' Mary/Ananda sounded almost petulant.

'There's no "must" about it, I'm afraid. We're not accusing you of anything, but we'd like you to tell us about why you wanted Mrs Aylett's baby.'

'It . . .' Mary/Ananda paused and did a lot of stuff with eyes and hands, while Stratton watched, impassive. Seeing that no help was going to be forthcoming from either himself or Ballard, she said, finally, 'It's all so complicated.'

Thinking he might as well enjoy the performance – for performance it would surely be – Stratton settled back in his chair and crossed his arms. Ballard, he saw from the corner of his eye, had done likewise. 'That's all right,' he said. 'We've got plenty of time. Why don't you start at the beginning?'

'Well . . . It was all *before*, you see.'

'Before what?'

'Before I met Mr Roth. I used to do the most terrible things.' She spoke as if she were about to recount a series of girlish pranks played on school chums. 'I was always telling stories, you see. Making things up. If someone had come along and told me to stop, it would have been much better, but they didn't, you see.'

'And Mr Roth did?'

'Oh, no.' Mary/Ananda looked askance. 'I would never tell fibs to Mr Roth. He sees everything.'

'Does he indeed?'

'Everything.' She nodded emphatically.

'So you've told him all of this, have you?'

'I didn't need to. He sees right inside you.' She leant forward dramatically. 'Into your heart. I think.' her eyes widened, 'that he must know *everything*.'

'Well,' said Stratton shortly, 'we don't know everything. So perhaps you can *enlighten* us.' As he said it, he disliked himself for the scorn in his voice, knowing that it was desire – however firmly controlled – that put it there. Mary/Ananda seemed to know it, too, because she crossed her legs with an exaggerated movement that made her skirt rise a little above one knee and smoothed the material down over her thigh with a slow, deliberate gesture before speaking.

'My trouble started when I was four, you see. My mother left my father. He told me she'd gone away because I was naughty, and that if I was' – here, she put on a little girl's high voice – 'very, very good, then she'd come back. I was sent to live with my aunt and uncle. When I asked them where my mother had gone, my aunt said the same – that I must be very, very good so that she would come back. So did my uncle. I had to be especially "good" to him,' she added, sardonically. 'He said, if I was good to him in secret, she would certainly come back. So I tried to be as good as I could possibly be.' She paused, appearing to hold her breath. 'By the time I was eight, I realised she wasn't ever coming back, so there was no reason to be good. And' – here, her voice hardened into a harsh bark – 'there was no reason to believe anything anyone said, either.' She tilted her head to one side and gave Stratton a long, challenging stare. He crossed his legs, deliberately casual, and stared back, willing himself not to blink.

'For a while I thought my mother must be dead, and they hadn't wanted to tell me. Then – quite by chance, when I was about fifteen – I learnt that she had simply run away. She wasn't dead – just vanished. And she never did come back. I knew that if I told anyone about what my uncle had done, I wouldn't be believed. By that time, I'd started making things up myself, and people *did* believe them – or if they didn't, they never said as much. I thought, why I shouldn't I? Everyone else does it. I'd always liked storybooks,' she added, wistfully. 'They were full of wonderful things – magical things – and they always had a happy ending.'

She stopped again, to see how this was being received, and Stratton, who'd begun to feel sorry for her, pulled himself back abruptly and said, 'So you carried on telling lies.'

Mary/Ananda looked hurt. 'It was just for fun, really. And then all that business about the hauntings—'

'Hauntings that you invented.'

'Well, people believed me. Edward, my husband – I suppose I married him to get away from home, really – he would have believed anything I told him. And then the other people who came, and . . . Oh, it was all such a *muddle*. It was Edward who contacted the newspaper people, the book man, you know . . .'

'Maurice Hill?'

'Yes. He made his money all right, I can tell you, but we didn't get anything out of it. We never had a moment's peace.'

'Was that why you did it?' asked Stratton. 'To make money?'

Evidently realising she'd made a mistake, she forced another laugh. 'Of course not, although we were certainly not well off, and when poor Edward got ill and had to retire, it was dreadful. He was in so much pain with his arthritis, and none of the doctors could do anything.' The way she said it made it sound as if she'd consulted every medical man in the country. 'We were living in Woodbridge then, and he was bedridden. His hands were drawn up like claws, and I had to feed him and do everything for him.' She inclined her head demurely in a way that recalled to Stratton the picture of the Madonna in Roth's room at the Foundation, mimicked so exactly by Miss Kirkland.

'So you nursed him devotedly,' he said. 'While at the same time pursuing an affair with an American serviceman named Carroll.'

Mary/Ananda did some more eye-and-lip work and then, seeing she was getting nowhere, spread her hands in a gesture of helplessness. 'It was all so difficult, Inspector. Edward was so ill and the neighbours would keep spreading rumours about me—'

'Some of the ones I've talked to,' interrupted Stratton, 'seemed to think that Edward Milburn was your father, not your husband. They also thought you'd neglected him in his last days, and that you'd carried on a sexual relationship with the doctor who attended him.'

'Then you've met them!' The eyes were huge now, imploring. 'You know what they're like – horrible people, the women especially. Real cats.'

'Very possibly, but you must have done something to give them that impression, Mrs Milburn.'

'Nothing. I swear . . . I nursed Edward. I'd never have . . . It isn't true!'

'But it is true that you were having an affair with this man Carroll.'

'He was so kind to me, and it was all such a *mess*. Then Edward died. That was for the best – he was suffering so much, poor man.' She made him sound like an elderly family pet. 'I didn't know what to do, and everyone was *against* me, saying these terrible things. Michael wanted to marry me, Inspector. He was going to take me back to America with him after the war, and that poor little boy needed a mother. I'd heard about him from someone in the village – that was people talking again, saying nasty things – and I felt so sorry for him. I thought he'd end up in some awful children's home, and I suppose I felt for him because I'd been abandoned by my mother, and—'

'You took him out of the kindness of your heart?'

'Yes.' Mary/Ananda nodded, eyes brimming. 'The moment I saw him, I knew—'

'Were you married to Mr Carroll when you took Mrs Aylett's son?'

Mary/Ananda opened her mouth to answer, then paused, as if calculating something. 'We can easily check,' said Stratton, 'so you might as well tell us the truth.'

'We weren't married,' she said quietly. 'Michael had been posted to Europe – he'd asked me to marry him, of course, and it was his suggestion I use his name because of how vile everyone was being. He thought it would make things easier for me.'

'Was Mr Carroll aware that you already *had* a child, Mrs Milburn?'

'I . . . I didn't . . . I wouldn't—'

A muffled thump from outside the door made her start. 'What's that?'

'Nothing that need concern us, I don't think,' said Stratton, who thought he'd guessed. 'You were telling me about your child, Tom. Born in . . .' he flipped through his notebook. 'Hard to keep track of all these dates, isn't it? Here we are. Born the twentieth of December, 1943. Don't tell me you've forgotten about him?

Then again,' he added, 'perhaps you have forgotten, because you left him with Mr and Mrs Wheeler in – let's see – May of 1945, and never went back for him.'

Mary/Ananda looked at him as if he'd just slapped her in the face – which, he supposed, he had. 'You see, Mrs Milburn,' he continued, 'I don't think that Mr Carroll *did* ask you to marry him. I think you'd told him you were pregnant so that he would marry you when he came back, and then,' Stratton knew he was skating on the perilously thin ice of partial knowledge and conjecture, but, sensing victory, pressed on, 'when you realised that he wouldn't be back in time to get married and for you to have a convenient "miscarriage" afterwards, you realised you'd have to produce a baby from somewhere. Tom, of course, was too old for your purposes by this time, so you managed to get hold of Billy – that was the child's original name, in case you've forgotten that, too – and you thoughtfully renamed him Michael, after the man who thought he was his father. And, for some reason which we have not yet been able to establish, you and Billy – now, of course, Michael – turned up at your former home, the Old Rectory in Lincott in the early months of 1948 and were taken in by Mr Roth. That's what happened, wasn't it?'

'No!' Mary/Ananda leapt to her feet. 'It wasn't like that! None of it! I won't . . . You can't . . .' Sobbing, she fled to the door and throwing it open ran straight into the arms of Tynan, who was not only right outside but, judging by his incredulous expression, had heard every single word.

CHAPTER THIRTY-FIVE

'What the hell's going on?' Tynan's jowls were vibrating with indignation, and his face had turned an alarming shade of puce. Mary/Ananda was crying hysterically into his chest, her whole body convulsing against him. 'What have you been doing to her?'

'Just asking some questions.' Stratton and Ballard, who had risen from their armchairs, now stood on either side of the coffee table.

'You're behaving like the Gestapo.'

'I can assure you we aren't, sir. We should, by rights, have conducted this interview down at the local station,' said Stratton, 'but,' he lied, 'we elected to do it here because we thought it would be more comfortable for Mrs Milburn.'

'Comfortable! When you're accusing her of ...' He stopped, realising what he'd been about to say would be tantamount to confessing he'd eavesdropped. 'Of God knows what.' He patted the still heaving Mary/Ananda on the back and she lifted her head and gazed up at him. 'I'll get you a drink, my dear,' he said. 'It's obviously all been too much for you.' Glaring at Stratton, he deposited her on a sofa and, crossing the room to where a row of decanters stood on a large and elaborately decorated sideboard, poured a hefty measure of what Stratton assumed to be brandy into the largest balloon glass he'd ever seen.

Mary/Ananda took it in both hands – the thing was so big she could hardly have done otherwise without dropping it – and sipped delicately. Stratton saw that, despite the storm of tears, her eyes looked only slightly pink. Catching a tiny chinking noise, he realised that despite the blaze in the vast, carved fireplace her teeth were chattering. Shock, thought Stratton – and it was clear that, for all his bluster and indignation, Tynan, too, was shocked. As the novelist sat down beside her and placed a thick tweed arm protectively around her slender shoulders, Stratton thought, you didn't know about any of this, did you, Sunny Jim?

By mutual unspoken consent, Stratton and Ballard resumed their seats. Tynan, looking as though he would dearly have liked not only to throw them out but to set the dogs on them, said, 'You're not thinking of continuing this interrogation, are you?'

'I'm afraid we are, sir.'

'But it's all nonsense!' Dropping the pretence that he hadn't been listening, Tynan said, 'All this business about having children and leaving them and getting them from people – it's rubbish, plain and simple, and, what's more, it's slander.'

'You heard what Mrs Milburn's been saying, sir.'

'Because you bullied her into it. It can't be true, it's just malicious claptrap, and I'm not having it.'

'I'm afraid it isn't claptrap,' said Stratton, 'malicious or otherwise.'

'Of course it is!' He gave Mary/Ananda's shoulder a comforting squeeze. 'There isn't a word of truth in it, is there?'

Mary/Ananda stared straight ahead of her, wearing an expression Stratton had seen a thousand times in the interview rooms at West End Central – that of a person who knows that her past, like an avalanche, has not only caught up with her, but is about to overtake her.

Gently, Tynan took her chin in his hand and turned her face to his. 'Ananda? Tell me it isn't true, my dear.'

Mary/Ananda said nothing. Tynan may not have been as familiar with the expression on her face as Stratton was, but he understood what it meant, all right. Withdrawing his arm, he flopped back on the sofa, defeated.

'As I was saying,' continued Stratton, 'we do have some more questions for Mrs Milburn, although,' he looked at Mary/Ananda, 'strictly speaking, I suppose I really ought to be addressing you as Mrs Carroll. You did marry him at some stage, I take it?'

'Now, wait a minute—' began Tynan, but Mary/Ananda cut across him.

'No,' she said in a small, clear voice. 'We were never married. Michael was killed in a car accident in Berlin after the war ended. I didn't hear about it for several months afterwards.'

The incomprehension on Tynan's face confirmed Stratton's view that all of this was news to him. Rallying, he said, 'If you're going to carry on with this, I'm staying here. And if there's any more of this sort of bullying and accusation, I shall report you to your superiors.'

It was an empty threat, and the novelist knew it. 'Very well, sir.' Stratton spoke with exaggerated courtesy. 'By all means stay, if you'd like – provided, of course,' he turned to Mary/Ananda, 'that Mrs Milburn agrees.'

She was staring at him with – for the first time, he thought – real fear in her eyes. She knows Tynan was listening, thought Stratton, and that there's more to come out that she doesn't want him to know. She was already imagining the questions afterwards, from Tynan and from Roth, and what they might mean for her future at the Foundation, and Billy/Michael's. Evidently realising that Tynan was prepared to stand, or rather, sit, his ground, and that if ejected he'd only go as far as the other side of the door anyway, she closed her eyes tightly for a moment, opened them again, and said, 'Yes.'

'Very well,' said Stratton. 'I assume, Mrs Milburn, that you are already aware of this, but, for the record, Rosemary Aylett's son Billy, who was born on the twenty-first of December 1944, is the illegitimate child of a American serviceman named . . .' he paused to consult his notebook, 'Patrick Brennan. When Mrs Aylett's husband was demobbed and discovered that there was, so to speak, a cuckoo in the nest, he made it a condition of the marriage continuing that she give the child away, which she duly did – to you, Mrs Milburn.'

Mary/Ananda, who now seemed to be clinging to the brandy glass for dear life, nodded dumbly, her head jerking up and down with exaggerated movements. Beside her, Tynan had withdrawn his arm and was now sitting hunched forward, pink forehead corrugated in a deep frown. He opened his mouth to speak, hesitated, and then closed it again when Stratton held up a warning hand.

'Why did you go back to the Old Rectory, Mrs Milburn?'

Mary/Ananda looked wildly about the room as if some answer might be hidden amongst the antique weapons and expensive *objects d'art*, then said, 'I hardly know. I suppose because it was my old home, and I had some idea . . . Mr Roth was so kind to me. He said I was meant to return, so I knew it was right, that we were in the right place . . .'

'But you didn't know that when you went there, did you? You just said you didn't know what you were doing. Did you even know about Mr Roth and the Foundation?'

'Someone had told me. Someone I met in London.'

'Who?'

'I can't remember his name, but he told me about the Foundation and then he said how much Mr Roth had helped him, so I thought . . . I . . .'

'You thought you'd see if Mr Roth could help you, too?'

'Yes.' Mary/Ananda looked relieved. 'Yes, I'd had a sort of break-down after I discovered Michael had died – I'd had months of not knowing, not hearing from him, and . . . I was so confused. I didn't really know what I was doing.'

'But you told us that Michael Carroll died "after the war ended" and you didn't discover that until some months later – so that would have been when, exactly?'

'I can't really remember . . . It was all so dreadful . . .'

Stratton noticed that Tynan had rearranged his position, leaning back now and inclined slightly away from Mary/Ananda, resting his elbow on the arm of the sofa. Leaning forward himself, elbows on knees, he looked intently into her face. 'Try.'

Mary/Ananda stared into the middle distance for a moment, then said, 'It's no good . . .'

You didn't give a damn about Michael Carroll, thought Stratton. If anyone had asked him the date of Jenny's death, he wouldn't have hesitated for even a second.

'I think,' she said, after a pause, 'that it was near the end of the year. I found out from another man who'd been on the same base. It was winter time – very cold.'

'So, that would be November or December of 1945?'

'About that time, yes.'

'And you had a nervous breakdown which lasted until the beginning of 1948? That's a pretty long time, Mrs Milburn.'

'Well . . .' Mary/Ananda hesitated, chewing her lip. 'I was all right at first, I think, but then with the baby and everything, it all got too much.'

'And where were you living at this time?'

'In London. A rented room.'

'And you met someone who told you about Mr Roth and you decided to come to the Foundation.'

'Yes, that's what happened.'

Tynan was now staring at her with undisguised hostility, nostrils flared and mouth slightly open, his lower teeth on view. Stratton could imagine what was going through his mind – the Maitreya was an Irish-American soldier's bastard, given to Mary/Ananda by his mother in order to placate her husband. Not exactly the nativity scene you imagined, was it, chum?

'Did anyone at the Foundation know that Billy – or rather Michael – wasn't your son, Mrs Milburn?'

Mary/Ananda shook her head.

'Not even Mr Roth?'

'No.' The word, whispered into her brandy, was barely audible. Tynan looked as if he wanted to grab the glass from her and dash the contents into her face.

'Did anyone else know? Apart from Mrs Aylett and her family, I mean.'

'No. I never told anybody.'

'The reason Mrs Aylett was on her way to the Foundation when she was killed was that someone had sent her an anonymous letter telling her that her son was there. Do you have any idea who that could have been?'

'No! I promise, I . . .' Tailing off, Mary/Ananda turned to appeal to Tynan, and recoiling at the look on his face, seemed to shrink into herself.

Ballard, who'd had been so still throughout this that Stratton had almost forgotten he was there, cleared his throat. 'Do you still have Billy's birth certificate? Mrs Aylett's sister told us it had been given to you.'

'Yes. I keep it in one of my suitcases. I've thought for ages that I ought to get rid of it – burn it or something – but I never got round to doing it. So many people about . . . To be honest, I'd rather forgotten about it. I suppose it must be still there.'

'Where do you keep the suitcase?' asked Ballard.

'That one's in my room at the Rectory.'

'That would be the one on top of the wardrobe, would it?'

Mary/Ananda stared at him. 'How do you know?'

'We searched your room this morning, Mrs Milburn. The suit-case was empty.'

'Well, you wouldn't see it if you just opened it up. I made a little cut in the lining and put it in and stitched it up again afterwards.'

'I think,' Ballard looked at Stratton, 'that we ought to see if the certificate is still there. I could ask PC Jackson to take a look.'

'Yes. Mr Tynan, do you mind if we use your telephone?'

'Of course.' Tynan rose, his sagging shoulders a definite contrast to his earlier demeanour.

'No need, sir.' Ballard put out a restraining hand. 'I know where it is. I took a call from the local station the last time I was here.'

'So you did.' Instead of sitting down, Tynan went over to the sideboard and poured himself a large measure of something golden-brown and expensive-looking, returning the decanter to the silver tray with a unsteady clang. He didn't offer Stratton anything – not that he could have accepted but it would, he thought, have been nice to be *asked*. Instead, Tynan took a large swig, bringing the glass to his mouth with an urgency that made Stratton think it was taking him quite a bit of willpower not to down the thing in one. He didn't return to his place on the sofa but instead, keeping his face averted from Mary/Ananda, slouched up and down in front of the fire, head lowered, like some huge animal trapped in a cage.

When Stratton turned back to Mary/Ananda, he saw she'd put her glass down on the coffee table and was picking at an invis-ible spot of lint on her jumper. Catching his eye, she arched her back very slightly, accentuating her breasts. A reflex, he thought, nothing more – the assured sexiness was gone, leaving in its wake a distinct and ugly twang of desperation. He, too, averted his face and in the lengthening silence wandered over to one of the cabinets and began examining the photographs propped on the top. A photograph of Tynan with Winston Churchill stood in pride of place, flanked by pictures of the novelist, cigar in hand, in the company of dinner-suited men with the assured expressions of the rich and powerful; Tynan with his arm round a pretty actress whose name Stratton couldn't remember, surrounded by the debris of an expensive meal; Tynan leaning against a Bentley, with Stewart Granger grinning back at him from the other side of the bonnet; Tynan alone at his desk, resplendent in a velvet smoking jacket ... On one side of this group, placed slightly apart, was a picture of a diminutive, haughty-looking woman in a hunting outfit, perched on top of an equally haughty-looking black horse. Stratton wondered if she was Tynan's wife, the Honourable Somebody-or-other, who according to Diana had died about six months previously. What had she made of the Foundation, Stratton wondered, idly. Had she been an initiate, too?

Standing alone on a cabinet a couple of feet away was a photograph of Tynan standing next to Roth and Miss Kirkland in front of Eros in Piccadilly. There were Christmas decorations in the shop windows behind the statue, and all three were clad in heavy winter coats. Both men were looking directly into the camera with the graciously benevolent smiles of visiting royalty, but Miss Kirkland was gazing up at Roth with what could only be described as adoration. When Stratton picked up the photograph for a closer look he saw, to the left of the statue, the end of a banner which had obviously been strung across the front of a building. The thick band of cloth had sagged slightly, but he was able to make out the words '-EST OF 1947!'

Interesting, he thought. When they'd interviewed Miss Kirkland, she'd told them she'd arrived at the Foundation *after* Mary/Ananda, who, according to Tynan, had gone there in 1948. What she hadn't said was that she'd known Roth before that – and quite well, judging by the photograph. Tynan had called Mary/Ananda Roth's 'right-hand woman' – which was exactly Miss Kirkland's position in the photograph. Had she, too, felt supplanted?

CHAPTER THIRTY-SIX

After some minutes, during which the silence seemed to open as wide as a chasm, Ballard put his head round the door and beckoned Stratton outside. As they crossed the grand and now dimly lit hall, Ballard shook his head and, when they'd reached a safe distance from the room, said, 'PC Jackson says it's gone, sir. And it was all stitched up again. Very neat, he said, both times. Blink and you'd miss it – which we did, of course.'

'Blow that,' murmured Stratton. 'It was your idea – well done.'

'Think Lloyd took it?'

'Him or one of the others, having a snoop around. Whatever they say or don't say, I'm not sure Mrs Milburn is all that popular at the Foundation. Not with the women, anyway, at least, not judging by what I saw of Miss Kirkland's reaction when she was mentioned – and presumably not with Lloyd, either, if he thought that her son was taking his place as favourite.'

'Do you think we should tell her and Tynan?'

'I don't see why not,' said Stratton. 'I mean, it's all got to come out. Whoever took it must have told Mrs Aylett where her son was – or told someone else who told Mrs Aylett, so either way ... don't you think?'

'I agree.'

'Here we go, then.'

They entered the room to find Mary/Ananda still on the sofa, nose buried in a handkerchief, and Tynan staring into the fireplace, jaw clenched, gripping his glass with a white-knuckled hand. Neither turned to look at them, and Stratton had the impression that they had not spoken to each other in his absence.

'Well,' he said, making no move to sit down, 'it's gone. Do you – either of you – have any idea who took it?'

Mary/Ananda raised her head and turned to glare at them with reddened eyes. 'It was Jeremy,' she said. 'He never liked me, or Michael. He was jealous. But I didn't kill him.'

'So you say,' said Stratton. 'Any ideas, Mr Tynan?'

As Tynan turned, Stratton saw that the man's normally ruddy face was the colour of lemonade. He's not just angry and puzzled, thought Stratton – he's worried. Very worried, by the looks of it.

Tynan gave him a weary shake of the head. 'If what she' – he indicated Mary/Ananda with a quick gesture of disgust, as if though she'd been a dog turd in the middle of one of his fine rugs – 'what she said about Lloyd taking the birth certificate was correct, and his death was connected with it, then I can assure you that both of us were at the cinema, and that we returned here afterwards. My staff will be able to confirm it.'

'We'll be asking them to do that, sir. And you're quite sure, are you, that none of your guns are missing?'

'We've been through that,' said Tynan impatiently. 'They're all here.'

'Good. Just one further question – for you, Mrs Milburn.' Mary/Ananda looked up at him warily. 'When you first arrived at the Foundation, in 1948, was Miss Kirkland already there?'

'Yes.' Puzzlement mingled with relief. 'Yes, she was.'

'Thank you. Well, I think that's all for the time being.' He glanced at Ballard, who nodded in confirmation. 'We'll be taking our leave now, but I must ask you – both of you – not to go anywhere. I presume, Mr Tynan, that Mrs Milburn can stay here?'

Tynan stared at him for a moment as if he'd made some outlandish and revolting request before giving a grunt of assent, and beginning to move towards the door.

'No need,' said Stratton. 'We can see ourselves out. Goodnight, and thank you both for your cooperation.'

'Blimey,' said Ballard, when they were in the car and heading back towards the village, 'they're going to have a lot to talk about, aren't they?'

'You bet. Do you think he was in love with her?'

'Well, if he was, I'm pretty sure he isn't now. You saw the way he was looking at her when we left.'

They passed beneath the magnificent archway, the moonlight shining on the fixed-back wrought-iron gates turning the spikes to a mixture of mercury and soot, and turned into the lane.

'Tynan's worried,' said Ballard. 'Not surprising, I suppose, given what he's just heard. Couldn't believe it, could he?'

'I think a lot of them do take the business about Michael pretty seriously,' said Stratton, remembering Miss Kirkland's reaction to his flippant remark about immaculate conception. 'But I'm sure,' he added, 'that they'll find a way round it. That's the thing with religions and what not,' he added thoughtfully, 'you can't reason somebody *out* of something they haven't been reasoned *into* in the first place.'

'I suppose not. But Tynan wasn't just worried, he was puzzled as well – it was written all over his face. Especially when Mary/ Ananda was talking about after the war – the nervous breakdown and coming to the Foundation.'

'Well, it was new to him, wasn't it? And he's a boy who likes to think he's got all the answers, just like Roth.'

'I did think there was something fishy about those dates,

though. That long gap before she came to the Foundation, when she said she had a nervous breakdown. I don't think we got the real story.'

Stratton snorted. 'She was probably living with some man who discovered what she was really like and threw her over, and she didn't want to tell us in front of Tynan. Anyway, it's not our problem.'

'Think she killed her husband? A pillow over the face, if he wasn't in a state to fight back . . . Easily done.'

'Wouldn't surprise me, but I don't see what we can do about it now. We've got enough on our plate with Lloyd and Mrs Aylett. I'll get onto Grove tomorrow, ask him to interview the Astley woman at Wimbledon and see if Mary/Ananda was where she said she was, and we'd better organise another search of Lloyd's belongings – make sure that birth certificate wasn't slipped inside a book or something.'

'Meanwhile,' said Ballard, 'we'll have to interview the whole bally lot of them again. I was thinking we should start with the students first, without mentioning the significance of the birth certificate – at least initially – and see if anyone gives anything away. After that, we can confront Roth with the whole shooting match, as it were.'

'Good idea. I have to say I'll be very interested to hear what Mr Roth has to say for himself.'

'Me, too. What was that about Miss Kirkland, by the way?'

Stratton explained about the photograph on Tynan's cabinet.

'Interesting,' said Ballard. 'I wonder why she lied.'

'I don't know,' said Stratton, 'but I *do* know she's not too keen on Mary/Ananda. I saw it when Roth was talking about her.'

'Mary/Ananda didn't mention her, though, did she? When you asked who might have taken the certificate.'

'No, but something tells me she doesn't worry too much about what other women think of her.'

'You might be right, at that. She's quite something, isn't she, our Mrs Milburn?'

'You can say that again. Easy to see how she could wind anyone – well, any *man* – around her little finger in no time.' He'd hoped to avoid any discussion of Mary/Ananda. The mixture of arousal and revulsion he'd felt in her presence didn't bear thinking about, let alone articulating.

'She's very odd, though, isn't she?'

'Odd how?' asked Stratton, cautiously.

'Well, she seems to be a mixture of very ruthless and manipulative – the sexy stuff, I mean – and completely off her rocker. If you want the truth, I felt pretty uncomfortable in there.'

'Yes,' said Stratton, 'I know what you mean. Do you fancy a drink? It's nearly closing time, but I'm sure Mr Denton won't mind.'

Ballard held his watch up to the window and squinted at it. 'Better not. Pauline . . . Don't want to, you know . . . But if you wouldn't mind running me home . . .'

'Of course not.'

Turning the car round after he'd dropped Ballard off outside his house, Stratton felt relieved. He knew what Ballard meant about uncomfortable, all right. The whole business had been bloody unsettling, and he could definitely do with a bit of time by himself.

He let himself into the pub with keys provided earlier by George Denton. Hearing 'Arseholes are cheap today, cheaper than yesterday,' sung to an opera tune he recognised from the wireless, with plenty of accompanying bangs and thumps, he concluded that the landlord, having just called time, was now tidying up in the bar. Doubting he'd be able to get to sleep anytime soon and definitely in need of diversion, however gloomy, he poked his head round the door and asked if he could borrow a newspaper.

'There you go.' Denton, who'd been rearranging the chairs in the snug with the dramatic violence of a lion-tamer, ambled over to the bar and produced a battered copy of the *Mirror* from somewhere underneath it. 'Afraid it's yesterday's. Fancy a pint to go with it? Don't mind my saying, but you look as if you could do with one. Take it up with you if you like.'

Stratton settled himself as comfortably as he could in the doll-sized, chintz-covered armchair in the small bedroom beneath the eaves. Placing both pint and ashtray within easy reach, he lit a cigarette and began reading the paper with fierce concentration.

ISMAILA FALLS: ALL-ALONG-CANAL RACE – AND THEN IT'S CEASEFIRE AT MIDNIGHT was the headline, with the triumphant tone of this first item – *Allies have fulfilled their mission, says French communiqué* – tempered halfway down by the heading, in smaller type, *Nasser calls in tanks* and some stuff about the first British casualties to be evacuated from the battle zone. At least, thought Stratton, wondering what Pete was doing and if he was all right, they were talking about casualties and not fatalities, which was something to be grateful for. In his mind's eye he saw the photograph of his son, proud in his new uniform, that stood on the mantelpiece at home. Millions of people had photographs like that, above the fire, except that Pete was – for the present, at any rate – still alive, and the vast majority of those sons, and husbands, and fathers, were dead. Was that photograph going to be all he was left with? That and a couple of snaps in the album, Pete grinning with his pals, mugs of tea in one hand and thumbs up for the camera in the other, looking out eternally from November 1956?

Remembering his last chat with his son made Stratton think of something he'd neglected: Reg. He'd not troubled to find out if there was anything wrong with him – because Pete had definitely been right, and Reg was looking under the weather. Still, nothing he could do about it right now, so . . .

Turning back to the paper, he thumbed through the rest and read items headed, *Garages will 'ration' petrol – supplies only for essential users; Women with rifles help in Hungary's last-ditch fight*, which was accompanied by a murky photograph of housewives with guns facing down a Russian tank amidst the ruins of Budapest, and then a couple of paragraphs about how Eisenhower was beating Adlai Stevenson in the US presidential election. Presumably, he thought, the people at the Foundation didn't take newspapers. He didn't recall seeing any there, or, for that matter, any wireless or television. This, he thought, was all of a piece with their notion of retreat from the modern world. Apart from seeing the expression on Roth's face when he told him about Michael, he wasn't looking forward to going there tomorrow. Christ, he thought suddenly, one of us is going to have to tell the boy. He hadn't thought of that before – too much else going on – and nor, he was pretty sure, had Ballard. Stratton groaned and reached for his beer. Having to tell a child that its mother wasn't its mother was bad enough, but this . . . 'Sorry, kid,' Stratton murmured, 'but you're not the Son of God after all.'

He threw down the paper, wishing he'd brought along his book. He wasn't a great reader of fiction, but he'd been enjoying *Lucky Jim*, borrowed from Don. Not that he knew anything about universities, but it was funny and he could sympathise with the bloke's attitude to life – getting drunk, making faces and the rest. Besides, it was a nice change from books about aristocratic types with superior sensibilities and grand passions and all the rest of it. *Lucky Jim* would have kept his mind off things, all right, or if he'd had some jazz to listen to . . . Anything really, to block out the barrage of thoughts and emotions that assailed his tired mind. Pete, Reg, Michael, Ananda, Tynan, Roth . . . Not to mention the fact that Diana would be here tomorrow night, waiting for him at her friend's cottage in the village of Wherever-it-was.

'Oh, hell.' Feeling too weary and dispirited to undress, he drained his pint and stubbed out his fag before wrenching off his shoes and tie, lying down full length on the bed and closing his eyes. After a while, he drifted into sleep. He dreamt that Diana was there on the bed, and that he was making love to her, and she was responding, and it was all as it should be, but when she propped herself up on one elbow and looked down at him, she'd changed into Mary/Ananda, and then she was pulling something soft and heavy over his face, so that he couldn't breathe ... He awoke, gasping, at a quarter-past three, to find that the light was still on and he'd somehow managed to pull the eiderdown over his top half, so that it had tangled around his head and neck. He clawed himself free and sat up, sweaty and shivering at the same time.

He undressed quickly, tearing at his clothes as if they were contaminated, trying to distance himself from what had just happened in his unconscious with the respectable safety of pyjamas. He stood for a moment, staring at the treacherous bed, before flinging open the casement window and thrusting his head out, hoping that the cold night air might blow away the ineffable compound of shame and failure, coupled with a sudden, and all the more powerful for being utterly illogical, wave of fear about the future.

CHAPTER THIRTY-SEVEN

After a long telephone call to West End Central, followed by several telegrams which were taken down with agonising slowness by PC Harwood, Stratton arrived at the Foundation to find Ballard standing on the porch, looking irritable and weary. 'You look like I feel,' he said. 'How's it going?'

'It's not. I've got three men searching the place – my guv'nor organised a warrant first thing and sent them over with it – but so far they've come up with bugger all. Nobody I've spoken to seems to have a clue about a birth certificate taken from Mary/Ananda's room, and Parsons isn't getting anywhere either.'

'Genuine, do you think?'

'Everyone I've spoken to so far, yes, and Parsons agrees with me. Did you talk to Grove?'

'Yes, and DCI Lamb. They've got all the information, and they're going to go through all of Lloyd's belongings with a tooth-comb. Grove's on his way to Wimbledon to talk to Mrs Astley. How far have you got?'

'Five to go, including Miss Kirkland, and then there's Roth. And the boy, of course. I'm not looking forward to *that* at all.'

'Me neither,' said Stratton, who, after waking from his dream, had spent a fair proportion of his sleepless hours dreading it. 'He is here, I take it?'

'Yes, I checked with Miss Kirkland when we arrived. I suppose we do have to tell him, do we? I mean, there's no getting round it?'

'I've been thinking about that, and I don't see how. It'll all have to come out in the end, and if we don't tell him now, he'll only get some mumbo-jumbo version of the story from Roth, and that'll only make it worse for him. The poor little sod's going to be confused enough as it is.'

Ballard, who'd been staring intently at an apparently feature-less patch of gravel during this, raised his head and said, 'You're right, of course. But at least he's got somewhere to go to.'

'Mrs Curtin, you mean?'

'Yes, although . . .' Ballard shook his head. 'God, I don't envy whoever gets the job of sorting out all that. Incidentally, hadn't we better get a policewoman up here?'

'Definitely,' said Stratton.

'I'll get Parsons to organise someone. You know what really browns me off,' Ballard added, sotto voce, as they went into the house, 'is that under all the pretence of being helpful – we've been offered three cups of tea in the last half-hour – what this lot are really saying is "Fuck you, Jack, we're all right. We've got the answer to life itself and your petty concerns don't matter."'

'We'll see about that,' said Stratton, grimly.

Inside the large hall, the air had the same eerie stillness that Stratton had noticed before, with no sound from anywhere. At first he thought the place was empty, but then he spotted a man kneeling behind one of the chairs, mouth rigid and eyes narrowed in concentration, piling logs into a basket by the grate with as much delicacy and precision as if they had been live hand grenades.

Quelling a surprisingly strong urge to jump up and down and shout 'Boo!', Stratton murmured, 'Talked to him, have you?'

'Yes.' Ballard jerked his head towards one of the doors. 'We're down the corridor, same as before.'

As he opened the door, Stratton saw that, as before, the earnest young chap was positioned outside the door of the room designated for their use. Bolt upright and staring straight ahead, he didn't turn to look at them as they came towards him, or even when Stratton stopped within a couple of feet of his chair. 'I'm afraid we'll have to ask you to move, sir.'

The man turned to them, his face pleasant, but firm. 'I must stay here,' he said. 'I am on duty.'

Stratton leant forward and put one foot on the crossbar on the side of the chair. 'So are we, sir,' he said quietly. 'Hop it.'

The man moved slightly away from Stratton's upraised knee, but his expression remained unaltered. 'I am here should you need—'

'We shan't need anything.' Stratton smiled, baring his teeth. 'We're happy all by ourselves.' He gave the chair a shove with his foot. 'On your way.'

Rising with as much dignity as he could muster, the man walked slowly away down the long corridor, stopping to glance back at the corner and, finding the pair of them still staring at him, vanished as abruptly as if he had been yanked by a rope.

The little room was arranged just as before, with a table, chairs, and a delicate vase bearing a spray of berried ivy and late autumn leaves. Parsons had just finished talking to the clumsy, moon-faced woman Stratton remembered from their first round of interviews, who'd spilt the tea on his crotch. Skirting them carefully, as if on the other side of an invisible cordon, she scurried off, leaving the policeman shaking his head. 'Hopeless,' he said. 'Not a dicky bird.'

'We'll take it from here,' said Ballard, pulling a sheet of paper out of his pocket. 'I've crossed off all the ones we've spoken to, so if you can find this lot – we'll have Miss Kirkland at the end, and Mr Roth last – and we're going to need a policewoman up here as soon as you can.'

'Right you are, sir.'

Parsons departed, returning a couple of minutes later with Mr Longley, who Stratton remembered as the chap who'd told them how Roth had cured his drink problem. He obviously had no clue about the birth certificate, and neither did Miss Mills, who followed him, or Mrs Welch. Stratton was hoping that Miss Banting, who arrived in the same arty, wooden-beaded get-up as last time, might prove more forthcoming, but after several questions both men decided that her puzzlement was genuine and allowed her to rattle off down the corridor.

As instructed, Parsons brought Miss Kirkland in last. The joyful smile, Stratton thought, had a slightly fixed quality about it this time. Asked to sit down, she perched herself on the extreme edge of one of the chairs, hands palm down on either side of her thighs and arms braced as if she were intending to launch herself from the room at the earliest possible opportunity.

'As you may be aware,' said Stratton, the formalities being concluded, 'we have been asking questions about an item which went missing from Mrs Milburn's room.'

'Then I am unable to help you. I know nothing about it.'

'Do you know what "it" is?'

'I gather,' Miss Kirkland said stiffly, 'that you have been asking about a birth certificate, but I am afraid, gentlemen, that I cannot shed any light upon the matter.'

Despite her precision of hair and dress she seemed, compared to the last time Stratton had seen her, to be somehow ragged about the edges, and he could see dark troughs of exhaustion beneath her eyes. 'Have you ever been in Mrs Milburn's room while she's been away?' he asked.

'Certainly not.' Miss Kirkland drew herself up. 'I do not make a practice of snooping.'

'No? But you didn't like her, did you?'

'I . . .' A deep blush suffused Miss Kirkland's pale face. 'I tried not to show it – not to think it. I knew it was wrong, what I was feeling, that it was just an idea – something I had to get rid of . . . give up.'

'Pretty difficult, I'd have thought,' said Stratton, 'to make yourself like somebody.'

'It wasn't easy. Quite apart from anything, it was the way she behaved with the men – she caused a lot of disturbance.' Remembering something he'd read somewhere – H.G. Wells, he thought – about moral indignation often being jealousy with a halo, Stratton imagined Miss Kirkland's initial assessment of Ananda's face and the contours of her body, and her dawning realisation that her own devotion would not, by itself, be enough to keep her in pole position. Miss Kirkland was staring down her tweed-covered knees. 'Sometimes . . .' her voice had dropped to a whisper, 'it was agonising.'

'You told us,' said Stratton, 'that you arrived at the Foundation *after* Mrs Milburn, but that wasn't true, was it?'

Another whisper. 'No.'

'You'd known Mr Roth for some time before she came along, hadn't you?'

'Yes. I met him in 1946. I was in London, working for the civil service, and I saw an advertisement for a talk he was giving and went along. And it was quite marvellous.' Miss Kirkland may have been tired, but as she said this her face was radiant.

'So,' said Stratton, 'you came here when?'

'I was here right from the beginning. The place was such a mess, you wouldn't believe . . . *So* much work to do.'

'And you looked after Mr Roth?'

'Yes. It was my particular duty at that time.'

'Until Mrs Milburn came.'

'Yes. Mr Roth said I was needed to look after the ladies here. He said they needed particular guidance, and that I could supply it. That was to be my work.'

'But you resented Mrs Milburn for supplanting you?'

'That wasn't important,' said Miss Kirkland, sharply. 'Only the Foundation is important. The work. The rest is,' she lifted a hand from the seat of the chair and waved it dismissively, 'irrelevant.'

'But all the same, you resented Mrs Milburn,' said Stratton, flatly. 'Just as Mr Lloyd must have resented Michael.'

'He never said so.'

'But he did, didn't he? The pair of you,' here, he saw her flinch at the bracketing, 'felt pushed out.'

'What are you suggesting, Inspector?' The voice was still fluting and the tones well-modulated, but the blush, Stratton saw, had concentrated into a hard spot of colour on each cheek.

'I wasn't suggesting anything,' he said mildly, 'but I am wondering why you lied to us. You may, of course, have decided it was your business to find out a bit more about Mrs Milburn, who she was, where she came from, and the . . . *provenance*, shall we say, of her son Michael?'

'I did no such thing. There was – and *is* – no reason for me to question Mr Roth's teaching on that matter, whatever I may think about his mother.'

No pretence now, Stratton noted, that she'd come to terms with her feelings towards Mary/Ananda. 'Actually,' he said, leaning forward and resting his arms on the table, 'there was a reason to question it, although perhaps – and I'm prepared to give you the benefit of the doubt, at least for the moment – you did not know it. Michael is not Mrs Milburn's son, and he certainly isn't the product of immaculate conception.'

Stratton wasn't sure if he'd expected Miss Kirkland to be shocked by this, but if she was she gave no sign of it. He gave her a brief summary of what they'd discovered about Michael's parentage and the reasons that Mary/Ananda had 'adopted' him, then said, 'The woman whose body was found in the woods is Rosemary Aylett, Michael's real mother. She'd received an anonymous note from someone in London to say that the boy was here at the Foundation, along with a photograph of Michael – so there was no chance of any mistake about *which* boy – and she was on her way to claim him back when she was killed. That is the reason we're asking about the birth certificate. It's Michael's – or, to use his real name, Billy's – and when we interviewed Mrs Milburn last night she told us she'd hidden it in a suitcase in her room. It isn't there now, and we think that somebody here took it and tracked down Mrs Aylett, in order to make trouble for the Foundation – and that somebody else,' he gave her a penetrating stare, 'apprehended her and killed her before she could turn up and put the cat amongst the pigeons by claiming her son. What do you have to say to that?'

'Well . . .' Miss Kirkland's beam was now so set that it looked as if some unlikely form of muscular paralysis had crept up on her. 'Who Michael is is not important, Inspector. What matters is *what* he is.'

Interesting, thought Stratton. She didn't deny anything he'd said, or attempt to argue with it. A mental adjustment was being – or had already been? – made. The recipe was being altered retrospectively, but the outcome, and its utter desirability – remained the same. 'You mean,' he said, 'that the whole business about him being the Son of God was just window dressing?'

The corners of Miss Kirkland's mouth turned slightly upwards in the superior and impenetrable smile of *one who knows*. 'Things can be understood on different levels, Inspector. Not all knowledge is acquired through facts, you know.'

'I can assure you that ours is.' Stratton couldn't stop himself.

'Some knowledge,' Miss Kirkland continued as if he hadn't

spoken, 'comes direct from the heart. And the scriptures have many levels of meaning, you know – from the coarsest to the finest and most subtle.'

'But we're not talking about something written hundreds of years ago. We're talking about a bunch of people here and now.'

'Yes, indeed.' Miss Kirkland looked at him with compassion – the way, he imagined, that she might look at a student who wasn't 'getting it'. 'And Michael is a very special young man. He was sent to us as a . . . gift, if you like. The rest is unimportant.'

'Whoever killed Rosemary Aylett didn't think it was.'

'But you have no proof of that, do you, Inspector? And, as you said, yours is knowledge that must be acquired through facts alone.'

CHAPTER THIRTY-EIGHT

'She had you there, all right,' said Ballard, as they sat smoking, waiting for PC Parsons to find out Roth's whereabouts. 'Smart cookie, that one.'

'Bet you wouldn't dare call her that to her face.'

'Too right, I wouldn't.'

'She's right, of course,' said Stratton, ruefully. 'We don't have a shred of evidence from the scene of Rosemary Aylett's death to link it to anyone in this building – or anywhere else, for that matter.'

'Sounded like a challenge to me.'

'It did, didn't it?'

'She couldn't have actually *known* about us having no proof, though.'

'Well, if we'd had proof we'd have said so, wouldn't we? She'd probably say that was an example of knowledge coming from the heart – even though it's just common sense. Making the ordinary extraordinary, that's what they do here.'

'She was still so bloody certain, wasn't she? Even after you'd explained about the kid.'

'Yes, and a bit too calm for my liking. I'm not at all sure it was the first time she'd heard all that. I think she's already had time to come to terms with it – reconcile it with her beliefs, or make it fit in, or whatever you want to call it.'

'Do you think she killed Lloyd and Rosemary Aylett?'

'I don't know. It's possible. She said Michael's origins were unimportant, but that wouldn't stop her wanting to prevent his real mother from taking him away as she obviously considers him to be an integral part of the place.'

'She told us she was here the night Lloyd was killed.' Ballard spoke thoughtfully. 'But at that point we were asking people about where Mary/Ananda was, not where *she* was—'

'And,' Stratton interrupted, 'Grove and his lot have been going door-to-door round Soho with Mary/Ananda's photograph, not hers.'

'I wonder if she can drive,' said Ballard.

'Only one way to find out,' said Stratton.

'I know. Interview the buggers all over again tomorrow. They just quote him all the time, don't they?'

'Roth?'

'Yes. It's as if he's actually in the room, inside their heads.'

'I know. Wait till you meet him.'

Ballard grimaced. 'Christ Almighty. I think I might just start foaming at the mouth if I have to go through this all over—'

Footsteps sounded in the hall, followed by scuffling noises and a remonstrating female voice, and then the door burst open and a man appeared, pulling with him Miss Banting, who was clutching grimly onto the sleeve of his jacket. The man strode across the small room, Miss Banting still attached, and stopped a couple of inches from Stratton, who recognised him as the chap who'd been piling up the logs in the hall on his arrival. He was trembling all over – so much that, for a moment, Stratton feared he was about to fall down in some sort of fit. Then he opened his mouth and, as loudly as anyone could without actually shouting, said, 'It is not true. You are a liar, and it is not true.'

Then, shaking Miss Banting off so that she took an unsteady step backwards and landed in a chair, he turned on his heel and left the room. Miss Banting leapt up, beads clashing, to go after him, but Ballard got to the door before she did and, closing it swiftly, stationed himself in front of it and said firmly, 'I think you'd better tell us what that was about.'

Miss Banting looked wildly round the room: at Stratton, who was wiping a fleck of spittle off his cheek, at the door, still guarded by Ballard, who gave her a decisive shake of the head, and then at the window, as if hoping she might be able to climb out of it.

Stratton stuffed his handkerchief back into his pocket. 'Sit down,' he said.

Hesitantly, as though she thought he might bite her if she got too close, Miss Banting, head down, slithered into a chair, Ballard remaining behind her to block her escape route.

'Now then,' Stratton said, gently. 'Perhaps you'd like to tell us *what* isn't true?'

Miss Banting rocked backwards and forwards and twisted her head from side to side so that her beads shook. 'I don't know,' she said, miserably. 'I mean, I know *what* he said, but it doesn't . . . He's got it all wrong.'

'Got what all wrong?'

'Well, it's . . .' She emitted a sudden staccato laugh, obviously intended to signal that what she was about to say next was absurd. 'He told me he'd overheard what you were saying to Miss Kirkland—'

'How?' asked Stratton.

'He was outside the window, fetching more wood, and—'

'Wait a minute.' Stratton turned to look at the window, one casement of which was ajar. 'He must have been standing in the flowerbed.'

'Well . . .' Miss Banting flushed and twisted her head about a bit more. 'I don't know – and of course he shouldn't have been eavesdropping – but he said you said . . . something about Michael. About it not being true.'

'What isn't true?'

'That he's not the Maitreya – not Ananda's child at all, but someone else's, not even legitimate . . . all sorts of rubbish. I told him it was nonsense and that he couldn't have understood you properly, but he wouldn't see reason.' She ducked her head and began fiddling with her bracelets. Head still down, she spoke in quick jerks as if desperate to get the words out. 'It's all been so *disruptive*. To the work. Everything. We were so peaceful here, and then there was the business over Jeremy, and . . . I know you have your job to do, but why can't you leave us alone?' Emboldened, she jerked her head up and stared at him defiantly. 'People who don't understand are bound to criticise, but you come and accuse us of stealing things, of murder, even, and it's *horrible!*'

Stratton, reflecting that things were bound to get a whole lot more horrible, felt pity for the woman. 'I understand why you're upset,' he said. 'And I'm sorry about it, but, as you said, we have our job to do.'

'Yes, well . . .' Now that her distress had been acknowledged, Miss Banting, who had turned her attention back to her bracelet, seemed unnerved by her outburst. 'It's just that people are getting a bit upset about it. And of course,' here, she looked at Stratton again, this time with a placatory expression, 'I know that Mr McCardle must have made a mistake. I mean, you don't know anything about it, so why you would say . . .' She shook her head lightly, as if apologising for a child who'd made an embarrassing error.

Stratton had thought that he'd kept his expression entirely neutral throughout this speech, but he must have given something away because suddenly she was goggling at him. 'You *did* say it, didn't you?' She leapt away from the chair as if it had burst into flames, upsetting it so that it crashed sideways to the floor. 'You really did say it!'

Stratton stood up with the half-formed intention of going to calm her, but she gave a high-pitched scream and backed away from him in horror, hands out as if to ward off a demon. 'What right have you, you ignorant – you, you . . .' Gasping, she put her hands to her mouth and emitted a series of low moaning sounds, as though she were about to be sick, and then, giving Ballard a violent shove away from the door, fled from the room.

CHAPTER THIRTY-NINE

'Christ!' Ballard, who looked as shaken as Stratton felt, righted the upset chair and sat down on it, hard. 'Should I have gone after her?'

'No. You'd have made it worse.'

Ballard nodded, then fished out his cigarettes and handed one to Stratton. 'The business about Michael ... They take it literally, don't they – I mean, they think he really is ...'

'Those two certainly do,' said Stratton grimly.

'That chap – McCard or whatever his name was – I thought he was going to ... And as for *her* ...'

'The hysterics were real enough, all right.'

'Do you think – her reacting like that – was just because she realised that you *had* said it, or because she's afraid you might be right?'

'I honestly don't know. I don't suppose she does, either. Do you know,' he added, thoughtfully, 'I don't think I've ever seen the ... *force*, I suppose, of a belief, quite so clearly.'

'I know what you mean. I suppose people must have carried on like this all the time in the Middle Ages.'

'Good job we weren't there then. We'd probably have been burnt at the stake or something.'

'You don't think,' Ballard glanced towards the door, 'that they're going to form themselves into a lynch mob, do you?'

'This lot?' Stratton shook his head. 'Far too polite – at least, after the initial . . . you know. I'm betting most of them will just rearrange their ideas a bit, like Miss Kirkland.'

'All the same, it makes you think, doesn't it?'

'About what they might do to preserve all this? It does that, all right.'

'Where the bloody hell's Parsons got to, anyway? I thought he was—'

Here, a discreet knock on the door heralded not the officer, but Miss Kirkland. If she'd encountered the hysterical Miss Banting, she gave no sign of it. 'Mr Roth sent me to fetch you,' she said coolly. 'He's ready to see you now.'

'Oh, is he indeed?' Stratton had intended that Roth descend from the heights and talk to them in the same place as his students had done, but clearly the leader was having none of it. 'Where's PC Parsons?'

'Mr Roth sent him off to the kitchen for a cup of tea. I understand that the policewoman you sent for is with him.'

'Oh, really?' Stratton and Ballard exchanged glances. 'Well, we can probably spare them for twenty minutes or so. What about PC Briggs?'

'In the classroom. Michael is having his lessons.'

'Well,' murmured Ballard, as they followed the neat figure up the stairs. 'That's something to be grateful for, anyway.'

Miss Kirkland ushered Stratton and Ballard into Roth's room and, after a muttered exchange with him, withdrew. At Roth's invitation, they seated themselves, but instead of joining them he went to stand with his back to the fireplace in a manner that made Stratton think of the headmaster of a public school who'd summoned a pair of pupils to account for some misdemeanour.

Deciding that it would be childish to prolong any sort of stand-off, Stratton said, 'As I'm sure Mr Tynan has told you, the dead woman found on the edge of his land has been identified as Rosemary Aylett, and we have very good reason to believe that she is the mother of the boy Michael.'

Roth produced his cigarette case and went into the theatrical smoking routine that Stratton remembered from last time. After what he felt was a particularly over-egged production of drawing in and slow exhalation, Roth said, 'So I gather. But where he came from is of no importance.'

'It is if it was the cause of Mrs Aylett's death.'

'I meant,' said Roth, 'that it is not important in the larger scheme of things. Mrs Aylett's death is certainly . . .' he brushed some ash off the knee of his trousers, 'unfortunate.'

'Or convenient, depending on how you look at it.'

'How is it convenient?'

'Mrs Aylett can't try to claim her son back. Which would have been pretty awkward for you, wouldn't it?'

'Awkward?' Roth pronounced the word distinctly, as though it were new to him.

'Yes, awkward. Given that you've put it about that the boy was the next great spiritual leader and immaculately conceived and all the rest of it.'

'I have never made such a claim—'

'Perhaps not in so many words, but you've certainly encouraged others to think so. We've just had a pretty graphic demonstration of that.'

Roth blew out a stream of smoke and shook his head with an air of amused tolerance, much as you would at a mischievous toddler. 'Michael is very special. You cannot alter that. There was a purpose,' he continued, his voice becoming declamatory and authoritative, 'in his coming to us. The performance of any action is the work of the appropriate instrument – in this case, Ananda

– but no action is possible in the physical world. That is merely the effect, and it is the effect of an action which was complete before the effect began, and may have been completed long ago.'

'So you are saying,' said Stratton, 'that the end justifies the means, no matter who is hurt in the—'

'That woman,' Roth raised his voice, so that it became a thunderous rumble, 'abandoned her child. She gave him up to Ananda. That is the fact of the matter. Whether or not that child is Michael, is . . .' he made an open-ended gesture with his hands.

Sod this, thought Stratton. Staring straight back at Roth, he said, 'Mrs Aylett did not abandon her child. She gave him up because she had no choice in the matter.' Ignoring Roth's scornful look, he continued, 'Mrs Milburn, however, *did* abandon a child. She left her son – her own son – with some neighbours, and never went back to collect him. The family haven't heard from her since. I take it Mr Tynan informed you of that as well.'

Roth had turned his head and was staring out of the window. 'Yes,' he said, quietly now. 'He did.'

'And you knew nothing of it – of either of these things – before?'

Roth paused to inhale more smoke and blow it in the direction of the window before shaking his head.

'So,' said Stratton, 'Mrs Milburn pulled the wool over your eyes good and proper, didn't she?'

Roth turned his head. The amused tolerance gone, he now looked wooden and irritated, reminding Stratton of his brother-in-law Don when he was teased into taking part in charades at Christmas. It struck him that Roth was not a man used to engaging in dialogue with an equal. Roth's default position when challenged, Stratton felt sure, was either to laugh it off, or, when he was unable to do that, to bully and hector. Apparently realising that neither course would be appropriate now, he seemed at a loss. His eyes flicked momentarily away from Stratton towards the door, and he attempted some more theatrical smoking, but

Stratton could tell that his heart wasn't in it. When he spoke, it was with an obvious effort at moderation. 'The truth is there to be discovered, Inspector Stratton. It's often shrouded in mystery. Once we remove the shrouds, it's quite simple, even though it doesn't always seem so on the surface. I'm sure you are aware of this. After all, you are, in your own way, a seeker after truth, and – also in your own way' – his tone suggested that, as ways went, Stratton's left a lot to be desired – 'you have taught me something.'

'So you're saying you were misled?'

'That is one way of putting it, yes.'

'And you had absolutely no idea, prior to Mr Tynan's telephone call, of the existence of Mrs Aylett?'

'None.'

'Somebody had, Mr Roth. Somebody found Michael's original birth certificate in Mrs Milburn's room, took it, and contacted Mrs Aylett to tell her her son was here. Do you have any idea who that could be?'

Roth hesitated, and Stratton thought he saw the ghost of a word appear on his lips, but he did not speak. 'I am sorry, gentlemen,' he said, formally. 'I am unable to assist you.'

'Unable, or just unwilling?' snapped Stratton.

'Unable.' He ducked his head in self-deprecation – though whether real or feigned, Stratton found it impossible to tell. 'On this occasion, I am entirely at a loss. But then . . .' He smiled, sadly. 'We all must work to free ourselves from our illusions, Mr Stratton, and you have done me a great service in freeing me from one of mine. Who knows? Perhaps I shall be able to return the service.'

CHAPTER FORTY

Stratton found that he had no idea what Roth was talking about, and at this point, he didn't much care. 'Make no mistake about it, Mr Roth, two dead bodies are not an illusion. I intend to get to the bottom of this, and I shall. Now, however, I need to have a word with Michael. He needs to be told the truth about his mother – but by us, not by you.'

Roth inclined his head. 'Very well. But I should like to be present.'

'Fine,' said Stratton, giving Roth some of his own eagle-eye treatment. 'But only on condition that you keep quiet.'

'I agree. You will find Miss Kirkland waiting outside. She can bring Michael to us.'

'We have a policewoman here, and I'd like her to be present.'

'Very well. Miss Kirkland will see to it.'

Ballard went to the door, and, after a few minutes, during which Roth stared silently at the garden, and Stratton tried to quell not only his anger but a mounting anxiety about what the next ten minutes might hold, Michael appeared with Miss Kirkland behind him. They were closely followed by the police-woman, who was accompanied, to Stratton's surprise, by a subdued and rabbity-eyed Miss Banting. Miss Kirkland and Miss

Banting made to leave immediately, but Roth stopped them with a gesture, indicating that they should sit down. To Michael, he said, 'I've asked you to come here because Inspector Stratton' – he indicated Stratton with his hand – 'wants to talk to you, and I want you to listen carefully to what he has to say.'

Stratton noticed that, as on the previous occasion, Miss Kirkland, head slightly to one side, mimicked the posture of the painted Virgin on the wall, and that Miss Banting, next to her, did likewise. The effect, judging by Ballard's face, was as eerie to him as it was to Stratton, and it was added to by Michael, seated next to them, handsome and collected, remaining bolt upright with a stillness that he was sure most twelve-year-old boys couldn't have managed for even ten seconds. Apart from the crackle and hiss of the fire, the only sound and movement in the room came from Roth who, seated in the armchair beside the fire, produced a cigarette from his case, tapped it, lit it, and began going through his smoking act.

Michael's expression, though polite, was blank and incurious. Stratton began explaining, in his gentlest voice, about the death of Rosemary Aylett. Afterwards, he could remember none of the words he'd used; they'd slipped out of his head at the first opportunity, leaving his part in the proceedings a merciful blur, his clearest impression being that Michael, although he listened with calm, even kindly, courtesy, wasn't really taking any of it in. Only when he got to the bit about Ballard's visit to Mrs Curtin, and was giving a (considerably bowdlerised) version of what she'd told them about how her sister had come to give him away, as a baby, to a stranger, did Michael's expression change. The boy narrowed his eyes as if weighing up the facts and, for a horrible moment, Stratton suspected that Michael thought he'd been summoned to Roth's presence in order to pronounce judgement, like a modern-day infant Solomon.

Stratton halted his narrative. 'Do you understand what I've been telling you, Michael?'

'I understand.' Michael's judicious expression didn't alter.

'Mrs Aylett gave away her baby son – you – to a lady who Mrs Curtin identified as your mother, Ananda.' Here, a flicker of apprehension passed over the boy's face, but he did not speak. 'This happened in the summer of 1945, when you were six months old. Ananda wanted you very, very much, and she promised Mrs Aylett that she would look after you.'

Michael looked uncertainly at Roth, as if, at his instigation, Stratton was setting him some sort of test. Roth gave him an encouraging nod and then turned his head back to gaze at the burning logs in the fireplace.

'Mrs Aylett called you Billy,' Stratton continued. 'She was very sad to part with you, but she felt – and you will understand this better when you're grown up – that she didn't have any choice.'

As Michael continued to stare at him, Stratton searched his face for signs of distress, but found none. Miss Banting had begun sobbing quietly, and Miss Kirkland had her eyes half-closed, as if in a trance. The boy, however, looked as if what was being talked about had nothing to do with him.

'Are you quite sure you understand what I've been saying?' asked Stratton.

'It isn't real,' the boy said flatly.

'I'm afraid,' said Stratton, 'that it is. Of course,' he added hurriedly, 'it doesn't mean that your mother – Mrs Aylett, I mean – didn't love you. She always loved you – she was coming here, to the Foundation, because she was trying to find you. She'd been trying for many years.'

Michael frowned slightly, but continued to gaze at him, polite and unruffled. Beside him, Miss Banting continued to weep, bracelets clattering as she twisted her hands frantically in her lap.

'Be still!' Although clearly aimed at Miss Banting, Roth's

command, which cracked across the room, made them all jump. The woman's hands ceased moving as, with a palpable effort, she clenched them together. Michael, however, seemed not to have registered it, and was continuing to stare at Stratton with an unnerving detached intensity.

'None of it,' he repeated, 'is real.'

'I'm very sorry,' said Stratton, helplessly, glancing round at Ballard, who'd been standing slightly behind him, for support.

'I think,' said Ballard, coming forward to squat down beside Michael's chair and patting him on the knee, 'that it might be better if we give you a little time to think about what Inspector Stratton has said. I know it's come as a bit of a shock—'

'It hasn't,' said Michael, brushing away Ballard's hand as though he were an importunate dog. 'Because it isn't true. It *can't* be true.' Sliding off the chair, he crossed the hearthrug and placed himself directly in front of Stratton, staring up at him with his perfect blue eyes. 'You see, I'm only ten years old. Ten and three-quarters. My birthday,' he added helpfully, 'is the twenty-eighth of February, and I was born in 1946.'

There was a gasp from Miss Banting, and Stratton saw that her face was split wide in a beam of radiant joy. Miss Kirkland, beside her, had her mouth pursed and her eyes pressed tightly shut, as if trying to contain herself by physical force. He stared at the pair of them, stupefied, until a rasping cough from Roth made him turn round.

'You see, Inspector? Out of the mouths of babes . . .' He took a last, deep puff on his cigarette, then threw his head back and expelled a triumphant cloud of smoke.

'Stop playing games,' snapped Stratton, 'and tell me who his father is.'

Roth looked at him with a face of leonine impassivity, then turned to Michael. 'Who is your father?'

'I have no father,' said the child. He gazed at Stratton for a moment with an expression of pity and then, obviously feeling that the matter wasn't worth any more of his attention, put his hands in his pockets and sauntered across the room to stare out of the window.

CHAPTER FORTY-ONE

'If that's a completely different kid up there,' said Ballard, as they clattered down the stairs, causing the students gathered over tea in the hall to stare at them reproachfully, 'then what the bloody hell happened to Billy?'

'Only one way to find out,' said Stratton, whose mind was reeling. 'Better get round to Tynan's place straight away.'

'If she's still there. She must have known we'd find out sooner rather than later.'

'Well, it's our best hope.'

'Explains Tynan's puzzlement, anyway. He may not have known anything about Billy or Mrs Aylett, but he bloody well knew the dates didn't fit.'

'Doesn't explain Miss Kirkland, though,' said Stratton, as they exited the lobby and made for the car, 'unless she'd never seen that birth certificate.'

Struggling to fire the cold engine, he added, 'If she had seen it, she'd have known that the dates didn't fit, too.'

'Perhaps she didn't know what they were. I mean, whoever took it could have told her about it without mentioning any dates.'

'I'd say it's more likely,' Stratton raised his voice over the sputtering motor, 'that she found out from Roth after Tynan telephoned him last night.'

'He doesn't seem to have told any of the others, though.'

'I suppose he thought they didn't need to know,' said Stratton, crunching the gears. 'Bad for their spiritual development or something,' he added bitterly.

'Perhaps it was some sort of test of faith. I mean, Roth must have seen Miss Banting was het up when she walked into that room, so perhaps he guessed she'd found out what was going on – he knew damn well what was going to happen, and that's why he asked her to stay.'

'Wanted an audience, more like it, for his piece of theatre. Did you see that little bow he gave us as he left the room?'

'Yes, thanks. Miss Banting didn't cotton on, though, when you said about Mrs Aylett handing over Billy in the summer of 1945.'

'Probably too upset to take notice of the date. Either that or she didn't know how old Michael is. I'm no expert, but he definitely looks older than his age. Shit!' Rounding a corner, Stratton braked sharply, just in time to avoid rear-ending a herd of cows ambling across the muddy lane.

'Hardly surprising living in that place,' said Ballard, as they waited for the creatures to pass, steaming and leaving splatters of khaki-coloured dung in their wake. 'Poor little sod. Took it well though, didn't he?'

'Seemed to. God knows what he was thinking.'

'Miss K. looked pretty stunned when we left.'

'Probably all the excitement. All that stuff about Mary/Ananda must have given them a bit of a turn, but right now they're probably all congratulating themselves on how much smarter they are than us – and they're right, aren't they?'

'They obviously couldn't give a toss about what happened to Billy,' said Ballard.

'Well, to them he's just some kid, isn't he? They're only interested in Wonder Boy.'

'Who presumably *is* Mary/Ananda's son – that's backed up by what Mrs Curtin told us about thinking she was pregnant, remember? Unless she picked up some other child along the way.'

'*Don't* . . .' Stratton groaned, then struck the steering wheel with the palm of his hand. 'Christ! It's unbelievable.'

'Not to them up there, it's not.' Ballard jerked his head sideways, in the direction of the Foundation. 'I think Tynan might have been a bit worried about Billy, though. I mean, he wasn't anywhere near as sanguine as Roth, was he?'

'Probably because he still retains a few of the instincts of a normal human being,' said Stratton sardonically.

Tynan was striding towards them before they'd had a chance to get out of the car. 'I had a call from the Foundation,' he said, leaning into the driver's window, face as haggard as if someone had attached weights to it in the night. 'I thought you'd turn up – but before you ask, Ananda's gone. Took off in one of my cars first thing this morning.'

CHAPTER FORTY-TWO

'I didn't find out until later,' said Tynan. 'She didn't come down for breakfast, and one of the staff told me.'

'What time was this?' asked Stratton.

'About half past nine.'

'What about when she left?'

'They weren't sure. Someone went out and found one of the cars gone. She wasn't in her room when the girl went up this morning.'

'Didn't anybody hear the car?'

Tynan shook his head. 'The man who drives me lives over the garage, but I'd given him a few days off – a death in family – so he wasn't there.'

'What about the gates?'

'Easy enough to open them – they're not padlocked.'

'And the keys to the car – how did she get hold of those?'

'My man has his own set of keys to both cars, but there are duplicates kept in the kitchen corridor, in a box on the wall. All the keys are kept there. She would have known that – she's used the car before, taking Michael for outings and so on.'

'Why didn't you telephone the station?'

'I did, straight away. Spoke to a man called PC ... Harman? Hardman? Something like that, anyway.'

'PC Harwood?' said Ballard.

'Yes, that's it. Harwood. I gave him the model and number of the car, and he said he'd pass on the message.'

'Well, he didn't.' Turning to Ballard, Stratton said, 'That must have been just after I'd left to meet you at the Foundation.'

'Just wait till I get hold of him,' muttered Ballard, shoving the car door open.

Opening his door, Stratton said to Tynan, 'May we come in, sir? We're going to need another statement.'

When they were settled in the sumptuous room with its collection of obsolete weaponry and smiling Buddha, bronze belly glowing in the weak afternoon sun, Stratton said, 'When we were here last night, you must have realised that the child Mrs Milburn was talking about couldn't have been Michael. Why didn't you say anything?'

Tynan, slumped on the sofa, rubbed a hand over his jowls. His eyes were bloodshot and, judging by the two clumps of white bristles Stratton could see on his chin, his shaving had been perfunctory. 'Shock, I suppose. I had no idea she was capable of . . . well, of any of it. I just couldn't believe what I was hearing. It was all so incredible.' Groaning, he leant forward and put his face in his hands.

Stratton remained silent and after a moment Tynan looked up and said, 'I needed to talk to Mr Roth about it first. I didn't know what I should do.'

'So you wanted Mr Roth to tell you?'

'Yes. I didn't realise at the time, but when I spoke to him . . . Mr Roth said to do nothing. He said no action was necessary. I was relieved. I felt . . . he'd taken it out of my hands.'

'And you were happy about that?'

'Not happy, but . . .' Tynan gazed despairingly out of the window. 'It was the best way. If you come under the discipline, you must accept—'

'Accept what? That you're going to hang up your common sense on a hook by the door?'

Tynan swung his head round sharply. 'Accept the direction of a wise man. "Common sense", Inspector, is very often the reverse of what it seems. We become caught up in the illusion and we don't always see what is in front of us.'

'What is in front of you,' snapped Stratton, 'is a charge of obstructing the police in the course of their duty by withholding information, and I can assure you that *that* isn't an illusion. But right now,' he added, nodding to Ballard, who pulled a notebook and pen from his jacket, 'we'll take the necessary statements and then we'll be off.'

Tynan waited outside while his manservant and the maid gave their version of events surrounding Ananda's departure, neither of which added to what he'd already told them. When he returned, Stratton took him through a brief summary of what had happened while they'd been there the previous evening, before asking, 'And when we left?'

'She went off to bed.'

'You didn't ask her what had happened to Billy?'

'I tried, but she refused to tell me. She was furious – blazing. I've never seen her like that before. When I asked her about the boy – Billy – she slapped my face and called me a bastard. She said I hadn't supported her and she'd never trust me again. Then she ran straight up to her room – Michael's room – and locked the door. I followed her, but I didn't want to make a scene – the staff – so I left it. To be honest, I didn't want anything more to do with her. I was . . .' he shook his head in disgust, 'appalled by the whole business. I came back down here and had a drink, and then I telephoned Mr Roth.'

'When you say you didn't want any more to do with her,' said

Stratton, 'are you implying that you'd previously had a liaison with Mrs Milburn – a sexual relationship?'

'No.' Tynan glared at him with burning eyes.

Stratton raised his eyebrows as high as they would go. 'Really, Mr Tynan? Mrs Milburn is a very attractive woman.'

'No! Absolutely not. I've just told you so. There was nothing of that sort between us.'

'He was lying about not having an affair with Mary/Ananda, wasn't he?' said Ballard as they were driving away.

'Through his teeth, I'd say.'

'Why, do you think? I mean, you'd just told him we were going to charge him with buggering us about.'

'Two reasons. One, he wants to pretend it didn't happen. I think he was pretty fond of her, and of course it was good for his ego, what with her being a smasher in the looks department, but now it's been proved that she's a liar and crazy and all the rest of it ... Well, that's not so good, is it? The other reason is Roth. We know he doesn't approve of anything like that. Tynan's like the others, under his thumb and desperate for his approval.'

'Which presumably he wouldn't have if Roth knew about it,' concluded Ballard. 'Extraordinary, isn't it? He's a grown man, rich, successful, obviously not stupid, and yet ...'

'I don't think any of them are stupid,' said Stratton. 'Fuck!' He slapped the steering wheel with the palm of his hand. 'We're back to square one, aren't we?'

'Yes,' said Ballard, 'we are. And when I find Harwood,' he added savagely, 'I'm going to kick his arse into the middle of next week.'

CHAPTER FORTY-THREE

After a hasty and extremely late lunch of curling bread, limp lettuce and sulphurous boiled eggs at the George and Dragon, Stratton and Ballard took their indigestion back to the local station, where they found Harwood doggedly picking his nose behind the counter. 'Message for you,' he said.

'We know,' snarled Ballard. 'Why didn't you telephone it through to the Old Rectory?'

Harwood crossed his arms and stared at him in amazement, as if this were not a question he could be reasonably expected to answer.

'Well?' said Ballard.

'I was busy.' Stratton looked around but was unable to spot any sign of industry, apart from a single page torn from a notebook.

'With what?' snapped Ballard. 'The contents of your nostrils?'

'Don't you want it, then?' Harwood indicated the piece of paper. 'Oh, give it here.'

Scanning it over Ballard's shoulder, Stratton read, *Black Vauxhall Velox, BFY 183, Mrs Melbourne, left this morning.*

'For Christ's sake,' said Ballard. Harwood stood back and stared at them reproachfully as Stratton lifted the hatch and they made for the office at the back.

'That wasn't much of a bollocking,' said Stratton, as they cleared a space on the single desk and sat down, one on either side. 'What happened to his arse and the middle of next week?'

'No point.' Ballard pulled the telephone towards him. 'He'll be just as useless in the future as he is now. I'll put out an alert for that car. Better check it first, though.' He crossed his eyes horribly and made a lolling movement with his head.

'Quite. And I'll call Grove.'

'There's only the one line,' said Ballard. 'I'll be as quick as I can.'

'Can Harwood make tea?' asked Stratton. 'Or will he burn the place down? I could do with something to get rid of the taste of that food.'

'That's just about the only thing he can do,' said Ballard, dialling.

'Right you are, then.'

'Bad news and good news, old son,' Grove's phlegmy rumble came down the line. 'We've done a search of Jeremy Lloyd's belongings, and we didn't turn up any birth certificate. But . . .' Grove paused, and Stratton could hear him spluttering into his handkerchief, 'we did find a slip of paper rolled up with the spills for lighting the gas fire – a bit torn, but it's got half of Mrs Aylett's name on it, and her address. Bit of a coincidence if that's nothing to do with it, wouldn't you say?'

'Definitely. What's the rest?'

'I've been to see your Mrs Astley. She says the Milburn woman was there, all right. The maid confirms it. Says Mrs M. spent most of the time in bed and she was up and down like a whore's drawers, carrying trays.'

'Was Mrs Milburn ill?'

'Well, according to Mrs A., the poor dear was "all done up and needed a good rest," and they didn't go out anywhere, not even the pictures. She doesn't take a newspaper, so she'd no idea we were looking for her guest.'

'What was she like?'

'Bit daffy, but all right otherwise. Wealthy widow, nice house, big garden. All above board, I'd say. Met Mrs M. when she – Mrs M., that is – was working in a dress shop up the road and they became friends after that.'

'When was this?'

'Just after the war, she said. She never saw Mrs M. with a child, or heard her mention one. She found the address for me, where Mrs M. was staying at the time – lodging house nearby. I spoke to the landlady, Mrs Harper, and she saw she didn't know anything about a child, either. *However*, she said Mrs M. was pregnant. Mrs M. didn't tell her, though – Mrs Harper said she wouldn't have known if she hadn't walked in on Mrs M. by accident when she was in the bathroom. Mrs M. told Mrs H. that she was a widow, husband killed in the war. Mrs H. said she felt sorry for her – or at least she did until Mrs M. did a moonlight flit owing two months' rent.'

'Do you know the exact dates?'

'Wait a minute . . . Here we are. Mrs M. arrived on September the twenty-fifth and left in the middle of November. Mrs H. had no idea where she'd gone, and never saw her again. Mrs Astley didn't know where she'd gone either, and she didn't see Mrs M. again until about a year afterwards, when Mrs M. suddenly popped up on her doorstep. She said Mrs M. never mentioned having a baby and told her she'd been ill and "living quietly in the country", nothing else.'

'Did she or Mrs Harper mention Mrs Milburn having any gentlemen friends while she was living in Wimbledon?'

'Nope. Mrs A. is also under the impression that Mrs M. is a war widow. Says she can't understand why she's never re-married.'

'So she walked out of Mrs Harper's and disappeared.'

'That's about the size of it, I'm afraid.'

'Bloody hell. Well, I'd better put you in the picture about what we've been up to ...'

When he'd finished, Grove said wearily, 'And I suppose you want me to relay all that to Lamb, do you?'

'I say,' Stratton put on a high voice and a lisp, 'you are a sweetie.'

'And you're a cowardy custard who doesn't want his dear ickle bollocks ripped off.'

'Too right I am.'

'Can't say I blame you. Still, you weren't to know about the kid, were you? Those weirdos are obviously playing silly buggers, and that Mrs Milburn sounds the most doolally of the lot.'

'I think,' said Stratton, 'we'd better try another appeal to the public. After all, Mrs M. dumped Tom on the Wheelers, so there's a chance she might have done the same with Billy somewhere else. Can you talk to Lamb about it? You'll have to be careful with the wording, though. The Wheelers were definitely in two minds about contacting us – they thought we'd take Tom away.'

Grove heaved a sigh. 'Fair enough. And I suppose you'd like me to stick a broom up my arse and sweep the floor at the same time?'

'So Mrs Curtin was right about Mary/Ananda being pregnant,' said Ballard, when Stratton had given him the gist of the telephone call to Grove. 'Michael told us he was born in February 1946, didn't he?'

'Yes, so Mary/Ananda must have been only a couple of months gone when Mrs C. spotted it. But according to Mrs Astley and the landlady, there weren't any men hanging around.'

'Perhaps he *was* immaculately conceived.'

Stratton lobbed a pencil at him. 'Don't *you* start.'

PC Parsons appeared, bearing two thick china mugs of tea. 'Compliments of PC Harwood.'

'All done?' asked Ballard.

'Yes, sir.'

'I take it you didn't find anything.'

'No, sir.'

'What were they up to when you left?'

'Having a meeting, by the looks of it. The one in charge—'

'Mr Roth?'

'No, the lady. She came to see us off. That's a strange old place, sir. I looked in a couple of the bedrooms while they were searching, and it was like a convent or something. I don't know if any of them are married, but there's no married quarters. And it's all plain, no photographs or personal stuff. I hope you don't mind, sir, but I brought Miss Wickstead back with me – that's our police-woman, sir,' he told Stratton. 'There didn't seem much point in her staying, and we need to make a start round the village with Mrs Aylett's picture.'

'That's fine,' said Ballard. 'Anything else?'

'I've got the copy of the birth certificate for Billy Aylett from records, sir.'

'Well,' said Ballard, 'now we need you to get one for Michael Milburn, born on the twenty-eighth of February 1946.'

'Do you know where he was born, sir?'

'Haven't the foggiest,' said Ballard, wearily. 'You might tele-phone Miss Kirkland at the Foundation and find out if anyone there knows.'

'Better ask about his surname as well,' said Stratton. 'We don't know that he's actually called Michael Milburn, do we?'

'Blimey,' said Parsons, who looked less than enchanted at the prospect. 'Nothing's straightforward with this lot, is it?'

'Did you get anything on the chap Mrs Milburn was supposed to be marrying in 1945?' asked Ballard.

Parsons' face brightened. 'Yes, sir. There was one that matched.' Licking a thumb and finger and grubbing through the pages of his notebook, he read, '*Michael John Carroll from Idaho, stationed at USAF Bentwaters as aircrew. Due to go home in the middle of September, but killed in an accident on the base on the twelfth. Accident thought to have been caused by his negligence – he was under the influence at the time, and had been disciplined for drunkenness several times.* Oh, and he was ...' Parsons scanned the rest of the page, 'twenty-five years old and unmarried.'

'Mary/Ananda moved into lodgings at Wimbledon on the twentieth, without Billy,' said Stratton, when the constable had gone. 'Couldn't even tell the truth about Carroll's death, could she? Car accident in Berlin my foot. She just lied to us for the hell of it.'

'I don't think she told the truth about *when* she found out about his death, either,' said Ballard. 'I reckon she heard about it a couple of days after it happened and high-tailed it down to London as soon as she could.'

'Managing to lose Billy somehow in the process.'

'How could any mother just *discard* her children like that?' said Ballard. 'Even if Billy was adopted. It's not natural.'

'Let's just hope she discarded him *alive*,' said Stratton, grimly.

Ballard leant back and stared up at the yellowing paint on the ceiling. 'You know, I keep thinking about that room in Rosemary Aylett's house, all the things she'd bought for him when she thought he was coming back. *That's* how a mother behaves, not ...'

He shook his head and they stared at each other in grim intimacy, leaving a wealth of unsayable things unsaid.

CHAPTER FORTY-FOUR

'Parsons said Michael Carroll was twenty-five,' said Stratton. 'In 1945, Mary/Ananda would have been in her late twenties, wouldn't she?'

'I don't imagine she looked it,' said Ballard. 'I'll bet she picked on him because he *was* younger. First time away from home, off some farm . . .'

'And it sounds like he had a bit of a problem with the sauce. Easy to wind him round her little finger, and that was her ticket out, all the way to Idaho.'

'Far from all the horrible people saying nasty things about how she'd done away with her husband and had it off with the doctor,' concluded Ballard.

'Exactly. Now, I haven't mentioned this to Grove yet, but I think we ought to get them to hawk a photograph of Miss Kirkland around Flaxman Court.'

'God!' Ballard slapped his notebook on the edge of the desk in frustration. 'I'd forgotten about that, what with everything else.'

'Of course,' said Stratton, 'we don't know that it's her. It might be one of the others. Or,' he added despondently, 'it might be someone else entirely.'

'I don't fancy trying to get hold of, what, twenty-odd photographs, and telling Grove he's got to go house-to-house with them, do you?'

'Christ, no. But we should try with Miss K.'s picture first. I think our best bet would be to ask Tynan.'

'Our only bet, you mean,' said Ballard. 'You heard what Parsons said about them not being keen on photographs at the Foundation. And they won't be too keen on us, either. Parsons said they had a meeting, and you can bet Roth's told them to close ranks against the Forces of Darkness, so I don't suppose we'll be able to get anything more out of any of them.' He shook his head dejectedly.

'Well, it's our best hope, so why don't we collect the photograph from Tynan, drop it back here to be sent to Grove and then call it a day? I don't know about you, but I could do with a drink.'

'God, what a complete balls-up.'

It was a quarter past six, and the only other customers in the George and Dragon were a sliver of a man with a grimly headscarfed wife. Stratton and Ballard chose a table as far away from them as possible and sat gloomily, nursing their pints.

'What do think will happen to him?' asked Ballard.

'Michael? Well, if he is Mary/Ananda's child and she's given him into Roth's care – legally, I mean – then he'll have to stay at the Foundation, won't he? He'll be a freak.'

'I suppose,' said Ballard, 'he won't know any different, will he? The adults in the place have chosen to be there. They've found the outside world wanting, so they've stepped out of that world and into Roth's, and they've invested a lot in it – spiritually and emotionally—'

'Not to mention financially,' put in Stratton.

'That, too. But Michael's there because he was *put* there. D'you know, I'd be surprised if he knows anyone of his own age.'

'Must be pretty lonely.'

'How do you think he'd manage outside?'

Stratton took a thoughtful pull on his pint. 'He'd have a lot of adjusting to do, that's for sure. Other kids would be bound to rag him something rotten if he went about telling them he was Jesus or something. And if he carried on doing it as an adult – well, he might end up getting put away. I'd say the longer he stays at the Foundation, the greater his chances of ending up in a loony-bin. But we can't do anything about that until we talk to Mary/Ananda.'

Ballard groaned. 'Wherever *she's* got to. Before we left the station I checked with Harwood in case there'd been any sightings and he'd forgotten to tell us, but there hasn't been a dicky bird.' He stared at Stratton for a moment, then passed his hand over his face in a gesture of unutterable weariness. 'Listen, if it's all right with you, I ought to be getting home.'

Stratton sat on by himself for a while after Ballard had left, watching the farm workers troop in and hunch down, monkey-like, over their pints. He tried to summon up the energy to trudge upstairs and run himself a bath, but even that felt like too much effort. After about ten minutes, during which the pub had gone from nearly empty to three-quarters full, Maisie Denton appeared to help her husband behind the bar.

Stratton watched her for a moment and then remembered, with a sudden pang of apprehension, that he was supposed to be meeting Diana at her friend's cottage.

CHAPTER FORTY-FIVE

Driving through the potholed country lanes in the moonlight, it took Stratton the best part of half an hour, including several wrong turnings and quite a lot of swearing, to arrive at the address Diana had given him in the village of Halstead Wyse. He supposed that, if he played his cards right, there was no need for Ballard – or indeed anyone else – to find out about Diana. Quite why this was so important, he wasn't sure; after all, neither of them was married. It was just the image he had of himself rushing back from a rendezvous, lipstick-smeared and fly buttons undone, having to explain himself to his incredulous former sergeant, that seemed furtive and indecent.

Telling himself that really, he *wanted* to see Diana – which he supposed he would have, if he hadn't felt so bloody tired – and that he was bound to perk up when he got there and actually *did* see her didn't seem to help much, and by the time he arrived he was in a thoroughly bad temper.

The heart of the village, being a jumble of Tudor and Victorian cottages around a small green, a general store and a church, alarmed him – far too many people to keep tabs on the comings and goings of a pair of strangers – but, enquiring at the pub, he discovered that the Lodge, which was the address Diana had given him, lay some way away from the centre. On being told it was hard by the 'burnt old hall' he began to feel that he had somehow got into the beginning of a very bad ghost story. This sensation was intensified as he drove out of the village and up to the top of the hill as indicated, where, by the feeble beams of his headlamps, he could make out an enormous pair of rusted wrought-iron gates hanging drunkenly open, with, in front of them, an overgrown and rutted track leading, presumably, to the burnt house that had, he supposed, once been the area's largest and swankiest property.

Beside the gates was a small and unnecessarily ornate house, all gables and over-large chimneys in fancy brickwork. Telling himself firmly that none of it was Diana's fault, he pulled up beside a decrepit-looking shed in the yard and clambered out of the car. On closer inspection, when he pulled his torch from his overcoat pocket, the house proved to be in a fair old mess, with half-timbering at crazy angles and moss threatening to overtake the balding thatch on the roof.

Staring upwards and caught unawares, Stratton jumped as the tiny front door swung open with a creak so stereotypically sinister that it could have been a sound effect, revealing a dishevelled-looking Diana with a candle in one hand.

'Darling! How marvellous, you've got a torch – I didn't think of it. Come in, quick – not that it's much warmer in here than out there, but all the same . . . I was hoping you'd be late so I'd have a chance to sort everything out and show you how efficient I am. Unfortunately, there's no electricity – Barbara forgot to tell me – and there doesn't seem to be any gas either. I spent ages stumbling about in the dark looking for *this*,' she brandished the candle in its enamel holder.

Christ, thought Stratton, that's all I need – an evening playing at Boy Scouts.

Diana must have spotted something of this in his face, because she carried on, her tone increasingly flustered and placatory. 'Fortunately, Barbara's got quite a stock of them, so we can have dinner by candlelight. At least, we can if I can manage to light the range, and then we can have hot water as well. Honestly . . .' she gave an embarrassed little laugh, 'it's more like camping than keeping house. I am sorry – I'm sure your pub is heaps more comfortable.' Here, looking contrite, she stopped to draw breath.

Feeling sorry for her, Stratton gave her a kiss, noticing as he did so that there was a smut of coal-dust on her face and that her fingers and the borders of her nails were black with the stuff.

'I'll fix the range,' he said, relieved, despite his annoyance, to have a practical task that would lessen the awkwardness he was feeling at being here, like this, in somebody else's house. Even though he knew that Barbara (whoever she was – he'd find out later) had given permission, it still felt uncomfortably like trespassing, or being the type who'd borrow another chap's flat for an afternoon rogering his mistress, or . . . well, something *not quite right*, anyway. 'I take it,' here, he glanced down at Diana's hands, 'that there is some coal, is there?'

'Lots. I brought a couple of buckets in, and the rest's in the shed round the corner.'

'Good. I'll soon have us warmed up, then. Where's the kitchen?'

'Looks just like our farmhouse when I was a boy.' Stratton shone his torch over the stone sink with its cold tap, the dresser, the table, and finally across the iron monster that took up one side of the small room, with its oven and boiler. 'My stepmother used to put the newborn lambs in our range to warm them up,' he said, bending down to look inside and remembering the little creatures beginning to recover and stagger across the flagstones on untried legs. 'You probably never went into the kitchen when you were a kid, did you?'

Diana's cheeks glowed in the light of the candle she was holding. 'Yes, I did. I used to have tea in there on Nanny's afternoon off. So there,' she added, sticking out her tongue at him.

'There's a bit too much coal in here,' said Stratton, 'and not enough kindling. Why don't I start again?'

'If I get the groceries and towels and things from the car,' said Diana, 'we can have some sherry while I'm cooking.'

'Any beer?' asked Stratton hopefully.

'Don't worry, I've got that too.'

'It's not been lived in for a while, has it?' said Stratton, when he'd sorted out the range and lit candles, sticking them on saucers all round the kitchen. The place looked so neglected that he'd been pleasantly surprised to find that water, and not dust, came out of the tap when he'd gone to wash his hands.

Diana, who'd poured them both drinks and was chopping vegetables with surprising dexterity, said, 'I don't think Barbara's ever lived here. That's why it's never been brought up to date. There's no bathroom, just an outside loo, and basins and ewers in the bedrooms.'

'Does she own the big house as well? When I asked in the pub, they said it had burnt down.'

'That's right: 1949, I think.'

'Was that ...' Stratton injected his words with deliberate nonchalance, 'a happy accident?'

'Insurance, you mean?' Diana chuckled. 'No such luck. The insurance company wouldn't pay the full sum because the walls were still standing, so Barbara's family couldn't afford to fix it – not that they could have anyway, with all the shortages of materials. There's a picture somewhere of how it used to look.' Putting down the knife, she took the candle back into the narrow hallway and returned with a black-and-white photograph in a wooden frame showing an impressive stone house with a colonnade in front.

'Georgian or Regency?'

'Or early Victorian. Lovely, wasn't it? Now it's just a shell, and not a very safe one, according to Barbara. She said not to go in. Pretty much all of the land's been sold to a farmer.'

By the time they sat down to dinner, Stratton was beginning to enjoy himself. Later, in a bed dried and warmed by some stone hot-water bottles Diana had found in one of the cupboards, when she'd hugged him and said, 'Isn't this *fun*, Edward?', he had to agree that it was – especially since he hadn't thought about the investigation for two whole hours.

It was odd, he thought, as they lay sharing a cigarette, that he'd never before thought of it as 'fun' with Diana. Not that he'd ever make a comparison between her and Jenny – at least not knowingly – but with Jenny it had always been fun, because it was easy and companionable and because, right from the start, he'd felt no heightened expectation from her, or any pressure for things not to go wrong, so they never had. That wasn't, of course, to say that he didn't care – he'd wanted to please her, all right, what man wouldn't have? But it was just . . . *easy*. With Diana, things were more complicated. Even at forty, her body was lovely. Stratton's feeling, the first time he saw her naked, had been one of awe – something uncomfortably akin to worship. This, he knew, wasn't just a physical thing. Another woman – pretty well any other woman, if you discounted film stars or royalty – could have had a body equally gorgeous, and it wouldn't have had the same effect. This feeling had, mercifully, subsided, but he was still taken aback by how at ease she seemed with no clothes on, and how, well . . . *active* . . . she was in bed. Not that that hadn't been a delightful surprise as well, but once he'd got over it he'd started to wonder who it was who'd taught her all those things. As it couldn't – surely? – have been either of her husbands, this didn't take too long, because the only possible candidate he knew of was Claude Ventriss. He knew it was stupid to be jealous – after all, given that Diana was several leagues ahead of him in every imaginable way it was a miracle he was there at all – but he still was. Images of the two of them together, which were quite capable of encroaching at just the wrong moment, filled him with a rage that, although he knew it to be irrational, still managed to grip him like a vice.

At least, he thought, Diana never came out with any excruciating romantic stuff. In fact, the only time he'd ever said something along those lines – largely because he felt it was expected of him – she'd put a hand over his mouth and seen to it that, for the next few minutes at least, he couldn't do anything more than gasp.

Diana nudged him. 'Penny for them.'

'Ohh . . . nothing much.' Stratton rolled over to look at her, propping himself up on his elbow. 'Nothing intelligent, anyway.'

Diana put the cigarette out and turned so that she was lying on her stomach, head cupped in her palms, and looked at him in a way which made it clear that he was expected to elaborate. Not being able to tell her what had actually been going through his mind – not a can of worms that could be opened in front of anybody, least of all her – he said, 'You know what I was saying when we were eating, about going to that Foundation place?'

'Yes?'

'Well, it was all a bit odd.'

'So I gathered.'

'But the oddest thing was the first time, just when I was leaving. The boy I told you about—'

'You mean Michael the Mighty-whatever-it-was?'

'Yes, him. We hadn't been introduced or anything – I mean, I don't think he had a clue who I was – but he suddenly told me that I was carrying a burden of guilt and that if I shed the burden, then I'd be happy. He was right, but I don't see how he could know that.'

'He probably didn't,' said Diana. 'But you could say that about practically anyone, couldn't you? Everyone's got something they feel guilty about, haven't they, even if it's not a particularly bad thing. Heavens, you should know *that*.' She rolled her eyes. 'You must see it all the time at work.'

'Yes, but just to come out with it like that . . .'

'He's only a child, Edward. He probably didn't know what he was saying.'

'That's not the impression I got. And I do feel guilty. About lots of things.'

'Such as?'

'Well, Jenny for one. I mean, I know that's in the past, and there's nothing I can do about it now, but all the same . . . And not being closer to Pete and Monica . . .'

'But you *are* close to Monica, aren't you? I've always thought that you and she – especially after that business . . .'

'Raymond Benson, you mean? Losing the baby?'

'Yes. I wondered if you'd been brooding about it when we were talking about her last week.'

'I can't really help it, Diana. I know she loves her work, but she ought to be . . . you know, settling down. Thinking about getting married, a family. Or at least seeing someone, and there's never . . . not that I'd expect her to tell me about it, or at least not straight away, but she's never mentioned boyfriends or chaps at work or anything like that. I can't believe it's for lack of offers. I know I'm biased, but she is a nice-looking girl and all the rest of it. I'm worried that the whole experience might have put her off men for life.'

'Are you?'

'Of course I am! What parent wouldn't be?'

'I suppose they would,' said Diana, stiffly. 'I don't really have any experience of things like that.'

'It's not a criticism,' said Stratton, hastily. 'I'm sorry, I always thought . . . Well, I suppose I *assumed*, that you didn't really want children. You once said – about that – that you'd lost a baby – more than one – but that you got over it, and I just thought . . . well . . . Oh, dear. I'm sorry, I'm being insensitive. Look, let's forget about it.'

Diana wriggled round and sat propped up against the pillows, shivering and pulling the covers up to her chin. She seemed, thought Stratton, somehow far more *human* than she had several minutes ago, when he was still in the afterglow of desire. 'No, don't let's,' she said. 'Or rather, let's forget about me because you're right, I never really have wanted children, but one does – or tried to do, in my case – what's expected . . . But hasn't it occurred to you that Monica might not want children, either?'

Stratton sat up, too. 'But that's not—'

'Not what?' said Diana. 'Not *normal*? People seem to make a hell of a lot of assumptions about what's normal, don't they? Especially where women are concerned. They think, if you don't want to be married and have children, you're unfeminine or sexless by nature and you won't find any fulfilment in life.'

Taken aback by the fierceness of her tone, Stratton said, 'Well, it *is* normal.'

'In that case,' said Diana, 'I'm abnormal, and so is Monica. And, by your reckoning, she's a lot more abnormal than I am.'

'What do you mean?'

'Well, I'm here in bed with you, aren't I?'

Stratton stared at her, bewildered. 'What's that got to do with it?'

'You're a *man*.'

Stratton's stomach lurched. Blood pounding in his ears, he said, 'What are you saying, exactly?'

'Oh, Edward . . . Look. What I'm saying,' she said, gently, 'and I'm sorry I said it like that, is that Monica – yes, *your* daughter – prefers women to men.'

CHAPTER FORTY-SIX

Stratton's sensation, as she spoke these last words, was that the air around him had suddenly bunched and become solid, so that he couldn't breathe. He felt distanced from everything, suspended with no past and no future, only this moment and Diana's words reverberating around the small bedroom, ricocheting off the wall-paper with its faded sprigs of pink flowers, the china basin and ewer on the chest of drawers and the brass bedstead as if they were trying to escape.

'Edward? Are you all right?' Diana put a hand on his arm and everything started to move and happen again.

Making a conscious effort to draw breath, Stratton said, 'No, of course I'm not *all right*. What the hell made you say a thing like that?'

'Because it's true. The girl Monica lives with, Marion – they love each other.'

'How can you know that?'

'I've seen them together.'

'What, holding hands? Kissing?'

'Of course not.'

'Then how—'

'It was obvious. Oh, they're very discreet, and Marion doesn't come to the studio very often, but it's the way they are with each other – the way they look at each other. You can tell.'

'Rubbish! You're imagining things. In any case, that sort of thing may be all very well for a bunch of actors and arty types, but not . . . not . . .'

'Not people like you and your family?' suggested Diana.

'Yes! Well, not exactly . . .' Stratton shook his head, trying to clear his mind. What he'd been about to say was nonsense. God Almighty, there were several policewomen at West End Central who were clearly . . . But they weren't *his daughter*, for Christ's sake. Which was nonsense, too, of course, but knowing that didn't make it any better. 'It was that bloody Benson, wasn't it? He's put her off men. But when she meets the right one, she'll—'

'She *has* met the right one, Edward. And the right one, in her case, happens to be a woman.'

'No. No! It isn't true. It can't be.' In an effort to keep calm, Stratton tried to light a cigarette, but succeeded only in spilling matches all over the eiderdown.

Diana took the cigarette from him and lit it. 'There you are.'

'But it can't be right. If she's always been so keen on women, why would she want anything to do with Benson in the first place? And she'd had boyfriends before . . .'

'Had she?' Diana looked up from picking up the matches. 'How many?'

'Well . . .' The truth was, not many at all. In fact, Stratton could only think of one, and that hadn't lasted long. He thought of Pete's words – Christmas, 1950 – he remembered that all right because it was just before Davies' trial: "You want to get your-self a boyfriend, Monica – or perhaps you don't." He'd thought, at the time, that Pete was just being Pete, needling people, but perhaps his son had spotted something he'd failed – or perhaps refused – to see . . . 'Anyway,' he finished, 'it still makes no sense that she would go with Benson, if—'

'Yes, Edward, it does. She was trying to convince herself that she was, as you would put it, *normal*.'

'How the hell can you possibly know that?'

'Because Monica told me.' The finality with which Diana said this removed Stratton's last shred of hope. 'Haven't you ever wondered, Edward? It's not as if you're narrow-minded, and you come across everything in your work—'

'Yes, but I don't expect to come across it in my own family!' As he spoke, his nephew Johnny, Reg's son who'd only narrowly avoided Borstal, flashed through his mind.

'Why not? Aren't your family like other people?'

'Of course they are. It's just . . . How long have you been having these cosy little chats with Monica, anyway?'

'It's not as if we're in league against you, Edward. We bump into each other sometimes at work, and . . .' Diana shrugged. 'You know how it is. You get on better with some of your colleagues than others, and you chat to them . . .'

'Yes, but about work, not about things like *that*.'

Diana put her head on one side. 'No, I suppose *you* don't, being a man. But Monica and I became friendly because of you, really. And she wasn't the one who raised the subject of Marion. I did. It was after Marion had come to the studio one day, and I saw them together and wondered . . .'

Realising that this was exactly what Pete had told him Monica had said about himself and Diana, Stratton said, 'Did you tell her about the two of us?'

'She asked me, so I said that yes, you and I were friends. That was one of the reasons I felt I could ask about Marion.'

'And Monica told you she was in love with her?'

'Yes.'

'And you think it's real? Not some sort of late-adolescent crush or . . . I don't know . . . arrested development or whatever doctors call it? Because I'm sure this wouldn't have happened if Jenny was still alive, if . . . Oh, *Christ*.' Stratton put his head in his hands. 'It's my fault, isn't it? I've been so stupid. I thought she could look after herself – she was always so sensible – and then after that awful business with that shit Benson . . . Sorry, Diana. But all of this is my fault.'

'No, Edward.' Diana grabbed his arm and shook it. 'You're wrong. *None* of it is your fault. Look at me. Please, Edward. Please . . .' Kneeling up, she put her arms around him. 'Listen to me. Monica is the way she is because that's the way she was meant to be and nothing you did or didn't do would have made the slightest bit of difference. She didn't want me to tell you. In fact, she asked me not to – she said that if you knew, you'd never want to speak to her again. She thinks *she's* failed *you*.'

Pulling away from her, Stratton said, 'Of course she hasn't bloody failed me! I've told you, it's the other way round. What the hell am I supposed to say to her now?'

'How about that you love her? You do, don't you?'

'Of course I do!'

'There you are, then.'

'It's not that simple, Diana, and you know it. People like that have terrible lives. They get laughed at, shunned . . . They're unhappy. They end up committing suicide. We see it all the time.'

'You see the tragedies. You don't see the happy ones who've found somebody they love and who loves them, do you?'

'No, but—'

'As I said, there you are. And I didn't tell you this to be spiteful or catty or anything like that, but because I thought you should know. I've thought so for some time.'

'Monica obviously didn't.'

'No, but she wouldn't, would she? But when *I* told you, a lot of things fell into place, didn't they?' Diana held up a hand. 'Don't deny it, because I could see they did. Would you rather I hadn't told you? Because you'd have been bound to cotton on at some stage, although I suppose you could have pretended it wasn't true and kept on telling yourself she just hadn't met the right sort of chap. But then it would have been a lot of lies, wouldn't it, between the two of you?'

Stratton rubbed his eyes with the heels of his hands. 'Yes, it would. And I don't want that. But it doesn't stop me from ...' Finding himself unable to express what it didn't stop him from, and, for that matter, what it had started him on, and caught up in a tornado of conflicting emotions, some of which he couldn't even put a name to, Stratton gave up on speech. Had Monica had eyes for Diana, too? Was that what had prompted her confession? Fighting to contain a sudden up-rush of sickness, he carried on rubbing his eyes until his head hurt and all he could see was a blizzard of black spots.

Diana rubbed his back. 'I'm sorry, Edward.'

'Sorry you told me,' he mumbled, 'or sorry about Monica?'

'I'm not sorry I told you. I'm sorry about how I said it – I was a bit stung by the not-being-a-parent business, I suppose. And I'm not sorry for Monica, because she's happy.'

'So,' said Stratton irritably, taking his hands away from his face, 'what – or who – *are* you sorry for?'

'You. That you've taken it so badly.'

'How the hell am I supposed to take it?' asked Stratton bitterly. 'As a cause for celebration?'

'No, but it's not the end of the world, either.'

'Possibly not, but it's not what you'd call good news, is it?'

Diana sighed. 'OK. Look, I spotted some brandy in the cupboard downstairs, and I think you could do with it. I'll be back in a moment.'

'You know,' she said, sitting on the bed with her arms round her knees and watching him drink, 'during the war, and then after, with all that business with Forbes-James and Claude, and then

leaving Guy and marrying James and him leaving me, and everything else that happened, it slowly began to occur to me – sort
of piece by piece – that a lot of the ideas and values I'd grown
up with, what I thought was right and the only way one should
do things, was actually wrong – or at least not the only way of
looking at the world. When I look back now, I see how impossibly naive I was, how unquestioning . . . I learnt that the hard
way. You helped me learn some of it, but a lot of it I learnt from
my own mistakes. I'm not the same person I was fifteen years
ago, and I'm glad of it. You're not, either, and the world's changed,
too. I know that all sounds pat, but it's true – and I think it's
important to recognise it because things are going to change
more before we're in our dotage. A lot more.'

'They're bound to,' said Stratton, wondering what she was
getting at, 'that is, assuming the Americans and the Soviets haven't
blown us up before we *get* to our dotage.'

Diana made an impatient gesture. 'I mean, Edward, look at
the two of us, here. We both know that I'm not ever going to be
Mrs Stratton. We – I mean, in the sense of you and I, together –
are living on borrowed time.'

'Is this something else you're trying to tell me?' asked Stratton,
wearily. 'I know I'm not good enough for you, and if you've met
someone else you've only to say—'

'Stop! In the first place, you're the best person I've ever known.'

'Doesn't say much for the rest,' Stratton muttered.

'Don't be silly. In fact, just shut up for a moment and listen.
In the second place, don't be so ridiculous, there isn't anyone
else, and thirdly, all I was going to say was that we might as well
enjoy it while it lasts because – as you've just pointed out – none
of us has any idea what's coming round the corner. After all,
that's why – or partly why – all those people at your strange
Foundation place are looking for a different way of life, isn't it?'

'I'd say so, yes.'

'Well, perhaps there's something in it. Not *them*, particularly, but . . . well, it just comes back to seeing things differently. Monica being the way she is is *not* the end of the world.' She leant over and kissed him on the cheek. 'And when I said you were the best person I've ever known, I wasn't just being kind. I meant it.' Diana took the glass from him, kissed him again, and blew out the candle. 'You should try to get some sleep.'

Stratton lay flat and closed his eyes, but he might as well not have bothered. His teeth were clenched, and every muscle in his body was rigid. Sleep was impossible. Logical or meaningful thought was impossible, too. *His daughter* was an invert. She was never going to settle down – at least not in the way he understood, marriage and children. He didn't know who he was more angry with – Monica for being . . . like she was, Diana for telling him about it, himself for practically everything, or God for doing all this – anyway allowing it to happen – in the first place. He glanced over at Diana who was curled up beside him, apparently asleep. It was all very well for her to be so matter-of-fact about it. Monica wasn't *her* daughter. And what about the rest of his family? Pete would be bound to treat it as a huge joke, at least on the surface, Doris would be appalled, Don would probably suggest Monica have treatment or a course of injections or some Christ-knows-what thing that was the latest in medical science, and as for Lillian and Reg . . .

What the fuck was he supposed to do? He could hardly rush off to Monica's cottage, drag her away from Marion and lock her up at Lansdowne Road until she came to her senses. That wasn't on, and anyway, according to Diana, she *had* come to her senses, which was why she was with Marion in the first place. And it wasn't as if Marion was some predatory older sort – he'd met her, hadn't he? She was Monica's age, and not in the least butch. He'd always supposed – inasmuch as he'd thought about it at all

- that one of them had to be mannish and the other feminine, but obviously that wasn't the case ... Stratton shook his head. He didn't want to think about it, but the problem was, he couldn't *stop* thinking about it.

What would Jenny have said? The answer to that was, nothing, because whatever Diana said, he was sure that if Jenny were still alive Monica would not have turned out to be - Christ, he had to stop shying away from the word - a lesbian. The thing with Benson he supposed he could understand, a bit - an attempt to convince herself she wasn't one - but the fact it had gone disastrously wrong couldn't have helped. She must have felt so lonely and scared. Knowing that she'd been scared of him, on top of everything else, made him feel about an inch high. *She thinks she's failed you.* That's what Diana had said. It was like Jenny, before she died, not telling him she was pregnant. Surely he couldn't be that much of an ogre? Or had Jenny and Monica both, in their different ways, thought they were trying to protect him? *He* was supposed to protect *them*, not the other way round.

In any case, who was he to judge Monica? She evidently couldn't help what she was, and here he was - with his *own son*, probably at this very moment, risking his life in a theatre of war - lying in bed with a woman who wasn't his wife. And it wasn't, as Diana had pointed out, even as if they were doing it on account, so to speak. Hardly on the moral high ground, was he? Of course, Monica and Marion weren't planning to marry, either, but then *they* didn't have the choice. The world really *would* have to change in totally unimaginable - not to mention completely implausible - ways before *that* ever became legal. Stratton made a vague stab at trying to imagine the sort of society in which it might even be considered as a possibility, but gave up almost at once and returned to considering his own position. Sleeping with Diana would be a thousand - a million - times worse, of course, if Jenny were still alive, but it still wasn't any sort of example to set to one's children. He wondered if they knew – or rather, guessed – that he and Diana sometimes slept together. Pete had, he was sure. What had he said? *Nice to know you're human like the rest of us.* If to err was human, then he was far too bloody human, in almost every way possible. That was the problem.

He'd been surprised – shocked, even, although compared to the other thing it was pretty insignificant – when Diana had come straight out with the fact that they both knew she was never going to be Mrs Stratton. She'd been so different when they were talking; forthright and sensible. Which, he supposed, she was in the normal course of things – nowadays, at least, being a career woman and all that – it was just that they weren't words he'd ever connected with her. She'd always been too special for that, too rarefied. But tonight, she'd begun to sound . . . well, almost like Jenny. He glanced across at her, but her eyes were closed and her breathing slow and even.

Stratton turned away from her and lay gazing at the window until the blackness round the edges of the curtains began to lighten, and the first birds began to sing. Then, slowly and quietly, he crept out of bed, shivering in the freezing room, retrieved his clothes, and slunk downstairs to dress before leaving so as not to disturb Diana. He stoked the range so that there'd be hot water for her when she woke up, and tore a page from his notebook to write her a note. He was standing at the kitchen table, pencil poised, trying to think of what the hell to write after 'Thank you for dinner', when he heard a noise on the stairs and a second later, she was standing in the doorway, wrapped in a dressing gown.

'At least let me make you a cup of tea, Edward.'

'All right.' Realising that this sounded churlish and ungrateful, and unable to think of anything to do or say that wouldn't compound this impression, Stratton left the room and went and stood outside the tiny front door, blowing smoke into the cold grey dawn, until Diana rapped on the window to signal that the tea was ready.

He tried to focus his mind on the day ahead, but couldn't remember what he was supposed to be doing in any sort of useful detail. Instead, his mind seemed to be juddering with echoes of what Diana had said, like a series of mental aftershocks. He pulled out his notebook and stared at what he'd written, but none of it seemed to make sense.

In the kitchen, he said, in a rush, 'I know . . . I realise . . . that I'm not glamorous like those other chaps, that I'm . . .' That he was what? What the hell was he trying to say? 'I'm sorry, Diana. I'm just so . . . so . . .'

'Confused, I should think.' Diana handed him a cup of tea, her eyes large and dark with concern.

'I was just thinking – or trying to think – about everything you said up there, not just about Monica, and I suppose I don't really know what you want, or why you . . . why we are . . . what we're doing. I'm sorry, that sounds . . . I don't mean . . .' Baffled, Stratton gave up and stared at her for a long moment. 'Help me,' he said, finally.

Diana, who'd been frowning into her tea as though she feared there might be a fly in it, raised her head and looked at him. 'That bit of it's simple,' she said. 'We enjoy each other's company, don't we? Well, I enjoy yours, anyway. And we like each other. Not just for . . .' she glanced upwards, 'that, but generally speaking.'

'Yes,' said Stratton hopelessly. 'Of course we do.'

'And you like women, don't you? I mean, other than wanting to go to bed with them. At least, you seem to.'

Stratton was about to tell her it was a silly question and of course he did, but pulled himself back. Did he? He'd never really thought about it. Suddenly, an image of Albertine, the jolly kid from the coffee bar, popped up in his mind. 'Yes,' he said. 'I like women. And girls. The nice ones, anyway.'

'And I'm a nice one, am I?'

'Yes.'

'And Monica's a nice one, too, isn't she?'

'Of course she is, but I don't understand what you're getting at.'

'Just that you must be able to see, if you like women – I mean, as opposed to just fancying some of them – that there can some-times be a bit of a gap between what they want and what they're expected to want. You expect Monica to want one thing, and she wants another and, now you know that, it might be a good idea to try to understand it a bit. I know,' she added, after a moment, 'that it probably won't be very easy, but all the same ...'

'I'll do my best. I can't let her down again.'

'You haven't let anyone down. You can't be responsible for someone else's happiness, Edward. No one can. All you can do is make sure that you're not helping to make them miserable.'

This was so much the kind of thing that Jenny used to tell him, delivered with the same totality of honesty and compas-sion, that Stratton felt a lump form in his throat. While he was trying to collect himself, Diana said, 'I think I should probably go back to London today, rather than staying on. All this ...' she gestured at the range, 'is a bit too primitive to be comfortable for long, and I was only planning on staying one more night anyway, so ...'

'It's probably best,' said Stratton, relieved to be led onto the safe ground of practicalities.

Diana nodded. 'I know you've got heaps of work to do, and I think you need some distance – space, really. It's a lot to think about.'

Backing his car into the overgrown and rutted drive, Stratton spotted an MG Roadster parked beside the house. He hadn't noticed it in the darkness the night before. He wondered, vaguely, if the colleague Diana had borrowed it from was the Barbara woman who owned the house, or someone else. Why did it matter, anyway? Despite the revelations of the previous night, there was a lot he didn't know and had never asked about Diana's life. He'd known, as he'd kissed her goodbye, that the balance of their relationship had changed irrevocably. What this meant for the future, he had absolutely no idea, and now wasn't the time to start speculating, especially about unimportant stuff like whose car she'd borrowed.

Without a conscious decision, or even a thought, Stratton turned his car in the direction of the burnt house. Coming round the corner, he saw that the circular front lawn was choked with brambles, which were beginning to encroach on the building itself. What was left of the once-white facade was scorched and cracked, and the great front door hung open, lopsided and forlorn. Stratton left his car and, skirting the brambles, made his way up the steps to look inside. He saw, amidst the mess of blackened rafters and rubble on the hall floor, a smashed pillar, which had clearly fallen from a height, crashing through the delicate iron balustrade at the top of the main staircase on its way down. He imagined it, hurled through the flames as if by some unseen infernal power, and felt a shiver down his spine. Beside it, a ray of sunlight pointed an accusing finger at the broken and twisted frame of an iron bedspread: a tortured skeleton.

Back in the car he felt foolish, although, he told himself, to proceed would have been equally foolish. Diana had told him it was unsafe, hadn't she, and in any case, what was there to see? Turning round, he drove back to the road, imagining the blackened horror of the rooms inside. He wondered if anyone had been killed in the fire. Presumably, if they had, Diana would have said so ... If anyone had told me that *that* house was haunted, he thought, I'd believe it. Suppressing a sudden impulse to stop at the Lodge and tell Diana on no account to go anywhere near the place, he drove back through Halstead Wyse and on to Lincott.

CHAPTER FORTY-SEVEN

As Stratton drove, he found himself struck by the resounding ordinariness of what he heard and saw, and his fear – because that's what it had been, no two ways about it – of the ruined house seemed not merely foolish, but idiotic. The mail van outside the village post office, the housewife in carpet slippers at her gate, the motorbike with a sidecar, the man and his dog glimpsed across a field, the distant lowing of cows ... everything was as it should be. The burnt house had made him suggestible, that was all, and his imagination had reacted accordingly. There was quite enough, he thought grimly, to bother him in real life – Monica, Pete, this flaming investigation to name but three – without getting het up about stuff that didn't actually exist.

It was just gone half past seven when he pulled up outside the George and Dragon, where any hopes of making an unobtrusive entrance were scuppered by the landlord, who was hauling dustbins about and hailed him with a sort of jovial menace.

Cursing himself for leaving it so late, Stratton said 'Morning,' in a businesslike fashion.

Clapping a lid on the nearest bin with a metallic clang, Denton said, 'Thought I hadn't seen you go up to your room last night.' Before Stratton had time to gather his thoughts enough to stammer out an excuse, the landlord tapped the side of his nose and said, 'Don't worry, squire. Don't ask, don't tell, that's my motto.'

Deciding that saying anything at all would only compound the situation, Stratton smiled weakly and went inside as quickly as he could without actually giving the appearance of hurrying.

After a wash and shave, he changed and, pausing only to ruffle up the bedclothes – knowing, as he did so, that it was shutting the stable door after the horse had gone, because Denton would undoubtedly tell Maisie – walked down to the police station to meet Ballard.

They spent an unedifying morning at the Foundation, re-interviewing all the students about everyone's movements on the night that Lloyd had died and the day that Mrs Aylett had been shot. As Ballard had predicted, they'd closed ranks. Now, their smiles were cold and invincible, the merest veneer of polite-ness overlaying outright hostility, as, one by one, they all claimed that, *as far as they knew*, nobody, bar Mary/Ananda, had been absent from the place during those periods. When asked if they'd seen Mary/Ananda or Tynan's Vauxhall Velox in the past twenty-four hours, they denied that, too.

If Tynan had told Miss Kirkland that they'd asked him for a photograph with her in it, she gave no sign of it. When at the end of four fruitless hours they asked to see Roth, she told him frostily that he and Michael had gone out, chauffeured by the man McCardle.

'Well,' said Ballard, as they left, 'even if one of them did know somebody'd been absent, they weren't going to tell us, were they?'

'No chance,' said Stratton. He was immensely relieved when Ballard made an offer of lunch at his house, because he'd been fearful that Denton, on seeing him again, would deploy his –

undoubtedly full – repertoire of verbal nudges and winks, which were bound to be impossible for his erstwhile sergeant to miss.

Pauline, who seemed a bit distant, said she'd already eaten but dished up bread, cheese and some extremely good soup and left them to their own devices, and afterwards they went to stretch their legs in the churchyard, smoking and enjoying the weak winter sun. Stratton wandered about by himself, peering at the names on the graves. Judging from the preponderance of Pooles, Lamberts and Warrens, these were the three main local families, although there were a fair few Leggetts and Buckleys as well. Some were hard to read, obliterated by lichen and centuries of rain on stones that were listing and neglected, but others – less appealing, he thought – had the rawness of new stone, with plainer lettering, name and dates only. An elderly woman, her blueish/grey hair in frozen waves and a basket on her arm, appeared from the church and nodded to him as he skirted the railed tomb of some landowning family and stopped in front of a grave that was blanketed with bunches of flowers, some brand new, others wilting and apologetic. It belonged to a child – Thomas Martin, who'd died, aged eighteen months, in 1912, and, according to the stone, been 'taken to the Lord'.

Ballard came up beside him, looked at the name, and shook his head. 'Billy wasn't even that when he disappeared.'

'She might,' said Stratton, who'd been thinking along the same lines, 'have just left him somewhere, of course. Hoped he'd be found.'

'Like Moses in the bulrushes?'

'She's certainly fanciful enough. God ...' Veering away from the subject, Stratton said, 'This little chap's pretty popular, isn't he?'

'I think that might be my Katy's doing. She's always trotting about redistributing the flowers so that everybody's got at least one bunch, but I've noticed that it's the children's graves who get the most attention.'

Stratton looked down the rows of gravestones and saw that indeed, everybody had at least one bunch. 'Obviously democratically minded, your daughter. There's one down there that looks as if it says Tynan – at the end.'

Following his gaze, Ballard said, 'Think it's his wife?'

They ambled across, past a row of Pooles and Warrens, and read: *The Hon. Dorothy Tynan, 27th January 1904–17th March, 1954.*

'Never noticed that before,' said Ballard. 'Not that I spend much time in here. Fifty years old – bit rough, that.'

Cancer, thought Stratton, remembering what Diana had told him. 'Did they have children?'

'Don't think so. Never heard of any, if they did. Wonder what she thought of it all.'

'The Foundation, you mean?'

'I was thinking more of Mary/Ananda.'

'I think I saw a photograph of her at Tynan's house. If it was her, she didn't really look the type for all the navel-gazing malarkey. As to the other thing, who knows? She's not around to tell us, and Tynan sure as hell isn't going to.'

CHAPTER FORTY-EIGHT

'I've managed to locate the birth certificate for the boy at the Old Rectory,' said Parsons, when they returned to the station. 'The Kirkland woman confirmed that his surname is Milburn. I don't have the actual copy yet, but I got them to read out the details.' He pushed a slip of paper across the counter, and Stratton read, *Michael James Milburn, Date of Birth: 28ᵗʰ February, 1946; Father: Reverend Edward Granville Milburn; Mother: Mary Ann Milburn, formerly Hamilton; Father's Occupation: Clergyman; Informant: M. Milburn, Mother, address given as 32, Dale Road, West Ham. Registration District: West Ham, Birth in the sub-district of West Ham North East (Forest Gate Hospital).*

'Literally a father in heaven,' said Ballard, 'given that Michael can't have been conceived earlier than the end of May and Milburn died in the middle of the month, didn't he?'

Stratton flipped through his notebook. 'Yes, the seventeenth. Unless the baby was late in coming and the Revd Milburn managed to impregnate Mary/Ananda on his deathbed.'

'Doesn't sound very likely, according to what Dr Slater said about his condition.' Ballard consulted his notebook and read out, '*Bedridden, crippled with arthritis, difficulty feeding himself . . .* He was quite positive about all that.'

'Mary had an affair with Slater about that time, didn't she?'

'Yes, if you can call it that.'

'So *he* could be Michael's father.'

'We'll probably never know the answer to that,' said Ballard. 'And from what we know of her, I'm beginning to wonder if she knows herself.' Turning back to the policeman, he said, 'Did you get anything else?'

'Nothing's come in on the car Mrs Milburn was driving, sir, but we have two sightings of Mrs Aylett getting off the bus at around three o'clock on the fifth of November. One said he saw her consult a piece of paper and walk off down Long Lane.'

'That's the way to the Foundation,' said Ballard. 'Presumably the paper was directions on how to get there. Lloyd – if it was him – must have put them in the letter. Did you manage to get round everybody, Parsons?'

'Pretty well. We haven't managed to talk to John Dunning yet. He's our local poacher,' Parsons told Stratton, 'so it's quite likely he was in the wood emptying his traps and what not. Adlard went round there – said his wife was cagey about his whereabouts.'

'He's been in trouble before,' put in Ballard. 'One of those blokes who's always committing offences and getting nabbed. They always speak up for him in court, so he gets out on probation and then they catch him all over again. Regard him as personal property, don't you, Parsons?' Ignoring the policeman's resentful look, he said, 'We're bound to catch up with him sooner or later – in fact, we could go round there now, if you like.'

'Why not?' said Stratton. 'As far as I can see, we've got bugger all else to do. Can we take the station car? I've almost run out of petrol.'

'Adlard's got it, I'm afraid, sir. There's been a break-in at Nelson's Farm. We can let you have a can, though – always keep some here. It's in the cupboard out back, with the mops and things.'

*

It took Stratton several minutes to locate the can and several more to transfer the contents to the Ford Popular and wipe the resulting splashes off his shoes and hands. When he returned to the station, Parsons was hunched anxiously over the counter telephone with Ballard beside him, muttering, 'Come on, come *on*.' When he turned, he had the look of a man witnessing something unstoppable and fatal – an unpreventable car smash or a parachute failing to open.

'Are you all right?'

'Did you sort out the car?'

'Yes. What's going on?'

'We need to get back to the Foundation, *now*.'

CHAPTER FORTY-NINE

'What's happened?' asked Stratton, as they shot out onto the road.

'A woman telephoned. She wasn't making a lot of sense, but she said that someone's been injured. A bunch of them were on the drive, and someone drove up, knocked a woman down, then turned round and went haring off again. Parsons is getting an ambulance, then he's going to call Tom Nelson's place – that's closer – and tell Adlard to get straight round there, see if anyone got a look at the car.'

As Ballard had predicted, Adlard had beaten them to it. The police car was pulled up halfway down the drive, and the sergeant was standing in the middle of a group of people in outdoor clothes. The woman who'd been hit was lying by the hedge, covered in a blanket, her head propped on a folded coat. Another woman, who Stratton remembered from the interviews – Miss Mills, he thought – was kneeling beside her, clasping her hand and a uniformed policeman, who he took to be PC Briggs, was hovering over them.

Getting out of the car, he suddenly thought of a spot-the-ball competition in a newspaper. What was missing from the picture? At every scene like this he'd attended, the onlookers were either milling aimlessly, or goggling, or showing signs of distress, but the people here, if they were doing these things, were doing them so discreetly as not to be noticeable. The students were standing quite still – some even had their eyes closed – but all of them were looking quite composed.

Seeing the car, Adlard broke away from the group. 'Where the bloody hell was Briggs when this happened?' shouted Ballard.

'Said he'd hung back for a smoke,' said Adlard, disgustedly. 'Said he was going to catch up with them, only he didn't get there in time. I've only just got here myself, sir, but I've got a description of the car. Black – everyone agrees on that, two of the men think it's a Vauxhall model, and one of them got the number plate: BFY 183.'

'Tynan's car,' said Stratton, as they got out. 'Did they see who was driving?'

'This lot didn't,' said Adlard, gesturing at the students. 'Too far off, they said.'

'One of them was near enough to read the number plate,' said Stratton, 'so they must have been able to see if the driver was male or female, at least.'

'Said he was concentrating on the car, sir. Most of them were over there,' he pointed to a wheelbarrow and a pile of leaves some seven hundred yards away across the grass, 'and by the time they'd got here, whoever it was had turned the car round and was driving off. They said it was heading that way,' he pointed left, 'towards the London Road.'

'Why don't you see to things here,' Ballard said to Stratton, 'and I'll get after it.'

With the immediate – if rather ignoble – thought that if there were any heroics going, Ballard was more than welcome to them, Stratton said, 'Good idea. The keys are in the car.'

As Ballard jumped into the driver's seat and turned on the ignition, Stratton poked his head in the window and added, 'Be careful, all right? I don't fancy telling Pauline she's a widow.'

'Will do.'

Stratton leapt clear as Ballard executed a neat three-point turn – which, judging from the way the edge of the grass was churned up, was more than the other driver had done – and disappeared at high speed. It looked as if the Vauxhall Velox had been travelling pretty fast, too – deep parallel tyre marks swerved across the gravel, a wave of which had been flung up and beached on the lawn. 'Left some rubber behind, by the looks of it,' he said.

'Yes, sir,' said Adlard. 'The chaps I spoke to said the car was going at a fair old lick.'

As the sergeant turned to go back to the group, Stratton caught his arm. 'Have you talked to the woman who was hit?' he asked.

'Not had time, sir. Thought it was more important to get the details of the car.'

'Quite right. See if you can get anything else – one of them must have got a glimpse of the driver. Come down heavy if you have to.'

'Yes, sir.'

'I'll deal with you later.' Stratton waved aside PC Briggs's stammered attempt at explanation and bent over the prone woman. It was Miss Banting, muddied and dishevelled, her mouth a quivering oblong and her eyes blank with shock. 'A broken leg,' murmured the woman kneeling beside her, who had the air of having taken charge of the situation. 'Two places, I think – and probably the ankle as well. I can tell,' she added briskly, 'because I trained as a nurse.'

'Miss Mills, isn't it? You'd best stay with her.' He squatted down beside Miss Banting. 'Can you answer a few questions?'

Miss Banting nodded. Her face was the colour and texture of marzipan, and, despite the cold day, sweat glistened on her forehead. Talking was clearly going to be an effort. 'Stay as still as you can,' he said. 'There's an ambulance on its way. You're obviously in pain, so I'll make this as brief as possible. Were you on your own when the car hit you?'

'No. With Mait— Michael and Miss Kirkland.'

'Miss Banting threw herself in front of Michael,' said Miss Mills. 'She saved his life.'

'Is he all right?'

'A bump and a scrape, that's all. Apart from the shock, of course.'

'You saw it?'

'Yes. I was just over there.' She pointed to a tree about two hundred yards away, were a rake lay abandoned beside another pile of leaves.

'Did you see who was driving?'

For the first time, Miss Mills looked uncertain, the crisp professionalism of her former self eroded by present uncertainty. 'I'm not quite sure,' she said.

'But you were close enough to see. Was it a man or a woman?'

Miss Mills hesitated. 'I thought I did. I mean, I thought I recognised . . . but . . .' She shook her head. 'She must have lost control of the car, because she seemed to be driving straight at Michael.'

'*She?* So it was a woman driving?'

'Yes, but—'

'It was Ananda.' Miss Banting's voice was barely audible. 'Mrs Milburn. Not an accident. She tried to kill Michael.'

'Is that right?' Stratton asked Miss Mills. 'Ananda was driving?'

'It looked like her.' Miss Mills's voice was full of disbelief. 'But it must have been an accident, because—'

'It wasn't.' Miss Banting's voice was faint but firm. 'She didn't want them to have him.'

'When you say "them",' said Stratton, 'do you mean Mr Roth and Miss Kirkland?'

'Yes.' Miss Banting's eyes blazed with vehemence. '*You* know.'

'I think,' said Miss Mills, 'that Miss Banting must be mistaken. Probably due to concussion.'

'I'm not mistaken,' said Miss Banting between gritted teeth. '*He* knows what I'm talking about.'

'*Do* you?' Miss Mills gave Stratton an inquisitorial stare.

'Yes, I think so. You may choose not to believe the evidence of your eyes, but Miss Banting does.'

'But it can't be right. Michael is Ananda's *son* – why would she try to kill him?'

'That,' said Stratton, 'is something we can only guess at – for the moment.'

'Spite,' said Miss Banting.

'No mother,' pronounced Miss Mills, 'would try to kill her own child.'

'Really?' Stratton stood up, taking hold of Miss Mills's arm as he did so, so that she had no choice but to stand up with him. 'I seem to remember,' he said quietly, determined to keep his voice level, 'that Goebbels' wife killed all six of hers.'

'That was entirely different,' said Miss Mills, with some authority. 'She must have been mad. Mr Roth says anyone in the grip of a strong idea is—'

'Never mind what Mr Roth says,' snapped Stratton. 'You think Mrs Milburn is sane, do you? After what you just witnessed?'

'I didn't see—'

'Oh yes you did,' said Stratton, firmly. 'When you said it couldn't be right, you meant it couldn't be right *because you can't believe it is*, and that means that you, Miss Mills, are "in the grip of a strong idea". Now, I suggest you start remembering what it was that you actually *saw*, because Sergeant Adlard will be taking your statement later and lying to the police is – as I'm sure I don't need to remind you – a very bad idea.' As he said this, he saw that although Miss Mills's face now registered bewilderment, her eyes had a calculating look, and knew that his message had got through. 'In the meantime, you can look after Miss Banting until the ambulance comes, and no trying to convince her that she's concussed or confused or any other nonsense.'

Turning away and dipping his shoulder in order to exclude her, Stratton bent and put his hand gently on Miss Banting's shoulder. 'It won't be long now,' he said.

'I saw her eyes,' whispered Miss Banting. 'She looked mad – almost demonic.'

Stratton, remembering Ballard had said that Dr Slater used the same word, could well believe it.

'You will make sure Michael is safe, won't you?'

'I'll do my best,' said Stratton. 'I can promise you that.'

Straightening up, he caught sight of Briggs, who appeared to be trying to merge with the hedge. 'Wait here till the ambulance comes,' he barked, 'and don't even think of buggering off again or I'll have you for dereliction of duty.'

As he strode off towards the house, he realised that, although 'his best' might protect Michael from future harm at the hands of Mary/Ananda, nothing he could do, short of turning back time itself, could protect him from the harm that she, and Roth, and all the rest of them, had already done.

CHAPTER FIFTY

The woman who'd telephoned the station turned out to be the one who'd spilt tea over him. Stratton imagined her clutching the Bakelite receiver in both hands, incoherent and tearful. Now, eyes still wet, she was staring around her in the manner of a demented person who is looking for something very important but can't remember what it is, and she didn't have anything to add to what Stratton had already been told. Miss Kirkland, who was sitting with her, kept an affronted silence, as though the uncontrolled display was distasteful to her. The woman, whose name was Mrs Palmer, had been raking leaves with Miss Mills and, at Miss Kirkland's bidding, had gone to make the telephone call. Miss Kirkland nodded in confirmation of this, and at Stratton's request stood up, self-contained as a cat, to follow him outside. Another woman student, sitting statue-like on a chair outside the door, rose on seeing them and glided silently past to attend Mrs Palmer.

Miss Kirkland had a smear of mud on her skirt, but otherwise looked remarkably composed. 'Ananda,' she murmured, looking round to make sure they were out of anyone's earshot, '*meant* to kill Michael. She drove right at him.'

'You're sure it was her?'

'Positive. She came roaring down the drive and straight towards him.'

'Does Michael realise that she was aiming for him?'

'I didn't speak to him afterwards – he obviously didn't want to talk about it, and we thought he ought to lie down and get over the shock – but he must have seen who was at the wheel. If Miss Banting hadn't rushed in front of him, I don't know what would have happened. How is she?'

'A broken leg, according to Miss Mills, and possibly more.'

'So brave,' murmured Miss Kirkland. 'Utterly devoted.'

And look where it's got her, thought Stratton. Aloud, he said, 'Did you recognise the car?'

'Yes. It belongs to Mr Tynan.'

'Have you,' asked Stratton, 'seen that car, or Ananda, at any point in the last twenty-four hours?'

'Yes, last night – or rather, early this morning.'

'Why didn't you tell me this earlier on?'

Miss Kirkland looked around again, and said, 'I think perhaps we'd better go somewhere more private.' She led him down the corridor to a small room, furnished as plainly as the other had been, but with the addition of two chintz-covered armchairs. Depositing himself in the nearest one, Stratton said, 'Well?'

Perching herself on the extreme edge of the other, as if fearful that contact with the soft surface would tempt her into some unpardonable laxity, Miss Kirkland said, 'I was concerned for the well-being of the Foundation. A connection with such a person might be harmful to our reputation.' She clasped her hands earnestly in her lap. 'We thought it unsuitable, and unhelpful to—'

'Wait a minute,' said Stratton. 'Who's "we"?'

'Mr Roth. When we discussed it, he—'

'So Roth saw her, too, did he?'

'Yes. It was Mr Roth she came to speak to.'

'I see. When was this, exactly?'

'About half past three this morning. Mr Roth is available to any student who wishes to speak to him,' she said, with some pride. 'At any time of the day or night.'

'So she woke you up, did she?'

'I was already awake. I've been having some difficulty sleeping, and I was standing at the window – my room faces the front of the house – when I heard someone coming up the drive.'

'In a car?'

Miss Kirkland shook her head. 'Footsteps on the gravel. I went downstairs and found her out there, in the corridor. She has a key to the back door. I asked her what she wanted, and she said she needed to speak to Mr Roth. She was very agitated. I had to tell her to keep her voice down.' I'm not bloody surprised, thought Stratton. 'We came up the back stairs in order not to wake the house, and I took her to him. Mr Roth asked me to bring them some tea, so I did.'

'Did she ask to see Michael?'

'No. Or not in my hearing.'

'You were present, were you, when she spoke to Roth?'

Miss Kirkland flushed slightly at this, and Stratton said, 'Don't tell me. You were listening at the door.'

'They were in Mr Roth's sitting room,' she said. 'I was waiting next door, in his bedroom, in case he needed anything.'

I'll bet you were, thought Stratton. 'So you heard everything, did you?'

'Not everything, but I couldn't help . . .' Miss Kirkland's colour deepened. 'I caught the gist of what was being said.'

'Which was?'

'That she had killed both of them – Jeremy Lloyd and Mrs Aylett.'

CHAPTER FIFTY-ONE

Stratton stared at her. 'You're telling me that you heard Ananda say she'd killed two people and you didn't think to tell me this morning?'

'Perhaps I should have done,' said Miss Kirkland. 'But I needed to consult Mr Roth, and he wasn't here, so—'

'There's no "perhaps" about it,' snapped Stratton, remembering that Tynan had done something very similar. 'Are you incapable of thinking for yourself?'

'I felt that it wasn't my decision to take.'

Stratton sighed. 'You mean that you weren't prepared to do it without Roth's approval.'

'No,' said Miss Kirkland quietly, 'I was not.'

'But circumstances have changed, have they? Or have you asked him?'

'No, Inspector, I haven't. There hasn't been time. But given what's just happened, I should have thought my reason for telling you was self-evident.'

You mean Michael's important but the other two aren't, thought Stratton. 'How did she kill them?' he asked.

Miss Kirkland stared at him as if she didn't quite understand the question, then said, 'As I told you, I didn't hear everything she said, but I heard her say that because she was hysterical – shouting. Mr Roth calmed her down, and then she spoke more quietly, so I couldn't pick up the words.'

'All right, then, why?'

Miss Kirkland blinked.

'Why did she kill them?' asked Stratton. 'After all, she knew that Michael wasn't Billy, didn't she? She had no reason to kill them. The moment Mrs Aylett arrived at the Foundation asking about her son, Michael could have told her when his birthday was. And if Mrs Aylett still didn't believe it, Ananda could have produced his birth certificate.'

'But then—' Miss Kirkland stopped abruptly, eyes flicking about the room and hands twisting in her lap.

'But then . . .?' prompted Stratton. When no answer was forthcoming, he said, 'But then the birth certificate would have revealed the name of Michael's father, wouldn't it?'

'I don't know,' said Miss Kirkland. 'I have never seen it. There was no reason . . . Mr Roth said—'

'Never mind what Mr Roth said, Miss Kirkland. Of course, the other reason Ananda had for not wanting Mrs Aylett to come here and start asking questions was that, once Mrs Aylett found out Ananda was here with a different child, she'd be bound to start asking what happened to Billy. Did she tell Mr Roth anything about *that*?'

'Yes!' Miss Kirkland leant forward, eagerly helpful. 'She said he'd died.'

'When?'

'As a child. She said she realised he was sickly soon after she'd taken him from Mrs Aylett, and she couldn't do anything for him, and the doctors couldn't help because he was too weak. He got pneumonia and died in the middle of September. She had him buried here, in Suffolk.'

'Did she say where?'

'Yes, Hasketon. She said her husband was buried there. Then she said she put up a wooden cross because she couldn't afford a headstone – and then she went to live in London. She said that was when she realised she was pregnant with Michael.'

'Given that she'd have been almost five months gone by that time,' said Stratton, 'I find that hard to believe.'

'Well,' Miss Kirkland, 'that is what she said. She told Mr Roth,' Miss Kirkland gave him a triumphant look, 'that it was like a miracle. One child had been taken, and another had been put in its place.'

'Well,' said Stratton, 'you seem to have heard *that* part of it all right. Did Roth ask her the name of Michael's father?'

'No.'

'Does he already know who Michael's father is?'

'No.'

'Do you know?'

'I have no idea. As I explained, Inspector,' said Miss Kirkland patiently, 'the individual is quite immaterial. As I believe I explained before, things can be understood on different—'

'You're not speaking to the students now, Miss Kirkland. What did Roth have to say about what Ananda told him about Billy?'

'Ananda said that she felt guilty about the child's death. That she blamed herself. Mr Roth said that was to do with a desire within the baby, and not with her.'

'What desire?'

'A desire,' said Miss Kirkland, in a voice of supreme assurance, 'not to obey the laws of the universe.'

Stratton wanted to throttle her. 'For the love of God,' he spat, 'what is wrong with you people? Next, you're going to be telling me that Lloyd and Mrs Aylett didn't want to live either, so somebody – some individual whose identity is quite immaterial,' he added, sarcastically, 'acted according to the "laws of the universe", whatever they may be – and killed them.'

Stratton saw that her face had changed. It was almost imperceptible but, added to the overwhelming certainty of her expression, he thought he saw a touch of pride.

As he glared at the prim little woman, Stratton knew that if he stayed any longer, he would say – or, worse, actually *do* – something he'd regret. 'I shall need to talk to you again,' he said, in the most measured voice he could manage, 'but right now I need to speak to Michael. Please take me to him.'

CHAPTER FIFTY-TWO

Outside Michael's room, which was along the landing from Roth's, Stratton indicated that Miss Kirkland should leave him and made a point of waiting until she was out of sight before opening the door. This was only partly because he feared she'd stay around to listen – after all, he could throw open the door at any time if he thought that's what she was doing – but more because he needed a moment to collect himself: the boy was bloody unnerving, no two ways about it. He was clearly unused to being treated like a child, so any hint of condescension was out of the question. Besides which – Stratton winced at the memory – he'd made a fool of himself in front of the kid once already, hadn't he?

It was no good trying to think about it. He'd just have to play it by ear. Swearing briefly but vigorously under his breath by way of preparation, he knocked once, and then, without waiting for a response, opened the door.

Michael's room was only slightly more marked by the tastes of its occupant than the few others he'd caught glimpses of through open doors. The small evidence of a life being – or having been – lived was a pile of textbooks on a desk, a battered-looking puppet dangling from a wooden crucifix and the moulded plastic sections of a half-constructed Airfix Spitfire. Michael himself was sitting alone on the bed, his blond hair a shining halo in the coned beam of an Anglepoise lamp on the cabinet next to him. He was dressed in an open-necked shirt and jersey, one flannel trouser leg rolled up, and staring down at the cotton wool pad that was stuck to his knee with strips of plaster. Without looking up, he said, 'I thought I told you—'

'Told me what?'

His head jerked up sharply, and Stratton saw that there was a bruise on his cheek. 'There was someone else here,' he said. 'Fussing. I told them to leave.'

'Someone who was looking after you?'

'I don't need anyone to "look after" me,' he said, irritably. 'Does Mr Roth know you're here?'

'No. And I'm here because I want to have a chat.' Stratton closed the door and, crossing the room, pulled the hard chair from under the desk and sat down.

Michael treated him to a haughty stare. 'I don't have anything to say to you,' he said, and turned his attention back to his injured leg. He was so self-assured that Stratton had to remind himself, before he spoke, that he was talking to a child. Crossing his legs, he said, easily, 'Oh, I think you'll find you've got plenty to say. Fancy a smoke?'

Michael's chin dropped, and he gaped in a mixture of adult outrage and boyish astonishment which, in any other circumstances, Stratton would have found funny. 'I shan't tell if you won't,' he said, digging into his pocket and extending the packet to Michael.

'Churchman's,' said Michael. 'Mr Roth smokes those.'

'Pinch his cigarettes when he's not looking, do you?' Two hard spots of colour on Michael's cheeks told him he was right. The boy stared at him for a further moment, then extracted one, clumsily one-handed, stuck it in his mouth and allowed Stratton to light it. Stratton lit one for himself, nudged the metal wastepaper basket forward with his foot to serve as an ashtray, and sat back in his chair, screwing his face up to contemplate Michael through one eye. The boy sat stiffly, self-consciously smoking; a parody of Roth, sucking in deeply but without actually inhaling, so that his cheeks bulged as he held the smoke in his mouth.

'Practise that, do you?' asked Stratton. 'Smoking like he does?'

Michael, unable to hold on to the smoke, exhaled in a rush, face puce and eyes watering. 'How do you . . .' he managed, then couldn't speak for coughing.

Stratton laughed. 'We all do things like that. It's how you learn to be grown up – by copying. I used to copy the way my dad did things. Mind you, my childhood was a bit different from . . .' he jerked his thumb at the door, 'all of this. We lived in the country, though – Devon. My dad was a farmer. I had two brothers, both older than me. They didn't half boss me about.'

Michael looked at him curiously. He's never been treated like this before, thought Stratton; people here are deferential, even his teachers. 'Why did they boss you about?' he asked.

'Well, it was a farm,' said Stratton. 'We all had to pitch in and help, so they had to tell me what to do. Mind you,' he added, 'some of it was just because they could, because they were bigger than me. But we did have fun as well. Harvest suppers and football matches, that sort of thing.'

'I've seen them playing football in the village.' Michael sounded wistful. 'It looks like fun.'

'Oh, it is,' said Stratton. 'Great fun. You don't know what you're missing. I'm sure if you asked Mr Roth, he'd let you go along and have a kick-about. You'd have to ask the boys in the village as well, of course, but I'm sure they wouldn't mind.'

Michael looked doubtful. 'I don't suppose they'd let me play. I mean, I've never had anything to do with them. I saw them at the bonfire. They were mucking about.' There was a peculiar mixture of emotions in his voice, as though this were something he ought to despise, but couldn't.

'Sounds like fun,' said Stratton. 'I used to enjoy a good burn-up when I was a kid. Still do, as a matter of fact. Who took you to the bonfire?'

'Miss Kirkland. But we didn't stay for very long. I didn't speak to the boys or anything.'

'Why not?'

'Mr Roth said he didn't want me to. He says I should keep away from them because they don't understand people here.'

And he certainly doesn't want you getting ideas about another way of life, thought Stratton, feeling the knot of fury that had been in his stomach since talking to Miss Kirkland clench tightly. 'That's a shame,' he said, equably. 'I think I'd have been very lonely if I hadn't had friends to play with. And my brothers, of course. Do you know you've got a brother, or didn't anyone tell you?'

Michael looked at him incredulously. 'You're making things up again,' he said, flatly.

'Not this time. His name's Tom, and I've met him. He's a couple of years older than you, so if you met him he'd probably boss you about, just like my brothers did me.'

Michael stared at him as if this idea was even more absurd than the notion of his having a brother in the first place. 'If I've got a brother,' he said, watching Stratton closely, 'then where is he?'

'Here, in Suffolk. He lives in a place called Dunwich. It's by the sea.'

Evidently deciding to humour Stratton, perhaps in the expectation of a joke, the boy said, 'Why does he live there?'

'That's where his parents live. Not his *real* parents, of course, but a couple called Mr and Mrs Wheeler, who adopted him to be their own. They've got other children, too, so Tom's got lots of brothers and sisters. I don't suppose,' he added thoughtfully, 'that he'd boss you *too* much, if you met him. He seemed a very nice chap.'

'So why is he there and not here?'

'That's a very good question,' said Stratton, 'but I'm afraid I don't have an answer for it yet.'

'I don't believe you.'

'That's a pity. But you will believe me when you meet him.'

'When we play football?' Michael's tone was sarcastic.

'I think Tom might have a bit of trouble playing football,' said Stratton.

'Anyone would have trouble playing football if they didn't exist.'

Stratton laughed, and Michael stared at him with barely concealed irritation. Not used to that, either, he thought. 'What I meant was, he'd have trouble with football because he's got an illness called polio. Makes it hard for him to run about.'

Michael stared out of the window for a moment, into the rapidly fading light, and then, in a voice that was a child's echo of Roth's intonation, said, 'People have illnesses because they ask for them.'

Keeping his tone deliberately light, Stratton said, 'In that case, a whole lot of kids must have asked for polio all at the same time, because there was an epidemic. Do you know what that is?'

Without turning his head, Michael said 'No, I don't.'

'It's when there's an outbreak of a particular illness, so that lots of people get it at once. Like measles.'

'I had measles.' Michael was looking at him now, uncertainty in his face.

'Did you ask for it?'

The boy frowned for a moment, and Stratton could see that he was struggling. 'I don't know.'

'Well, did it happen because you were bad? Because you deserved it?'

'No!' Now, he looked outraged.

'There you are then,' said Stratton, leaning over to twitch the cigarette from the boy's fingers and stub it out on the side of the wastepaper basket. 'Sometimes bad things happen to good people. Life isn't always fair, you know.'

'Then,' said Michael, not like Roth now, but with the black-and-white absoluteness of childhood, 'it's stupid. It doesn't make sense.'

'Some things don't make sense. Take what happened this afternoon.'

'I don't want to talk about it.' Michael ducked his head and started to tug at one of the plasters on his injured knee.

'I can understand that,' said Stratton. 'But I'd like you to tell me about what happened.'

Michael did some more fiddling, then raised his head and said, abruptly, 'It was my fault.'

'What makes you think that?'

'She came back because I kept on thinking about her. Mr Roth said not to, but I couldn't help it.'

'Telling yourself not to think about something doesn't mean it won't pop into your mind every now and then,' said Stratton. 'But it certainly wasn't your fault.'

'Mr Roth says thoughts are very powerful things,' said Michael, stubbornly.

Giving this up as a bad job, Stratton said, 'So you were out for a walk, were you?'

'Yes. With Miss Kirkland and Miss Banting, and then the car came. She was staring at me.'

'Ananda was?'

The boy's face clouded at the mention of his mother's name. 'She's gone mad, hasn't she?'

'Is that what Mr Roth said?'

'Not exactly. But when she ... went away, and you came, I

asked him what was happening, what everyone was talking about – because nobody would tell me, they just said we shouldn't talk about it . . . Except that they *were* talking about it, about Mr Lloyd and the lady in the wood, when they thought I couldn't hear, but when I asked Mr Roth where my mother was, he said something about people falling by the wayside. He said it as if it wasn't important . . . he kept saying that the Work was what mattered, and we mustn't get caught up in other things, and then you came and told me about the other boy, and then . . .' Michael was blinking fast, now, trying to hold back tears, 'she tried to kill me! I know she did. I wanted to jump out of the way, but I couldn't move. Miss Banting jumped right in front of me and the car hit her.'

'Sometimes,' said Stratton, 'when we're scared of something – really scared – we sort of seize up. Our brains send the message to our muscles all right, but our muscles refuse to obey it. It's nothing to be ashamed of.'

'It didn't happen to Miss Banting,' said Michael. 'She *did* something. I just stood there.'

'She wanted to protect you. That was her idea, and it was a good one, wasn't it? She stopped you from being injured and she might even have saved your life.'

'What you're saying,' Michael's tone was flat, 'is that she was better than I was when it happened. I'm supposed to be better than her, all the time, but I'm not, am I? And now she's been hurt, and it's my fault. She's not . . . not going to die, is she?'

'I shouldn't think so,' said Stratton. 'We think she's got a broken leg, and people don't usually die of those. And you mustn't think that's your fault, because it isn't. You didn't make any of this happen.'

'But it did happen! I only wanted my mother to come back because I missed her, and then . . . then . . .' The boy's face quivered and broke apart, tears coming now. 'I don't understand!' He leapt up and hurled himself at Stratton, an explosion of wind-milling fists, puny blows catching him on the chest and arms. 'Everyone thinks I do, but I don't! And she tried to kill me, and then you said I've got a brother I didn't even know about, and they all whisper and talk about me behind my back – they think I understand everything Mr Roth talks about, and how ... how ... important it is, and they won't even tell me stuff about *her*, and ...' Stratton, closing on him, pinned the struggling form in a bear hug. Unable to fight any more, Michael went suddenly limp, allowing Stratton to rub his back.

'Steady on, steady on,' he murmured, as the boy gulped and hiccupped.

Stratton thought suddenly of his own children at the same age, and of Tom and his siblings, playing in their garden, and felt ready to bash someone. Stifling his rage, he said, 'You must be tired.'

'I am, a bit,' Michael admitted. 'We don't have to talk about this stuff any more, do we?'

'Not if you don't want to.'

'Then ...' Michael hesitated, his mouth still open.

'If you stand like that for much longer,' said Stratton, 'you'll catch a fly, like the old lady.'

'Which old lady?'

'In the song.' Feeling foolish, Stratton stumbled through the barely remembered tune. 'There was an old lady who swallowed a fly, I don't know why she swallowed a fly. Perhaps she'll die.'

Michael gave a yelp of laughter. 'That's not how it goes. You're not very good at singing, are you?'

'Not very. Do you know it?'

'Yes. Miss Banting used to sing it to me when I was little. She used to put me to bed when my mother ...' A flicker of wistfulness, almost entreaty, crossed his face, swiftly replaced with a hard, closed expression. 'When she was too busy, which was mostly. Miss Banting,' he brightened again, 'knows lots of songs.'

'Well, let's try it now, shall we? Even though I'm not very good. Let's get your shoes off, and then you can lie down.'

Michael sat on the bed and allowed Stratton to kneel down and undo his laces. 'Why don't you get under the eiderdown? It's a bit nippy in here.'

'I suppose it will be all right, will it? I mean, I'm supposed to be having lessons and things.'

'I don't think anyone's going to worry too much about that,' said Stratton.

'All right, then.' The boy lay down and, as Stratton covered him over, said, 'You will stay with me, won't you?'

'Yes, until you're asleep. Now, close your eyes. You might want to close your ears, too, once I get going.' Michael giggled, but did as he was told.

Stratton began to sing quietly, staring out of the window at the almost darkness and dredging his mind to reconstruct the words from dim memories of when Monica and Pete were small. Somewhere around swallowing the cow to catch the dog, he got muddled and stopped, expecting Michael to prompt him. When he looked over at the boy, he saw that he was fast asleep. There was something about the depth of it that reminded him of the way Monica and Pete had slept when they'd been feverish as children and how, in slumber, they had seemed to be healing themselves in front of his eyes.

If he'd ever had a stranger conversation, he was damned if he could remember it. As he looked at the boy's beautiful, peaceful face, he thought of the first time they'd met. Michael had told him he was carrying a heavy burden, but it was nothing to the one on his own slender shoulders, the one he would have to try and make sense of – and escape from, if that were possible – in the years to come. And, unlike Stratton's, it had been deliberately placed there. With the best of intentions, but *intended*, all the same. What would his future be?

Children are resilient, he told himself. People are. But all the same ... 'Poor old lady,' he murmured. 'She swallowed a horse. She died of course.'

CHAPTER FIFTY-THREE

Jaws clenched, Ballard shot round a narrow corner too wide, narrowly missing a baker's van that was coming in the opposite direction, barrelling past him with the bray of a horn and an inarticulate shout. Swearing, he ground the unfamiliar gears, praying that the thing wouldn't stall. So far, he'd seen a couple of lorries, a petrol tanker and three cars, none of which was a Vauxhall Velox, and he was nearly at the London Road. Where the hell was she? Most of the turn-offs he'd passed had been farm tracks or lanes that led to villages. Reasoning that the fastest means of escape would be to stay on the larger roads, he'd ignored them, but what if he'd been wrong?

He stamped his foot on the accelerator and shot round another bend, spotting fresh manure and hoping like hell that he wasn't about to run into a herd of cows. A blindingly vivid flash of himself slumped forward, the steering column embedded in his chest and the buckled wreck of the car surrounded by steaming, flailing, bellowing bovine flesh, made him squeeze his eyes shut. When he opened them again, a second later, it was just in time – Fuck! – to swerve around the last black-and-white rump as it disappeared through a gate in the hedge. Sweating with relief, he hurtled on down the road and through a village, spraying gravel where the road was being mended, and, wincing at the imagined impact of an unsuspecting lorry ploughing into his side, straight across a junction. The road was wider now, and straight, with detached cottages dotted amongst the fields on either side. The engine's whine turned to a scream as he flogged the car up a hill at sixty-five miles an hour, eyes popping with adrenalin as he crowned the ridge and scanned the countryside below. As he shot down the other side – seventy – seventy-five – the whole car rattling like buggery and his teeth with it, foot jamming the accelerator against the floor – he saw the boot of a black car disappear round a bend about a quarter of a mile away. If it was the Velox, it would certainly be faster than Stratton's Ford Pop., even assuming that it had been serviced recently which, by the sound of things, wasn't the case. Crouched rigidly over the steering wheel, he shot after it, blind across another junction and onwards, narrowly missing a kid on a bicycle and swerving round one bend, then another, too close to the edge of the road – no ditch, thank God, but the bare branches of the hedge clawed at the side of the car as he struggled to keep it on course. The car was now rattling so much that it felt as if it might break apart like something in a circus, the vibrations juddering his entire body so that he kept his mouth tight shut, fearful of biting his tongue.

Moments later, he saw the black boot of the car disappearing around another corner. He sped after it and caught sight of the letters BFY on the registration plate before it went round another corner. Then, on the straight, he saw the whole registration number and, inside the car, dark hair and then a flash of wild, white profile as the driver looked round, and knew that it must be Ananda. Closing on her, Ballard leant forward and switched his headlights on and off a couple of times to indicate that she should stop, before both cars careered round another corner, the Ford Pop. almost riding on her bumper. They rounded another corner, then another, and then the Velox jinked suddenly left and swerved across the road. Ballard just had time to realise that one of the tyres must have burst when, with an almighty metallic bang, the car went straight into the sharp corner of a large white house. Caught by surprise – he was so intent on the Velox that he hadn't even registered the building – Ballard wrenched the wheel round and stamped on the brake pedal, fighting to control his car as it skidded past the crash and embedded itself, in the last, frantic seconds of a high-speed nightmare, some yards up the road in the opposite hedge.

Ballard heard the tinkle of falling glass and opened his eyes to see, through the crazed glass of the windscreen, the stabbing branches and the buckled, steaming bonnet rising up in front of him. Not dead, then. His body, in its own collision with the steering wheel and instrument panel, felt not his own. He raised his head, inched himself back slightly in the seat and stared down stupidly at his chest, groin and knees. What were they doing there? What was he doing?

Hearing tapping on the window of the passenger door, Ballard turned his head and saw a man in an apron and shirtsleeves tugging at the handle, and, behind him, a dozen silent faces staring at him with the closed intensity of mourners looking into a coffin. A sudden absurd impulse to wave to them made him lift his hand, and then the air inside the car seemed to break apart as everything – sense, memory, pain – rushed back on the high, piercing clarity of a scream from across the road.

CHAPTER FIFTY-FOUR

Tugged and manipulated by willing hands, Ballard managed to extract his legs from under the dashboard and crawl across the passenger seat. He shook his head at attempts to help him stand up, and, lowering himself gingerly onto the muddy verge on his hands and knees, struggled into a sitting position, leaning against the back wheel of the car. The aproned man squatted down in front of him, and a pair of liver-spotted claws draped a tartan blanket round his shoulders. Looking up, he saw a lizard-skinned grandmother with a fox fur round her shoulders, and next to her a barrel-shaped woman – or possibly a middle-aged, middle-weight wrestler impersonating a woman – in a too-small hat, with a fat, tightly buttoned child goggling puggily at him from behind her skirt. Now they'd seen that he was alive and – to some extent at least – mobile, all three adults looked censorious.

Ballard's chest hurt. He ran a tongue over dry lips and tried to work some saliva into his mouth. 'What's happened to her?'

'Your girlfriend?' said the aproned man. 'Well, she's not too clever.'

'Having a race, were you?' said the barrel-shaped woman, who sounded, utterly incongruously, a great deal like Ron's girlfriend Eth from *Take It From Here*.

Ballard shook his head. 'Policeman.'

'You?' The woman wagged her head in disbelief.

'Get away,' said the aproned man. 'That's not a police car.'

'It was an emergency. She's a suspect.'

'Well,' said the man, unconvinced, 'the manager's called the police, just now. And,' he added in a triumphant tone, as if it was conclusive proof of wrongdoing, 'you've got a cut on your forehead.'

Ballard put his hand up and felt the wetness of blood. 'What manager?' he asked.

''s a hotel.' The man stood up, waving the onlookers back. 'See?'

Ballard looked up at the white building across the road. Box-shaped, with a square, pillared porch, on top of which were two poorly executed stone lions, it had a green pantiled roof on which, painted in large white capital letters in order to be visible from far off, were the words 'Car Park'. Milling around in the road in front, bewildered at stepping into the chaos of someone else's life from the safety of their morning coffee, were the guests. Most of them were of a similar age to the beefy woman, who now stood slightly to one side of him. She was looking down at him with her lips pursed, her disbelief even more obvious than the man's.

Over to the left, the bonnet of the Velox was concertinaed against the corner of the hotel, steam hissing from the broken radiator. The front wheel Ballard could see was buckled inwards at a crazy angle, the headlamp smashed and hanging to one side like a detached silver eyeball, and the windscreen completely gone. A humped shape bowed over the steering wheel told him that Ananda was still in there, and he struggled to get to his feet, batting away the hands that reached out to restrain him. Weaving slightly, he approached the car, pushing away two other men in aprons who tried to intercept him, but as he got to within a few feet, the driver's door swung open and, as if detaching itself by its own agency, clattered onto the oil-stained tarmac. Ananda, hair falling over her face, stockings laddered, coat open, staggered out and performed a strange half pirouette before sinking to her knees in the road. Despite her obvious state of shock, the movement seemed to Ballard to be self-conscious and knowing – like the flourish of a dancer at the end of a perform-ance. For a moment, her head was thrown back, and he saw the fragments of the shattered windscreen glinting in her forehead, and a tracery of blood on her cheek and neck. Then she collapsed onto her back and lay still, clothes twisted about her thighs and legs splayed so that Ballard caught a glimpse of one stocking-top and the darkness beyond. Behind her, in the car, the front seats and the footwell were covered in glass. She turned her head and stared at them as if she'd left something – part of herself, perhaps – inside the car.

He approached hesitantly, hearing agitated murmurs behind him, aware of people backing away, and knelt down beside her head. Her eyes, which had been closed, now opened wide and stared straight at him, engulfing him in a brown velvet gaze. Her smile seemed – no, it actually *was* – sexual, inviting. For God's sake, said a disgusted inner voice in Ballard's ear, the woman's hurt. Stop it. Then he saw her lips part and pucker and, for an appalled split-second, he thought she was blowing him a kiss but instead she said, 'Oh, it's *you*.'

CHAPTER FIFTY-FIVE

Hearing a tentative knock on the door, Stratton tiptoed across Michael's room, opened it a fraction, and sidled into the corridor. Miss Kirkland was standing there, eyes lowered. Putting a finger to his lips and miming sleep with his hands palms together against his cheek, he motioned her to follow him onto the landing.

'We had a telephone call from the police station. They'd like you to call them at once.'

'I see.' Stratton glanced over the banisters at the hall below and saw Mr Roth sitting in an armchair by the chimney breast. No one else was present and he was staring into the fire. Stratton, who had a good view of three-quarters of his face, saw that his features were settled in a broad, expressionless mask. Wondering what – or possibly who – was hiding behind it, he said, 'I'll need to talk to Roth, too, afterwards. Did the ambulance come for Miss Banting?'

'Yes, they've gone. Miss Mills is with her.'

'Good. Then,' he added, 'you'd better find PC Briggs and tell him to station himself outside Michael's door and not to move until I tell him otherwise.'

Miss Kirkland nodded meekly.

'Where's the telephone?'

'Downstairs, in the office.'

'Right. If you'd take me ... And you need to make it clear to Briggs that no one – and I *do mean* no one – is to disturb Michael.'

'... a pity about your car, sir,' said Parsons, evenly. 'We're sending a truck to tow it back.'

'Never mind that,' snapped Stratton. 'What about DI Ballard? Was he hurt?'

'Just bumps and bruises as far as we know, sir. There was a doctor present – one of the hotel guests, apparently – and he was able to confirm that there was nothing serious.'

'Thank God for that.'

'He was very lucky, by the sound of things. The chap who telephoned us said it was a miracle neither of them was killed – Mrs Milburn's car ran straight into a wall. They've taken them both to hospital, so we'll have a report soon, I daresay.'

'How bad is she? Do you know?'

'Not sure, sir. There may be injuries, but she was conscious. She's been charged with the attempted murder of the boy, but apparently she didn't respond.'

'There's someone with her, is there? Apart from Ballard, I mean?'

'Of course, sir.' Parsons sounded reproachful. 'A police guard.'

'Well, let's hope he's a bit more efficient than Briggs was,' said Stratton. 'I've got a couple more things to do here, and then I'll be straight down to see her. Adlard can take me in the car. Send that policewoman back here, will you? I'm concerned about the boy, and I don't see Briggs being a lot of use ... Oh, and we've another job for you, Parsons. Can you find out if there's a William or Billy Milburn – or possibly Carroll – buried in the churchyard at Hasketon? He'd be about ten months old.'

'Right you are, sir.'

Stratton put the telephone back on its hooks and let out a long, ragged breath of relief, then went down the corridor to see if Roth was still in the hall.

He was. In fact, he did not appear to have changed position at all in the last few minutes. He was attended by Miss Kirkland, who sat beside him, her hands demurely folded on her now clean tweed skirt.

'How is the boy?' Roth's tone, kindly but remote, suggested that he might have been enquiring after a distant relative or a missing cat.

'Still asleep, I hope.' Stratton turned to Miss Kirkland. 'You fetched PC Briggs, did you, and told him what I said?'

'Yes. He's up there now.'

Stratton acknowledged this with a curt nod, and turned his attention back to Roth. 'You may like to know,' he said, savagely, 'that DI Ballard managed to catch up with Ananda. Her attempts to evade him resulted in her crashing Mr Tynan's car, and she's been taken to hospital.'

'Do you know her condition?' asked Roth. The impassive, leonine mask was still in place but Stratton thought that the man's face looked greyer now, with a rubbery quality, as though it might be possible, by touching the flesh, to mould it into something other than it was. 'Not as yet,' he said. 'Apparently she was conscious, but it's very likely she's been injured.'

Roth's sunken eyes did not change their expression, but his mouth curved upwards, prompted, Stratton thought, by some inner joke. 'Conscious,' he repeated quietly, nodding his head in approval. 'That's good.'

'I should like to speak to you alone.'

Miss Kirkland looked as though she were about to say something, but Roth said sharply, 'Leave us.' Stratton took the vacated seat, and both men sat in silence as she crossed the hall and stepped through the vestibule doors, shutting them behind her with a snap. Roth did not speak but stared after her, cloudy-eyed and mouth slightly agape. In spite of the prominent belly, his body had the slack, shrunken look of a deflating balloon.

'I know that Ananda came here to see you early this morning.'

'I imagine Miss Kirkland told you that,' said Roth, his eyes still fixed on the doors. He gave a half smile. 'I thought she might.'

'You didn't see fit to tell me yourself?'

'No,' said Roth, judiciously. 'Not then.'

'But you knew Miss Kirkland was listening when you spoke to Ananda?'

'Yes. What has she told you?'

'I'm not here to answer questions. I want to hear what you have to say.'

Roth uttered a long sigh, like a child resigned to having to recount a series of events it considers wholly unimportant and has half forgotten. 'Ananda told me about the boy.'

'Which boy?'

'The boy who died.'

'What did she say about him?'

'She explained the circumstances of his . . . adoption, shall we say – which of course I knew, thanks to you.' Roth inclined his head graciously. 'She then told me that he had died several weeks later.'

'And you believed her?'

'You may think it surprising,' Roth wagged his head at Stratton, 'but yes, I did.'

'You believed her when she said she had no idea she was pregnant until Billy died?'

'I see Miss Kirkland did tell you everything. Yes, I did. Stranger things have happened, Inspector.'

'Yes,' said Stratton shortly. 'And most of them seem to be connected with this place. What else did she tell you?'

'What else?' Roth raised his eyebrows. 'There was nothing else to tell.'

'She didn't mention the deaths of Jeremy Lloyd or Rosemary Aylett?'

Roth looked at him enquiringly, and then his glance flicked momentarily towards the doors. 'No,' he said, simply. 'She did not.'

'Mr Roth, I am already considering charging you – and Mr Tynan, and Miss Kirkland – with obstructing the police by withholding information. There have been two murders – possibly more – and you need to tell me the truth. I am going to ask you again if Mrs Milburn said anything about the deaths of either Lloyd or Mrs Aylett, and I would advise you to think very carefully before you reply.'

'There is nothing to think about.'

'So you stand by what you've said, do you?'

'I stand by what I've said because it's the truth.'

'In that case, perhaps you'd care to tell me what happened after Mrs Milburn told you about Billy's death.'

'I have a duty to the students, Inspector, and especially to Michael. I told her to leave and not to come back. She left soon afterwards.'

'Did she threaten you or Michael in any way?'

'No.'

'But she came back this morning and tried to kill him.'

'Yes.' Roth gave a deep sigh. 'Ananda was not in her right mind when she came to see me. She was confused, overwhelmed by distress and anger. Men turn their anger outwards, Inspector. They lash out at others. Women turn it upon themselves ... or upon their children, who they perceive as being a part of themselves.'

Stratton nodded, remembering a case the previous year of a subnormal woman, persecuted by her neighbours, who claimed she'd killed her two children because she couldn't afford to feed them. When he'd gone to her house, he'd found kitchen cupboards packed solid with every kind of food imaginable. And there'd been others like her, too ... 'If you knew that,' he said, 'surely you knew that she might come back?'

Roth bowed his head. 'There, I'm afraid, I was at fault. I should have anticipated it.'

'Why didn't you?'

'Because I had told her not to come back. I had said that she wasn't to attempt to see Michael again.'

Christ All-fucking-Mighty, thought Stratton. The man actually believed he was infallible.

As if reading his thoughts, Roth said, 'For a man like me, the temptation is egotism. On this occasion, I succumbed to it. For many of my students, the temptation takes an inverted form – masochism. I don't mean in its grossest, physical form, but the desire to purge or discipline themselves, seen in a false light. But both these temptations lead us away from the truth . . .'

Stratton was about to tell Roth that he didn't have time to listen to him talking in riddles when the man leant forward as far as his stomach would allow and placed a hand on his sleeve. He gave a surprisingly kindly smile, although the hooked nose and wide mouth caused Stratton's imagination, for a second, to superimpose on him the face of Mr Punch, trickster in cap and bells. 'As a child, I had strange episodes. The best way of describing them is as a downpour inside my head. It didn't hurt at the time, but afterwards the pain could become severe and I was compelled to lie quite still . . .' Wondering what was coming next – a revelation, perhaps, or possibly an attempt at exoneration, or at least explanation – Stratton nodded encouragingly.

'After a while,' said Roth, 'these episodes stopped. Many years went by without one – until the end of the war, in fact. I was in Berlin. People have told me that things were bad here, but . . .' Clownish mouth turned down at the corners, Roth shook his head. 'It was terrible. Barricades in the streets, old trams turned over and railway carriages filled with rubble, destroyed tanks, wreckage and smashed houses . . . There were child soldiers wandering about in uniforms made for men and people living in cellars that stank with excrement, with no light, only coming out to scavenge for food like rats. I saw a dead horse in the street once. People crowding round it with their knives, sawing the meat off it. When I touched it, it was still warm ...' He was talking to himself now, apparently unconscious of Stratton's presence. 'Hundreds of people committed suicide. They were afraid of what the Russians would do to them. There'd have been more suicides if people had had gas. They'd have put their heads in the ovens ... There were corpses wrapped in newspaper, buried in gardens and parks. Had to do it at night to avoid the soldiers. The Russians were looting, raping women ...'

Roth stopped and stared down at his feet. Stratton remembered that Dr Thorley of the Psychical Research Society had said that Roth claimed to be from Russia, but it didn't sound as if he'd been a soldier. In any case, Stratton thought, unless he was a lot younger than he looked, he'd have been in his fifties then, too old for active service, so perhaps he'd been an official of some sort. If Jewish, he surely would have been in a camp, although, if this were the case, he'd have been bloody lucky to survive, especially if they'd known he was epileptic, which was certainly what the 'episodes' he'd described sounded like. If Roth *were* a survivor, Stratton supposed he could have got back to Berlin afterwards – assuming (here, he remembered, with horrible clarity, the newsreels of Belsen he'd seen at the end of the war) that he was in any condition to go anywhere ...

Had he really seen all the things he'd described, or were they part of some terrible collective memory?

'Were you in a concentration camp?'

Without looking up, Roth batted the question away with his hand as if troubled by a fly. 'That was when the rain inside my head began again. It became very clear to me at that time that the most important thing was to find the truth and teach it to others. With truth would come justice. At the beginning, I imagined that if mankind could be taught a new way of thinking and acting, wars and their consequences might be avoided. I saw that I could either spend my life doing that, or I could spend it in a half-sleep, getting through it as comfortably as I could. There was, of course,' he raised his head and chuckled throatily, 'no choice.'

'Does Michael have a choice?' asked Stratton.

'Michael is young,' said Roth, 'but he will know what to do when the time comes. I have made sure of that.' He averted his head, as if in dismissal. Stratton left him staring into the fire and dashed up the stairs to give a contrite PC Briggs a graphic account of what would happen to him if he deserted his post even for a minute.

When he descended again, Stratton saw that Roth had neither moved nor, apparently, changed his expression, but he felt a withdrawal of presence as evident as a drop in physical temperature, as though the door to a roaring furnace had suddenly slammed shut.

CHAPTER FIFTY-SIX

'They've gone to the cottage hospital, sir,' said Adlard, in the car. 'Won't take long to get there.'

Stratton sat back in the passenger seat and closed his eyes. It struck him that – whatever *he* might think of Roth – the man, like Billy Graham, understood the extent to which people might hunger after something that was greater than themselves, and how this made them behave. His own philosophy of life, in so far as he had one, was his father's often repeated 'do your best'. For the students at the Foundation, this clearly wasn't enough. He could understand how such types might fall in love with someone who represented such authority and wisdom, and subjugate themselves to him to get what they craved, just as they did to political leaders. Rather, he imagined, like members of the Communist party, who despised individuality as 'bourgeois'.

Mary/Ananda was a bit different, though. She – rather like Tynan, he thought – wanted to be both in the thick of things and simultaneously rise above them. It was also a form of superiority, of self-selection, like her claims to have been visited by ghosts.

Had Miss Kirkland been lying to him, or had Roth? If Roth had, as he'd claimed, expelled Mary/Ananda from the Foundation, then he had no reason to protect her. Except, of course, that he did want to protect Michael, and she was, after all, his mother. 'A duty', he'd called it. All the same, she'd made a fool of him.

In a way, she'd made a fool of Miss Kirkland, too. Miss Kirkland, with all her certainty, who thought that individuals did not matter – but who'd been supplanted by Mary/Ananda, and who seemed to want, above all else, to please Roth. But clearly, accusing Mary/Ananda wouldn't please Roth, or he would, Stratton thought, have done so himself when he had the opportunity. Instead, he'd insisted that she'd made no confession.

He'd just have to hope that Mary/Ananda was in a fit state – and could be prevailed upon – to tell them herself. As for the business about Billy . . . Stratton opened his eyes and stared out of the window into the darkness, dazed by everything he'd seen and heard, unable to come to any conclusions.

The hospital was small, a pretty Victorian building with an ugly post-war addition sticking out on one side. Stratton was directed down a corridor where he found Ballard chatting to a uniformed policeman outside a door, as purposeful nurses with serious eyes squeaked across the new lino on brisk, rubber-soled feet. 'In there, is she?'

'Yes, sir,' said the policeman. 'Quite safe.'

Ballard's face was pale and somehow out of focus. Dazed, thought Stratton. 'How are you?'

'I'll live.' Ballard grimaced. 'No real damage. Hell of a bruise coming up on my chest, though. Sorry about your car.'

'We can worry about that later. The main thing is that you're all right. How's *she* doing?'

'Not too clever, I'm afraid. Have a look.' Ballard motioned him towards the small window cut into the door behind them.

Stratton looked. He wasn't sure what he'd expected – a scene of hysterics, perhaps, or at least agitation – but it wasn't what he saw. Mary/Ananda, propped up by a bank of pillows, was sitting up in bed, gowned, a bandage obscuring the top of her cloud of dark hair. The rest of it massed, dishevelled, around her shoulders. She was staring straight ahead of her, slack-jawed, a nurse beside her, fingers on her pulse, peering down at the watch she'd lifted from her starched bosom. Apparently satisfied, she gave Mary/Ananda's hand a kindly but impersonal pat, and, becoming aware of Stratton's gaze, gave him an almost imperceptible shake of her head before moving to the end of the bed to make a note on the chart. Mary/Ananda seemed to realise that she was being watched, because she turned her head.

There were the enormous dark eyes and sultry mouth, but she seemed oddly unrecognisable, and it took him a moment to realise why. She wasn't looking at him, but through him, as though he were part of the small window, and her gaze seemed somehow inhuman. Turning to Ballard, he asked, 'Is she drugged? Have they given her something?'

'The doctor didn't mention it – other than for the pain, that is. She was quite badly cut, and she had a hell of a bump on the head—'

'So she's concussed?'

'The doctor didn't seem to think so. He spouted a bit about delayed shock, but he obviously thinks something funny's going on, because he's telephoned for a psychiatrist to take a look at her. Told me he'd be along soon, if we wanted a chat.'

'Have *you* tried talking to her yet?'

Ballard shook his head. 'I was waiting for the all-clear from the doctor.'

The two men stood back as the nurse emerged from the room. 'May we go in?' asked Stratton.

'Dr Hicks said you could have five minutes, no more.' She glanced down at her watch in order to emphasise the exactness of this amount. 'I shall wait here.'

Mary/Ananda was once again staring straight ahead of her and didn't turn her head as they entered the room. 'Good evening, Mrs Milburn. I'm DI Stratton and this is DI Ballard. Do you remember us?' She did not move or even appear to acknowledge their presence. As they seated themselves on either side of the bed, Stratton saw that, close to, her cheekbones were as perfectly sculpted as he remembered, but there was a faint tracery of lines about her eyes and the skin of her jaw was just beginning to sag. Her hands were palm down on the bed covering, the bony knuckles of her wrists projecting like manacles from the sleeves of the hospital gown. Gazing at her, he found himself floundering, groping after words.

'We'd like you to tell us what happened this morning, please, Mrs Milburn,' said Ballard.

Still, she did not move or speak.

'We appreciate you've had a shock,' said Ballard, 'but we do need you to answer some questions.'

Nothing. Stratton stared at her almost flawless profile and wondered if she were faking.

'You have been charged with the attempted murder of Michael Milburn,' said Ballard. 'Several witnesses have told us that you tried to run him down in your car. What do you have to say about it?'

As the silence lengthened, Stratton suddenly remembered visiting the tramp, Shitty Sid, when he was dying in hospital. It hadn't been anything to do with work, simply a feeling that, as the station had been unable to discover a next of kin, *someone* ought to go and see the poor sod before he pegged it. Sid had been pretty far gone, but you still knew it was him, and not just from the smell, either. It was because of something *inside* him – his consciousness of himself, Stratton supposed you'd call it. Presence, that was the word. Mary/Ananda, on the other hand, seemed to be *absent*. It wasn't just a question of her not understanding what was being said: her not-thereness was so entire that she might as well not have been in the room.

Mary/Ananda was going on – or rather, not going on – as if she wasn't aware of her own existence. The contrast with their previous meeting – when she'd seemed very much aware of it – was extraordinary. He stared past her cheek to Ballard, who seemed to be mouthing something at him.

Ballard got up, jerking his thumb in the direction of the door. Stratton nodded and went to join him. 'Hopeless,' murmured Ballard. 'Might as well be talking to a waxwork. What say we wait for the trick-cyclist?'

Turning in the doorway, Stratton saw that Ananda's eyes were still fixed on the opposite wall.

CHAPTER FIFTY-SEVEN

Twenty minutes later the psychiatrist Dr Wardle, a large, expansive individual, emerged from examining Mary/Ananda and swept Stratton and Ballard down the corridor and into a consulting room.

'I understand that you require an evaluation of Mrs Milburn,' he said, parking himself behind the desk and waving at them to be seated. 'She is – as I'm sure you observed – in a bad way, but I haven't got a lot to go on. Perhaps you could fill me in on the details . . .'

It took Stratton almost half-an-hour to take Wardle through Mary/Ananda's history, including what she'd told him about her childhood, during which the psychiatrist nodded a great deal and took copious notes.

'Well,' he said finally, capping his pen with a flourish, 'one's always wary of giving diagnoses in these situations, and obviously I shall need to observe the patient more closely . . .' He paused, eyebrows raised in a vigorous dumb show, for the pair of them to acknowledge this, then continued, 'Judging by what you've told me, I'd say this is a case of narcissistic injury.'

'Meaning?' asked Stratton.

'In psychiatric terms, narcissism can be seen as a self-perceived form of perfectionism. It's not just a matter of liking to view oneself in a mirror – although that may come into it – but of having an elevated sense of self-worth, so that the sufferer believes him, or in this case, *her*, self to be more important than other people. These sorts of individuals can sometimes – although by no means always – have immensely fragile self-esteem and be unable to tolerate any form of criticism. Their grasp of reality is, therefore, somewhat tenuous. They tend to pursue selfish goals and exploit others for their own ends. This can, as you've mentioned, sometimes taken the form of fraudulence or deception. At the same time, they tend to require constant praise, attention and often, sympathy. Reinforcement, if you like. Those individuals who are not, for whatever reason, able to collude with the narcissist, or to be useful to them, are often perceived as worthless.'

'Surely,' said Ballard, 'that doesn't include their own children?'

'In a severe case, yes. As to the boy . . .' Wardle glanced down at the notes he'd made, 'Michael . . . he appears to be an important source of self-esteem for his mother. Very often, a narcissistic parent requires, shall we say, a specific *performance* from a child in order to aggrandise him or herself, and that would seem to be the case here. Such people often object when the child begins to develop independently of themselves – attempting to cut the boy off from the outside world would seem to be a symptom of that, although there were some other factors in this case – related, of course . . . Failure on the child's part to respond adequately – as they see it – may give rise to anger, criticism, attempts to instil guilt, and so on. Or, in some cases, outright rejection.'

'Or attempted murder?' asked Ballard.

'It's unusual,' said Wardle, 'but not unknown. But remember,' he raised a warning finger, 'we are talking hypothetically here.'

'I'd say you were spot on, so far,' said Stratton.

'Oh, good.' The psychiatrist sounded faintly sarcastic. 'Now,

touching on what you've told me about Mrs Milburn's own childhood – the matter of the mother's disappearance, and the behaviour of other family members, particularly the uncle. Assuming
that this is to be believed, it sounds as if she was the victim of
emotional and sexual injury at a young age, which may well be
linked to her subsequent behaviour.'

'What about the state she's in now?' asked Stratton.

'Based purely on what you've told me, I'd say that it's a drastic
reaction to a situation in which she feels both rejected – by the
people at this Foundation – and humiliated by being 'found out'
by them, and also, of course, by you yourselves. A psychic blow
– on top of which, of course, there are the physical effects of the
car accident. It's a defence mechanism. In some cases, it takes
the form of anger – irrational accusations and so on – and in
others, complete withdrawal from something that cannot be
faced. What it comes down to is that she can't square her reality
with your reality, and her ego will not allow her to make a compro-
mise between the two.'

'Will she recover?' asked Stratton.

Wardle gave an open-handed shrug. 'Impossible to say.'

'Well, what's the likelihood?'

'That, I don't know. I'm a psychiatrist, Inspector, not a bookie.'

'Pretty accurate, I thought,' said Ballard, as Adlard drove them
away from the hospital. 'Have you got a cigarette on you? I can't
find mine – think they must have fallen out of my pocket when
I pranged your car.'

'Here.' Stratton lit two and passed one over his shoulder.

'Thanks.' Ballard inhaled gratefully. 'I needed that. You know,
I'd swear she recognised me when she was lying in the road. She
looked up at me and said, 'Oh, it's *you*,' as if she'd expected somebody else – you, I suppose. But when we were in the ambulance,
she got downright weird.'

'Did she say anything?'

'No. It wasn't just that, though – to be honest, it reminded me of that film, *Bride of Frankenstein*. Elsie Whatsit. You know, married to Charles Laughton.'

'Elsa Lancaster. Something like that, anyway. What about her?'

'When she's first brought to life by the doctor and she doesn't know where she is or anything, and she's looking round all sort of twitchy and jerky with her eyes blazing. That's what she looked like – as if she'd been electrified or something, and she had no idea who anyone was, or even why she was there. When we got to the hospital and they opened the doors, she just sort of stopped moving, as if the current had been turned off, and she was . . . Well, you saw. How did you get on?'

'So,' said Ballard, when Stratton had finished, 'do you believe Roth, or Miss Kirkland?'

'I'm not sure I believe either of them. And I'm not inclined to believe what Mary/Ananda told Roth about Billy dying and then discovering she was pregnant, either.'

'Does seem a bit unlikely. I mean, Mrs Curtin didn't say anything about Billy being ill when she took him. I suppose it might have come on suddenly, but all the same . . . Do you think Miss Kirkland was lying about it?'

'No, I don't. She was far too specific about it – much more than when she was talking about what Mary/Ananda had said about Lloyd and Aylett, when she claimed she couldn't hear properly. She said Billy was buried at Hasketon, so I've asked Parsons to check up on it.'

'That reminds me,' said Ballard, 'we didn't speak to Dunning, did we? We could go and do that now – he's just outside Lincott.' He squinted at his watch. 'It's just gone half past six. Bit early for him to be prowling round the woods, I'd have thought, so we'd probably catch him.'

'Sure you're feeling up to it? I mean, if you want to go home, I could—'

'Not likely,' said Ballard. 'Quite apart from anything else, I'll get a royal bollocking from Pauline when she sees the state of me, and I'd like to put that off as long as possible.'

'Well,' said Stratton, as they pulled up in front of a tumbledown cottage, with light shining from its uncurtained windows, 'someone's in, at any rate.'

As they walked through the muddy, cratered garden, past the mangled remains of bicycle frames and prams and a single, stunted currant bush, six or seven children, tattered and shameless, piled out of the front door and paused for a second to stare at the pair of them defiantly. Then, as suddenly as if a starting pistol had gone off, they charged, shouting with ferocious energy, towards the looming darkness of the woods.

'Bloody clear off!'

Stratton, who'd been staring after the children, swung round. A man who he supposed must be Dunning was standing in the doorway. He was small, with the desiccated look of a jockey past his prime, shabby clothes, and fingertips and teeth stained ochre by years of rough tobacco.

'Sorry, gents. I meant them, not you . . . Always getting under my feet, they are. What can I do for you?'

'DI Ballard,' said Ballard, producing his identification. 'And this is DI Stratton. We'd like to ask you where you were on the fifth of November, in the afternoon.'

'Fetching wood for the big bonfire, wasn't I?' Dunning sounded defensive. 'Mr Tynan always lets us help ourselves.'

'I'm sure he does,' said Ballard, soothingly. 'That's not what we're here about. We need to ask you if you saw anyone in the wood.'

Dunning thought for a moment, then said, 'Yes, I did, as it happens. Two of 'em.'

'Two . . . ?'

'Women. Smart-looking, they were.'

'Did you recognise them?'

'One of 'em, I did. Couldn't tell you her name, though.'

'Does she live round here?'

'Up at the rectory . . . Or what used to be the rectory.'

'The Foundation, you mean? Where the vicar used to live?'

'That's the one. Funny lot up there now, and she's one of 'em. Keep 'emselves to 'emselves, but I've seen her in the village a fair few times, with the boy who lives there. Very stuck up, she is. Wouldn't give me the time of day. Not that I tried to talk to her, or the other one – they didn't know I was there, because I didn't go close, just saw 'em through the trees.'

'What does she look like?' asked Stratton. 'The one you recognised, I mean.'

'Smart-looking, I told you. Small, thinnish. Tweeds and a head-scarf. That's what caught my eye. Blue, it was.'

'What sort of age?'

Dunning's forehead crinkled up in thought. 'Fifty or thereabouts, I'd say. Fifty-five, maybe. A good bit older than the other one, at any rate. Sounds like this.' Screwing up his mouth, Dunning said, 'How do you do?' It was a surprisingly good imitation of Miss Kirkland's flutey voice.

Stratton and Ballard exchanged glances. 'Know her, do you?' asked Dunning.

Ignoring this, Stratton asked, 'You'd be able to identify her, would you?'

Visibly alarmed, Dunning fingered his grubby collar, as if he were imagining it being felt by an official hand, and was starting to say he didn't know about that when Ballard cut him off. 'It would be a great help to us, Mr Dunning.' Staring intently at the poacher, he added, 'I'll make sure that PC Parsons remembers it.'

A calculating expression passed across Dunning's wizened face. 'I don't want any trouble, you understand . . .'

'We'll make sure of that, Mr Dunning,' said Stratton. 'What about the other one? What did she look like?'

'Younger, like I said. She had a scarf, too. Flowers or summat. Light-coloured coat, boots. Bit of a looker, from what I could see. It's her that was killed, isn't it? I heard about that.' The thought of reporting it, Stratton thought, clearly hadn't crossed his mind.

'Would you be able to recognise her again?' he asked.

Dunning goggled at him. 'You mean you want me to—'

'From a photograph.'

'Dunno about that. Only saw her from the side, you see, and I never set eyes on her before.'

'Fair enough. Were either of them carrying anything?'

'I don't know about her – couldn't see – but the other 'un had a bag.'

'What sort?'

Dunning looked nonplussed. 'Just an ordinary handbag. What women have.'

Remembering what the pathologist Trickett had said, Stratton thought that, while you certainly couldn't get a rifle into the average-sized handbag, a pistol was a different matter – if they could just find the bloody thing.

'What were the women doing when you saw them?'

'Just walking. Nothing particular.'

'Talking?'

'Yes. That is, I heard voices but I never heard what they were saying.'

'What time was it?'

'Maybe three o'clock, but I can't be sure.' He held up his right wrist to show he wore no watch. 'Still light, any road.'

'What was it Miss Kirkland said about knowledge?' asked Ballard, as they walked back to the car.

'She said,' Stratton made a quivering attempt at falsetto, '*that ours was knowledge that must be acquired through facts alone.*'

'You're not half as good as Dunning,' said Ballard. 'He had her spot on.'

'It's not conclusive though, is it?' said Stratton. 'Not enough to hang a case on, at any rate. Assuming that it *was* Mrs Aylett and Miss Kirkland that Dunning saw, because the descriptions certainly fit – all it actually tells us is that Miss Kirkland was the last person to be seen with her.'

'You could fit a pistol into a handbag,' said Ballard, who'd obviously been thinking along the same lines as he had. 'It's probably at the bottom of the lake by now.'

'And Mrs Aylett's bag with it. Assuming she had one, of course.'

'I was thinking about that. Mrs Curtin said that she'd never have left home without it. She told me they had the same bag – bought them together. She showed me hers. A crocodile thing with a gold clasp – or some sort of metal, anyway.'

'You know,' said Stratton thoughtfully, 'Michael told me that Miss Kirkland took him to see the bonfire on the green. She could have disposed of Mrs Aylett's bag then.'

'Bit obvious, a woman wandering about with two handbags then throwing one of them on the fire in front of everybody.'

'Not necessarily. There'd be a lot of people milling about, chucking on all sorts of rubbish. The clasp wouldn't burn, would it? Gold would melt, of course, but if it were made of something else, that would still be there. And if there is, we can compare it with Mrs Curtin's bag.'

'They've probably raked it over pretty thoroughly, but I suppose it might be worth a look. We can do it tomorrow. No point trying to mess about with torches now – if it's there, it isn't going anywhere, and we'd be bound to miss it in the dark.'

'I suppose so,' said Stratton. 'What about a drink, then – bit of Dutch courage before you face Pauline? You look as if you could do with one, and I could certainly use a pick-me-up.'

CHAPTER FIFTY-EIGHT

The saloon bar of the George and Dragon was empty but for a couple of farmers arguing about myxomatosis. 'Put your money away,' said Stratton, as they waited for the landlord to come through from the kitchen. 'I'm buying. You're the hero of the hour, and all that.'

'I say, thanks most awfully.' Ballard affected a toff's bray to hide his embarrassment.

When Denton appeared, Stratton, who'd completely forgotten the events of the morning, found himself on tenterhooks. All it needed was an innuendo about him being out the previous night . . . He made a point of staring at the man with meaningful intensity as he ordered their pints, but apart from a sly smile and a wink as he handed over the change, Denton gave no sign of what he'd surmised.

'Well, cheers,' said Ballard, when they'd settled themselves in a corner by the fire. 'It's beginning to look as if we might actually get a result.'

'Don't count your chickens,' said Stratton, fishing his cigarettes out of his pocket and offering the packet to Ballard. 'We thought that before, didn't we – about Billy – and look what happened.'

'That's true. Roth was happy enough to string us along, wasn't he? Do you think he's behind the whole thing?'

'What, the evil mastermind? No, I don't. He may be wrong-headed, but he's not . . . *malignant*. The Foundation isn't like . . . oh, I don't know . . . something in one of Tynan's novels. Worshippers of Satan trying to take over the world. I'm beginning to wonder if – behind all the carry-on – he isn't as confused as we are. Not that he'd ever admit it, of course.'

'Perhaps you're right. Goodness, I'm tired. Tell you the truth, I feel as if an entire rugger team's been using me as a trampoline.'

'I'm not surprised,' said Stratton. 'Want to call it a night?'

Ballard shook his head. 'Pauline'll have a go at me, all right – but, to be honest, that's not the only reason I'm not keen to get back.'

'Oh?'

'It's the business over the baby. What I told you.'

'She seemed happy enough to me,' said Stratton. 'Not that she'd tell me if she wasn't, of course,' he added hastily, 'but she didn't seem angry or upset.'

'She is, though,' said Ballard. 'We can't seem to get away from it. I try to forget about it – the baby, I mean – and a lot of the time I *do* forget about it. Because it doesn't affect me . . . you know, *directly*. But sometimes – last night, for example – Pauline behaves as if . . . Well, if she thinks I might have forgotten about it for a single moment, even when I'm at work, then I must be a monster. And now she's bringing the Foundation into it—'

'How do you mean?' asked Stratton.

'She's been going to lectures there. She says they're "kind" and, what's more, she can "talk to them". Apparently I've got all the wrong ideas about her. Preconceived ideas, she said. It's not like her at all – she's just parroting what she's heard up there, and it's all to do with this bloody baby she isn't having.' Ballard finished his drink and said, bleakly, 'tonight there'll be more of the same, and if you want the truth, I'm dreading another row.'

Stratton stood up. 'She won't miss you just yet. Let me get you another drink.'

'What, and go home pissed? Because that's how she'll see it. Proof that I'm an uncaring bastard and all that.'

'Just a half, then.'

'Oh . . .' Ballard looked round the pub as if seeking permission from the assorted fixtures and fittings. 'All right, then. Thanks.'

'You know,' said Stratton, who'd had time to think while standing at the bar waiting his turn after some new arrivals, 'I can see that the divine plan, or whatever you want to call it – that your fate will always be what you deserve – is a lot more attractive, especially to someone in Pauline's position, than the idea that, however good you are, life is just a series of random incidents with no guarantee of a happy ending.'

Ballard stared down at his glass. 'It's a pretty frightening thought, isn't it? No wonder people look for alternatives. Especially with everything that's happening at the moment. It doesn't seem fair, that we went through all that during the war and now our former allies could press a button and wipe us out and there's fuck all we can do about it.' He did a bit more staring into his glass, then said, 'With Pauline, it's not that I'm not sympathetic, because I am.' Taking a swig of his drink, he continued, 'But the way she was talking last night, well . . . I lost my temper. Not much, but enough. And I said perhaps thinking she *had* to have another baby was a wrong idea, too.'

'Thing is, though,' said Stratton, 'it's a bit more than that, isn't it? More than an idea, I mean. Women get so . . . *set* on it, don't they? It's a physical urge. I don't think it's something we can really understand.'

'Well, I'm buggered if I do.' Ballard looked intently at the bar, where Denton was pulling a pint for an elderly chap whose hat looked as if it had wilted on his head, and said, 'I came down this way this morning, about four o'clock. Couldn't sleep, so I went for a walk. Thought it might help clear my head. Didn't see your car, though.'

'Didn't you?' Stratton made a conscious effort to keep his voice level. 'I must have left it around the back.'

Ballard looked him straight in the eye for just long enough for Stratton to realise that he knew this not to be the case, then said, quite neutrally, 'Yes.'

For a moment, there was the potential for Stratton to return the confidence and tell Ballard about Diana and perhaps even Monica. In a way, he supposed, it was the decent thing – a sort of personal version of buying one's round – but he couldn't bring himself to do it, not yet. He could hardly frame it for himself, never mind trying to explain it to anybody else. 'I remember, now,' he said, hoping he wasn't overdoing it. 'Got a bit of a scare this morning, when I came out and it wasn't there.'

'I'll bet,' said Ballard. There was no trace of sarcasm in his voice, only agreement, but he was, Stratton thought, disappointed by the lack of trust. He wanted to explain that it wasn't that at all, but saying this was even less possible than talking about the other things.

CHAPTER FIFTY-NINE

After dinner – two small and very dry lamb cutlets, followed by one of the new-fangled instant desserts, which he didn't much like – Stratton borrowed Denton's copy of the *Mirror* and sat reading in the snug. *SOVIET ARMS BUILD-UP; FRENCH KILL 26 REBELS IN ALGERIA; Sir Anthony Eden's Government beat off a Socialist censure motion on Suez in the Commons last night* . . . After a couple of desultory conversations with other patrons, he said goodnight to Denton, getting a leer in return, and went up to his room. It was still early – not yet ten – but he felt exhausted. He sat down on the edge of the bed, heeled off his shoes, loosened his tie and, resting his elbows on his knees, stared without really seeing at a small but heavily framed painting of a winsome child clutching a kitten, and attempted to get his thoughts into some sort of order.

After a while, he took out his notebook and pencil, but that didn't help. When he looked at his wristwatch and realised that half an hour had passed, during which he'd smoked three cigarettes and done a not-very-accurate doodle of his car, he decided to give the thing up as a bad job and go to bed.

Lying back on the pillow, he closed his eyes – then opened them again in seconds. This wasn't going to work, either. The moment he'd emptied his mind of the case, Monica had filled it, and now the words MY DAUGHTER IS A LESBIAN seemed to have written themselves like newspaper headlines on the insides of his eyelids.

What *would* Jenny have made of it, he wondered. He thought again about what Diana had said, and realised how ridiculous it was to imagine that, if her mother had not been killed, Monica would now be happily married with children. Jenny would have been shocked by the news, of course, but he suspected that once she'd calmed down she'd probably have agreed with Diana. Women were often surprisingly sensible about these sorts of things, and practical; at least in situations where circumstances allowed them to be honest.

Somewhat comforted by this train of thought, Stratton eventually drifted off to sleep, waking at half past three, crumpled and uncomfortable, his mouth like sandpaper and his bladder full to bursting. A glance under the bed told him there was nothing for it but to descend the narrow, uneven stairs. There were two other rooms beside the bathroom on the next landing but, unsure whether they were inhabited, he decided against putting on the light – he'd just have to hope he didn't wake anyone up by falling down and breaking his neck. He groped for the banister and clung to it, wincing as the floorboards creaked like pistol shots, but nobody stirred – or if they did, they didn't show themselves.

There was just enough moonlight shining in above the net curtain halfway down the bathroom window for him to see what he was doing. He relieved himself, did up his trousers, and washed his hands as best he could in a meagre dribble of water to avoid making a noise. Feeling euphoric with relief, as if he'd achieved something marvellous, he grinned at what he could see of himself in the flyblown square of shaving mirror propped on the narrow shelf above the sink.

He thought about the last time he'd seen Monica, a fortnight before. She'd paid him a visit on a Sunday afternoon and they'd walked up to the allotment together. She'd brought him a cake she'd made specially, and some cheese straws, and she'd been jolly and relaxed, excited about the film she was working on and groaning at his puns and jokes like she'd always done. Picturing her face, the smiling eyes and the fall of glossy dark hair, he felt a fierce rush of protective love towards her. What was it Tynan had said about getting caught up in something and not always seeing what is in front of us? At the time he'd thought it was just more poppycock, but in one way, the man had been right. He had been so appalled by what Diana had told him that he'd forgotten that Monica was actually very happy. That was the important thing. 'I want Monica to be happy,' he told his reflection, 'that's all that matters.'

Still grinning – now at the fact that altering your point of view could be just as simple and effective as emptying your bladder – he negotiated his way back to bed, changed into his pyjamas and, within minutes, was asleep. He dreamt of Jenny for the first time in months. In the dream, he was walking along Tottenham High Road on his way to catch a bus when he saw her crossing the road ahead of him. He felt a surge of relief – Jenny was alive, everything was all right again – and love for her. She looked young, the age she'd been when they were courting, and she was wearing a blue dress he'd particularly liked that had been a favourite of hers at the time. When he caught her eye, she smiled at him and waved briskly before turning away and walking on. Then a line of buses came past right in front of him and he lost sight of her.

Waking, he lay wet-eyed in the darkness, and knew that Jenny had given both him and Monica her blessing.

CHAPTER SIXTY

They spent almost three hours on the village green, poking through the soggy, scattered remains of the bonfire in a persistent drizzle, before Ballard came upon a blackened metal clasp.

'Thank God for that,' said Stratton, when they were crouched in front of the station's inadequate gas fire trying to get dry.

'We'll need to get a comparison with Mrs Curtin's bag,' said Ballard. 'I need to tell her about poor Billy. I'd best go after lunch, and I can pick up the bag while I'm there. Then we can send it and our clasp to Trickett and his minions. Parsons,' he added, as the policeman appeared with two mugs of tea, 'you're a godsend.'

'Thank you, sir. Got some information just come in about the baby buried at Hasketon.'

'Fire away.'

'Well, for one thing Billy was cremated.'

'So bang goes our chance of an exhumation if we need one,' said Stratton. 'What was the name?'

'William Thomas Milburn, sir. Ten months, as you said. The vicar remembered it particularly because he knew Mrs Milburn's husband.'

'I wish he'd mentioned that before,' said Stratton, 'but I suppose he thought we knew about it.'

'I don't know, sir,' said Parsons, 'but the ashes were scattered beside Reverend Milburn's grave and there's a wooden cross to mark the place.'

'That's cosy,' said Ballard. 'Keep your victims together.'

'If they are victims,' said Stratton. 'We don't know that.'

'I don't suppose we'll ever know about those two. I'd best go over and tell Mrs Curtin after lunch – I can pick up the bag while I'm there. Parsons, can you try and get hold of the kid's medical records?'

'If he's got any,' said Stratton, darkly. 'Think about it – she told Roth she didn't have any money, hence the wooden cross, and there wasn't any National Health in those days.'

'Well,' Ballard told Parsons, 'give it a go, anyway. She might have been able to sweet-talk someone – or blackmail them as she did with Slater. Not that any doctor's going to come forward to say so . . .'

'Unless, of course, she's able to give us the information herself.' Stratton glanced at his wristwatch. 'I'll ring the hospital this afternoon.'

After a hasty and not particularly pleasant sandwich lunch, Ballard departed for Mrs Curtin's home at Wickham Market and Stratton telephoned Dr Wardle about Mary/Ananda.

'There's no change,' said the psychiatrist, 'you'd be wasting your time.'

'She hasn't spoken?'

'Not a word, and I have to say I'm not optimistic. At least, not in the short term.'

Wardle promised to inform him if there was any change to Mrs Milburn's condition, and rang off. A second later, Grove called. 'This is your lucky day, old son.'

'Oh?'

'Two sightings of your Miss Patricia Kirkland on the night of the thirtieth. One walking along Wardour Street and the other in Ingestre Place, getting out of a car that the informant identified as a Hillman Minx.'

'Excellent! Remind me to buy you a drink when I get back. What time was this?'

Grove sucked his teeth. 'Neither was what you'd call exact – in fact, between you and me, the chap who saw her in Wardour Street said he was three sheets to the wind. Only remembered her because he'd nipped down Duck Lane for a piss and collided with her when he came out again. A real sourpuss, he said – as if she was sucking a lemon. It was only when he got home he realised his flies were still undone.'

'Duck Lane's off Broadwick Street, isn't it?'

'Yes, right before Wardour Street, so she'd have been almost opposite Flaxman Court. The chap said it was sometime around eleven, because the pubs were shutting, but he couldn't be more specific than that.'

'What about the one in Ingestre Place?'

'He works in a small club in a basement down there. Said he saw her about an hour before closing – that's at midnight – when he came up for some air.'

'Right.' Stratton flipped through his notebook. 'Mrs Linder said she was in by quarter past eleven, and she said Wintle came in at quarter to twelve.'

'Sounds like she must have been in and out by eleven fifteen, then.'

'He must have let her in,' said Stratton. 'If you're right about the time, the only other person in the house was Mrs Hendry, and she said she didn't hear anything, never mind answer the door. Mind you, I think she might be a bit deaf.'

'Wouldn't have heard any sounds of a struggle, then,' said Grove. 'I must say,' he added, 'that if I was going to do someone in I wouldn't go armed with a pair of scissors – unless she picked them up on the spot, of course.'

During the last part of this, Parsons barged into the office and, ignoring the fact he was on the phone, began talking very fast. 'Sorry, Grove, it looks as if I need to go. I'll call you later . . . What is it, Parsons?'

'The Old Rectory, sir. Call from Wickstead. Says there's been an incident involving the boy, and can you get up there at once?'

The light was just beginning to fade as Stratton, driven by Adlard, turned up the avenue of trees that led to the Foundation. Bare branches twisting against the darkening sky, they had a tormented look to them. And was it his imagination, or did the building itself look spikier and more oppressive than usual?

Adlard shivered as they got out of the car. 'Creepy, isn't it? I never really noticed before.'

'It's certainly very quiet.'

There were no lights on in the hall, the dusk had cast a grey veil over everything in the place, and Stratton felt the air pressing in on him, giving a prickling sensation at the nape of his neck as though the building were invisibly alive, with eyes and ears of its own, waiting for something. He felt suddenly afraid, with a sort of split-second sensation that something monstrous was about to happen, and the house knew it. 'I can see why Mrs Milburn managed to convince people that the place was haunted,' he murmured to Adlard. 'Where the bloody hell is every—'

His words were cut off by a scream of 'No!' from somewhere above their heads, a piercing, desperate sound that might have come from a woman or a child.

'Christ!' Adlard made for the stairs at a run with Stratton just behind him. As they raced upwards, there was another scream, followed by the sounds of running feet as various of the students dashed across the landing towards the source of the noise. Adlard pushed his way through the knot of people clustered outside Roth's room, Stratton in his wake, and stopped in the doorway as if held back by an invisible cordon. Policewoman Wickstead, white-faced, scrambled sideways through the crush to his elbow, her voice an urgent whisper. 'I'm sorry – I couldn't stop him – there wasn't time—'

Stratton silenced her with a chopping motion of his hand. 'Stay there and keep quiet.'

Inside the room were four figures, frozen in position. Roth by the window, his hand with its cigarette suspended halfway to his mouth, Tynan beside him in a chair, looking stricken and Miss Kirkland behind him, mouth agape, were all staring at Michael, who stood in the centre of the room, his back to the onlookers at the door.

'Keep them all back,' Stratton said to Adlard, and stepped past him into the room. As he did so, he saw that the boy held a gun and was pointing it directly at Roth.

CHAPTER SIXTY-ONE

There was a moment of heavy, thrumming silence, followed by a howl of pain and rage that made the crowd around the door flinch and draw back. It took a moment before Stratton realised that the sound was coming from Michael. Tynan's eyes were tightly closed and his heavy face screwed up grotesquely as though folded in on itself, and Miss Kirkland had clapped her hands to her ears, jerking backwards and forwards in a frantic attempt to block out the noise. Only Roth appeared unmoved.

'You lied to me,' shouted Michael. 'You lied to everyone, and they believed you!' He began sobbing, his words breaking up, body heaving, the gun jumping in his hand. 'You – did – this! You! All of it! You made her do it ... you *told* her things, you used her to ... to ... And you used me ... And you couldn't— You don't care about anything! You think it doesn't matter!'

They must have been arguing for some time, Stratton thought, because any rationality Michael might have been able to summon at the start had clearly gone out of the window. 'What do you think of this?' he yelled at Roth. 'I don't care about you! You're not important – you're just a big, fat *liar*!'

Roth, whose eyes were fixed on Michael, made growling noises in his throat as though preparing to speak, but no words came.

A wail, thin and pitiful, burst from Miss Kirkland. 'What about this?' screamed Michael, brandishing the gun. 'Does this matter?'

Shit, thought Stratton. I'm responsible for this. That conversation. Could he have put the idea of defying Roth into the boy's mind? This was a hell of a lot more than just defiance, but all the same ... How had he managed to get hold of a gun? And where the hell was Briggs?

Michael had fallen silent. He lowered the gun and swung it back and forth by his side, staring down at it as though mesmerised.

'Michael.' Stratton took another step into the room. The boy remained quite still, as if he had not heard. 'Michael.'

The boy turned slowly, still holding the gun by his side, and stared into Stratton's eyes. Holding his gaze, Stratton felt as though invisible ropes were binding them together as a single entity. He took another pace forward, holding out his hand. Another step, and he'd be able to touch Michael. He was aware of the tension in his muscles, of the effort of keeping his face neutral, of the concentration of Adlard and the knot of people behind him, of Roth, Tynan and Miss Kirkland, all focused on the gun in the boy's hand. Don't look at it, he told himself. Just keep looking at *him*.

Michael's eyes shone electric-blue, with the wide, perfect stare of a child. They drew him in so that it seemed that there was no space between them, just absolute stillness, as though they were the centre of a vortex.

'I understand,' Stratton told him. 'It will be all right, I promise.'

The boy remained motionless, his expression unchanged, and Stratton had no idea if he'd understood or even heard him. 'Michael, please give me the gun.'

The boy gave him a brief, emphatic shake of the head and then, before Stratton or anyone else could move to stop him, whirled round and shot Roth, point-blank, in the chest.

*

Stratton heard a scream from somewhere behind him. Michael staggered backwards and then, righting himself, stared at the gun as though he'd never seen it before and, dropping it, hurled himself at Stratton, burying his face in his chest and bursting into noisy sobs. Roth was slumped against the wall, blood staining his grey waistcoat, cigarette still burning beside the upturned sole of his left shoe. His head was hanging, as if he were staring down at the wound, one hand clawing upwards at his chest, the other limp at his side. Miss Kirkland, who'd flown across the room, was kneeling beside him, keening and pawing at his clothing. Behind him, Adlard was herding the watchers onto the landing, with instructions that they were to remain where they were.

'You,' Stratton snapped at Tynan, who was still sitting, slack-jawed, in his chair, 'telephone for an ambulance. And don't even think of leaving the premises.' Policewoman Wickstead pushed past him as he left and, shooing Miss Kirkland away from Roth, knelt down beside him and began unbuttoning his waistcoat. Stratton saw that a small amount of blood had pooled on his white shirt front and clamped Michael's head more firmly against his chest so that he shouldn't see.

Adlard appeared at his side. 'I'll make sure no one leaves.'

'Keep an eye on Tynan,' said Stratton. 'He'll be in the office.'

Adlard nodded and disappeared again, shutting the door after him. As his footsteps retreated down the corridor, there was silence, apart from Michael's whimpers and the hoarse rasp of Roth's breath.

Stratton stroked the boy's head. 'Can you get him out of here?' he asked Wickstead. 'Take him to his room and keep him quiet.'

Michael, limp now and placid, allowed himself to be led away. Kneeling beside Roth, Stratton could see just how hopeless the situation was. The bullet hole was over Roth's heart. The small amount of visible blood was, he thought, a bad sign rather than a good one – the bleeding would be internal. 'The ambulance'll be here soon,' he murmured, pushing up Roth's cuff to feel a pulse that was barely there. As he disengaged his hand, Roth gave a great groan. The force of this last expulsion of breath moved his head slightly, so that his face was a mere three inches from Stratton's own. His skin was the colour and texture of putty, the lips a purplish blue. He wasn't looking *at* Stratton, but *through* him, and his eyes were wide, fixed in an astonished stare.

To the left of him, Miss Kirkland, slumped in a chair like a marionette with its strings cut, gave a single sharp cry and put her hands over her face.

Stratton stood up and, facing her, said, 'Patricia Kirkland, I am arresting you for the murder of Rosemary Aylett and Jeremy Lloyd. You are not obliged to say anything, but I must warn you that anything you do say will be taken down in writing and may be given in evidence against you.'

When she neither moved nor acknowledged this, Stratton leant down, put a hand on her shoulder and said, 'You told me that my knowledge must be acquired through the facts alone, and I have acquired them.'

Miss Kirkland took her hands away from her face. For a moment, her gaze rested on Roth, and then she looked up at Stratton. Her expression, he thought, bore the imprint of a long and exhausting struggle that she had lost.

'Someone . . . saw me?'

'Yes. Come on,' said Stratton. 'Let's get you out of here.'

CHAPTER SIXTY-TWO

Stratton stood on the driveway, watching the retreating tail-lights of the police cars taking Miss Kirkland and Michael back to the station. The boy, who had not yet been charged, had not spoken, but simply allowed himself to be led away by Wickstead, head bowed.

'Parsons is going to telephone Trickett from the station,' said Ballard, who'd arrived from Wickham Market while they were waiting for cars to be brought from Sudbury to collect the pair and gone straight inside to supervise things. 'The ambulance people can take the body to the police mortuary. I asked Parsons to get hold of the welfare lady for Michael.'

'It shouldn't have happened,' said Stratton. 'I should have stopped him.' He shook two cigarettes from his packet and handed one to Ballard. 'Chilly out here. You want to go back in?'

'Rather stay put for a moment, if it's all the same to you.' Ballard bent his head for the match. 'If you want the truth, I never want to set foot in the bloody place again.'

Stratton turned towards the house, where light was spilling out from gaps in the curtains, behind which the students, who'd been marshalled downstairs into the hall, were having their statements taken by two other policemen who'd been sent for from nearby villages. He'd sensed their excitement when they'd arrived – this, they knew, was something that happened only once in a lifetime of country policing.

'Me neither. Christ, I should have stopped him. I could have.'

Ballard shook his head. 'Too quick. Adlard told me what happened. Nobody could have—'

'I don't mean then, so much, I mean before. I should have realised when I spoke to him—'

'You didn't tell him to kill Roth, did you?'

'No, but I must have put the idea into his head, you know, telling him that things weren't really the way Roth said they were.'

'He probably had no idea he was going to do it when you spoke to him. He was asleep, wasn't he, when you left?'

'Definitely.'

'There you are, then. And you didn't know he had a loaded gun in his room, did you?'

'No. How the hell did he get it, anyway?'

'God knows,' said Ballard. 'But guess who searched his room?'

'Don't tell me – Harwood.'

'The very same. The boy'd hidden it behind the skirting, down by his bed. Miss Wickstead said he had it out of there and in his hand in a matter of seconds. She thought he was asleep.'

'What the bloody hell was Briggs doing?'

Ballard sighed. 'The Gents. By the time he got back, Michael was in Roth's room with the gun.'

'For Christ's sake. Right, I think we'd better see Tynan – try and clarify what happened.'

Tynan, sitting on an upright chair by the empty grate in the library, rose awkwardly as they entered. He looked smaller than before, as if he'd shrunk, and very shaken. Stratton noticed a tremor as he raised his cigarette to his lips.

'Mr Roth?' he asked. 'Is he . . . ? I didn't hear the ambulance.'

'He's dead,' said Stratton brutally. 'Sit down.' Looking around him, he saw a strangely cheerless room, made more so by the absence of a fire. There were no armchairs – nowhere cosy to curl up and read – and the books on the shelves, apart from the Bible and Shakespeare, were the same jumble of funny stuff he'd seen in Lloyd's room in London. There were no novels, not even Tynan's, or anything that could be called 'light reading'.

Pulling up a chair, Stratton said, 'Perhaps you'd like to tell me what happened.'

'Michael just appeared,' said Tynan. 'He was so angry – shouting – Mr Roth tried to talk to him, but he wouldn't listen. He kept saying something about a trick, and it being Mr Roth's fault. He was so . . .' Tynan shook his head, looking dazed. 'Just like her.'

'Like Mrs Milburn?'

'Yes. That rage, that energy . . . I tried to take the gun from him, but he was too fast for me.'

'Do you know where he got the gun?'

Tynan sighed. 'I gave it to him.'

Stratton stared at him. 'You *gave* a loaded gun to a boy who is not yet eleven. Are you insane?' Tynan's customary indignation wattled his face momentarily, but was then replaced by something else that Stratton couldn't quite read. 'What sort of gun is it?' he asked.

'A revolver. Webley Mark IV, .38. There's no doubt – I recognised it.'

'You do realise you could be charged with aiding and abetting, don't you?'

'I've been teaching Michael to shoot, Inspector. Several months ago he asked me if he could have a gun to practise with—'

'But that's a service weapon. You don't shoot game with it.'

Tynan swallowed. 'Target practice – tin cans on a wall and so on. That was the one he chose.'

'So he asked for it, and you gave it to him without a second thought?'

'Michael . . .' Tynan leant forward.

Thinking he saw the familiar look – the initiate in smug possession of knowledge explaining to the outsider – on the man's face, Stratton pounced. 'Yes, we know. Michael's a special case.' Nodding meaningfully, he added, 'Well, if he wasn't a special case before, he certainly is now. Very special. Thanks to you people, he stands a very good chance of spending the rest of his life in a special institution. And – just before we go – I feel I should tell you that I have arrested Patricia Kirkland.'

Tynan gave Stratton a look of total incomprehension. 'Why?'

'For the murder of both Jeremy Lloyd and Mrs Aylett.'

Tynan shook his head. 'I don't understand. Do you know what happened to the other boy?'

'Billy? He died, Mr Tynan. Very soon after Mrs Milburn "adopted" him.'

Tynan put his elbows on his knees and buried his face in his hands.

CHAPTER SIXTY-THREE

Wickstead was waiting for them at the police station. She looked shell-shocked, Stratton thought, as well she might. 'He's in the interview room,' she said. 'The welfare lady's with him. Her name's Mrs Dane.'

'Has he said anything?'

'Not a word. He must be wicked,' she burst out suddenly, as if the thought could not be contained, utter revulsion in her face.

'He's not wicked,' said Stratton wearily. 'He's a child. He's angry and confused and probably very frightened.'

'Some of the children round here are no better than animals,' said the policewoman. 'It's their families – houses like stables – the way they live. You might expect it from them, but *him*!' She fell silent, blinking back tears.

'I know,' said Stratton, gently. 'And you can tell us about it later. But perhaps, for now, you might bring us some tea?'

When she had gone, Stratton and Ballard exchanged glances. 'Can't blame her,' said Ballard. 'Delayed shock. She's just had the fright of her life, and she's only young, too. And,' he added, 'she's got a point. You can imagine what a jury will make of it.'

'Interesting that Tynan said Michael reminded him of Mary/ Ananda, though,' Stratton said. 'Perhaps it's hereditary.'

'Usually is, isn't it, madness? But we both know it's about a lot more than that.'

Stratton sighed. The collective lunacy that had brought Michael to this point was going to be well-nigh impossible, even for a clever defence barrister, to explain in any way that was comprehensible to the average person.

Ballard cut across his thoughts. 'I take it Mary/Ananda hasn't improved, then?'

''Fraid not. And I get the impression we shouldn't hold our breath.'

Mrs Dane, solid and unflappable with a long face and downy hair on her upper lip, made Stratton think of a police horse. By contrast Michael, huddled in a chair next to her, looked small, cold and horribly vulnerable; a child entirely alone but for such official comfort as the state could provide. Of course, thought Stratton, he had always been alone, in the sense of being treated virtually as a living god and having no shared experience with friends his own age. He hardly knew he was a boy at all. But now, in the course of a week, he'd lost everyone and everything he'd ever had.

If I hadn't seen it with my own eyes, Stratton thought, I'd have a bloody hard job believing he'd killed a mouse, never mind a human being. Glancing at Ballard, he could tell that he was thinking the same thing.

Realising how imposing the pair of them must look, Stratton hunched over the table in an effort to appear smaller. The tea being brought, Wickstead retreated to a chair by the door and stared at Michael, as if she didn't quite believe that he wouldn't produce another pistol and kill them all.

'How are you feeling, Michael? Are you warm enough?'

'Yes, thank you,' said the boy, automatically polite. After a second's hesitation, he added, 'Is Mr Roth dead?'

'I'm afraid so.'

'Are you sure?'

'Quite sure.' Suddenly realising that Michael was having a hard time understanding that Roth *could* die he added, 'A person – even Mr Roth – is no different from a partridge in that respect.' This got him a reproving look from Mrs Dane. 'We're all mortal, I'm afraid. Even you. Now, I'm going to have to charge you with killing Mr Roth. Do you understand what that means?'

'Yes. Mr Hardy – he's my tutor – he told me about the law.'

'That's good.' Clearing his throat, Stratton said, 'Michael James Milburn, I am arresting you for the murder of Theodore Roth. You are not obliged to say anything, but I must warn you that anything you do say will be taken down in writing and may be given in evidence against you.'

Michael blinked. 'How will I know it's right?'

'Well, you can tell us what happened in your own words, and DI Ballard here is going to write it down. Then you can read it and see if it's right and a true record of what you said, and then, if it is, you sign it. That will be your statement. After that, we'll need to take your fingerprints, and then we'll get you some supper, and you can stay here overnight. Is there anything you'd like to ask me at this point?'

Michael hung his head, picked at a loose thread on the knee of his trousers for a moment and then said, 'I won't be on my own, will I? You won't lock me in and leave me?'

He looked so forlorn that Stratton felt an actual physical pang in his heart. 'Of course not. There'll be someone here all the time. You can bang on the door if you need anything. Now, why don't you tell us what happened.'

'I didn't want to kill him.' Michael sounded as plaintive and uncomfortable as a boy trying to explain a cricket ball through a window. 'I don't know why I did it. I was angry, that's all.'

'Why don't you go back a bit?' asked Stratton. 'Tell us about your life at the Foundation.' Michael looked at him doubtfully. 'Tell us what it was like. So that we understand. It's all a bit unusual to us, you see.'

'People were always telling me how lucky they were to know me,' said Michael. 'They said I was lucky, too.' He frowned. 'Actually, I don't think they meant "lucky" like winning something, but more that it was meant to happen and it had, so that was good . . .'

'Why did they say that?'

'Because of my mother. They said she brought me to Mr Roth so that I could fulfil my function.' The last part came out in a flat, mechanical tone, as if learnt by rote. 'I didn't understand it at first, but I didn't mind. Later, when I was bigger, I asked my mother about it, and she said I was special, like Jesus.'

'How old were you then?'

'I don't know. About eight, I think. She said I was special . . . I didn't think about it much then. Not properly, I mean. But Mr Roth was always asking me things. He'd make me sit very still for a long time and say I must empty my mind and then he'd ask me what I'd seen – observed, I mean, and I didn't know . . . I tried to do what he said, but I couldn't, and I didn't understand what he wanted me to say. He wanted me to be special, like they all said, but . . .' Michael blinked and shook his head. Mrs Dane was gazing at him in appalled fascination.

'Go on,' said Stratton. 'You're doing fine. Take all the time you want.'

'They'd made a mistake, hadn't they?' blurted Michael. 'I knew they had. I *knew* it! It wasn't me they wanted. I tried to tell my mother, but she just got cross. She said I was being ungrateful, that people were depending on me . . . that I had to be their guide. I tried to tell her that it wasn't me and they'd got it wrong, but she wouldn't listen.'

I'll bet she wouldn't, thought Stratton. 'Did you try telling Mr Roth?'

'No. I couldn't. She said I wasn't to say those things to anyone else. She was so angry with me... Mr Roth kept asking me how I felt and if I got headaches and ... I didn't get any headaches, but I said yes and he said he used to get headaches and I wasn't to worry because it was part of the process of finding the spiritual ... spiritual source ... inside myself. So then I worried because I didn't get headaches, and I used to pretend I did. Try to be like they wanted. Mr Roth gave lots of talks and they went on for hours. It was hard to listen to what he was saying when I wanted to go out and play. Everyone thought I understood it all and they kept on asking me things. I'd try and repeat the things that Mr Roth said so they'd leave me alone, but they didn't. They wouldn't leave me alone!' Michael let out a howl that rocked his whole body. It seemed to Stratton to contain all the frustration he must have felt.

'And you just wanted to be a normal boy,' he said. 'You didn't want to be special.'

'I thought it must be my fault.' Michael's voice had dropped to a whisper. 'I thought, when they realised, they'd say I was a liar and I'd tried to trick them, but I didn't. Honestly, I didn't. Sometimes I really did believe that I was ... what they said ... and then I'd think I did deserve to be in that position with everybody, you know, looking up at me, and then it would be all right for a while, but a lot of the time it was just ... just ... not right. Jeremy knew, though. He was the only one who did.'

'Jeremy Lloyd?'

'Yes. He used to teach me sometimes. Once when we were by ourselves he said to me, "Don't think it'll last for ever. I was his favourite once, and it'll come to an end for you just like it did for me. He'll move on to someone else." We'd been down to the village and just before we got back to the house he grabbed my arm and said it.'

'How old were you then?'

'Same as I am now, ten.'

'So it was earlier this year?'

'Yes. He left soon after. Well, quite soon. About a month, I think. I told Mr Roth what he'd said, and he told me I mustn't worry about it. He said he would talk to Jeremy.' Michael frowned, trying to find words to explain. 'I didn't want it to last for ever, or be a favourite. But I was frightened, especially after Jeremy left, because if we had to leave, too, and it was my fault, then ... my mother would be angry like she was before, and she wouldn't forgive me, and I didn't know where we could go or what we could do ... Sometimes, if we'd been somewhere and we were coming back in the car, I used to look at the houses, if there were children there playing in their gardens, and wonder what it would be like. Once, we were in the car – Mr Roth was there, and Jeremy and Miss Kirkland, and the tyre was flat so I helped Jeremy to put on a new one and there was a house next to us, with boys in the garden. They were playing, swapping cigarette cards. They'd put them all on the grass. I heard one boy saying he had the whole set. It was aeroplanes, and I wanted to see ... Just to have a look, that's all, because he had all the different sorts. I kept trying to see, but I had to hold the tools for Jeremy and he was getting cross because I kept on dropping them. Then a lady came out and called them in for their dinner – it was lunch, really, but she called it dinner – and they picked up the cards and rushed inside and they were laughing.

The lady was laughing, too – she said, "Ooh, get inside, get on with you." It looked such fun, and I wanted to be with them. It took ages to mend the tyre and I kept on wondering what they were doing in there.' He paused, caught up in the memory of it, then said, 'I tried to imagine what it would be like if we lived in a house like that, an ordinary one. I wanted to make a picture of it in my head, so it would be something to think about, but

I couldn't. And it was bad, trying to do that, because Mr Roth says you shouldn't indulge in daydreams because it stops you paying attention to what you're meant to be doing ... If you daydream, you're not awake and you have to be. Present, here and now, and nowhere else.' Again, these words trotted out with a mechanical ease. Stratton wondered how many times Michael must have heard them.

He was about to ask the boy another question, when Michael suddenly said, 'Mr Roth ... Are you *really* sure he's dead? Did a doctor tell you?'

'He died while I was with him, Michael.'

'A doctor confirmed it later,' added Ballard. 'When the ambulance came.'

'I didn't mean to do it. I was so angry with him. All the stuff he'd been saying ...' Michael's words broke up into sobs. Mrs Dane put an arm round him, but he clawed it away, shrugging her off and moving his chair so that she couldn't reach him. 'You don't understand!' he shouted at Stratton. 'None of you. You don't!'

'No,' said Stratton. 'We don't. Not really. But we're trying to understand.' Beside him, Ballard nodded in vigorous agreement.

'You were upset about your mother,' said Stratton.

Michael stared at him through flat, expressionless eyes. 'She tried to kill me. Before, when we went there, I think it was because she wanted to get back to her old home and be the lady over everyone. She wanted to be better than them. They believed all the lies she told and Mr Roth made it worse, he told all those people so they would ... they would ...' Convulsed with weeping, Michael was unable to continue. Mrs Dane produced a handkerchief from her handbag and held it out to him. The boy shook his head, and wiped his nose on his sleeve so that a trail of snot glistened on the expensive material. 'I know she didn't care. That woman – the one who was killed – she cared about her boy, the one she thought was me, because she came to find him, didn't she? But *my mother* didn't care!' He let out a long howl of despair that seemed to contain all the pain in the world.

When he'd subsided, shaking and shying away from Mrs Dane's attempts to pat his arm, Stratton said, 'Can you tell us about the gun, Michael?'

Michael hiccupped. 'Mr Tynan – he gave it to me about two weeks ago. It was only because I wanted it for practice – bottles and things. I knew he would give it to me if I asked him.' A calculating look crossed his face. 'He wanted to be my friend, you see. He said we should make a pact, pricking our fingers, you know, that we wouldn't talk about it. I thought they'd listen to me if I had the gun. Mr Roth was always talking about the truth, as if it was just one big thing and if you knew it you could explain everything else, but he couldn't, could he? I thought he could tell me why she'd tried to kill me. He said that people who knew the truth were guided by it, but when I went into the room – when I asked him – he said my mother was confused and she made a mistake. That was all he said, "a mistake". As if it didn't matter! He said my mother was going away, and I was going to stay with them and everything would be all right. But I don't *want* to stay there, I want to live in a proper house, like those boys, but I don't even know any other boys, and now . . .' Letting out a great, tearing sob, he covered his face in his hands.

Stratton got up and walked round the table to put a hand on his shoulder. 'It's all right, Michael. You've done very well, explaining. Now, I see you haven't drunk your tea – perhaps you'd prefer some cocoa? Would you like that? Then we're going to ask the doctor to have a look at you, and you can have a rest.'

Michael looked up at him, eyes glistening. 'I would like some cocoa.'

'Good. Do you know, I wouldn't mind some myself.' Looking over Michael's head at Wickstead, who was staring at the boy as though transfixed, he said, 'Do you have any cocoa?'

'I'm not sure,' said the policewoman, stiffly.

'I am,' said Ballard. 'Mr Parsons keeps a tin in his cupboard. I'm sure if you asked him, he'd give you some.'

'There we are, then,' said Stratton heartily. 'Cocoa all round, I think. And while we're waiting, I'd just like to ask you about the bonfire in the village. You said you'd gone to see it with Miss Kirkland.'

'Yes. I had one of the potatoes they were cooking on the fire. It had gone all hard inside so I threw most of it away.'

'Did Miss Kirkland have one, too?'

'I'm not sure. She went round to the other side of the fire – it was a big one, with people putting things on all the time, like wood and old furniture and stuff.'

'Did she have anything with her?'

'Well, she had her bag, and she had a small case, like a suit-case. She said it was old things we wanted to get rid of – you know, if they were broken.'

'Did she show them to you?'

'No, she just went and emptied them on the fire.'

'And you didn't see her do that?'

'She was on the other side. Is it important?'

'We're not sure.'

'You spend quite a lot of time with Miss Kirkland, don't you? Do you like her?'

Michael looked surprised. 'I suppose so. Miss Kirkland's very clever, and she does everything right, but she's quite serious . . . I don't think she liked my mother very much, really. It was because she used to look after Mr Roth until we came along, and then he asked my mother to do it.'

'What sort of looking after?'

'Well, he has funny turns sometimes at night, so Miss Kirkland used to sleep at the foot of his bed so that she could give him medicine and help him get back to sleep. She told me it was because he took other people's pain and suffering away from them, so that it made *him* ill, instead.' Obviously, thought Stratton, the 'strange episodes' Roth had mentioned to him, that sounded like epilepsy, hadn't really gone away at all. 'Miss Kirkland was very angry when my mother had a bed put in his room for herself.'

'Did they have a row about it?'

'They never have rows if they don't like things. They just accept them – or that's what they pretend.' And under that smug, polite surface, Stratton added to himself, there's a massive, roiling under-current of resentment and fury and Lord knows what else. 'I asked my mother why Miss Kirkland was so cross about it and she said that before, she had slept on the floor of Mr Roth's room because she thought that a person should suffer if they wanted to make spiritual progress. My mother said it was nonsense. She said Miss Kirkland should have become a nun if she wanted to do things like that.'

'What did you think about that?'

'I thought she was right. A couple of times when I was ill, Miss Kirkland slept on the floor of my room, and I didn't like it. If I woke up in the night, I'd find her staring at me. I told Mr Roth and he said she was devoted to us and it was her way of showing it and we had to be nice to her. I felt she could see what I was thinking – if it was about wanting to go out to play or fly in an aeroplane or something – and that was bad enough, but if she could see my dreams as well, that was worse, because you can't stop dreams, can you? When she was there I didn't want to go to sleep in case I was doing wrong without knowing it and she might tell Mr Roth and then I'd be in trouble.'

CHAPTER SIXTY-FOUR

When Michael had signed the statement and the cocoa arrived, Stratton, who badly needed some time alone, excused himself and went to stand outside on the porch under the lamp, smoking and gazing out into the wet darkness. He felt exhausted. What poor old Ballard must be feeling like was anybody's guess. And as for Michael . . .

Stratton thought how many of the taken-for-granted pleasures of childhood had been denied him. During what must have been hours and hours of stupefying non-activity waiting for the next pearl of wisdom to fall from Roth's lips, he'd been denied even the pleasure of day-dreaming because the bloody man had managed to police his private thoughts. With little, or severely curtailed, interior life, how the hell would you know who you were? Not that a ten-year-old *did* know, of course – too young – but Roth appeared to have had a damn good go at short-circuiting the process of him ever finding out. He'd seen enough abused children in his time, maltreated, starved, violated, sometimes deliberately, sometimes through ignorance and neglect, but never anything like this. This child had been put in a position where, at one moment he believed he was some sort of living God, and, at the next he was in the depths of despair about being able to live up to Roth's billing, never mind his mother's. Coercion, indulgence and the omnipresent, unspoken threat of the total withdrawal of affection, nurture and every other bloody thing if he didn't comply – not to mention living in the human equivalent of a goldfish bowl … It was enough to drive anybody stark, staring mad.

He'd see what the doctor had to say about Michael, and then they'd need to take a statement from Miss Kirkland. I know what I'd like to do to her, Stratton thought savagely. I'd like to grab her by her scrawny little neck and shake her till her teeth rattle. Taking a mental step back from this – no good steaming in there with his fists clenched, after all – he supposed that, in a way, she was a victim of Roth, too. But if she was, she'd been a willing one, coming to the Foundation of her own volition. That was also true of Mary/Ananda, although whether she was a victim of anyone but herself was a moot point. Poor Michael, on the other hand, hadn't had any choice in the matter.

Pausing only to ask Adlard to return to the Foundation and collect some clothes and washing things for Michael, Stratton went back to the interview room to find an elderly man with a lugubrious expression and a carbuncular nose waiting for him.

'DI Stratton.'

'Dr Sidgwick. I'm afraid it's too late to make alternative arrangements for the boy, but I've given him something to help him sleep, and Mrs Dane's getting him settled down.'

'What's your opinion?'

'Well, he's obviously upset, but that's hardly surprising. Mrs Dane said he was surprisingly lucid – quite a vocabulary for a child of his age, she said.'

'Not so surprising when you remember he's grown up with only adults for company. Adults who seem to spend most of their time speaking in platitudes.' The doctor raised an enquiring eyebrow. 'Have you ever been to the Foundation?' asked Stratton. 'In a professional capacity, I mean.'

'Several times. Can't say I ever thought much about it, but . . . they really are something, aren't they? As to the boy's mental state . . . He'll have to be seen by a specialist, of course, but only time will tell. That and where he's placed. If he ends up in a borstal – when he's a bit older, I mean – I'm afraid he's doomed. He'll either get himself killed, commit suicide, or end up in a mental institution for life. Poor little chap. Judging from what DI Ballard said, life's not going to be easy for that young man, whatever happens. Honestly,' he gave a wheezy sigh. 'It makes you despair of humanity.'

'Thanks for looking on the bright side,' murmured Stratton as he went down the corridor to find Ballard and Parsons. Sidgwick did have a point, though. The thought of Michael, six years hence, surrounded by callous, jeering young thugs, was awful. If that happened, God knew how he'd end up . . . Just have to pray that someone further up the line's got some sense, he thought.

Ballard and Parsons were waiting for him outside the cells. 'How's Miss Kirkland?' he asked.

'Not a peep out of her,' said Parsons. 'Last I looked, she was sitting there, bolt upright, with her eyes shut.'

'Floating on an astral plane,' said Ballard.

'Well,' said Stratton, 'let's hope she's making the most of it, because she's about to come down to earth with a bump.'

CHAPTER SIXTY-FIVE

'It was Mr Dunning, wasn't it?' Miss Kirkland smiled benevolently at a knothole in the table as she said this.

'Mr Dunning saw you in the wood with Mrs Aylett,' said Stratton. 'We also have two witnesses who saw you near Jeremy Lloyd's address in London on the night he was killed. And we found this.' Stratton pushed forward the bag containing the debris from the bonfire. 'We believe that you removed Mrs Aylett's handbag after you killed her, and placed it on the village bonfire on the night of November the fifth. We also believe that the remains of this bag will show that it is identical to one purchased by Mrs Aylett's sister, Mrs Curtin, who confirms that they bought the two articles at the same time. What do you have to say about it?'

'Well, gentlemen.' Miss Kirkland looked up, smile now on full beam. 'There's no sense in beating about the bush. I killed Mr Lloyd. I also killed Mrs Aylett, and afterwards I disposed of her handbag in the way you have mentioned. I threw the gun into the lake.'

'How did you obtain it?'

'From Mr Tynan. He's got quite a collection, as I'm sure you know. Mr Roth had asked me to deliver some papers to him. I was to leave them in his study. I entered the house from the back, and while I was there I went into the gun room – there was no difficulty as it wasn't locked – and took what I needed. The staff were busy elsewhere, and nobody saw me.'

Stratton raised his eyebrows at Ballard, who shook his head and murmured, 'Told me they were all present and correct – obviously hadn't looked properly.'

'When did you do this?'

'Two or three days before Mrs Aylett's arrival.'

'Were you expecting her?'

'I had an idea that she would come, yes.'

'Because Lloyd had told you?'

'Yes. I'd received some correspondence from Jeremy Lloyd during the preceding months. One would not usually communicate with anybody who has left – it is neither desirable nor helpful – but I made an exception in this particular instance.'

'Did you send him money?'

'Yes, I did. I felt he'd been rather hard done by. Ananda had done her best to make it impossible for him to continue at the Foundation, and her treatment of him had left him unhappy and embittered, and, as she had taken over the secretarial work for Mr Roth, he felt that he wasn't required in that capacity, either. She really had taken against him, Inspector. In part, I think, it was because he was the only man who was immune to her ...' Miss Kirkland's mouth twisted slightly, 'her *charms*.'

'And Lloyd told you he'd discovered that Michael was not Ananda's child,' said Stratton.

'Yes. He said he had evidence. That he intended to expose Mr Roth. He was very angry, Inspector, and he must have thought I would be, well, sympathetic to his cause. I went to London with the intention of persuading him not to contact Mrs Aylett. He told me that he'd sent her a letter that morning, and that he was planning to include the information in the book he was writing about the work of the Foundation. We argued, and I'm afraid ... Well, it was as you saw. The scissors were on the desk, Inspector. I picked them up, and ... It was as if someone else, someone quite outside myself, was acting and I was merely watching her do it. That, I believe, was what gave me the physical strength to kill him.' She nodded solemnly. 'Afterwards, I searched the room and took a parcel of manuscript I found in a suitcase under the bed, and then I left.'

'Do you have the parcel?'

'I didn't care to see what it contained. I burnt it without opening it.'

'If you had,' said Stratton, 'you might have seen Billy Aylett's birth certificate and realised he couldn't have been Michael – because you didn't know about the dates, did you? You didn't realise until you heard me talk to Michael about it.'

Miss Kirkland shook her head. 'I considered that my first duty was to make sure that nothing should undermine the Work. I felt there was no other course of action open to me. The Maitreya had to remain inviolate – the students were not ready for ... not ready to hear anything like that. What mattered was to act directly, with indifference. I sought guidance—'

'From Roth?'

'From a work of scripture called the Bhagavad Gita. It is a conversation between the prince Arjuna and the Lord Krishna that takes place at the start of a great battle. Arjuna is in moral turmoil because he will have to fight and kill members of his own family, and Krishna explains his duties by saying that death involves only the shedding of the body; mortality is illusory, but the soul is permanent and cannot die. It is Arjuna's duty to uphold the path of Dharma, which is duty in accordance with Divine Law, through warfare. He must perform this duty for the greater good, without any attachment to the results. I took great strength from those words. Ananda,' she sounded scornful, 'had swanned off somewhere, as she was in the habit of doing, and my duty was to protect Mr Roth and the members of the Foundation. I was determined not to fail them.'

'And determined to show Roth that he needed you more than Ananda,' said Stratton.

For the first time, Miss Kirkland looked rattled. 'I was his help-meet from the beginning. Others came and went, but I remained by his side. That was my place.'

'But when Ananda came along, Mr Roth thought it was *her* place.'

'She had her duties, yes. Mine were to oversee the welfare of the students in our care. It was a great responsibility.'

'But you resented not having exclusive access to Mr Roth.'

'I needed to speak to him about the students. To ask his advice. Ananda made it very difficult for me.'

'And Roth preferred her company to yours.'

'Mr Roth was a wise man. I never questioned his devotion to her.'

'Roth tried to protect her, didn't he?' Miss Kirkland looked puzzled. 'When he told you not to tell us that Ananda had come to see him. He wanted to give her time to get away – he'd no idea she was going to come back, of course. But he didn't try to protect you, did he?'

Miss Kirkland was frowning deeply, shaking her head. 'I don't understand.'

'He knew you'd been listening, and he knew you'd spoken to me. I asked him if Ananda had said anything about the deaths of Lloyd and Mrs Aylett. I think that's when he realised what you'd done. He could have shielded you by blaming Ananda for them, but he didn't.'

Miss Kirkland looked at him in alarm. 'He didn't know!'

'As you yourself said, Miss Kirkland, some knowledge comes from the heart . . .'

She shook her head with a frantic look – someone trying to fit pieces into a jigsaw that kept reassembling itself under their hands. 'You're twisting my words!'

'Not at all,' said Stratton, mildly. 'And it seems to me that, far from remaining unattached from the results of your actions, self-preservation has been uppermost in your mind from the very beginning.'

'No, Inspector. You see, I am not important. I am merely the instrument in this.'

'But nobody *made* you do it. And – despite what you've just told us – you consider yourself to be mentally competent, don't you? You know the difference between right and wrong?'

Miss Kirkland stared at him with outraged eyes. 'Of course!'

'In that case,' said Stratton, 'you must be aware that you are facing a lengthy prison sentence at best, and, at worst, the ultimate sanction of the law. I'm sure I don't have to remind you that, whatever your philosophy may say on the matter, the Bible says "thou shalt not kill" and the law of this country agrees with it. And you won't get away with it because you acted on duff information from Lloyd, either. Now, perhaps you would like to tell us exactly how you went about killing Mrs Aylett?'

Miss Kirkland took a deep, shuddering breath. 'I wasn't sure when she'd come, so I kept a lookout from my room. It's at the front of the house and you can see across the garden to the woods, which aren't too thick at this time of year. I said I was unwell and wasn't to be disturbed. Of course, I didn't know what Mrs Aylett looked like, but I know most of the villagers by sight and we don't get too many strangers visiting, so I felt reasonably confident. I have a pair of binoculars – I used to be a keen bird-watcher, Inspector – which was a help. When I saw her coming down the road, I went to intercept her. I had the gun in my handbag. I made it seem as if it was a chance meeting – in fact, it was she who stopped me to ask for directions. She had very little idea of what the Foundation was; in fact,' Miss Kirkland chuckled, 'she appeared to think it was some sort of boarding school. It was easy enough to get her to tell me why she'd come, and when I suggested I escort her, and we take a short cut through the woods, she agreed quite readily. I think she was glad to have someone to talk to, because she told me the whole story. To be honest, Inspector, I felt quite sorry for her – for her weakness and lack of discrimination. That was what had brought her to this point, you see.'

'Even though you thought she was Michael's mother?'

'Yes. I was doing the right thing, Inspector. For the greater good.' The invincible smile flared for a moment, then faded away uncertainly.

'And you shot her from behind.'

'Yes. I confess I was a little worried about that part. I'd never handled a gun before, but in the event, it was quite straight-forward.' She beamed, again, as if they'd just been discussing the successful conclusion of some innocuous task.

Stratton opened his mouth, then closed it, defeated. 'Of course,' Miss Kirkland continued, 'the work here cannot continue without Mr Roth, but wherever there is a need, such men will arise to meet it. And believe me, gentlemen, there has never been a greater need than there is today.'

Stratton glanced sideways at Ballard and saw that his eyes were bulging with appalled disbelief. 'But,' he said, apparently unable to help himself, 'you've killed two people for no good reason.'

'Nothing,' said Miss Kirkland, 'is ever entirely without meaning.'

Stratton thought that if the neat, upright little woman before him had screamed and hurled vile abuse, he would have been less horrified. He sat silent while Miss Kirkland read and signed her statement, and was just about to ask Wickstead to accom-pany her to her cell when she said, 'I wonder if I might ask you to contact my sister. Her name is Mrs Fielding, and you'll find her address in the room I occupy at the Foundation. I presume she still lives in the same place – we have not had any contact for several years.'

'Since you arrived at the Foundation.'

Miss Kirkland inclined her head, beaming as though he were a student who'd given some particularly useful insight. 'That's right!'

'I don't know about you,' said Ballard, as they went back the lobby to talk to Parsons, 'but I could do with a drink.'

'And how!' Stratton shook his head wonderingly. 'I don't suppose I'll ever forget today as long as I live.'

They were interrupted by Parsons. 'Got Mr Tynan here, sir. I put him in there,' the policeman indicated the office, 'because he's in something of a state, sir.'

Tynan was sitting at the desk, head bowed and hands clasped in front of him as though in prayer. He turned slowly as they entered, and Stratton saw that his ruddy face was streaked with tears. He held up his hands as if in supplication and said, 'Forgive me, gentlemen. I must see Michael.'

'I don't think—' began Stratton, but Tynan, who looked as if he were choking, cut him off with a gasping sob.

'I have to. I need to tell him . . . This is all my fault. I've done a terrible thing.'

'I'm sorry, sir,' said Ballard, seating himself on one corner of the desk, 'but you're going to have to tell us what you're talking about.'

Tynan shook his head miserably. 'Miss Kirkland came to me a few weeks ago – asked me if I knew who Michael's father was. If I'd only told her the truth, none of this would have happened.'

'What did you say?' asked Ballard.

'I told her I didn't know.'

'But you *do* know, don't you?' said Stratton. 'At least,' he put his head on one side, 'as far as you can be certain.'

'Yes . . .'

'You're his father, aren't you?'

'Yes.' He spoke slowly, testing the words for the first time. 'I am Michael's father.'

CHAPTER SIXTY-SIX

'All that business Mrs Milburn gave us about nervous breakdowns and what she told Roth about discovering her miracle pregnancy after Billy died was eyewash, wasn't it? I accept that you knew nothing about Tom or Billy, but you didn't tell us you knew Mrs Milburn before she arrived at the Old Rectory with Michael. You'd known her in Suffolk, in the summer of 1945, and that's when Michael was conceived. What was it, a fling?'

Tynan nodded. 'I had no idea about the American soldier or ... any of that.'

'I'm prepared to believe that. Mind you, she seems to have been pretty free with her favours – we know of at least one other candidate, possibly two, so how—'

'Michael is *my* son!' Tynan spoke loudly, his mouth open wide, mucus strands at the inner corners of his lips. 'I'm sure of it.'

'When did you first meet her?'

'I can tell you exactly.' He fished a small black book out of his overcoat pocket. 'Diary for 1945. Keep them all. After Ananda'd taken my car and gone, I was going over it all in my mind – the dates – and I looked it up. Here.' He tapped a page with his forefinger. The entry for 1st May read *7.30 p.m. USAF Debach*. 'It was a dance,' he said. 'I'd been invited there to dinner, and we looked in afterwards. That's when I saw her. I'll never forget that moment . . . I thought she was the loveliest thing I'd ever seen.'

'Excuse me for asking,' said Ballard, 'but wasn't your wife there?'

Tynan shook his head. 'It was to do with some business I'd undertaken – can't go into details.'

Stratton, who remembered what Diana had told him about Tynan and Colonel Forbes-James, said, hastily, 'That's not important. So you danced with her, did you?'

'Yes. Rather a lot, as I remember. We made an arrangement to meet the following week.' He pointed to an entry for 7th May, which read *Rose Hotel 1 o'clock*. 'We had lunch,' he said, 'and then we went for a drive in my car.'

'Did intercourse take place on that occasion?'

'Yes. Several times that month, in fact. She told me that her husband was dead and she might be going abroad to live.'

'Did she say where?'

Tynan shook his head. 'Just that she'd had enough of this country and wanted to travel and see the world. I was crazy about her. She was so beautiful, so *vital* . . .'

'How did you contact her?'

'I wrote to her in Woodbridge. Then she told me she'd moved to London, and that she was pregnant.'

'By which time,' Stratton said, 'Michael Carroll, the American airman, was dead, Billy – conveniently, because he was too old to be your son – was also dead, and she'd decided that you, despite being married, were her best bet.'

'Michael is my son!' Tynan banged a fist on the desk. 'I may never have acknowledged him before, but I've always done right by him.'

'You gave him a loaded gun,' said Stratton.

'I acted like a fool, Inspector. Shooting was something we always did together, and I wanted us to . . .' He shook his head, momentarily lost for words. 'To make up for not . . . not . . .'

'For keeping him in ignorance?' said Stratton. 'For allowing this ridiculous charade to continue?'

'Yes ... But I looked after Ananda when she was expecting him, and gave her regular money for his keep. Ananda never liked living in London, and I didn't like them being so far away. I'd planned to bring them to the Foundation early on, but the place needed a lot of work before it was suitable for a child to come into. So, when Michael was two, I introduced him and Ananda – Mary, as she was then – to Roth. I said I'd met her at a party in London and told her about the Foundation and its work and she'd been interested ... Roth took to her immediately, and he obviously liked the idea of having a child about the place, so he asked her to stay.'

'So you had your mistress and your son conveniently to hand, although I don't imagine that Roth was aware of that.'

'I couldn't tell anyone,' said Tynan. 'That was out of the question. It wasn't only because of Roth, there was my wife as well. Dorothy was a wonderful woman in many respects, but I never felt for her the way I felt for Ananda.' Tynan shook his head, sadly. 'But I didn't know her at all, did I? I simply had no idea ... And even when all this happened, I'd been silent for so long, I just couldn't ... I thought it was more important for the Foundation – the damage it might do ... God!' he groaned and sank his head into his hands. 'What a *mess*.'

'Mr Tynan.' Stratton put a hand on the man's shoulder. 'I don't think it would be wise to see Michael tonight. The doctor's given him something, and I imagine he's already asleep. Why don't you come back in the morning?'

Tynan raised his head and got slowly and painfully to his feet. 'I have to make amends,' he said. 'Whatever happens to him, I'll be there.'

CHAPTER SIXTY-SEVEN

Stratton put down his *Daily Express* and rubbed his eyes. He was glad to be home and looking forward to a couple of days off, but he must have read the same piece – *TITO TELLS RUSSIANS: QUIT HUNGARY* – at least five times, because all he could think of was Michael: how small and vulnerable he'd looked in the box at the Ipswich magistrates' court that morning, where both he and Miss Kirkland had been remanded in custody. The clock on the mantelpiece chimed nine o'clock. It was a bit early for bed, and anyway, he knew he wouldn't be able to sleep any better than he had the night before. He didn't fancy the wireless, but *Lucky Jim* was upstairs on his bedside table. Perhaps that would hold his concentration better than the newspaper.

He'd just decided to go up and fetch the book when there was a knock at the front door. When he opened it he found his brother-in-law Reg standing on the porch. He did not speak, and made no move to enter and, for a moment, his arrival had a tentative feeling, as if he'd been a holiday acquaintance arriving unexpectedly after a year's lapse, unsure if he'd be welcomed. Pete had been right, Stratton thought. Reg was definitely thinner, grey about the gills, and, as if this weren't enough, the whites of his eyes looked like boiled rhubarb. Masking his anxiety with a hearty,

'Don't stand on ceremony, come on in!' he ushered his brother-in-law into the hall.

Reg, who usually made himself at home straight away – and rather too much for comfort by immediately pointing out things like damp patches and chipped paintwork – gazed around him uncertainly. He looked, Stratton thought, rather like a man who, bidden for the first time to a secret gathering, was afraid he'd come to the wrong house and didn't want to utter the password for fear of giving himself away.

'Are you all right?' asked Stratton, helping him off with his coat.

This question would normally have elicited a detailed run-down of the more troublesome aspects of Reg's bunions, bowel movements, and so forth, but instead, his brother-in-law asked, 'I'm not disturbing you, am I?'

'Of course not. I was just reading the paper – trying to find some good news, for a change. Go on through and I'll put the kettle on.'

'You needn't do it on my behalf.'

Stratton's eyes widened involuntarily. This was becoming bizarre: Reg never turned down anything on offer, even if he'd just come from having a great deal of whatever it was at home or in the pub. 'No, no,' he said hastily, retreating down the passage into the scullery, 'I was just about to have a cup myself.'

Reg came after him, fixing his red eyes on Stratton as he filled the kettle from the tap and then accompanying him into the kitchen to put it on the gas, not speaking but watching as if he thought Stratton might disappear in a puff of smoke if he let him out of his sight for even a second. Having offered a couple of usually reliable topics for conversation to no avail, Stratton, feeling increasingly out of his depth, made the tea, plonked cups, saucers, milk and sugar on a tray, and went through to the sitting room, trailed by his brother-in-law.

'Are you sure you're all right?' Stratton asked when, tea poured, they'd settled themselves in the armchairs.

'Bit under the weather,' said Reg. Then, glancing down at the newspaper Stratton had left on the floor, added absently, 'Don't seem to understand the world any more ... all these new things happening. Wonder if I ever did understand it, really.'

Stratton felt seriously alarmed. In the family – and, for all he knew, outside it as well – Reg's reputation for unearned world-liness was legendary; given half a chance, and sometimes not even that, he'd make pronouncements on anything and every-thing. He was just about to ask what the matter was, when Reg looked straight into his eyes and, said, 'I'm not like you, Ted. Or Don. I've never been popular. Not at school, or work, or with other chaps. I'm not even popular with you two, am I?' Holding up a hand like a traffic policeman to forestall anything that Stratton might have to say, he continued, 'Oh, you tolerate me all right. Don't have much choice, I suppose ... When I was younger, I made myself into a character, hoping it would make people like me – or at least hoping they might find me amusing. By the time I realised it wasn't working, I was stuck with it.' Glancing down at the newspaper once more he said quietly, as if to himself, 'Ah, well. Nothing to be done about it now.'

'Reg,' said Stratton helplessly. 'I ... I don't know what to say.'

'Then don't,' said Reg, matter-of-factly. 'No sense wasting your breath lying about it, when we both know the truth.'

Mention of the word 'truth' made Miss Kirkland flicker, momentarily, across his mind. What he'd just been listening to, he thought, was true self-knowledge; raw, absolute and appalling. And he could see from Reg's face that there was more to come.

'I haven't always been as kind as I should to Lilian. I've been damn lucky to have such a forgiving wife, really ... Johnny's a different thing altogether. Despises me, and I can't say I blame him for it. I'm just sorry he's gone down the wrong path. I never did thank you, Ted, for helping to keep him out of prison like that when he was younger. I can hardly bear to think of my behaviour then, going off my head like that . . . but I am grateful to you and I wanted you to know that. I've always admired you, you see.'

By the end of this little speech, Stratton, who'd been adding together his memories of what Pete had said, the Billy Graham business and the physical evidence in front of him, thought, Reg is ill. No, he corrected himself. He's more than ill. He's dying. That's why he's here, saying all this – he knows he's running out of time.

He's telling me first, Stratton thought suddenly. He's not told anyone yet, even Lilian. He couldn't have said quite how he knew this, but he was positive that it was true.

'. . . had a friend from before he was married,' Reg was saying. 'They'd known each other before Dad met my mother. They spent all their free time together, making model boats. That was his hobby . . . the pair of them used try them out in the tin bath in our back yard, and sometimes they'd take them to the ponds at Hampstead Heath. They used to talk about them all the time. I never remember my parents going anywhere together, it was always him and Joe.' Stratton had no idea how he'd got onto this topic, and wondered, with trepidation, if it was leading to some awful revelation. 'We used to call him Uncle Joe. Saw him almost every day – he lived in the next street. He even came on holiday with us a couple of times, when Dad started earning a bit more and we could get to the seaside. My mother didn't resent it.' Reg stopped suddenly, frowning and shaking his head. 'No . . . the truth is, I don't know if she resented it. She never seemed to, but then I never asked her, so I can't say. That was just how it was, and I suppose she made the best of it . . . It was Joe who was with him when he died, not her. He used to come and see Dad every day when he was bedridden. My mother'd put a tray on the bed to make a flat surface, and they'd play cards for hours. We'd hear them in there, talking about the boats and laughing. We knew he was going downhill, of course. One day, Joe came downstairs and told us he'd gone. He died quite soon after Dad did.'

Reg fell silent and stared into the fire. Stratton couldn't imagine what on earth he was supposed to say in response to this. Reg surely couldn't be telling him what he *seemed* to be telling him, could he? If so, why was he telling him? Was it – could it possibly be – meant as an oblique reference to Monica? No . . . Not Reg. Surely not . . .

He racked his brains for something that wouldn't sound either prurient or banal, and settled for offering more tea as the safest option, realising, as soon as he'd opened his mouth that Reg hadn't drunk the first lot, and neither had he. How long had he known he was ill, Stratton wondered. He must have gone to the doctor, assuming his symptoms to be caused by some minor, if irritating, ailment, and been given the news . . . And he was what? Sixty-one? Sixty-two? Only just retired. He and Lilian must have made plans for days out and there'd been talk of him helping Mr Kendall with the scouts. Presumably, none of this would now happen . . .

'My mother never mentioned Joe's name after he died,' said Reg, cutting across Stratton's train of thought. 'She'd talk about Dad, sometimes, but him, never. I've wondered, over the years, about their friendship. It's easier, sometimes, not to admit . . . if there was anything *to* admit, of course. I don't know. He certainly never showed any signs of being . . . well, *that way*, and neither did Joe. But, you know . . .' Reg sounded wistful. 'My father was a popular man. Well thought of. People looked up to him. I suppose, with these sorts of things, it doesn't make any difference in the long run. It seems better not to . . . make a fuss about it.'

'I'm sure you're right,' said Stratton, after a pause.

'Are you?' Reg sounded suddenly wary, as if fearful Stratton might burst into a loud guffaw of finger-pointing laughter.

'Yes,' said Stratton firmly. 'I am.'

Reg turned back to the fire for a moment, then said, 'It's good of you to listen to me. I suppose you must be wondering why I've been telling you all this.'

'Well, I was a bit, yes.'

'The reason . . .' Reg cleared his throat. 'I've been told I have cancer. There's nothing they can do. One's always reading about new scientific discoveries, but . . . Well, you can't expect these chaps to do everything, so there it is.'

'I'm sorry, Reg.' Even as he said it, Stratton was aware of the pathetic inadequacy of his response.

'You don't seem surprised,' said Reg.

'Well . . .' Stratton hesitated. 'You have been looking a bit, well, poorly, and I did wonder . . .'

Reg gave a faint smile. 'Ever the detective, eh?'

'It wasn't only me,' said Stratton. 'Pete noticed too. He was worried about you. Told me before he left.'

'Did he? That was kind of him.' Reg nodded. 'Yes, very thoughtful, to think of me like that. But all the same . . .' he leant forward slightly and Stratton saw the loose flesh on his jawline sag, hanging away from his face, 'I'd prefer it if you didn't . . . broadcast the fact. At least, not at the moment.'

'Of course,' said Stratton. 'I shan't say anything if you don't want me to. But I think you should tell Lilian. I'm sure she must be worried.'

'Yes.' Reg sighed. 'She is. The thing is, I don't know how long . . . Didn't ask the doctor. It seemed a bit much – after all, they're not soothsayers, are they?'

This was such a far cry from the self-dramatist Stratton knew that it made him feel ashamed for all the times he'd laughed at the man, by himself or with Don, so that he stared down at his slippers, unable to look Reg in the face. 'No,' he said, finally. 'Of course they're not. But I think, with Lilian, it's only fair.'

'I know. I will tell her. It's finding the right moment. She's been very good to me, all things considered.'

'She loves you, Reg.'

'Yes.' Reg stared down at the cup of stewed tea on the small table beside his chair. Stratton, following his gaze, saw that there was a small stain, a round beige spot, on the white embroidered tablecloth. Reg must have noticed it too, because he frowned and extended a finger, as if to touch the place. Withdrawing it, he said, 'She loves me. Extraordinary, when you come to think of it.'

'We will look after her, you know,' said Stratton. 'Her and Johnny.'

'Yes . . . I just wish he'd settle down. Get a decent job and find himself a nice girl – not one of these flashy types he goes about with.'

'I'm sure it's just a matter of time.'

Reg shook his head. 'I wish I could believe that. But if you'd just try and put in a word for him. I mean, if the need arises. I've no idea what he's up to. I'm sure it's pretty shady, a lot of it, but I should hate him to go to gaol. It may be what he deserves, but all the same . . . it would break his mother's heart.'

'I'll do my best.'

'I know you will. Anyway,' said Reg, with finality, 'there it is. Now,' he got to his feet, 'I mustn't keep you. I'm sure you've got a busy day ahead. I just thought it best to set the record straight. You know,' he added, 'between the two of us.'

Stratton rose, too. 'If you're sure. There's no need to rush off—'

'I should go,' said Reg. 'Seem to get very tired nowadays . . .'

In the hall Stratton helped Reg put on his coat, noting, as he

did so, how the garment hung off his shoulders, the extra material bunching at the waist as he fastened his belt. 'Same size now
as when I was thirty,' said Reg. Even his hat, always too small so
that it left a pink ring around his sparsely-haired scalp, was
looser.

'You going to be all right?' asked Stratton. 'Want me to walk
home with you?'

'No need. I'm not quite that much of a crock yet, but I really
do appreciate . . . everything.'

'And I appreciate your coming to tell me, Reg.'

'Ah, well . . . There it is.'

They shook hands awkwardly on the porch, and Stratton
watched as his brother-in-law made his slow way across the garden
and into the street, standing in the doorway until Reg turned
the corner and he could see him no more. Then, returning to
his armchair, he sat for a long time in silence.

CHAPTER SIXTY-EIGHT

'But she seemed so nice.' Pauline stabbed the needles through the ball of wool and laid her knitting aside.

Ballard leant forward to lump another log on the fire. 'They all seemed nice.'

'How could she try and kill her own child? And I don't understand how anyone could just abandon a baby like that, either.'

'Well, if it's any consolation, I don't understand *any* of it. They're all quite mad, if you ask me, and the sooner this place is shot of the lot of them, the happier I'll be.'

'The Foundation, you mean?'

'Yes. I went to see Miss Kirkland's sister this afternoon, up near Diss. Nice woman – perfectly ordinary—'

'That must have been a relief.'

'It was. Horrible for her, though, finding out about the murders. Burst into tears and kept saying she couldn't believe it – I was jolly glad Policewoman Wickstead was there, I can tell you. She kept telling me Patricia – that's Miss Kirkland – never used to be like that, and how close they'd been as children, and how happy . . .'

'I suppose she was trying to show you there was another person – a normal person – underneath it all.'

'That's exactly it. She kept on saying what a loving person Miss Kirkland was, and how kind – talked about the pets they'd had, how well she'd looked after them, things like that. Mind you, she did say that the family'd often wondered – later on, this was – if Miss Kirkland might take holy orders or something.'

'Was it a religious family?'

'No, that was the thing. But apparently she was very keen on going to church, very serious and conscientious about everything . . . Spending hours over her homework, always ticking the sister off for being slack, not wanting to go out and play much, even when she was quite young. Mrs Fielding – that's the sister – made a bit of a joke of being told off all the time, but it's obviously why a person like Mr Roth must have appealed so much. Judging from what Mrs Fielding said, she hadn't undergone a personality change – no brainwashing or anything – but the Foundation just sort of . . . *reinforced* what was already there. She said Miss Kirkland had never shown any interest in getting married or anything like that. According to her, Miss K. was the brainy one. She went to university to study economics and then she went off to London to be a civil servant, so the family didn't see much of her, and after she met Mr Roth and went to live at the Foundation they never saw her at all. I remember she – Miss K., I mean – said something to us about Roth not encouraging outside distractions, so I suppose family was one of them. They didn't even know where she was living. When the parents died, Mrs Fielding had no idea how to contact her, so I don't think she even knows they're no longer with us.'

'Perhaps she guessed and that was why she asked you to contact her sister, not them.'

'Could be. Mrs Fielding said she'd like to see her, but she didn't know if Miss Kirkland would want it.'

'That's really sad. I can't imagine not wanting to see my family, can you?'

'No, I can't. It seems all wrong to me, but Miss K. obviously thought she was doing the right thing, didn't she?'

'But,' Pauline gave him a shrewd look, 'By isolating people from their families, Mr Roth had more control over them, didn't he? If the Foundation became their family . . .'

'They wouldn't have any outside influences,' finished Ballard. 'That was the point. To start afresh, as it were.'

'Well, I think it's wicked!' Pauline got up and began tidying up the tea cups. 'That poor woman . . .'

'It's what Miss Kirkland wanted.'

'*Thought* she wanted,' said Pauline. 'Nobody could *want* to kill somebody – not unless they were mad, or in a war. And the boy didn't have a choice, did he?'

'No,' said Ballard. 'He didn't join it, he was put there. But most of the people who did join it are probably just like us, really.'

'Speak for yourself!' Pauline swept up the tray and took it into the kitchen.

'What I meant,' said Ballard, when she came back a minute or two later, 'is that they were probably asking quite ordinary questions – why am I here, what happens when we die, why are some people born rich and others poor . . . things like that. And when they met Roth, they thought they'd found the answers.'

'More fool them, then.' Pauline sounded angry. This was, Ballard realised, in part with herself for being impressed by the Foundation in the first place.

'How about a glass of sherry?' he said. 'And let's talk about something else, for God's sake. I've had it up to here with all that stuff.'

'I'll get it.' Pauline went over to the sideboard. Her back to him, pouring from the decanter – a present from her parents which stood in pride of place on a doily – she said, 'Thank you, Ben.'

'What for?'

'For not saying "I told you so".'

'Don't be silly.' Accepting a glass of sherry, he added, 'I did find out something odd, though – I think Stratton has a secret.'

'Oh?' Pauline kicked off her slippers and curled up on the other end of the sofa, legs tucked underneath her. 'Tell me.'

'It might be nothing, but after we had that row – you know, the second time . . .' he stopped to gauge Pauline's reaction.

She raised her eyes in good-humoured acknowledgement and said impatiently, 'Go on . . .'

'Well, I didn't sleep very well – you know, thinking – so I got up at about four—'

'Yes, I remember. You woke me.'

'Sorry. I was trying to be quiet.'

'You sounded like a herd of elephants. Anyway, never mind that.'

'I went for a walk, down the hill and past the pub, and I noticed that Stratton's car wasn't there. I asked him about it later – I didn't make a big hoo-ha about it, just mentioned it – and he said that he'd left it round the back. But I know he didn't, because I went down the lane – you know, the one that leads past the back of the pub, where there's a bit of space – and it wasn't there, either.'

'Perhaps he'd gone back to London.'

'In that case, why not tell me? I mean, if there'd been an emergency at home, or something . . . He said he'd forgotten where he'd parked it, but it didn't ring true.'

'Are you sure you're not making something out of nothing?'

'I wondered about that, but I don't think so. He's not that kind of bloke. I mean, he doesn't tell you all his business, but he's honest. Open. Always has been.'

'Maybe it was something to do with the case.'

'Then he'd *definitely* have told me. He's never been the type to keep things back then claim the credit – that's not his style at all. Anyway, I'd know by now, wouldn't I?

And afterwards – at the pub, I mean – when we were talking about other things, he seemed a bit . . . well, distracted. Of course, I don't know what he'd been up to, but . . .'

'What, though? Do you think he's got a woman tucked away somewhere out here?'

'I don't know. It did cross my mind, but it seems a bit unlikely . . . And I was under the impression that he was a one-woman man.'

'"Was" is the operative word. His wife's been dead for – what? – ten years, now?'

'Nearer twelve.'

'There you are, then,' said Pauline triumphantly. 'He's got a ladyfriend. It's like that bunch at the Foundation – people aren't always what you think. Even me.'

'You're absolutely right,' said Ballard. Finishing his sherry in a single gulp, he crossed the room, bent over her, and kissed her on the mouth.

CHAPTER SIXTY-NINE

Passing the war memorial on the way to the allotment on Sunday, Stratton stopped to look at the bank of wreaths left there the previous week. He noted, as he always did, the recurrence of certain surnames and wondered what on earth the woman of the house must have felt like when she received the second – and, in the case of one poor family, third – telegram. He'd not had a letter from Pete, but then his son had never been much good at keeping in touch. Perhaps he had a girl to write to . . . Pete had brought several girls home in the past, but he'd always been pretty casual about it. They'd always seemed nice – at least, as far as he was able to gauge on such a slight acquaintance – and certainly attractive, but he'd never had the sense that they were being . . . what was the word? Presented? Offered for inspection? And when he'd mentioned them later, choosing his words carefully so as not to seem overly inquisitive or – far worse – lascivious, Pete had dismissed them. He'd certainly never seen any of them again. His son had always contrived by his offhandedness to give the impression that he'd tired of them, but Stratton supposed it could have been the other way around . . . Still, so long as he came back safe and unharmed, what did it matter? He'd have his life ahead of him.

Unlike poor old Reg, whose life, now, was all behind him. He'd fought in the Great War – there was a photograph somewhere of him in uniform, posed self-consciously beside a papier-mâché tree stump in some photographer's studio, in front of a back-drop of painted fields. He must have lost some pals, thought Stratton, but he'd never spoken of them ... He'd never spoken of it at all, really, other than to remind you, at intervals regular enough to be extremely bloody irritating, that *he was there.*

Sometime around three o'clock that morning, lying sleepless and listening to the rain, Stratton had reignited the – surely insane – notion that Reg's story about his father's unusually intense friendship with another man was an oblique attempt to counsel him about Monica. Despite dismissing the idea as nonsense, it had refused to leave him, and he'd spent the next hour constructing increasingly elaborate explanations as to how Reg might have spotted something that he could not or would not see about his own daughter. Looking at the thing now, in the cold light of day, it seemed clear enough that Reg had spoken because he'd never told his suspicions about his dad to anyone and simply wanted to give them voice. Or so Stratton imagined. That had to be it, didn't it? As asking Reg about it was clearly out of the question, and he'd bet his bottom dollar that his brother-in-law wasn't going to mention it to anyone else, he might as well drop the whole thing.

He turned away from the memorial, lifting his collar against the wind. As he reached the allotment, he realised that he'd simply gone there out of habit with no intention of actually *doing* anything. Ah, well ... nothing much to do in November, anyway. He'd be better off in the shed at home, scrubbing pots, except that somehow he couldn't fancy it.

He stood and stared at his patch, which was covered by a drift of leaves from the trees by the fence, pounded by the recent rain into a mulch out of which poked a few dismal-looking cabbages, a cluster of bamboo sticks with bits of string flapping from them and the gooseberry bush. Ought to prune it, he thought, and then: another day. The sky had the dark and unsteady look of a muddy, windblown puddle, and the air, still wet from the heavy early morning rain, was like a damp handkerchief around his face. There was only one other man on the site, bent over a spade – more fool him – while his two young sons, bored and restive, tumbled over each other like cubs in the slippery mud beside the plot. They'd be eight or nine years old, he thought; not all that much younger than Michael Milburn. How long would it be, he wondered, before Michael was released? And what sort of person would he be by then? Christ! Angrily, he yanked the bamboo sticks out of the ground, threw them down on the path and kicked them into a pile.

'Dad! *Dad!*' Stratton looked up to see Monica running towards him, pink-cheeked and breathless, with shining eyes.

'Hello, love. I didn't expect to see you.'

'I know, but I just thought . . . with Pete away and everything . . . Anyway, here I am.' Monica surveyed the allotment. 'Bit of a mess, isn't it? Shall I give you a hand?'

Looking at her, Stratton suddenly saw her as fourteen again. He remembered how she'd come up here with him the year after Jenny died, when the war was ending and she and Pete had finally come home. She'd offered to help then, too. Pete had never taken much of an interest, but she had, and she'd turned out to have quite a knack for growing things. I'm lucky to have a daughter like her, he thought. No, he was more than lucky. What he actually felt, in a barely definable – and wholly unsayable – way, was blessed.

'Are you all right, Dad?'

'Wh— Oh, yes. Fine. Why?'

'You've got your crumpled look.'

Stratton glanced down at his mackintosh. 'I know it's not exactly

Savile Row, but . . . Anyway, you're a fine one to talk. You're wearing overalls.'

'Not *overalls*, Dad.' Monica lifted up her own mackintosh. 'They're called jeans. It's the latest thing from America – I bought them from someone on the set. Hardly anyone's got them yet, but everyone wants a pair.'

'I can't think why. They've got rivets, for God's sake. You look like a battleship. You don't wear those to work, do you?'

'Course not! But you wait, everyone'll be wearing them soon.'

'I won't.'

'No, the *young* people.'

'Well, they'll all look like cowboys. What's wrong with a frock, anyway?' Stratton fell silent, suddenly remembering the many times Reg had held forth on the topic of women in trousers. He was, of course, against it – or, as he put it, 'agin it'. He thought of this now with something approaching affection, although when it was actually happening his feelings had been the usual mixture of boredom, irritation, and embarrassment on his brother-in-law's behalf.

'Honestly, Dad . . .' Monica rolled her eyes. 'Anyway, when I said crumpled, I didn't mean your clothes, I meant your face. That sort of funny smile where your mouth goes half up and half down, as if you're pleased about something and sad at the same time. You're looking like it now.'

'Oh.' Stratton made what he hoped was an improved (or at least less melancholy) face. 'Sorry about that. I'll try to do better in future. I'm pleased to see you, at any rate. Have you heard from Pete?'

'He hasn't got time to write to me – he's got a girl, didn't you know?'

'No. He dropped in before they left, but he didn't say anything.'

'Well, he's a dark horse,' said Monica, easily. 'Bit like you, Dad.'

Stratton raised his eyebrows, but decided not to pursue that.

'Actually,' he said, 'I was wondering about that this morning. Pete, I mean. He told you about her, did he?'

'Not very much. He telephoned a couple of weeks ago, from Catterick – said he was coming to see you – but I couldn't get much out of him. By the time he'd told me her name, we'd had our three minutes and he didn't have any more money. Or so he said.'

'So what is her name?'

'Alison. He met her at a dance, and he sounded quite soppy about her – well, soppy for Pete, anyway. He's probably scribbling away to her right now.'

'Did he say anything else?'

'No. I told you, we ran out of time.' Monica bent down and started picking up the bamboo sticks. 'Are we going to do any gardening or not? If we stand still much longer, I should think we'll go mouldy, like your old cabbages.'

Stratton grinned at her. 'That's enough cheek from you and your funny trousers. Let's go home, shall we? I'll take one of these mouldy old cabbages, as you call them, and we'll have it for lunch.'

'All right, then.'

'How's Marion?' he asked, as they walked back, arm in arm.

Monica looked up at him, surprised. 'She's fine. Why?'

'Just wondered . . . You didn't bring her with you.'

'Well, no. I didn't think . . . I mean, I always come by myself.'

Stratton looked down at his daughter. Was it his imagination, or were her cheeks a bit redder than before? Deciding that this was the time to say something – if he were *ever* to say *anything* – he squeezed her arm against him with his elbow. 'She's always welcome, you know. Be nice to get to know her a bit better, that's all. Because you're quite fond of her, aren't you?'

'Yes, I am.' Monica's reply was quiet but firm, almost defiant.

Ignoring the hint of challenge, Stratton said, 'I can see that you're very happy. That's all that concerns me, you know. I am aware ...' he knew he sounded pompous, but it was the best he could do, 'that we're not all alike.'

'No,' said Monica, thoughtfully. 'We're not, are we?'

'On balance,' said Stratton, carefully, 'I'd say it's probably just as well. Now, I was hoping you might volunteer to cook lunch. I know we've got some potatoes, and Doris has left something under a cloth in the scullery, but I've got no idea what it is, so ...'

'Don't worry, Dad. I'll make sure it doesn't bite you back.'

'Good.' Giving her arm another squeeze, he added, 'What would I do without you, eh?'

CHAPTER SEVENTY

When Stratton had been to see him the previous Thursday, DCI Lamb had been remarkably sanguine about all the news from Suffolk – including that Mary/Ananda might never be compos mentis enough to be interviewed about Michael or Billy or anything else – and he was suprisingly composed about Stratton's car, too. After a lot of guff about it being highly irregular, he'd admitted that not only had he discussed it with his opposite number in Suffolk, but that they'd agreed that the money for the extensive repairs should come out of their joint budgets. When, after this news, Lamb had produced a packet of Players and offered him one, Stratton was so astonished that he'd practically swallowed the thing.

Looking at the chaos on his desk, he decided he'd better sort out the mess before he read any more, and, having scraped all the papers into a rough heap, began weeding out the ones that weren't witness statements. Burglary in furrier's shop . . . Report of someone selling liquor in unlicensed premises . . . Stabbing after fight in club . . .

A new witness had come forward for that last one, which was unusual. It was the type of thing where everyone in the place suddenly came over all vague and short-sighted, or said things and then retracted them twenty-four hours later. Stratton was looking over the statement when a call was put through from Ballard.

'Just had the pathologist's report on Roth. There's a copy on its way to you, but I thought you'd like to know – it seems he isn't Jewish after all.'

'Not circumcised, you mean?'

'Not according to Trickett.'

'Well, he should know . . . He certainly looked it, and Roth's a Jewish name, isn't it? Sounds a bit as if it's been shortened from something longer – German or Russian or something like that. Assuming Roth *was* his real name, of course.'

'We haven't found anything at the Foundation to prove that it isn't, but if he came over here as a refugee—'

'Which was what the chap at the Psychical Research Society seemed to think . . .'

'There were thousands of those buggers, so if he entered the country with one name – which might not have been his own, either – and then started calling himself something else, we don't have a hope of finding out who he really was.'

'Did you speak to Tynan about it?'

'Yes – insisted he was called Roth when he met him and he'd never heard of him being called anything else. Tynan's still pretty shaken up, and I think he'd tell us if he knew anything. In fact, I'm sure of it. He's not the type to stay down for long – I get the impression that he's attempting to recast himself as the man who blew the whistle on an evil organisation that was threatening the fabric of society with occult practices and so on . . . Suit him down to the ground if Roth turned out to be a Nazi.'

'I suppose it's possible,' said Stratton. 'When Roth told me he was in Berlin at the end of the war, I did wonder. That accent wasn't German, though . . .'

'Doesn't mean he wasn't a Nazi.'

'Doesn't mean he was, either. But *if* he was, all he had to do was get hold of some new clothes, adopt a Jewish name, get his hands on some papers – easy to do, I should think, if you had a bit of money – and he already looked the part, so . . .'

'Bob's your uncle.'

'Well, not quite – I mean, he'd probably have had to walk across half of Europe – but certainly not impossible. If it's true, that is.'

'If it is,' said Ballard, thoughtfully, 'then no wonder he was so keen on telling people that the past wasn't important.'

'Well, quite. I don't suppose we'll ever know for sure, but – for whatever reason – he was dead keen to start again . . .' Remembering the conversation they'd had in the pub, Stratton added, 'I hope it didn't come as too much of a shock to Pauline. She was rather keen on the Foundation lot, wasn't she?'

'She was a bit. I think she was kicking herself rather – you know, for being taken in. Anyway, all's well.'

This wasn't just a put-on, thought Stratton, Ballard really did sound contented. 'I'm glad,' he said.

'And your business?' said Ballard. 'That went off all right, did it, whatever it was?'

'Business?' echoed Stratton. Then, realising that Ballard hadn't believed a word of his explanation about forgetting where he'd parked his car the night he'd been with Diana, he said, hastily, 'Oh, yes. I see what you mean. Fine, thanks – nothing to worry about.'

'Jolly good. Oh, and I saw Miss Kirkland's sister, too. Quite sad, really. Apparently they were very close as children . . .'

Listening with half an ear, Stratton thought about Diana. Whether she actually wanted to see him again or not, he wasn't sure. And, more confusing, he wasn't sure what *he* wanted, either, at least, not for the long-term future. If they weren't so far apart in just about every way imaginable, it would be different. But they were, and there was no point in pretending otherwise. And what he felt for her wasn't love – at least, if it was, it wasn't the kind of love he'd felt for Jenny. Years before – just before he'd left the farm, in fact – his father, who'd rarely talked about anything except farming, and then only when absolutely necessary, had made his one and only (to Stratton, anyway) pronouncement about marriage. Pointing at their horses, Blackie and Dora, standing side by side between the shafts of the great farm cart, he'd said, 'You've got to pull together.' Stratton could not now remember – and he certainly couldn't imagine – what had given rise to this observation, or what he'd said in response, but he knew his dad had been right. If you were a lord or a millionaire or something, with a lot of servants to do things for you, then it probably wouldn't matter so much if you were pulling in different directions, but for people like him . . . And he couldn't imagine it with Diana. Apart from anything else, if the pair of them were horses, they'd each be pulling a different sort of carriage – probably, in his case, a cart. And, surprise him as she might with her common sense, Diana was too flighty, somehow. Too insubstantial. But despite all this he *did* want to see her again – and in any case, he ought to contact her, if only to thank her for what she'd said about Monica, for which he was genuinely and profoundly grateful.

'. . . Anyway, there it is,' Ballard concluded. 'I'll let you know if we turn up anything at the Foundation.'

Stratton replaced the receiver in the cradle and went to collect his coat and hat from the stand. It was three o'clock, and, as this was Diana's half-day, she'd probably have reached home by now. No time like the present, he thought. He'd nip out now and give her a call from one of booths in the tube at Piccadilly Circus.

He'd got halfway down the corridor to the foyer when Feather, the desk sergeant, came hurrying towards him, a huge and horrible grin on his big pink face. 'It's your friend Mr Heddon again.'

'Heddon?'

'You know. Just stepped out of his own personal flying saucer.'

'Bloody hell. What does he want?'

'Another urgent message from the Interplanetary Parliament, I would imagine. That's why he wants to see you – far too important for the likes of li'l old me.'

'You could have told him I was out.'

'No point. He'd only have waited. I know the type.'

'I suppose so,' said Stratton, with bad grace.

Heddon, small and dapper as ever, was sitting on a bench between an earnest-looking youth with a row of pens and pencils in his top pocket and a fat woman carrying a bulging handbag, so misshapen that she might have been carrying a dozen pounds of walnuts. Seeing Stratton, Heddon leapt to his feet, shiny-eyed and nose twitching slightly, as if he hoped to be thrown a biscuit.

'I have a communiqué,' he said, 'from Venus. They wish you to know that Condition Green is currently in operation.'

'Condition Green?' Stratton repeated the words loudly in the hope of masking Feather's sniggering.

'Yes. The threat of war has passed. Human life has been declared safe.' Feather snorted loudly and Stratton flapped a discreet hand in the direction of the desk in an effort to shut him up. 'Your agencies,' continued Heddon, 'may stand down. There may, of course, be other occasions – it is, I fear, an unstable time – but, for the time being, we may consider ourselves in the clear.'

'I'm very pleased to hear it,' said Stratton.

'I thought I should let you know immediately. After all, we don't want resources diverted with these other crises going on.'

'No, indeed,' said Stratton faintly. 'I'm most grateful.'

The little man acknowledged this with a brisk nod of his head, then, snapping into a salute, barked 'Over and out,' and, turning smartly, marched across the lobby and out of the door. The young man with the pens and the woman with the bulbous handbag stared after him, mouths agape. Stopping in front of Feather just long enough to mutter, 'Thanks a bunch, pal,' Stratton followed, turning left down Vigo Street on his way to Piccadilly Circus. There weren't many people about at this hour – businessmen and shoppers, mostly, not pausing to look in the windows but hurrying under the sullen sky with their packages, seeking tea or buses or taxis before the next lot of rain fell. Stratton descended to the underground and, finding an empty telephone kiosk, squeezed himself in and closed the door.

The receiver was waxy against his ear, the mouthpiece rank with the ghost breaths of a thousand conversations. The operator's voice came on the line, followed by a jumble of whirrs and clicks, and then, rising out of it, Diana's voice, crisp and clear, '. . . 653?'

Stratton pressed button A. 'It's Edward,' he said. 'I just thought you'd like to know that the world isn't going to end after all.'

A BRIEF NOTE ON HISTORICAL
AND PERSONAL BACKGROUND

The roots of many of the doctrines of the 'alternative religions' that comprise what we now tend to refer to as 'New Age' beliefs can be traced back to the Theosophy Movement begun by Madame Helena Blavatsky (1831–1891) which, in turn, spawned various spiritual leaders, the best known being Rudolf Steiner (1861–1925), G.I. Gurdjieff (1866?–1949), P.D Ouspensky (1878–1947) and J. Krishnamurti (1895–1986). However, the mid-fifties saw both the end of Britain as a world power (in Suez) and the alarming intensification of the Cold War (in Hungary) with the attendant prospect of nuclear holocaust, and this, together with the post-war decline in adherence to established religions, seems to have provided fertile ground for a bumper crop of all sorts of gurus.

The societies and organisations founded at this time took inspiration either from Eastern religious traditions and practices (meditation, yoga and the like), or from science fiction, then growing in popularity, with their leaders claiming to have received visitations from extra-terrestrial beings. All, however, represented a rebellion against spiritual orthodoxy, and, for those attracted to them, provided answers to the questions that we all, at some point, ask ourselves, such as, 'Why I am here? What is the point of it all? What happens when I die?', and so forth. Responses from outsiders ranged then, as they do now, from baffled incredulity to trepidation about whether their friends and relatives are being brainwashed, but for those within, there is only one mystery: why doesn't everybody else see the light and join up as they did?

My parents found answers to their questions – and later, each other – when they joined such an organisation (independently, for they had yet to meet) in the late fifties. The organisation's name is immaterial, but, in common with many others of its type, it was founded by a charismatic egotist who formed a connection with an Indian guru; it spiritualised the trivial and mundane; it had very strict rules governing everything from day-to-day conduct to gender roles, and it took up a hell of a lot of everybody's time and practically all of their mental space.

I, unavoidably, also became a member, and remained so until my early twenties. As Alexander Waugh remarked when discussing his famously Catholic grandfather, the great novelist Evelyn Waugh, 'the zeal of the convert is seldom passed down on the hereditary principle'. It certainly didn't get passed down to me. In the case of my parents – intelligent, kind, conscientious and wholly delightful people – their enthusiasm and commitment knew no bounds. My father remained a member of the organisation until his death in 2010, and my mother still attends. For me, it was different. I was constantly told, from an early age, how fortunate I was to be in contact with the teachings of a man who was in a higher state of consciousness, with the implication that I must have done something quite wonderful in a previous life to have been accorded such a privilege in this one. I spent half my time wondering if there hadn't been some hideous cosmic mistake, and the other half feeling like an undeserving fraud. We were also told that those who had been wicked in previous lives were born disabled or disadvantaged. I never heard any of the adults question this pronouncement, or others like it, and the resulting atmosphere of serene, intolerant complacency was one that I grew to find unbearable. One thing I learnt quite early on was that people are never more dangerous, or – at least 99 per cent of the time – wrong, than when they 'know' they are right, especially if the 'knowledge' has a spiritual underpinning. (Oddly, my experience didn't turn me into an atheist. I suppose it should have done but, like DI Stratton, I feel that God seems somehow more 'factual' than logical explanations for faith allow).

Although I wasn't around in the 1950s, I have drawn extensively on my memories of how people in the organisation looked, behaved and spoke in the writing of A Willing Victim. I've left out a lot of the dottier stuff on the grounds of implausibility – there are still some things I can hardly believe myself, even though I was witness to them – but I've tried to give an accurate and, I hope, entertaining account of the sorts of things that go on in such organisations.

I have taken a small liberty with the dates of Billy Graham's 'London Crusade'. The American evangelist (b. 1918) made his first visit to London in March 1954, preaching to thousands of people at north London's Haringey Arena (in use as a sporting and events venue until 1958). Billy Graham has visited the UK many times since, although not in 1956.

The book begins on the 31st October 1956, which was in fact a Wednesday, not a Tuesday. I have altered the days of the week in order to fit the time scheme.

Lastly, cinema buffs may have noticed a reference to a film about an alligator. This is based on an anecdote told by the actor Donald Sinden about a film in which he starred with Jeanie Carson, Diana Dors, James Robertson Justice and Stanley Holloway. It was called An Alligator Named Daisy – hence the consternation when the creature proved, in a way which left no room for doubt, that it was male. It was directed by J. Lee Thompson for the J. Arthur Rank Organisation, and went on release in the UK in December 1955.

L.W.
January 2012

ACKNOWLEDGEMENTS

I am very grateful to Tim Donnelly, Claire Foster-Gilbert, Stephanie Glencross, Nicholas Green, Jane Gregory, George Harding, Liz Hatherell, Maya Jacobs, Claire Morris, Lucy Ramsey, Anna Webb, June Wilson, Jane Wood and Florence Mabel Basset Hound for their enthusiasm, advice and support during the writing of this book.